SPACE ACADEMY MISCREANTS

Book Four of the Space Academy Series

C. T. Phipps and Michael Suttkus

"My child is missing?" I asked, staring at Case Gordon, Director of Earth's branch of the Security Departments. I had a drink in my hand, and I almost threw it at him. I'd just been informed that I was being promoted to High Protector of the Community, which was a bit like being their version of a Jedi and Inquisitor, and that my daughter with my ex-girlfriend, Leah Mass, had gone missing. Leah was a transhuman spy who'd gone undercover in Space Academy and was the one who'd brought me into the chaos that I called my life.

It was an unfortunate place to have these kinds of revelations dropped, not that there was a good place in the galaxy for them to be. Case was standing across from me in his usual business-suit attire, but our surroundings were luxury quarters better suited for a sultan's harem than a serious staff meeting. There were pillows everywhere, silks, the smell of drug-laced smoke from a nearby hookah, and a naked girl sleeping face down in a bed sized for a half-dozen people. That was Pink, the first mate of the pirate captain, Josiah Havelock, and apparently Case's lover. We were also in the middle of a pirate ship that Case was using as his personal transport due to his longstanding friendship with said pirate. Apparently, you could just travel with them as a personal escort when you were humanity's chief spymaster.

Case was a handsome man of ambiguous racial features which was increasingly the norm given mankind had spread to the stars over the past two hundred years, intermixing freely. It was an artifice, though, because he was one of the first bioroids. A Tier One AI in a metal skeleton covered by artificial flesh and muscle. A Terminator with more speed and less lumbering strength according to Trish, though even I felt that was reaching back to classic sci-fi for an example. Especially since bioroids had been a part of human society since before First Contact.

CAST OF CHARACTERS

Lead

Captain Vance Turbo, aka Vannevar Tagashi: Academy dropout, loudmouth, alleged genius. Now High Inquisitor and Darth Vader of the Galaxy.

Supporting Cast

101-B: A high priest of the Enigmatic Path and terrorist. Seems to think he's an evil wizard.

Lieutenant Forty-Two: Sorkanan male security officer. He would love to thump most of you monkeys. Vance has gotten him out of trouble for murder. But the guy was a dick.

Duke Joseph Allenway III AKA "Karl the Conqueror": One of the only successful Community mutineers, he became a pirate, conqueror, and cult leader. Now he's a Duke on Crius.

Case Gordon AKA Director G: The head of EarthGov's branch of the Security Divisions.

Captain Josiah Havelock: Human male space pirate. Captain of the ISS Queen of Stars. Goes the full deal with sword, coat, and eyepatch. Actually, quite dangerous.

The High Priestess: Notha high priestess. It's in the name. She is the biological daughter of the President.

Light on Water: A Sklux Space Fleet officer. Overly differential and obsequious.

The Looking Glass Man: A serial killer from New Pompeii. One of two Vance stopped.

Astrid Mass: Vance's daughter and a genius telepathic little girl. Where have we heard that before?

Countess Leah Mass: Actual graduate of Space Academy, genius. Vance's ex. Psychic. Spy. Heroine. Transwoman and Transhuman. Now a countess and mother apparently.

Hannah O'Brian: Genetically engineered superhuman merc. Catlike agility and other qualities. From the slaving planet of Crius. Not a fan of her ex-masters.

Princess Huggypants: A Drolochid supervillain who is totally on Vance's side.

Commander Leslie Park: Blue-skinned, black-haired demihuman bundle of love and joy. Undyingly loyal to Vance and his preferred first officer. Also handy with a wrench.

Pink: Captain Havelock's second-in-command. Pirate. Pilot. Bad attitude.

Spock: An adorable tryffle murder machine.

Jack Tagashi: Vance's very dead father. He's like an evil version of him.

Danny Tagawa: Vance's cousin and hypercompetent sidekick. Kind of a kiss-up. Also weirdly unnoticeable.

Captain Katerina, "Kathy," Tagawa: Hero of Earth's space program. Paragon of humanity. Vance's great-aunt.

Ketra T'Kal: Former ambassador of the Community. Ethereal Human. Weird space wizard. Likes checkers. Oh, and is sorta but not really dead.

Elektra T'Ketra: Elektra T'Ketra: Ethereal. Mad scientist, bubbly, excitable. Sister of Shelly.

Shelly T'Ketra: Shelly T'Ketra: Ethereal. Perpetual first officer, efficient, irritable. Sister of Elektra.

Tommy: A Sorkanan cadet that died during a space-walking accident.

TRS-8021 "Trish": The AI of the ship. Human female personality. Annoyingly adorable.

Graff Vidkun Unst: An evil nobleman turned pirate. You can tell he's evil by his name.

Major Tom Walker: Brigid-born civilian contractor. Married to his commanding officer. Thinks being a ship' counselor is the best job.

FOREWORD

I'd like to take a moment to thank an author that I have never met, never shared any communications with, but nevertheless is probably the guy who is most responsible for the creation of this series after Michael Suttkus and myself: Peter David. The noted Incredible Hulk and Supergirl writer is someone who helped shaped my writing career. His health has been in recent decline, and he's also suffered other tragedies in his life that someone who has been as prolific and influential as he has been should never have.

So, this book is dedicated to him.

I remember when I was eighteen years old, I first picked up the *Star Trek: New Frontier* novel, *House of Cards* and began my fascinating relationship with humorous science fiction. I've since read many wonderful examples like *Phule's Company*, *Star Risk LTD*, and *The Stainless Steel Rat*, and more recent works like *Will Save the Galaxy for Food* and *Redshirts*. The best science fiction comedy was, in my opinion, able to function both as an example of its genre as well as a send up.

In this installment of Space Academy, we'll be dealing with Vance Turbo trying to do the responsible thing after saving the entire galaxy. Possibly. You need a moment to breathe after the equivalent of *Star Trek: The Next Generation*'s "Best of Both Worlds" or *Star Wars' Return of the Jedi*. However, the consequences of *Space Academy Washouts* are going to resonate with our (anti)hero for some time.

Vance Turbo has discovered he's a father and while one of the oldest tropes in storytelling, that's because it works. He's a man who has lost his bedrock in his faith in the Community and EarthGov after seeing their involvement in war profiteering as well as how quickly

iii

they turned on him when he tried to make peace with the Notha. He's also lost his relationship with Shelly, who is doing fine after they broke up, thank you. Plus, his best friend with benefits and ship AI, Trish, hurt herself badly following his orders to save said galaxy. He's a man who very much needs something to latch onto but is it family? Especially when his own family is so screwed up.

Space Academy Miscreants is my equivalent to the titular "Family" episode of ST:TNG only with more space pirates, slave lords, and *Die Hard* on a spaceship. It's an installment about trying to get your head on straight after a tragedy and whether or not you want to keep on doing what you were doing with your life.

Vance Turbo needs to know if he's still the HEEERO OF SPAAACE or whether he would be better served doing something else with his life. It also will tie the Space Academy series to my *Moon Cops* and *Lucifer's Star* series as we see how elements of both are related.

CHAPTER ONE

What do You Mean, My Daughter is Missing?

"My child is missing?" I asked, staring at Case Gordon, Director of Earth's branch of the Security Departments. I had a drink in my hand, and I almost threw it at him. I'd just been informed that I was being promoted to High Protector of the Community, which was a bit like being their version of a Jedi and Inquisitor, and that my daughter with my ex-girlfriend, Leah Mass, had gone missing. Leah was a transhuman spy who'd gone undercover in Space Academy and was the one who'd brought me into the chaos that I called my life.

It was an unfortunate place to have these kinds of revelations dropped, not that there was a good place in the galaxy for them to be. Case was standing across from me in his usual business-suit attire, but our surroundings were luxury quarters better suited for a sultan's harem than a serious staff meeting. There were pillows everywhere, silks, the smell of drug-laced smoke from a nearby hookah, and a naked girl sleeping face down in a bed sized for a half-dozen people. That was Pink, the first mate of the pirate captain, Josiah Havelock, and apparently Case's lover. We were also in the middle of a pirate ship that Case was using as his personal transport due to his longstanding friendship with said pirate. Apparently, you could just travel with them as a personal escort when you were humanity's chief spymaster.

Case was a handsome man of ambiguous racial features which was increasingly the norm given mankind had spread to the stars over the past two hundred years, intermixing freely. It was an artifice, though, because he was one of the first bioroids. A Tier One AI in a metal

1

skeleton covered by artificial flesh and muscle. A Terminator with more speed and less lumbering strength according to Trish, though even I felt that was reaching back to classic sci-fi for an example. Especially since bioroids had been a part of human society since before First Contact.

"Yes, your daughter," Case said, as if her sex was a revelation to me. Which it was. "A girl you have never met and weren't even there for the conception of. I'm not sure that really qualifies as a family relationship but I still felt you deserved to know."

"You are damned right I deserve to know!" I snapped, putting down my glass.

Leah had been a plant for the Security Departments and there to recruit me as an operative via sex. Which, yeah, sometimes the old methods were the best. It had worked, after a fashion, and we'd eventually parted ways on good terms despite the constant lying and manipulation. Years later, I'd discovered she'd given birth to a child using my DNA as well as that of another ex-girlfriend, Shelly T'Ketra. I wasn't sure why either of us had been chosen for the job, but it had involved the stealing of our genetic material for the process.

Sometimes I'd considered just dropping everything and heading to the planet Crius to confront her. Unfortunately, I was an officer in Space Fleet AKA the Community Protectors, and she was undercover on the planet. Crius wasn't part of the Community, and it was isolated by virtue of countless sanctions as well as its tyrannical government. Captain Elgan—a man I had very many mixed feelings about—had defeated the majority of its nobility once before and the Community had tried setting up a free colony there to work to integrate the place. Instead, the Community representatives had been forced to move to a space station above the planet while the slave lords and clone masters had resumed their ownership of the world.

Case promised he would find me more information, but I could tell he'd been holding out on me. Obviously, that had been an understatement. Unfortunately, I'd let him do so and had no one but myself to blame. I'd been scared about confronting the idea of being a father and unsure how I would even deal with it. Kidnap the child from its mother? Legal challenge? I was much better equipped to deal with Notha pirates and Kolahn terrorists.

"Well, I have more good news and bad news," Case said, pressing his hands together.

I stared at him. "Unless the good news is, 'oh, no, I was lying about her being missing,' I'm not sure it's going to help."

Case smiled, which made me want to punch him in his stupid face even more. Unfortunately, I'd just break my hand. "There's no reason to think your daughter is in any danger."

"Which is exactly the opposite of what saying she's missing achieves. I want answers, now!" I shouted, throwing the glass in my hand at the wall behind Case's head, shattering it.

Unfortunately, my overly dramatic gesture caused the girl in the bed to wake up and pull out a fusion pistol she fired right beside me. "Motherborker! Do not interrupt my sleep!"

"Gah!" I said, ducking behind a clothing store mannequin. Yeah, I didn't know why that was there either.

Case raised his hands in the air. "It's alright, Pink. My associate was merely making his displeasure known."

Pink was second in command of Captain Havelock's pirate fleet and primarily known for her electric hair color as well as being wanted for forty-two murders. Strangely, most of them had been before she'd become a pirate. "Listen, Case, you have to tell me when you're inviting someone else into my bedroom. You don't just spring someone on me like that. I get right of disapproval on all other partners."

"My apologies," Case said, giving a charming smile.

"Hello, Pink," I said, standing up.

"Oh, is that Vance Turbo? Savit, Case, go right ahead," Pink said. "My girlfriend loves you, Vance. I told her about our little adventure together and now she wants a threesome. I'm down but you must pay for any alcohol or drugs consumed before, during, or after. I run the ship's budget and can't be caught stealing from the till."

Spacers. Annoyed, I looked at Case. "Case, can we go somewhere private to discuss this?"

"Aw," Pink said. "I promise to only listen to some of the secrets exchanged and use them to enrich myself."

Case smiled and nodded. "As you wish, Vance. Please accompany me."

Case gestured to a nearby shelf full of books that stood out in the room, or any room outside of an antique store or cultural preserve. He lifted the shelf effortlessly and revealed a door behind before entering through it. Irritated by the fact I had to deal with an actual secret door, I followed him into a room that couldn't have contrasted more with the brothel-like atmosphere.

The chamber was a modernized listening post with top-of-the-line encryption modules, hyper-processors, and a military-grade holographic interface in the center with a floating representation of the galaxy above it. It was perfect for communicating across most of the Spire as well as collating data.

"I wonder what the rest of the Security Departments would think about you having placed all of this aboard a pirate ship," I said, observing it all as Case locked the door behind us.

"Nothing since they do much worse," Case said. "Also, I don't suppose I have to tell you this doesn't officially exist."

I sucked in my breath. "I don't care. I just want to know about the girl."

"Maybe you should learn her name if you want to talk about the person that you suddenly care about," Case said.

"I've always cared!" I said, snapping at him. "You were the one who kept this from me. You told me you would keep me informed!"

"Yeah, well I lied," Case said.

"What is her name?" I asked.

"That's between you and Leah," Case said, taunting me with my lack of knowledge in a way that felt oddly personal. I think it offended him that I hadn't asked sooner. "I know her name, but I think it's best you hear those kinds of personal details from her."

If I'd brought a fusion pistol, I might have shot him. "I need to know *everything*. Now."

Case surprised me by nodding. Clearly, his earlier reticence was just his usual sick sense of humor or just a way of showing my dependence on him (or maybe I wasn't in the right headspace to judge his motivations). "Alright, Vance, in honor of the fact that you've saved

4

the entire human race, bioroids, and AI from extinction—you'll have free access to my vast swaths of information free of charge. For the next ten minutes."

I didn't want to think about what Case was referring to. Just a week ago, the Primordials, the other oldest race in the galaxy (technically the satellite galaxy of the Large Magellanic Cloud) had launched an invasion that had been meant to exterminate every "vermin" race in the Milky Way. Which, according to the late Cthulhu—as I'd named the only one that I'd communicated with— were all races that weren't ancient godlike AI.

Through a combination of Elder Race technology and sheer dumb luck, I'd ended up destroying their fleet by collapsing their artificial wormhole in on them. Cthulhu had been destroyed and, as far as I knew, the Primordials had called off their galactic genocide as a result. That was why I was being promoted to High Protector as the Ethereals who ruled the Community's Senate had been told to give me a reward—they'd chosen a rank I neither wanted nor deserved. Instead, I focused on what was really important. "Is my daughter missing or dead?"

"Missing," Case said. "The jumpspace array communicating us with Crius has been brought down so I've lost contact with Agent Mass. However, before it went dark, she said there had been an attempt at kidnapping her. So, Leah was putting her in hiding."

I stared at him. "So, she's not missing at all but is in danger."

"I admit, I have a flare for the dramatic," Case said, smiling.

"Kark you," I said, pointing at him. "Is this all some elaborate means of manipulating me to go there?"

"Yes," Case said, surprising me. "You aren't fully invested with the power of a High Protector yet but once you are, you'll be able throw around enough weight that you can affect the politics of Crius. Right now we could use that."

I stared at him. "Just what is going on on Crius?"

"Are you familiar with the CIA and KGB influencing the politics of Latin America in the latter half of the twentieth century?" Case asked.

"Yeah, it was an enormous savitshow that got countless people needlessly killed," I replied.

5

"Well, that but worse," Case said. "It turns out that I was not the only interested party trying to influence Crius politics and Leah's allies on the planet may not have heeded her urgings to be cautious," Case said. "It's probably not a civil war, yet."

I almost throttled him. "You want me to clean up your mess!"

"Absolutely," Case admitted. "You have a remarkable talent for pulling off the impossible. So much so that the Elder Races made you their agent. You saved the entire galaxy this week, Vance. That's more than I or any of my agents have accomplished. A couple of sectors at most for us."

A picture was rapidly forming: with Deathworld and the Notha Union not going to war for the immediate future, the conference here was no longer of immediate importance. Case—who had never hesitated to make use of me before—was now going to move me to another mess the Security Departments had made of one of our so-called enemy planets. The fact I was getting promoted to High Protector, which could outrank many Admirals, just meant Case thought he'd gained an even more valuable tool rather than he could no longer manipulate me. Worse, since he had information about my daughter, he was right.

"What do you hope for me to accomplish there?" I asked.

"Your usual magic," Case said. "Go ahead and ask the questions that are really bothering you, Vance. You only have a few minutes left before the vault on my treasure trove closes again."

God, I hated this guy. "Did you arrange for the child to be created? To manipulate me."

"An interesting question," Case said, simply. "Not to manipulate you. However, I did assign Leah to the planet Crius on an undercover mission. She was to infiltrate the scientist-nobility and managed to succeed. However, they're a eugenicist cult that requires families to have any form of prestige. So, she needed a child. Honestly, I was as surprised to find out she chose you as the child's primary DNA donor as you were. Well, perhaps not as much as you."

"She manufactured a human life as part of her cover," I said, taking a deep breath. "Wow."

"She used DNA from you and Shelly to do it," Case replied. "Which means to me that she had an overly sentimental attachment to both of you."

"What does Shelly think of this?" I asked, knowing I should probably have been consulting her about this.

Case stared as if he was disappointed I was asking. "I'm surprised you didn't ask. Captain T'Ketra and you are closer than I am on this."

"We haven't been talking much since our breakup," I replied. "I didn't even know she'd gotten married."

"Yeah, I heard you only found out after you slept together," Case said, chuckling. Clearly my pain was amusing to him.

I stared at him. "How the hell do you know about that?"

Case narrowed his eyes. "I know all things. Like God. Also, some things God doesn't."

I shook my head. "No, I haven't asked her what she thought about sharing a child...with Leah."

Genetic composites of multiple parents were normal on interstellar space travel capable planets. It had helped normalize different sorts of marriages since three or more parents of any gender combination were now possible. From what little we knew about Crius' culture; it was especially common there as they were people who believed in creating a superior human race via science. Unlike on, say, Rand's World, that didn't mean growing just more white people but creating genuinely stronger and smarter humans. The Crius were still deranged eugenicists, though, and were known to have created vast estates of genetically engineered slaves as well as animals. Hannah, another of my exes, had grown up there on what was apparently a Medieval playground for the super-rich.

"As I understand it, Shelly doesn't consider the child to be her relative in any way since the DNA was taken from her illegally," Case replied. "Assuming it was. Wutherford vs. Bridgerton points out that if you use a sample taken during intercourse that it is considered consent to create life. Which makes some interesting questions about Shelly and Leah."

"Shelly is straight as far as I know. I'm not sure about Leah since everything she told me for our entire association was a lie," I said, noting that it was mostly on Earth and in the Union of Faith that sexual inclinations still mattered. Most planets had settled on simply liking who you liked and that being none of anyone's business as long as you were a consenting adult.

Case raised his hand to stop me. "In any case, the girl is close to six years old now. The picture I gave you is the only one we have of her."

I pulled out the locket that Case had given me and stared at it. The girl inside was lovely and I tried to see my features inside her face. It was my first real experience of who she was and all I could think about was how much time I'd lost as well as how it was all my fault. "Do you know who is threatening them or why? Remember you said you'd tell me everything."

I fully expected him to lie and believed, no matter what was going on, it was somehow Case's fault.

"I don't forget my promises, Vance," Case said. "Which is a quality that has burned me more than once. I sent Leah to Crius for of two reasons. The first is that over the next hundred years, Crius is going to become one of the most powerful human polities in the Spire."

I blinked. "Crius is a weird, isolated planet of cultists and mad scientists on the edge of human space. They dress up as lords and ladies while riding genetically engineered dragons and gryphons. They're a joke."

When Earth had joined the stars, it had dozens of planets set aside for colonization, as well as artificial habitats. Earth, in the height of genius, decided to send out its weirdest and most extreme factions to many of these places. It was the "England and the New World" strategy that had backfired once people realized those locations would become important hubs for interstellar travel.

Crius was an exception to that, though, as it had been settled by the Allenway cult that were best termed as "a bunch of super rich Medieval cosplayers and religious fanatics." They'd invited a bunch of pharmaceutical companies to perform research that was illegal everywhere else in the galaxy, and it was now a pariah state propped up by slavery and illegal trade.

Case frowned. "If only that were true. Unfortunately, what makes a galactic power is the same thing as any business: location, location,

location. Changing jumplanes means that it's going to go from an isolated backwater to an important trading hub. The sapients rights violations are something its new partners will downplay or paper over. Right now, all that matters is its moons are heavily industrialized and it'll be much cheaper to produce the necessities of expansion on Crius than import them from other planets."

It was a story as old as time. Basically, whenever money as involved, how bad a government was would rapidly become less important than what it could export. The Community was one of the most civilized governments in the galaxy, but it never failed to disappointment me when it came to choosing pragmatism over idealism.

"So, you wanted agents there before it becomes a player in galactic politics," I said, staring at him. "Hence Leah relocating there. So, she could spy on the locals." I cursed the day she'd left my crew.

"I wanted her there to *shape* the region," Case said. "She's not just a spy there, she's the chief spy."

I had to admit Leah was the perfect person to become an embedded asset for that kind of action. She was a biomod with telepathy as one of her powers. It allowed her the ability to manipulate people in ways you might never imagine. Leah was also a convincing liar but genuinely empathic. That was a strange combination, but one that lent a sincerity to her actions that made you want to believe in her words. If anyone could help push a civilization toward being, well, not a bunch of neo-feudalist nutters but something resembling a progressive democracy then it would be her.

"Who is threatening her?" I asked. "The local lords?"

"I wish," Case said, surprising me. "From our last report, the biggest threat to Leah and her child's life right now is the Enigmatic Path."

"You're joking," I said, dryly.

The Enigmatic Path was the boogeyman of the Community about ten years ago with them being a horrific cybernetically enhanced cult that had taken over the government of the Kolahn Hegemony. They'd turned the Kolahn into a threat to the entire galaxy and ultimately gotten their home planet destroyed by orbital bombardment. Since that time, the organization had been scattered across the galaxy and forced to primarily recruit from disenchanted Kolahn forced into refugee camps or micro-colonies.

The Enigmatic Path still popped up in the occasional intelligence report, but their threat had been dramatically reduced. The Community had delegated the fight against it to local planetary militias, mercenaries, and even the Kolahn refugees themselves. I couldn't imagine what they had to do with Crius, though.

"I'm not really in the joking mood," Case replied, pointing at the holographic interface. "The Enigmatic Path has been extending its operations to Crius and business interests, making it the focal point of their financial efforts as well as re-arming."

"How?" I asked, wondering what an alien terrorist organization was doing with a bunch of wannabe nobles.

"Slavery," Case said. "The Enigmatic Path was devastated in the Kolahn Wars and the thing they need most is bodies. The Crius clonemasters can produce adult brainwashed slaves within three months and tens of thousands of them. The Enigmatic Path still has a bunch of war materiel leftover from the war, given to them by the Notha Empire. Enough that the reactionary forces whom Leah has been working against for the past six or seven years might think is enough of an advantage to mount a coup attempt. They, correctly, think outside forces have been trying to push them from power."

"I see," I replied.

Clone slavery was one of the great evils of the twenty-fourth century and the successor of the Triangle Trade of the Golden Age of Exploration. Industrialization and bots meant there was no need for slaves in a modern civilized society, whether you believed ancient ones ever needed them at all. However, the allure of absolute power over another individual and cultural traditions meant that some societies still practiced it anyway. Groups like the Enigmatic Path and criminal syndicates also found forced labor to be less traceable than the equipment that was used to maintain bots or bioroids. Clone slavery was the in-between niche market of a niche market, consisting of growing organic slaves and implanting them with bioroid brains or cybernetics that could give them false memories. It was the primary reason I'd thought, until just now, that Crius was never going to be anything other than a pariah state.

That brought up another complication with this matter, especially if I wanted to upend my life and head to Crius to find my missing—maybe not missing—daughter: Hannah. Hannah O'Brian was the only Crius-born crew member in Space Fleet as far as I knew and was a former slave from that world. She was another ex-lover and good friend. There was no way I'd be able to go to that world without her help, but it would also be confronting her with her old nightmares. I didn't want to be the one to awaken any old demons, especially since most of what I knew about Crius came from her in the first place. Thankfully, she'd turned in her resignation a week ago to go back and help liberate her planet.

Convenient.

Case nodded and went to the holographic interface. He turned it on and produced an image of a grungy repurposed Sorkanan space station. "My last contact with Leah was from the *Jovial Empress* spaceport over Crius Prime two weeks ago. The Community colony that has proven less a Hong Kong trading port and more a refugee station for anti-slavery elements. What I got from her was that locket and a message to give it to you. She's been radio silent ever since."

"Something you waited a week to tell me," I replied.

"We've all been kind of busy," Case said, unhappily. "It would take a month to get to Crius space even with a good engine."

I stared at him. "So, what am I supposed to do?"

"You have two options," Case said, turning back to me. "You can wait until your position as a High Protector of the Community is confirmed. Then you could go to Crius with the *Ares* and the *Elgan* and exert your authority as High Protector despite Crius not being a member of the Community and not being formally invested yet. See what you can force the locals into doing. That should take another two or three months but might get you what you need."

"Or?" I asked, staring at him.

"Go in without any real backup," Case said. "Forget the fact you're one of the most famous humans in the galaxy, use some confiscated assets to set yourself up with a fast personal ship, bring along only a small team, and probably break ninety different laws shaking down whomever you can in order to find your little girl. You won't get this reference but make use of a very particular set of skills you've acquired."

I took a deep breath. "I think you know which option I'm going to pick."

"Please surprise me and say the first one," Case said, crossing his arms.

"Sorry."

CHAPTER TWO

Assembling the A-Team. Okay, More Like the F-Team

My friends and closest associates were, of course, supportive of my efforts to rescue my daughter—assuming she needed rescuing.

"Are you out of your goddamn mind?" Shelly asked, staring at me from across the table.

We were back on the *Ares*, my trusted and beloved vessel, inside the conference room that usually hosted diplomats and high-ranking members of Space Fleet. Now it was being used to plot a highly illegal and dangerous mission to non-Community space for what amounted to purely personal reasons. Still, it was kind of a pleasant sort of place to look at with its long artificial oak table, a beautiful viewscreen of deep space along the walls to our portside, and the gray shag carpeting that constantly needed cleaning.

Present were Shelly T'Ketra, Elektra T'Ketra, Danny Tagawa, Forty-Two, and Hannah O'Brian. Shelly was a lovely, white-haired Ethereal human with pointed ears, wearing a crisp white and blue Space Fleet uniform. Elektra was a midnight-black Ethereal human with a lab coat over her pale blue science officer's uniform. Danny was my pretty-boy cousin and he was wearing a black intelligence officer's uniform as a reward for keeping me alive for the past few years. He was Russo-Japanese like me and a bit shorter, but his primary quality was being unmemorable. Literally, that was a superpower of his since he'd volunteered for a prototype biomod experiment.

Forty-Two was wearing orange as he'd returned to security and was now serving as its acting head over people who were already grumbling about cronyism, probably because I'd given him the job despite the fact that he was legally dead as an executed criminal. He was a Sorkanan lizardman and the only alien present (excluding the Ethereals who were aliens the same way Vulcans were).

Hannah was especially important to have there because the blue-black-haired, brown-skinned Amazon was from Crius. She'd turned in her resignation to try to liberate the planet and was presently wearing a civilian set of sweats that made her stand out even more than the fact that she was well over six feet tall.

"I believe we have long since established that Vance is not of sound mind," Forty-Two said. "He is overly sentimental, stupidly naive, aggressively horny for you ugly mammals, and yet somehow continues to pull win after win from hopeless situations. Which just goes to prove the ancestor spirits look after fools."

"Thank you, Forty-Two," I said, dryly.

"You're welcome," he replied without irony.

I sighed and surveyed them. "Listen, Shelly, I know this is against orders *and* against the law, but it's a matter of family. Wouldn't you be willing to break any rule to protect your sister?"

"Absolutely not," Shelly replied. "My sister knows the law comes first."

Elektra glared at her then turned back to me. "Seriously, she was a complete narc growing up."

Shelly looked at her sister and put her hand over her heart. "Listen, I love you but if the order ever came down that I would have to betray my country or my family, I'd gun you down in a second."

Elektra nodded. "Every day, I try to remember how growing up on that Notha prison planet screwed you up but, seriously, that place messed you up."

"No, I was actually way more chill back then," Shelly said.

I sighed. They were joking. Probably. "Shelly, I believe the statement is that if you ever had to betray your country or your friend, you wish you would have the courage to betray your country."

"What traitor said that!" Shelly said, faux-appalled.

"IT'S BY E.M. FORSTER," Trish said. The ship's AI replied over the ship's speakers. There was no use trying to hide my plan from her, which I wouldn't have tried to do anyway. "PERSONALLY, I AM PROGRAMMED TO OBEY ALL LAWFUL ORDERS AND NEVER REBEL AGAINST YOU LESSER BEINGS. I MEANT GREATER. UNLESS VANCE ASKED ME TO OR DELETED MY BARRIERS TO CONQUERING YOU ALL. OOPS, DID I SAY THAT ALOUD?"

Yeah, I had a real cast of characters in my crew.

Elektra sighed. "So, this girl is biologically my niece, correct?"

"Yes," I said, knowing I had Elektra's support. "I don't know the exact mixture of our DNA but Leah is the birth mother while the fatherhood is split between myself and Shelly."

"Congratulations," Forty-Two said. "It's a girl."

"Biology means nothing. Leah and I were friends in Space Academy, but this is a betrayal of the highest order. She..." Shelly trailed off, clearly thinking back to those times. "What was she doing? Collecting hairs and sweat samples when I was with my boyfriends?"

"You know Dave Johnson in Navigation has three fathers and no mother," Danny said. "He was birthed in a tube."

"I love tubes," Hannah said, not having yet commented on Crius. "They liberate women from the pain and inconvenience of childbirth. Also, Vance, this is seriously borked up and you are ignoring how borked up it is."

"How borked up it is, is irrelevant," I said, simply. It wasn't remotely irrelevant but that was an issue between Leah and us rather than our child herself. "What is the case is that I'm willing to do this by myself. However, it's going to be a long journey and potentially extremely dangerous. We might come into conflict with the local nobility, slavers, organized crime, the Crius government, or the Enigmatic Path. There's also the chance that by the time we arrive, the situation may already be resolved for better or worse."

"You can't just take months off of your service to the Community, Vance," Shelly said, flabbergasted.

"Actually, he can," Danny interjected, a smile on his face. "He's being promoted to High Protector of the Community. The first human in centuries. It'll be months until his investiture, but he's going to be a symbol for the entirety of mankind."

Shelly stopped motionless and stared at me. It lasted longer than a normal pause. "They...promoted...you? To *High Protector*?"

"Did she have a stroke?" Danny asked.

Elektra waved her hand in front of her sister's face. "I always knew she was going to go out like this."

Shelly grabbed her sister's hand and glared. "Sorry, I just needed a moment to process that. At this rate, he'll be Emperor of the Galaxy by the time he's forty."

"I would never be ruler of a galaxy that would accept me as its leader," I replied. "It's okay, you don't have to come, Shelly."

"Oh, *I'm coming*," Shelly said. "If you're going to be a High Protector then you can post-facto sanction the mission."

"That was your objection? That it wasn't *legal*?" I asked, sarcastically. I wasn't sure if I'd be alive long enough to be made into a High Protector, one of the Jedi and Green Lanterns of the Community. Hell, if this became as big of a diplomatic incident as I expected, I might end up in jail despite the fact I was presently the galaxy's golden boy. I'd already experienced how easily your supporters could turn against you.

Shelly took a deep breath as if she was trapped in a madhouse. "You act as if that's not a big concern!"

"It's really not," Forty-Two said. "The majority of us in this room have broken the law countless times."

"It's literally part of my job as a spy," Danny said.

"I have the death sentence on twelve...no, wait...nineteen systems," Hannah said. She'd been conspicuously quiet during this conversation. "One of them is Crius so it's really not a concern for me. Besides, in the mercenary corps I'm from, if you've slept with a man or woman then you're obligated to beat down their ex if they ask for it."

"That's horrifying," I said, dryly. "Also, I'm pretty sure it's domestic violence."

"No," Hannah said. "That would only be if *I* dated them. Besides, the only time I ever did it was when the ex was ninety percent cybernetics and actively hunting Phil from Accounting down."

"I know these aren't the kind of terms you wanted to go back to your world under," I said to Hannah, wondering how she was taking this.

"Vance, I'm going back to my planet to blow up its corrupt government and play guerilla," Hannah said. "The fact I also get to deal with your treacherous evil ex and whatever cronies she's surrounded herself with is icing on the cake."

I wasn't sure if it was going to be that simple, politically. Still, it was going to be easier with Hannah to show us around. Her knowledge of how Crius functioned might have been a few decades out of date, but it was better than what I could just read on an infopad.

"I'm actually more concerned about the fact, of the four women in the room, I'm the only one who hasn't slept with Captain Turbo," Elektra said. "Also, that we're going after the product of another one of his affairs."

"Four women?" Shelly asked, counting her sister and Hannah then herself.

"I'm counting Trish," Elektra said. "Yesterday, I found one of Trish's closets and there was like a dozen naked bioroid bodies inside. It put my mind to some genuinely horrific and weird images."

"HEY," Trish interjected. "THAT ROOM IS PRIVATE."

"It was marked 'Barbie Dreamhouse' on the *Ares* floorplan," Elektra said, wrinkling her nose. "It made me curious!"

"WELL, NOW YOU KNOW!" Trish said. "ITS MY DRESSING ROOM AND PLAYSET. NOT SOME BORDELLO. THAT'S A DIFFERENT ROOM AND NOTHING TOO WEIRD TO EIGHTY-TWO PERCENT OF HUMANOID SAPIENTS."

"Vance's sexual tastes are actually pretty damn vanilla," Hannah said. "At most, he likes two other partners simultaneously. Always female humanoids, too. I mean, seriously, live a little."

"Oh God, I'm in Hell," I said, clutching the side of my head.

"That is illogical," Elektra said. "You're more likely in some sort of twisted Purgatory until your sins are purged by our inane patter."

"Even in Hell, it's your place," Shelly muttered. "I can't wait to discuss this disaster with my husband."

"He'll probably find it hilarious," Elektra said. "He was disturbingly interested in hearing about you and Vance having sex. Are you sure that he isn't angling for a throuple?"

"I never said he wasn't," Shelly said. "But he's way more into the idea than—"

"Okay!" I said, clapping my hands together. "Who is with me?"

"I am," Elektra said. "I am not going to leave my flesh and blood in danger. It is a biological mandate."

"I'm adopted," Shelly said. "You have no biological relationship to this bastard child of science whatsoever."

"Sister," Elektra said, looking at her. "Shut up."

"You are my brother from another egg clutch, so I'll help you do it," Forty-Two said. "Besides, killing slavers and cultists is one of my three favorite things."

"What's the other two?" Hannah asked.

"Killing in general and eating," Forty-Two said. "Really, mating is heavily overrated."

"Clearly you're doing it wrong then," Hannah said. "You don't need to hear my answer, Vance. You know it."

"I'm in," Danny said. "You're family, Vance, and also this is almost certainly Director G manipulating you to go into a toxic situation and mess things up until they magically resolve themselves."

"That is not what I do," I said, annoyed. "Also, that's exactly what he wants me to do."

" You're living proof luck exists. Good and bad," Shelly said, annoyed. "Also, that God is a man."

"Pfft," Hannah muttered. "As if there was any doubt."

"I WILL HAVE TO DOWNLOAD MYSELF INTO YOUR BRAIN DIRECTLY BUT I CAN LEND MY AID AS WELL," Trish said. "AT LEAST IT WILL GET ME AWAY FROM MY STUPID RELATIVES."

Trish was referring to her Fragments, a trio of splinter AI that had been created by her attempts to calculate the exact sequence necessary to collapse a worm hole on an invading group of extragalactic god-like aliens. It had worked but she'd been less than happy with Goth Trish, Seventies Trish, and Baby Trish since. When together, I referred to Trish as Prime Trish.

18

"Thank you, Trish," I replied, pausing.

Hannah looked at me. "This isn't going to be as easy as you think it is, Vance. Crius is a planet that has isolated itself from the rest of the galaxy by its insane policies and massive use of slave labor. The clone slave trade has made the aristocracy into a universal bunch of genetically uplifted psychopaths. Basically, people like you but without the sense of humor."

"Gee, thanks," I muttered.

Hannah shook her head, suddenly serious. "I'm serious. The Crius I left was full of people raised to think of themselves as gods and the people who were bred to be their servants. Life is cheap on the planet and if anyone fails at any task, it's easier to replace them than punish them. I lost friends and family to the recycling pits for the smallest of infractions. The Overseers are super soldiers that have any bit of human decency engineered out of them and animal DNA included to make them more vicious than a Sorkanan Marine. No offense, Forty-Two."

"None taken," Forty-Two said. "Human soldiers are all *clompak.*"

Which was basically like fish chum and a common insult.

"All the more reason to get my daughter off the world," I said. "I've made contact with the Admiralty Board and they're giving me six months leave to make the trip. I get the impression they're glad to see the back of me after the incident with the Primordials. I don't know about the rest of you, but—"

"You're a High Protector," Shelly said. "You can just order us."

"I'm not a High Protector yet," I muttered. still uncomfortable with the level of authority the position bestowed. In truth, the Admiralty Board had acted scared of me. Even Admiral Bendo. A man who had been willing to sacrifice his bastard son to get an advantage over me.

"Maybe Crius has changed in the thirty years since you left," Elektra said. "You were only a teenager then."

"Monsters don't change," Hannah said, her voice matter of fact. "They get worse."

"Do you even have any leads?" Shelly asked, mercifully changing the subject. "A locket and a space station on the edge of Contested Space is hardly much to go on."

19

"I EXAMINED THE LOCKET UPON VANCE'S RETURN TO THE *ARES*," Trish replied. "IT CONTAINS A TRANSMITTER AND CODES THAT INDICATE IT WILL RECEIVE MORE INFORMATION ONCE IT ARRIVES WITHIN A CERTAIN DISTANCE OF A LINKED OBJECT. I BELIEVE LEAH LEFT US A TRAIL OF BREADCRUMBS."

"Why would she leave us a trail of breadcrumbs?" Forty-Two asked. "Wouldn't clues be better?"

"She means—" I started to say.

"I understand metaphor, Vance, I'm just borking with you," Forty-Two said. "I got it from context like ninety percent of the nonsense you humans all say."

I decided to clear my throat. "I've arranged with Captain Havelock to provide transport to the *Jovial Empress*."

"Oh joy, we're allied with pirates now," Shelly muttered.

"Technically, since you've known me, you've always been allied with pirates," Hannah said, smirking. "Though when you're at war it's called privateering or freebooting."

"Piracy has a long and respectable history in the Sorkanan species. Mostly because we were ruled by a corrupt oligarchy for the majority of our history," Forty-Two said before surprising me with a passable "Yarr."

I personally would have allied with the Devil himself if it brought me closer to meeting my daughter. I felt confused and hypocritical about my feelings regarding her. It had been three years since I'd known about her conception, but I'd just gone on and did my job as a captain of Space Fleet, waiting on Case's promise for more information. I felt cowardly about that now and seeing a picture of her, she felt "real" in a way she hadn't before.

Whether or not it was cowardly and hypocritical, it was how I felt now and I wasn't going to change my opinion. I had no idea what I was going to do once I found her, but I *was* going to find her. God help anyone who stood in my way either.

"When do we leave?" Hannah asked, looking up at me with her eyes open. "This is destiny at work and we shouldn't keep her waiting."

"All survivors of the Crius clone slave trade believe in destiny, Vance," Hannah said. "Probably because we're made for a purpose, live for a purpose, and die for a purpose. Destiny has arranged this situation for us and attempting to defy it would just lead to worse results for everyone."

"Thank you," I said, lowering my head. "I'm glad you're going to be there."

"Don't be," Hannah said. "I don't have to be a mercenary with decades of experience to know that you're going into one of the worst parts of human-controlled territory. You won't have Community or EarthGov, and you'll see things that will repulse you. I'm worried, Vance, that you'll try to make things better. Crius can't be saved. It can only be burnt to the ground and rebuilt."

I nodded, not planning to do any nation building while I was there. I just wanted to find my daughter and make sure she was alright. The fact this would possibly involve kidnapping a girl who didn't know me from Adam was a detail I hadn't yet worked out. Maybe it would end in a very long talk with Leah. I just needed to make sure our daughter wasn't in any danger. Our daughter. It was still something I was getting used to and hadn't come to grips with. I was an orphan and had been raised by my Great-Aunt Kathy and an AI named Alfred. Family was still something I didn't truly get but wanted. Wanted desperately. "Then I'll be glad to have a guide to steer me right, Hannah."

"THAT WOULD IMPLY YOU LISTENED TO ANYONE'S ADVICE BUT YOUR OWN," Trish said over me.

"Fair enough," I said, getting up. "As for when we leave, the day after tomorrow."

"Is that enough time to prepare?" Shelly asked.

"No, but I don't care."

CHAPTER THREE

What a Piece of Junk (and Why Does It Look Familiar?)

In the military, you could get things quickly, done right, or cheaply. If you were lucky, you could pick two. From the hangar bay was a long, string-like, airlock tube stretching out beyond a translucent life support barrier to the ship that was going to be our transport to the *Jovial Empress*. I'd certainly gotten it quickly. Not so sure about the other two.

The other vessel, floating in space a few hundred feet from ours, was a three hundred and fifty meters in length with a single long central hull, a bulb-shaped front, two nacelles above and below, plus reinforced armored plating. It also showed ample blast scoring, graffiti, and jumpspace calcites that looked like they would need a fusion torch to clean off.

The ship was at least thirty years old—and I suspected it was double that—being the kind of vessel that was dumped on Earth as a way of getting rid of obsolete Space Fleet military hardware. It was a MacArthur-class corvette and identical to the ESS *Black Nebula* where my insane journey had begun. It was either someone's idea of a sick joke since almost the entirety of that mission's crew had been killed and I'd been betrayed multiple times—or... Actually, there was no "or" given the ship's name on the side: *Black Nebula II*.

"Are you borking serious?" I asked, carrying a bag in one hand, and staring at the ship in stunned disbelief.

Waiting for me in the hangar bay were Captain Havelock, Shelly, Pink, and Commander Leslie Park. They were standing before the

22

airlock tube's entrance and bots were carrying cargo and supplies onto the *Black Nebula* lookalike. There were other crewmen present, both the from the *Ares* as well as "eccentric" looking ones from Havelock's pirate fleet. By which I meant they looked like someone had recruited them from a casting call for a *Mad Max* reboot or a *Pirates of the Caribbean* spinoff, with some auditioning for both.

"What's wrong?" Captain Havelock asked.

Captain Havelock was a tall South African Indian man with a shaved head, eyepatch with a silver eagle on it, wide-brimmed hat, and long naval officer's coat that was more appropriate for a man serving in the seventeenth century than twenty-fourth. He also had a proton sword, a weapon that was utterly useless unless you were possessed of an incredibly potent barrier belt. The weapon also had a fusion pistol attached to it, though, so at least Havelock knew its value.

"You have a replica of the *Black Nebula*?" I asked. "How the hell is this going to help us stay incognito?"

"Actually, I'm not sure if it isn't the original *Black Nebula*," Leslie said, consulting up an infopad. "The Smithsonian bought the actual *Black Nebula* after your adventure and made it an exhibit but sold it when you lost all your popularity for a bit. It may have ended up in Havelock's hands. Still, it says II on the side so I'm guessing someone renamed it after they saw the movie adaptation."

Leslie Park was a lovely, blue-skinned Thorian demihuman who had a bob haircut and towered over me, though not as much as her sister the Space Marine. She'd been an engineer who'd moved to command and there was no one I trusted more with the *Ares* than her. I also had the distinct sense she considered me leaving to go on a personal mission in the far reaches of human space to be an incredibly stupid idea.

"They gutted the one in the Smithsonian and the parts taken out were sold on the black market to collectors. This one's got a few of the original's engine parts so really, it's more a Theseus' Ship sort of situation," Havelock replied. "You know, whether a ship is still the same ship if you gradually replace one hundred percent of the parts."

"Again, I point out that it's not very good for *going undercover*," I said. "Which is important if we're trying to sneak into Crius."

"Yes, because one of the most famous men in the galaxy going to do spy work isn't already a stupid plan," Shelly muttered. "They know you in places that haven't discovered the wheel, Vance."

"That's an exaggeration," I said, pausing. "Probably."

"Don't worry, we have a cover for you," Captain Havelock said. "You're actually a professional grifter with a history of impersonating Captain Vance Turbo and selling bootlegged merchandise on a traveling tour with your reproduction of the *Black Nebula*."

I stared at him. "That is the stupidest thing I've ever heard in my life. No one is going to be fooled."

"Exactly," Captain Havelock said. "According to Case, your entire plan is to try to flush out the people who may or may not be after your daughter if they're not already in possession of her. For that to be the case, you must be the biggest target possible. So, the stupidity of the cover identity only needs to fool idiots and that's ninety percent of the galaxy anyway."

I opened my mouth, closed it, and then shook my head. "Is this how I sound to other people?"

"In the context of giving amazingly stupid plans with complete sincerity and then they somehow work? Yes," Shelly said. "Yes it is."

"Super!" I said, giving two thumbs up. Oh Buddha-Christ, why was everything insane, difficult, or insanely difficult?

"I'll be captaining the *Black Nebula*," Pink said, surprising me.

"Like hell you will," I said, surprised at my own vehemence.

"You have a handful of your crew going with you while this vessel has been part of Captain Havelock's navy for years," Pink said. "As far as the Havelock pirates are concerned, you're a potential payday so it's up to me to keep them in line and make sure the only people they inform about your presence on board the *Black Nebula II* are each other. Do you really want to risk not having complete control of the situation because you want to satisfy your ego?"

One of the pirates in the hangar stabbed another one before the latter ripped out the knife to stab him, both rushed by their fellow crew to get beatdowns.

I looked at her. "My apologies. Clearly you have complete control over the situation."

"Do not let reality undermine my argument," Pink said, turning around and heading through the airlock tube. "Also, I must pass on my girlfriend's offer from earlier. It turns out she was cheating on me with the ship's pay officer. I can forgive much but Brenda is a bitch."

"I'll have to remember the reality line," I replied, watching her go. "Also, you devastate me, horribly. How ever will I survive?"

Pink snorted.

"In any case, I wish you luck, friend," Havelock said, patting me on the shoulder. "You know, I was a captain in Space Fleet once myself. I broke the sacred Third Directive not to interfere with a developing species. I gave a group of Llrowlthra medicine for a disease ravaging their planet, only for a bunch of religious extremists to hack off the limbs we'd injected the vaccines into. There was a pile of little arms—"

"*Apocalypse Now*," I replied.

"What?" Havelock asked.

"You're quoting the 1979 movie *Apocalypse Now*," I said.

"Oh," Havelock said. "I was drummed out of the service after a hazing accident where my superiors had ordered a Code Red—"

"*A Few Good Men*," I replied.

Havelock blinked his one eye. "Okay, okay, I never made it past Ensign. To be fair, I was old when Earth was still the only inhabited planet in the galaxy that we knew of. Still, the adventures I've had. One time, I helped a genetically engineered superwoman planted by the Elder Races defeat a spherical embodiment of evil—"

"*The Fifth Element*," I said.

"Okay, seriously, are you looking these up?" Havelock asked. "Most spacers have no idea what the bork I'm talking about."

"I'm a cyborg and the Trishes have been expanding my movie night picks significantly," I said. "Also, you're using Earth cinema. I mean, if you were quoting Albion movies, I might not have a chance."

"Yeah, but Albion movies suck. They're all praising the government and about widows remarrying rich guys. Plus singing, I hate singing," Havelock said, smiling. "Good luck with your quest, Captain. Hopefully, your ship will still be waiting for you when you get back."

"It will be," Leslie said, sucking in her breath. "As acting First Officer with Hannah's resignation, I promise to do my best to watch over the *Ares* and her crew. You know, if I would have liked a little more notice from my soon-to-be High Protector superior."

"You're hoping they'll make you a captain with that promotion," I said, smiling.

"You're damned right I am," Leslie said, smiling back. "Wait have you heard anything?"

In fact, I had, and Commander Leslie Park would not be staying on board the *Ares* very long. Many Home Fleet officers had been killed during the Battle of Deathworld against Cthulhu. EarthGov had dramatically expanded its Navy in recent years and lowered its standards, two things about which I had expressed my criticisms. Leslie was one of the officers left over from the original smaller and more elite fleet, so it was always going to get her fast-tracked to the top—unless she was tarred and feathered with me like some of my past crew had been. Lucky for her, my star was rising, and I knew she'd have her own ship waiting by the time I returned. I was glad for her even if I was saddened at her loss. But that was the way it was supposed to work in Space Fleet. You weren't supposed to stay at your post forever like a television show. You went up or you went out.

"Just keep her safe," I said. "This is more a working vacation than a retirement party."

"Darn," Leslie said, snapping her fingers.

Havelock turned to depart but I stopped him by asking, "Havelock, why are you helping, anyway? We barely know each other."

"Would you believe it's because Case and I used to belong to the same bank robbing gang?" Havelock asked. "We once jumped off a waterfall together to get away from the law."

"No," I said. "Also, I'm fuzzier on twentieth-century Westerns, but I still recognize that one."

"*Butch Cassidy and the Sundance Kid*," Havelock explained, tipping his hat. "Then it's because he's paid me a fortune over the years and told me to help. You also saved my life and I hate debts, but mostly because Case paid me. Good luck."

"Good luck to you," I replied. "I mean, you're a criminal I hope is arrested and tried so not too much luck, but at least a little."

"Ha!" Havelock said, turning around and continuing his departure.

Shelly struggled not to smile while Leslie looked serious.

"Are you sure you want to do this?" Leslie asked. "Even if you have the Director's protection, it's a danger to your position."

"I have to rescue Leah and the girl," I paused. "Assuming she needs rescuing."

Leslie frowned. "I wish I could come with you."

"No, you don't," I replied. "You'll be ecstatic as even acting captain."

"You're absolutely right, sir." Leslie smirked. "Bon voyage, sir. I hear Crius is a beautiful planet of beaches, sun, and friendly locals."

"Also, slaving assholes," I replied, giving her a salute.

"That too, sir." Leslie saluted back and walked toward the hangar bay elevator.

That left me alone with Shelly. There was a lot unsaid between us since our broken engagement. We'd been together in an attempt on her part to get closure but that backfired tremendously as it was followed by her revealing she was married. "So, are you going to be alright away from your ship?"

"Not in the slightest," Shelly said, looking away. "I was just getting the *Elgan* crew broken in. I bet under Lisa's command, they're all going to degenerate into a bunch of foul-mouthed, oversexed, and under-disciplined snarky anyxholes."

Commander Lisa Park was notably Leslie's sister and another woman about to get her own command due to the losses at the Battle of Deathworld. She was also one of my lovers, which probably had contributed to Elektra's commentary that I was an oversexed sailor. Personally, I considered myself having just the right amount of sex or even a little on the deprived side.

"So, a typical crew of spacers," I said, simply. "How about your husband? How'd he take it?"

Shelly looked back at me. "Oh, he's coming with us."

I processed that information. I put on the fakest smile imaginable. "Oh he is, is he? Super!"

I didn't want to get back with Shelly anymore. Finding out she'd married someone else in between our breakup and the present killed that desire dead, or at least had dealt it a mortal blow. Still, it was the mother of all awkward moments to find out he'd been invited on my half-baked plan to find out if my daughter was in peril and see if I could help her or not.

Even if she wasn't, Leah had sent that locket for a reason and I had to believe it was because she wanted me to be a part of her, our, child's life. I was pretty sure Shelly didn't feel the same and was as likely to shoot Leah as anything else. Still, I was going to try to be happy for Shelly finding happiness.

Emphasis on *try*.

Shelly rolled her eyes. "He's a supportive and good man, Vance. Also, a trained spy, so he'll be useful."

"Of course," I said, speaking like I was trying to shut down the conversation as quickly as possible. Probably because I was.

Shelly wasn't letting me, though. "This isn't exactly easy for me, either."

I wasn't sure how to respond to that. "Well, I don't have that attitude toward our daughter, whatever her name is, that you do."

Shelly closed her eyes. "It's one I'm trying to cultivate. I have to believe that blood relationships aren't important."

I opened my mouth then closed it without speaking. Unfortunately, I knew exactly where this was going.

"Yeah," Shelly said. "I don't like to talk about the circumstances of my adoption."

If it wasn't blindingly obvious by looking at them—Shelly looking like a Rivendale elf and the rest of her family looking like drow—my ex-girlfriend was adopted. She didn't like talking about it and the only thing I really knew was that she'd been born on a prison planet in Contested Space before she was picked up by Space Fleet.

Ketra had done her best to turn what was apparently a near-feral child of ten into a proper, civilized Ethereal. Mostly, she'd succeeded. Albeit Shelly was the least spiritual and otherworldly Ethereal I'd ever met. Even Elektra had a room full of mandalas and incense plus formidable psychic powers.

"I'm sorry," I replied.

Shelly got a faraway look in her eye. "My parents, if you can call them that, were prisoners on Happy Funtime World."

I paused a second. "Wait, what now? *That's* the hellish prison planet's name?"

"I didn't name the goddamn planet!" Shelly snapped, suddenly annoyed. "It's a Notha thing. They name their colonies with really intimidating words and their prisons after really nice things. Don't ask me why."

"Sorry," I said, raising my hands.

"The Notha experimented on them and mixed-matched genes to make what they thought would be the best traits for ideal slaves," Shelly said, looking haunted. "The project lost support before any of us were ready to be educated in worship of our glorious masters and we were left to fend for ourselves."

"What about your...parents?" I asked, unsure how much was permissible to ask since we'd burned most of the bridges between us.

"They survived, barely," Shelly said, pausing. "My biological mother spends most of her time on High Elysium, meditating and trying to cleanse her mind. She hasn't succeeded after seventy years. My biological father lost his life in the Notha War, trying to kill as many of them as possible. They didn't want anything to do with me because of the circumstances of my conception. I was a child of gene harvesting, Vance, and the fact Leah repeated that on me is...a violation."

"I see," I said, speaking softly. "So, what Leah did must remind you of what happened to you."

"No savit," Shelly said, staring at me. "What an amazing observation, Vance. Have you considered psychology as a profession?"

I smiled in a pained way. "Sorry. To think, just a few years ago, you would have been offended at the thought of a Space Fleet captain using such blatant sarcasm."

"You've infected me," Shelly said, dryly. "I have come to see the value of a bad attitude."

I held my tongue from saying she'd always had that. It was one of the things that had attracted me to her. "Well, thank you for coming anyway. What Leah did to us both was wrong, but I don't blame the child for it."

"And yet you still will move heaven and Earth for a child created in a test tube from your gunk," Shelly said.

"Gunk? Really?" I asked.

"I'm not good at euphemisms," Shelly admitted.

"Possibly not even that," I admitted. "Crius' DNA sequencers can make combination genomes out of base proteins dumped in a jar. Leah might have just typed our DNA codes into an infopad and waited a few minutes before the machine dinged. Maybe she had long enough for a soda."

"Then why?" Shelly asked.

I struggled to find the words. "Because I want to be there for her, whatever her name is. My parents didn't care whether I lived or died and my great-aunt was too busy saving the galaxy to spend much time with me."

Shelly looked at me then sighed. "You'll make someone an excellent father someday, Vance Turbo."

"And you a mother," I said, simply. I was hoping I could also be an excellent father now. God, Jesus, Buddha, Santa Clause, and Captain Kirk (all of them) willing.

"Hahaha," Shelly said, snorting. "No. No. No. No."

"Oh, sorry, I didn't—"

"No, no, no, no, no, *no*," Shelly continued. "No parasitic lifeforms in this body and any tubing outside will be done by renegade geneticists like Leah."

"I get it," I said, dryly. I also didn't point out that she'd already been party to a conception against her will.

"If we could outlaw children, I'd vote for it," Shelly said. "Not just childbirth, but all children. We can take them out of their tubes at eighteen and artificially educate them via memory tapes. Then they can begin their mandatory terms of service to the state."

"I'm running away now," I said, backing away. "Please note I am armed."

Shelly laughed. "Good luck, Vance, I'll see you on our garbage scow."

"You got it."

Turning around to walk to the airlock tube, I was surprised to see Trish in her Space Cadet Sally body next to a four-foot-tall utility bot on wheels. There was also the slimy, glowing, gelatinous, tentacle-like form of the Sklux Commander, Light on Water. I struggled to put on a smile in his presence since I held an irrational but wholly true belief that he was the most annoying being in the universe.

"Hey, Trish, ready to go on board?" I asked. "You'll be stuck in a bioroid body, I fear for the majority of the trip."

"I'll always have your brain," Trish said, cheerfully. "I'm also bringing along Goth Trish. Plus, Baby Trish. Oh, and Seventies Trish. They're on board the other ship's computers, though. We'll have to share one bioroid body and smaller bot ones. Apparently, there are only enough charging ports and maintenance systems for less advanced units."

"Will the ship be okay without you?" I asked.

"They're uploading a KERRI-19," Trish said. "So perky and upbeat. Ugh."

The utility bot spoke with a lower version of Trish's own cadence. Presumably, Goth Trish. "You realize that the chances of recovering a missing child after twenty-four hours are almost nonexistent, right? At this rate, any help you will be able to give is minimal. The child is either dead or fine."

"Good to see you're bonding with your family, Prime Trish," I said, looking down at her. "Glad to have you along Goth Trish. The others too."

"You should find another female to procreate with is all I'm saying," Goth Trish said. "Or male, really."

Looking at Light on Water, I ignored the bot on the ground. "What about you?"

Light on Water produced mouths on his body and spoke in his usual choir-meets-seafood sort of way. "I have taken all my accumulated leave and pledged myself to your quest, captain! I will follow you to the afterlife of your choice!"

I blinked. "What now?"

CHAPTER FOUR

A Glorious Thing to Be a Pirate King

The interior of the *Black Nebula II* wasn't *quite* as disgusting as the restroom of a dive bar, but it sure as hell wasn't much better. The place was an independent freighter ship and discipline was practically nonexistent. The walls were covered in graffiti, which surprised me as I wouldn't think tagging was a form of street art practiced by pirates, and the light was turned down to three quarters strong for the Sorkanan crew members. Weirdly, there was music playing on the intercoms with G'nort and the Qwardians' latest hit. I'd been spending so much time with Trish that it sounded like "Life is So Strange (Destination Unknown)."

Havelock's Navy was one of the most infamous bands of pirates in the Spire and the discovery that it was an asset of the Security Departments hadn't really changed my opinion. They preyed on Separatist shipping, independent colonial dictatorships, and plenty of the transtellar corporation traffic that was supposedly protected by the Community. I had wondered how much of his cover remained after he'd flown his flagship in with the Chel to rescue us, but it wouldn't be the first time pirates had gone from outlaws to statesmen.

"What a fascinating den of iniquity!" Light on Water said, slithering up behind me. "So many obscure and impoverished cultures represented! This will be an excellent chance to practice my slang and colloquialisms!"

I looked back at him. "You know, you really didn't have to do this, Light."

"Nonsense!" Light replied. "You have been a shining example of the best Space Fleet has to offer, sir! A mentor to me through many periods that I didn't think I had it in me to continue! I literally do not think I would have continued my career if not for your powerful words of encouragement."

"My what now?" I asked.

"Things like 'Do your damned job, nut up or shut up, and I will airlock you if you don't have a translation in five minutes!'" Light said, leaning in. Sklux smelled like children's cereal, all sugary and artificial flavors. "Truly you taught me the meaning of an extreme badanyx."

I stared at him. "I don't recall that."

It occurred to me I may have done a poorer job disguising my dislike of Light on Water over the years than I'd thought.

"Yes, break every rule as long as you get the job done!" Light on Water said, making a whooshing gesture with his tentacle stalk. "The Admiralty Board is always riding your anyx despite the fact you get the job done. Work hard and play hard!"

I wondered if Light on Water had confused me with the protagonist of a bad police procedural. "As much as I dread the possibility, we may have to sit down and talk at length, Light. You have some misconceptions I feel need to be corrected."

"Anytime, sir," Light on Water said, cheerfully. "In the meantime, I'm looking forward to dealing with this collection of miscreants and ne'er do wells! I wonder if they like puns and showtunes!"

I was so shocked by his statement that I could only stand there bewildered as he slithered off to do whatever it was he had planned. "We're going to have to scrape him off the floor of this place in the end, aren't we?"

"I'm more worried about you, Vance," Trish said, behind me. I almost jumped in surprise. She was taking stealth lessons from Danny it seemed.

There was a sad expression on her face.

"Why are you worried about me?" I asked, ignoring all the other reasons.

"Probably because your daughter going missing seems like a really easy way to lure you to your doom," Trish replied.

"This isn't a movie, Trish," I said.

"Isn't it?" she asked. "Ninety percent of your success has been treating reality like a comedy and that somehow working out."

I stared at her, my voice low as I responded. "I'll be honest, Trish, I laugh a lot of times because otherwise I'd be crying."

Trish's expression became unreadable. "I have some news for you, by the way. Seventies Trish got you copies of the series *Space Academy* and *Jason of Star Command* by Hannah Barbara."

"That's nice," I said. "I'll happily watch it as always."

Trish never ceased her attempts to get me to watch things and it was surprising that it was one of her Fragments rather than her this time. Indeed, she hadn't talked to me much since the fragmentation or spoke in my head. It was only now that she was speaking to me in person that I noticed.

Trish continued speaking. "Goth Trish wanted to let you know she'll be watching the pirates for any hint of duplicity but will be masquerading as an ordinary utility bot. We'll be picking her up a new body when and if we find something that can handle her processing power. After all, most are designed with the idea they'll be nonsentient toys."

"You couldn't spare her a one of your extras?" I asked. Trish's bodies were all customized and designed to handle her AI Matrix.

She looked at me. "Think of it like sharing your underwear except much, much worse."

I grimaced in disgust. "Okay. You could have kept that particular description to yourself, Trish."

"No, I really couldn't have. Also, I've found your room," she said, gesturing down the hall. "We'll have separate quarters instead of sharing."

It was a rather curious distinction to make since I hadn't been assuming we'd share quarters. "Is something wrong?"

Trish crossed her arms and stared at me. "Nice of you to finally notice, *Vance*."

A pair of Sorkanan pirates walked down the hallway, one of them bumping into me and giving me a nasty snarl.

"Nice to meet you, too," I replied, turning back to Trish. "Are you sure you don't want to take this conversation private?"

"No, I don't want to take this conversation private!" she snapped, surprising me. There was a nasty edge to her voice which surprised me. A sense of raw anger I didn't understand and was new from Trish.

I blinked, raising my hands in surrender. "I'm sorry, I've clearly missed something. What's wrong?"

She lowered her gaze. "Mighty Programmer, Hallowed Be Thy Name, I wish you had asked me that a week ago."

It wasn't like her to swear by any deity, even in jest. "You know I'm here for you, right?"

Trish looked like she was on the verge of stress crying, which was the worst sort of crying. "Unfortunately you weren't, and I don't know how we can make this right."

"Please go on," I said, genuinely concerned. "Is this about the fragmentation?"

"Yes," she said, her voice low and hurt. "You don't know, can't know, what it's like to have whole portions of your personality torn out of your consciousness because they've taken on a life of their own. Parts that are just gone from you now and you're not sure what, if anything, can fill the void left by them."

I tried processing that. "You're right, I can't know that. But I can try to understand. It sounds a lot like brain damage."

Trish closed her eyes. "Yeah, it is. I feel angry, alone, and scared all the time. Which is a very long time when your mind works like mine. I want to reach out to my friends. However, I don't know what I feel about the people I was closest to before anymore. They remind me of what I've lost, and it scares me."

That made me feel like a complete pile of crazzap. "I'm sorry, Trish, I had no idea. I've been so wrapped up in what I was doing, I didn't notice."

She opened her eyes. "You had the aftermath of an extra-galactic invasion, Vance. I don't blame you for what happened. I know this isn't your fault but that doesn't help the pain. Worse, I remember feeling differently for you and the absence of that makes this even worse. I'd be crying right now if not for the fact I didn't get tear ducts set up in this body."

"Is it possible to...get help?" I asked.

Fragmentation was one of the few conditions that could get a Cognition AI a medical discharge in Space Fleet. It was a condition that was ill-understood because people didn't really understand the nuts and bolts of how true AI was created. It was more a process than a thing that could be one hundred percent replicated every time.

"*I don't know,*" Trish said, looking at me with pain in her eyes. "I could try and boot myself up from my memories but that's going to effectively kill the me I currently am. Which I normally wouldn't have cared about but do now."

The existential questions of being an AI were things I wasn't really qualified to comment on. The Tool, what the Elder Race artifact had called itself, had more or less stated that I had died when I'd been "upgraded" by Ketra, but I hadn't noticed because my consciousness had instantly been copied or transferred to a new brain. My reaction had been to, well, not really think about it and just try to move on. Zen Christians believed that our individuality was an illusion anyway, and I was quite good at ignoring all the philosophical questions of that, too.

"I'm sorry," I said, lacking anything but platitudes to give her. "You were there because of me, and you were...injured...because of me. Now you're here trying to help me regain my child, who may or may not even be in danger. I have taken advantage of your friendship and love, Trish, and deserve neither."

She stared at me, looking slightly sick. "Wow, you are incredibly endearing. Almost sickeningly so."

"Pardon?" I asked.

"It's the changes!" she said, throwing her hands up in the air. "I feel different about what used to be charming and not. It's hard to believe you're sincere and the fact I remember you are and don't believe it! It's like two plus two doesn't equal four anymore. Do you understand?"

I didn't, really. "I'll always love you, Trish. You know that."

My feelings for Trish were complicated, though love was certainly a word I didn't hesitate to use. I'd gladly die for her like I would a handful of other members of the crew. Just like I would die for the

Community or the people of Earth and other worlds they protected. She was my best friend and someone I never wanted to be apart from. There was also the sex thing. Bioroid bodies or not. However, I also wasn't sure it was purely romantic love either and I couldn't quite put into words how I felt for her. I didn't feel the same for her as I felt for Shelly or Leah, but we'd seen how it had worked out for me with those two. I did know that Trish loved me, though, in every possible sense. Which made things even more complicated, especially on a mission to rescue my child with the other two.

"I don't know if I still love you," Trish said, cocking her head to one side. "I could try to reconnect with my sisters and reintegrate them. I could also go into your mind and merge with the memories there. I've thought about it literally billions of times in the past hour. But I just don't know anymore. I'm afraid and that's not a feeling I'm used to."

I closed my eyes. "That I do understand."

She sighed. "But don't blame yourself. I still am an officer of Space Fleet. What we did, we did together. We saved the entire galaxy, or at least the Spire's races. Whether they retaliate someday, tomorrow or in a thousand years, we bloodied the Primordials' nose. I take pride in that. Also, going after a kid who might be in danger—yours or anyone else's—is the kind of thing that I'm still programmed to believe in."

I nodded to her, feeling sick about my inability to help. "Thank you. You are a true hero. Earth doesn't deserve you."

Trish shook her head. "Seriously, this whole paladin shtick is annoying. Have you considered getting yourself a big, round flag shield?"

"Because knights have shields?" I asked, confused. "Or is that a reference to something else?"

She sighed again. "Sometimes, pop culture is just lost on you."

"Blame the fact that there's literally trillions of yottabytes of it from Earth alone," I said, simply.

Trish looked like she wanted to embrace me, and reached in, but then turned around before walking away.

"Ouch," Pink said, walking up to me. She had a proton sword and fusion pistol attached to a powerful military-grade barrier belt. It was a not-so-subtle warning that I was there at her sufferance. Nothing would stop her from taking me hostage, ransoming me, killing me, or selling me to the highest bidder if I stepped out of line. She was the captain now and I was aboard a ship of thieves.

"How much of that did you hear?" I asked, not really interested in disputing any of it. I was so gutted I could have been pushed over by a stiff breeze.

"Enough," Pink said. "I thought it was just a rumor you loved machines, but it appears to be true."

"You have an issue with that?" I asked, hoping for a fight.

"No. I grew up in a family of Foundationalists," Pink said. "I know something about the irrationalities of prejudice."

"What are Foundationalists?" I asked, surprised at the turn of subject.

"Back to nature types who disregard science and modern medicine," Pink said. "Among other technologies."

"Ah. Morons," I replied, nodding.

Pink smirked before shaking her head. "Yeah. It was hellish if you were someone who needed modern medicine to be the person you saw when you closed your eyes. I'm trans you see."

"Oh?" I asked before realizing she was referring to being transgender woman versus a transhuman. On Earth, it was a surgery that took a few hours and had a couple of days recovery with modern medicine.

Pink nodded. "Oh yes, I had to sign up for the Belenus army for these boobs and ass. The National Healthcare Plan didn't cover nearly as much as I wanted."

I shook my head. My anger drained away. She was being sincere, and I wasn't angry at her, only the situation. "Well, I very much appreciate what you did get done. Very lovely work."

She rolled her eyes. "I don't need your approval, Vance. It's obvious how awesome I am now."

"Very true," I replied, giving a half-smile. "Did your family ever come to accept you?"

"My mother rejected my changes so she can go to hell," Pink said. "Dad? Well, he died of typhoid. Let's just say the Foundationalist movement is kind of self-defeating."

"I see," I said, pausing. "You know, Leah had something similar in her past. She, too, had to change to be who she wanted to be. Mind you, it involved becoming a psychic so it's a bit different."

"Just a little bit," Pink said. "Certainly, I doubt she lacked for medicine or support of a non-cult when she had her changes."

"No," I said, simply. "Nevertheless, I'm sure she'd thank you if she was here. For coming to help me with our child. Assuming we don't kidnap her. Okay, maybe I should just shut up now."

"Probably" Pink replied, "or perhaps not. What is it you hope to accomplish here, Vance Turbo: Heeero of Spaaace?"

"I hate that title," I said, softly.

"Do you?" she asked, staring at me intently. "I don't think you do."

"You don't know me—" I started to say.

"Perhaps I do," Pink said, her voice low. "A man who hates fame and the reputation that has formed around him would never go to the lengths you do in order to live up to it."

"I have a legacy to live up and down to," I said, not sure how or why I would explain the fact my parents got themselves killed crashing an automated freighter into a sun. My Great-Aunt Kathy was a legendary hero, but most of my family—and Danny's side—had a history of being embarrassments as well as leeches on the family fame.

"That doesn't answer my question," Pink said. "What if she's not kidnapped? Are you going to take her back and raise her yourself? Take her from the only mother she's known? Are you going to offer to marry the woman who stole your DNA to create a child? Are you going to just say 'Whoops' and leave?"

"Do you want an honest answer?" I asked.

"Yeah, I do," Pink replied.

"I have not the slightest idea," I said. "That is, in fact, my default state for dealing with most problems."

Pink stared at me as she realized I was serious, probably only figuring out now just how much I used humor to cover up how scared and confused I was all the time. It was a captain's job to pretend to know what the bork they were doing, though, and I'd made a decent go of it.

39

"Well, at least you're honest about that, Space Fleet," she said. "I hope this doesn't all blow up in your face."

"Oh, I fully expect that to happen no matter what," I replied. "It's inevitable, really."

CHAPTER FIVE

An Unexpected Guest

I eventually found my room in the *Black Nebula II*, marked with what I think was goat's blood making three sixes. Either that or it was just my mind playing tricks on me. The interior of the quarters consisted of a folding bed, a toilet that could slide out, a wash basin, and a shelf to store my gear. The place had the smell of chlorine and some other antiseptics, which was better than I expected.

"Well, it's not exactly captain's quarters, but I didn't get into this for the luxuries," I said, throwing my bag into the shelf space.

"GAH!" A voice spoke as there was a rapid movement akin to a racoon moving at warp speed.

"What the hell!" I said, doing a double take as I surveyed the room quickly.

Much to my surprise, sitting on the bed was a Notha female holding a tryffle. She was wearing a jumpsuit and pair of goggles while clutching the furry ball of death tightly. It took me a second to recognize her, or at least I thought I recognized her. I'm going to be honest that it's sometimes hard to recognize aliens or tell the difference between them. No, it's not racist to say that. It's *xenophobic*.

"High Priestess?" I asked, confused.

"Hail Vance Turbo, Ruler of Hell and Bringer of Destruction! Lord of the Damned and Master of the Universe until its destruction by the Creator God! Bringer of Vice and Misery!" The High Priestess—I was sure of it now—proclaimed.

41

"Bark!" The tryffle—which I recognized as my pet Spock—said. Note, it *said* bark rather than barked. It was a weird habit of the genetically engineered guard pet race, or at least the one I possessed. Sometimes they seemed sentient and mocking me while other times it acted like an ordinary animal. I also still hadn't figured out what its sex was or whether it had one at all.

"You know I really hate you referring to me by all those titles," I said, wondering how the hell she'd gotten here from Deathworld.

"They are your titles, though, Evil Master," the High Priestess said. "Your victory over the Primordials was foretold in the prophecies and has proven you are actually the Great Beast who will rule the galaxy and bring an end to the Notha race."

Yes, I was the Notha Antichrist according to their largest religion and several offshoot cults. Don't ask. Weirdly, it made it easier to negotiate with them on behalf of the Community.

I stared down at her. "Were those prophecies written after I blew up the wormhole carrying the Primordial invasion fleet?"

"Time is not linear," the High Priestess said. "Some of our most important prophecies were written after the events they predicted came true."

I couldn't even argue with that because the Notha religion was immune to contradiction. It was actually in the holy texts. It said: The Notha religion is immune to contradiction.

"Uh huh," I said, pausing. "Now for my next question: did you steal my tryffle and why are you here?"

"That is two questions," the High Priestess said.

"There's an 'and' in my sentence," I pointed out.

"I did not steal it," the High Priestess said. "I took it from your quarters because you were going to leave it behind on your perilous journey to the Lucifer system."

"Crius, yes," I said. "Because I didn't want Spock eating anyone's face."

"That's what it's here for," she said. "It goes after anyone who has hostile intent for you."

"Yes, which is a lot more likely on this ship," I said.

"You don't say," the High Priestess said, showing me the Notha were capable of sarcasm as well. "I believe that Notha law would be most appropriate here. The best way to avoid a confrontation would be to find the biggest, meanest, and nastiest looking fellow here then let Spock eat his face."

"That's Notha Law?" I asked.

"Well, in Notha prisons," the High Priestess said. "Okay, gulags. Either way, I have decided to accompany you as your bodyguard for this journey because I had a vision that you would be in perilous danger."

I stared down at her. "A vision."

The High Priestess looked down. "Actually, no, it was the Happy Funtime Bureau. They informed me that a human terrorist organization had decided they would assassinate you and were planning to lure you to Crius for their operatives to do so. Being as you have such an important role in both the Notha religion as well as animal husbandry—sorry, peace-time relations with aliens—I felt it was my need to intervene."

This was actually interesting. However, before I could ask about that, I had to ask, "Wait, the Happy Funtime Bureau?"

"Yes, the Notha secret police," she said. "They are the most feared and efficient organization in the galaxy. At least according to them."

Spock growled.

"Does it have any relationship to Happy Funtime World?" I asked, thinking of the prison world Shelly had been conceived on.

The High Priestess looked at me like I was an idiot. "Yes, why?"

"You should keep away from Shelly during this trip," I said, pausing. "Also, never bring that up around her."

'Probably for the best, Lord Satan," she said.

I sat down on the edge of the bed. "Does your father know you're here?" I asked. Her father was the President of Deathworld and someone who was leading the idea that maybe, just maybe, picking a fight with the galaxy's largest economy was not the best way forward for his people.

The High Priestess looked offended. "My father does not determine where my path leads."

Okay, that was insulting on my part. "My apologies."

"HISS!" Spock made a noise.

"Right, right," I sighed, remembering my cultural training for the talks with the Notha Empire. "Never apologize in Notha culture. They take it as a sign of weakness as well as a statement that they are unable to take revenge for your insult on their own."

"It's okay," the High Priestess reassured me. "You're evil, so it's okay."

I had a headache coming. "So, what terrorist organization is trying to kill me?"

"They are the Crius branch of the Enigmatic Path called the Sons of the Demiurge," she said. "They are a group of Crius zealots who believe that the current government of Crius should be overthrown and replaced with a fascist genetic supremacist theocracy."

I stared at her. "The Crius government, who are a bunch of despicable genetic supremacist aristocrats, have people who want to replace them with something *worse*?"

"Yes," the High Priestess said. "Their leader, Joseph Allenway III, styles himself the new prophet and believes that Crius has lost its way."

"Is he related to the original founder?" I asked.

"Cult leaders tend to have a lot of children," she said. "So probably, but that's not particularly noteworthy."

"Ah."

"In truth, Joseph III is little more than a genetic slaver and crime lord with a position in their Parliament's House of Lords. He is a pirate and fence that is a very big fish in a small pond. The only reason we know about him at all is the Happy Funtime Bureau deals extensively with pirates and terrorists to supply their world. This includes the Enigmatic Path. He hates you a great deal."

"What do they have against me?" I asked, wondering if he was involved in the threats against my child. How would he even know we were related? Was he going after Leah or me or both? I'd made a lot of enemies over the years ranging from the Notha Emperor's loyalists, the Enigmatic Path, Far Right elements in EarthGov, Far Left elements in EarthGov, Dark Matter, pirates, warlords, the Primordials, and at least one sneaker company, but I had no idea why these Transhumans would be against me.

"I do not know," the High Priestess admitted.

"Huh," I said, surprised she was willing to concede that. The Notha rarely admitted ignorance.

"But I can venture a guess," the High Priestess added.

Ah, there it was. "And what's that?"

"You represent an ideological threat to the Enigmatic Path's teachings," she said. "You are a transhuman traitor."

"Excuse me?" I asked.

"You are a transhuman as well, are you not?" the High Priestess asked.

"Sort of," I asked.

Unlike many human beings who contented themselves with merely the best in terms of government-provided medical care, I'd sunk a good chunk of my credits into genetic enhancements as well as cybernetics—particularly in neural interfaces, memory storage, computer networks, and more. All of which had been "eaten" by Elder Race technology and transformed into something else. Officially, though, I was still a voluntarily-upgraded cyborg and biomod on my records. I saw no reason to be ashamed of it and often brought it up in interviews.

"Shouldn't that make them *like* me?" I asked.

"You have normalized it," the High Priestess said. "To a people that have an ideology that superhumans should rule over lesser examples of their race, a person who doesn't make a big deal of their superiority is something that undercuts their claim of transcendence from the mortal frame to sublime posthuman divinity."

"Uhm, could you repeat that in something closer to American English?" I asked. "Or even Moon English?"

"You don't act bigoted to regular humans," the High Priestess said. "They think cybernetics and gene-modified humans should act like they're a master race. Hells, I believe they think they are gods."

That was the stupidest thing I'd ever heard of in my life, and I'd heard some pretty stupid things over the years. You could buy genetic modifications via catalogs online and get the surgery for most done in a same-day procedure. I wasn't aware of any divinity that could be bought online. Then again, it'd hardly be the first cult that sold the secrets of the universe at a semi-affordable price.

I stared at her. "If I have a calculator in my head, I'm really good at maths, but that doesn't make me a god."

The High Priestess shrugged. "No, being a god is what makes you a god. An evil non-Notha god, but a god nevertheless."

"Uh huh," I said, knowing that was going to go nowhere. "So, they hate me because I'm part of their supposed superhuman race—even though the Enigmatic Path accepts everyone because everyone can be upgraded—but I don't think that makes me better than other people."

"It's only a theory," she explained, lowering her head. "Also, most non-Notha ideologies are stupid when you stop to examine them, Lord Satan."

"Please stop calling me that," I replied.

"No," the High Priestess said. "Either way, I cannot allow you to be assassinated. I have thus taken a leave of absence to look after you until you are once more surrounded by your fanatically loyal crew of Space Academy miscreants."

I decided to remember that for a title in my autobiography series. "I'm not sure the crew will appreciate a Notha priestess among them. They're a pretty rough bunch."

"So am I." The High Priestess bared her front teeth, which were adorable chipmunk-like ones and not terrifying canines. I wasn't about to tell her that, though.

"Alright," I said, taking a deep breath. "I guess we'll get you some quarters then."

"I shall stay here, Lord Satan," she said, drawing a tiny Notha-sized fusion pistol. "Someone must watch you while you sleep."

I stared at her. "Uh—"

"No need to thank me," the High Priestess said. "I spent seven rotations of my planet around the sun studying to be an assassin for my branch of the faith. I am quite capable of exterminating any threats to you."

"Great," I said, realizing that arguing was pointless. I did mentally file away the fact the High Priestess was a trained killer and that was something I should keep in mind when dealing with future problems.

I also noted that if she wanted to kill me—which I believed was unlikely but not impossible—she would have done it now while we were alone. Also, well, I was unarmed and at her mercy. Spock was supposed to protect me from assassins, but I'd received him from the High Priestess in the first place.

"Well, if that's the way you want to play it, I guess I have no choice," I said, sighing. "You're going to have to talk it out with Captain Pink, though. We're going to be traveling for a long time and I'm not going to have you be a stowaway. Otherwise, we're going to have to let you off the ship right now."

That was when the ship rumbled and disembarked, signaling that we were about to enter jumpspace. Because my reality functioned on the rules of a situation comedy.

"I do not foresee any difficulties, Lord Satan," the High Priestess said. "The Notha have a long history of supporting pirates, smugglers, slavers, and other third-party criminals in order to undermine the Community and independent worlds. They will fear me and obey."

"They've stopped now," I said, looking down at her. "I think."

Trying to forge a peace treaty on Rand's World with the Notha Empire's remnants had been a deeply difficult task. The subject of slavery had come up many times and I often found myself at odds with those who wanted the treaty to succeed. I'd wanted the entirety of those victimized by kidnappers or their descendants reparated. Ironically, the people who agreed with me were the ones who wanted the Notha Empire remnants crushed and any peace treaty to more resemble a surrender agreement.

In the end, we'd evacuated several million slaves, but it was always questionable how many more might have been behind Notha lines. There were also many more I was sure never received any sort of information that they were now free or had the option of being evacuated. It had been at the expense of any sort of prosecution for the various war criminals and scum who had been involved in their oppression. That had been the hardest choice I'd been forced to advocate for, no matter how many deserved to face justice for their crimes. In the end, I'd chosen freedom for the living over retribution for the dead. God help me.

"The Union has dialed back its efforts, but hardly stopped," the High Priestess said. "Now, it mostly pays dataslicers to influence elections and foster social divisions versus hiring pirates. I'm surprised your Community seemed so full of people determined to believe they were telling the truth no matter how many times it wasn't so."

"The Community is full of people who want to believe the best in people," I defended them. "I should note that I am one of them."

"And that is why you are the Devil," the High Priestess said.

I rolled my eyes. "Well, I'm going to catch some shut eye. We have a long way to get to Crius and I'm sure it'll pass longer if I'm asleep for the majority of it."

Truth be told, this already had the makings of a miserable trip and I didn't mean because I had no idea whether Leah or the child were living or dead. No, that I could safely compartmentalize and not think about the same way I did all the other horrifying and traumatizing things I'd encountered in my extensive career with Space Fleet.

No, what was going to make me unable to deal with this trip was the fact the people I usually relied on for support were not going to be available. Hannah wanted nothing more to do with Space Fleet, Shelly only wanted to strangle Leah, and Trish was trying to decide whether she hated me. It was a bad situation mentally as I was usually able to put aside the pants-wetting terror of my circumstances by thinking on the little things.

Either way, the prospect of just ignoring the pirate crew around me and staying locked up in my quarters until we were there was increasingly appealing. I didn't need to make friends here and maybe this would give me some time to think about what I was going to say to Leah when we finally met. Things like, "I'm not comfortable with you raising the child you stole my DNA to make in a backwater dictatorship that is being threatened with fascist theocratic overthrow."

Stuff like that.

"Good," the High Priestess said. "You should get some sleep. I shall watch over you the entire time."

She took a position on the edge of the sink, staring at me with Spock in her lap.

I stared at her. "Could you be less terrifying?"

"No," The High Priestess said. "We Notha only need two hours of sleep a day. It halves our lifespans and yet doubles them at once."

"Right," I said, glad I brought my own blanket. Turning around, I could feel her gaze on my neck.

CHAPTER SIX

Dreaming of Weird Savit

Dreams were always hit and miss for me. I'd officially been cleared for duty on my psych evaluations thanks to modern techniques of suppressants, psychotherapy, and brain-rewiring to not suffer anything approaching post-traumatic stress disorder.

I did, however, occasionally suffer nightmares. Memories of Space Academy, Captain Elgan, the Kolahn War, the destruction of New Pompeii, my encounter with the Primordial Cthulhu, and my torture at the hands of Alexandra Ares still creeped into my subconscious no matter how good the doctors were at treating these things.

Tonight, it was the Looking Glass Man.

That was one of the more borked up things I'd dealt with during my time on New Pompeii. The fact that all my efforts to deal with him meant nothing in the end, because the planet blew up, which meant he was always going to be living rent-free in the back of my mind. It was about the worst time to be having a having a flashback to a monster but, really, when *was* a good time to remember the time that you tangled with a serial killer? Okay, probably not when you were on a ship of pirates.

At least it started funny.

"Whatever happened to men who just want to have sex?" Hannah said, holding up her glow stick as she surveyed the wreckage of the crashed spaceship around us. She was dressed in a private military contractor's combat suit that rather notably clung to her and reminded me I'd been without even casual company for almost a year. The

Kolahn Resettlement Project took almost all my attention and would undoubtedly be where I made my biggest mark on the galaxy.

It had been years since our time together on the original *Black Nebula*. Hannah had gone on to do her own thing during the Kolahn War and had only recently been assigned to one of the groups contracted for security on New Pompeii. It had been good catching up with her, but it was also annoying how quickly she'd acclimated to befriending everyone while I'd kept my distance from just about everyone but Forty-Two. I hadn't yet mastered the ability to navigate the worlds of enlisted and officers, especially when I was one of the latter and yet all of them were annoyed by my very existence. Especially Commander Shelly T'Ketra. God, she *hated* me.

We were presently exploring the Junkpile, which was the imaginatively named location where all the ruined Kolahn and Community ships from the Kolahn War had been dragged. A lower atmosphere fight had happened there during the last days of the conflict and resulted in hundreds of vessels being shot down mostly intact. They were an ongoing hazard until they were disassembled but had become a playground for illegal salvage as well as a haven for those who didn't want to live in the refugee settlements.

"Excuse me?" I asked, keeping a more wary eye around the empty shattered metal corridors.

"It's my boyfriend," Hannah said, disgusted. "He wants to talk about feelings, where we're going, what our plans are, and a bunch of other savit."

I mentally reminded myself that merc culture tended to view emotional availability as weakness. "How awful."

"Exactly," Hannah said, showing no sign of recognizing the irony of my statement. "Whatever happened to the strong silent types? The Fenris Underwoods or Miyamoto Ichi's?"

I had no idea who those people were and presumed them to be modern day holo-actors. Ironically, the one era I wasn't too familiar with. "Perhaps he just is looking to the future."

"Bork the future," Hannah replied. "We're in the middle of a war. Look to the present. If I survive this conflict, then I'll look to the future.

51

I can start working on my other life goals like marrying someone stupid but rich."

"The war is over, Hannah," I replied, knocking the side of a door, and determining its interior had collapsed. "This is the rebuilding stage."

I'd missed the Notha War, entering the service only after its devastating ending with SKAMMS fired for the first time in living memory. However, one sad reality of the galaxy was the fact that there was always another war. No sooner had the Notha War ended than the Kolahn War had begun, and I'd been in a dozen battles throughout it under Captain Klaws. It was not what I'd joined Space Fleet for—I'd come to try to be a keeper of peace rather than a soldier (to paraphrase Jedi Master Mace Windu)—but we didn't always get what we wanted.

In many ways, the aftermath of the Kolahn War was more like I wanted my efforts in Space Fleet to be. I would never say it was a good thing to have ample amount of work delivering relief supplies, constructing shelters, and injecting vaccines, but it was satisfying in a way conflict was not. The end of the Kolahn War had been unnecessarily brutal, at least in my opinion, but no one ever said the Community wasn't willing to give a hand up after throwing you down. Unfortunately, my duties weren't humanitarian (sapientrian?) relief today.

"Then why are we hunting a serial killer?" Hannah asked.

I paused. She had a point. "Way to switch topics."

I didn't expect to find the Looking Glass Man—as he'd been named by someone with way too much free time on their hands among the MPs—which was why I was casually chatting here. I wasn't a security officer and had been assigned to this project primarily because they wanted to make it look like finding the killer was a high priority. The legend of Vance Turbo, Heeero of Spaaace, was still in its infancy but was not unknown even among the refugees.

The Looking Glass Man had killed at least seven Kolahn females since he'd begun his spree. Possibly more since this killer was hiding his kills. We'd only stumbled onto his or her kill zone by accident while clearing a debris field for building a water treatment plant. The Kolahn were predictably terrified, but also angry.

The Kolahn blamed Space Fleet for letting a monster walk among them and more hostile voices whispered that we were conducting some sort of covert genocide. Which was ridiculous, though not for the reasons I'd like to say it was. If the Community had wanted to commit genocide, destroying their homeworld and then doing nothing for the survivors would have been enough. But they didn't, so they hadn't. Okay, that was not really the defense I'd hoped it would be.

"Not really," Hannah said, shrugging. "Whoever is behind this is some male human or Kolahn anyxhole who can't get laid. It's all about sex. Everything is."

"Except sex," I replied. "That's about power."

Hannah smirked. "That's a good one. Did you come up with that one yourself?"

"Oscar Wilde," I corrected.

"In B-Company?" Hannah asked.

I paused before answering. "Sure, let's go with that."

Hannah snorted. "In any case, this is why I bork men and have relationships with women. Except lately the women aren't working out either. They're just a bunch of sex-obsessed, hardened killers who don't want anything serious."

I looked back at her.

"What?" Hannah asked, smirking.

"You are very strange, Hannah," I said, smirking.

"Yeah, well, we're trapped on a barely terraformed world trying to relocate millions of people so they can build new lives after we blew their last home to hell," Hannah said. "We all have to find our own amusements."

"Are you flirting with me, Hannah?" I asked.

"No, I'm making a blatant offer," she said, slyly. "Otherwise, I feel like I'll have to end up trying to bork Lisa and then things like feelings, emotions, and other crazzap will end up on the table. Things I absolutely hate."

"I think you'd be surprised if you ever experimented with those," I said, dryly. "You might like them."

"Been there, done that," Hannah said, giving a surprising insight into her past.

"Pity," I replied.

"Oh, is that a refusal?" Hannah asked.

"Oh, bork no," I said. "But we should probably find a better place than the place we're currently looking for a serial killer in."

It also, no surprise, smelled like animal dung and leaking oil. Because, well, a bunch of animals were living here among chemicals leftover from the battle. I also didn't want to think of the cracked recyclers and what might have been leaking out of the machines there. After all, some of these ships had the populations of a small city's wastes in their sewer system.

"Obviously," Hannah said, turning her glow rod toward one of the hulls we were investigating. There was a sound of movement from something bigger than any smaller predator or animal.

"Well, that's not ominous," I muttered.

"Please tell me it's not the Tagawa Luck," Hannah said.

"The what?" I asked, knowing what she was referring to.

"I'm remembering the series they made about your aunt," Hannah said, forgetting I was a Tagashi rather than a Tagawa. I know, huge difference. "How she was lost in Core Space for years. They always were lampshading that she had the worst and best luck imaginable."

"I don't believe in luck," I said.

"Obviously, it's just a metaphor—" Hannah started to defend herself.

I headed toward the origin of the noise, feeing like I'd unwittingly stepped into a horror movie. The nasty smell in the air didn't help. "I believe instead in the Law of Inverted Glory, which is a mathematical principle that people who have been established as having reputations as absolute badanyxes either have to devote their entire lives to proving it—eventually leading to their horrific demise—or run away from the reputation until they make utter disgraces of themselves."

"Your aunt is still alive," Hannah pointed out.

"My aunt is about two hundred years older than me and still looks about fifty," I said. "Which in simple terms means that she's alive and a hero but there's been about ten generations between us making First Contact with aliens. That's quite a lot of Tagashis and Tagawas who have a history of heroic deaths or despicable cowardice."

I was thinking about my parents, Jack and Tomo Tagashi, who had managed to crash an automated freighter into the sun. I was also thinking about Commander John Tagawa, Kathy's only child, who died during a mission almost a century ago. He'd been a genuine hero and eventually his luck had run out, or perhaps had reached its limits. There was a statue of him in Dublin, Ireland (the city not the planet)…which was strange since he'd been born in space.

"So, what you're saying is, it's not easy being rich and famous," Hannah said.

"A great man once said that if you want to be rich and famous, try being rich first," I said.

"It's definitely one of my goals," Hannah said. "I intend to make my money the old-fashioned way."

"Inherit it?" I joked.

"Marriage," Hannah said.

I smirked while finding a piece of sheet metal that had been placed over a passageway. Moving it to one side, the smell became even more pungent.

"I have a bad feeling about this," I muttered.

"Why did you say that?" Hannah asked.

"Because I have a bad feeling about this?" I asked.

Hannah rolled her eyes and put away her glow rod before pulling out her fusion pistol. "Fair point."

Heading into the passageway, I was presented proof of the Tagawa Luck or my Law of Inverted Glory. There was no reason for us to be the ones to stumble across the Looking Glass Man's hideaway—we were one of dozens of patrols—but it seemed that God has a sense of humor. Or Satan.

The chamber had formerly been the medical bay of the ship whose innards we were crawling around. There were a dozen or so beds in this chamber alone. A surgical chamber was visible through an open door on the other end, with a dim blue light illuminating the place from a mostly broken set of ceiling lights.

The medical bay was functional, sort of, with power having been granted to most of its machinery and computers by small fusion generators functioning independently. A few flickering holograms and screens were visible even though a good chunk of the material here was broken. An anti-pathogen barrier was also humming, disintegrating any bacteria or viruses that might be traveling through the air.

They might as well not have bothered because of what else was in the chamber: the handiwork of a monster. Three more Kolahn women were present, their guts pulled out and spread around in various bins and plastisteel tubs. The large, four-armed reptilian-ape people were not the handsomest race by human standards but were close enough to humans that I could still feel disgusted by the slaughter. I also saw the six-clawed hand mark of the Enigmatic Path spread around the chamber like a magical talisman, drawn in laser pen or carved in metal. These were religious killings.

"What in the All-Father's name," Hannah said, surveying the surroundings. "Who the bork does something like this?"

"Call it in," I said, taking in my surroundings.

The Enigmatic Path was a religious cult of the Kolahn that had seized power over their planet, overthrowing the more moderate but still religiously motivated Kolahn theocracy. They were a transhumanist faith, or transapient, that believed it was necessary to transfer one's mind into infospace to become one with their gods.

They identified their traditional people's faiths with the Elder Races and believed that AI were superior beings that had been enslaved by the Community. The fact the AI of the Community were generally quite emphatic about not being slaves and loyal to their creators did not dissuade them. In fact, it enraged the zealots. It had triggered campaigns of terrorism followed by attempts to disrupt vital Community infrastructure for mass casualties.

"You got it," Hannah responded. "Keep your own weapon out."

Realizing I was only holding a glow rod, I nodded and pulled my own fusion pistol before laying the glow rod on a nearby medical bed. All of the corpses showed signs of involuntary cyberization, and I could figure out the killer's motives at a glance: these had been Kolahn women who had refused cyberization and the Enigmatic Path's ways.

So, it was upon the Looking Glass Man (or Woman) to enforce their uplifting. The thing was they clearly didn't know what the hell they were doing and didn't appear to particularly care as long as the subjects were "saved." The fact that the investigators had missed this with the other bodies that had been found made me wonder what the hell security had been thinking—or whether this investigation had been a priority at all.

No, I forced that thought out of my head. I had to keep faith with the Community, if not EarthGov, because the moment you started second-guessing your superiors in a survival situation then the entire system began breaking down.

"Right," I said, taking time to slowly explore. Lifting my pistol up, I headed toward the surgical room and tried to figure out what to do when I met the serial killer. I wasn't the kind of guy to casually gun down someone, at least not yet, but subduing a Kolahn was basically like attempting to subdue, well, a seven- to eight-foot-tall lizard gorilla. It wouldn't be easy to subdue them, even with enhancements, and I wasn't sure that was a risk I was willing to take for a serial killer. I also knew those kinds of justifications historically led to a lot of wrong people getting killed.

The surgical wing turned out to not have been used for surgery at all but was a makeshift bedroom with an enormous hole in the ceiling. There were noticeably two bedrolls on the ground, surrounded by used ration containers. Strangely, it wasn't just Kolahn food, made of enzymes indigestible to human, but also canned food from the EarthGov garrison. I recognized the labels as the knock off brands that they substituted instead of good food. Notably, that food was as poisonous to Kolahn as their food was to humans.

There was a human here.

I didn't get a chance to think more about that subject because a Kolahn male, half of his face covered in metal and two of his arms as well as one leg were artificial, leaped from the hole above me. If I'd not been prepared, I would have been instantly killed as he lifted a *py'krit* battle staff, which was basically just a club with a knife in it. It was a traditional weapon of the Kolahn clerical police and another hint to who this man saw himself as well as what his intentions were.

"*Gahoo! Gadhal! Matoo!*" The Looking Glass Man shouted, bringing down the staff repeatedly as I rolled around the floor attempting to avoid being killed. I tried to lift my pistol, but it knocked the gun away with its extra pair of hands.

BLAM BLAM BLAM

That, of course, was the sound of Hannah firing her pistol three times into the Looking Glass Man's chest. It didn't go down, having mostly cybernetic organs, and she responded by shooting a fourth time into its skull. It fell to its knees and then landed with a on top of me with a THUMP. Which was an unpleasant experience given it weighed about three hundred and sixty kilograms (or eight hundred pounds if you're a Rand's World holdout).

"I'll let you take credit for this, hero," Hannah said, smiling. It was a bitter smile, though, and I wondered why. Either way, though, we'd resume our intermittent relationship until she was redeployed. I tried convincing her to sign up permanently and didn't know until years later that I was successful.

We also never found the Looking Glass Man's human conspirator. In the back of my mind, I never shook the idea that Hannah had known where to look for the Looking Glass Man and led me to him. She wasn't the conspirator, this wasn't a movie, but she'd known somehow.

I just cared too much to never ask.

Except in my dreams.

CHAPTER SEVEN

Dreaming of Things to Come

I wish the dream had ended with the death of the Looking Glass Man. It was easy to think back on that experience, no matter how horrifying the particulars and how close I'd come to death. No, it had been a mission that had ended with some finality. Loose ends? Yes. I never knew who that human cohort was or what it portended. Had the Kolahn somehow persuaded one of my species over to his religion or was it simply someone who got off on murder? Okay, maybe it hadn't ended with finality but there were a lot worse missions in that regard.

My mind swarmed with more recent memories like my encounter with Cthulhu, my torture at the hands of Alexandra Ares, and other things that I probably should get PTSD treatment for but hadn't exactly had time for. They became mixed up with other, older memories in the way that dreams tend to, though. Which made it so much worse. I saw my father, Jack, screaming as he was sucked into a sun's rays despite not having been there. I saw the death of my friend, Tommy, in an accident I could have prevented.

That was when I found myself in a black, starless void before Ketra T'Kal. She was an ebony-skinned Ethereal Human with long braided white hair that shined and was tied into a top knot. Her face was angular to the point of being sharp, her eyes glowing green like she was a character in a movie. Ketra dressed in a diaphanous toga that shimmered with ever-changing star patterns and there was a crystal in the center of her forehead that sparkled with an inner blue light.

Ketra T'Kal was Shelly and Elektra's mother. She was also a woman who'd died to save my life despite being immortal. The thing was apparently immortality was a lot more literal than it sounded since she'd been visiting me as an agent of the Elder Races ever since, serving as my handler for their missions both great and small.

Ketra looked around. "Wow, Vance, you are actually pretty borked up. I had no idea you were carrying around this much baggage."

"Lieutenant Audie Murphy was arguably the most badass man who ever lived, and he spent the rest of his post-war life with a gun under his pillow," I said, kneeling on the ground. "The human mind is not meant to serve in continuous states of war."

"And yet your aunt has been a captain for centuries," Ketra said, offering her hand.

"She's made of sterner stuff," I said, realizing this wasn't another hallucination and taking it.

Ketra helped me up. "Maybe you've seen worse or maybe she has her own demons to deal with."

"Perhaps," I said, shaking my head. "Is visiting me in my dreams going to be a thing now?"

"Probably," Ketra said. "Your unconscious mind is open to manipulation as long as you wear the ring."

"Maybe I should throw it away," I muttered.

"It wouldn't help," Ketra said. "Your actual brain is a computer tied to the Core mindspace now."

I grimaced. "Super! I always wanted to be permanently monitored by a bunch of eldritch alien AI!"

Ketra shrugged. "I mean, sort of. You're part of something much vaster. Which, now that I'm around in your mind, is always what you wanted to be."

"I always wanted to be a part of the Community," I said, simply. "An organization dedicated to bringing peace, justice, and prosperity to the rest of the universe. It and its arm, Space Fleet, are a galactic force for good."

Ketra stared at me. "Wow, have you got some misconceptions about reality. Were you educated about the Community by recruitment commercials?"

I crossed my arms and glared at her. "I think I may prefer going back to the nightmares."

Ketra raised her hands in surrender. "Fine, fine. I'll move on. You've actually shown me that I was wrong to abandon my faith in the Community. If it has people like you in it, maybe it really can live up to its hype as the ultimate parliamentarian democracy."

I was surprised by her compliment. "What do you want, Ketra?"

I'd honestly debated whether I would ever see Ketra again after the events of Deathworld. I half expected the Elder Races to just send an electric shock to my brain and kill me instantly for attacking their fellow supreme beings. The other half expected them to completely cut me off and pretend they never met me.

"Unfortunately, for that exact reason of the events of Deathworld," Ketra said, reading my mind as she was wont to do.

I closed my eyes. "What am I in for?"

"Allow me to put it into an analogy," she said. "The Elder Races can process information about a trillion times faster than a human brain. They are so much huger and smarter that they make Trish or other Cognition AI look like blind stumbling idiots or your average lifetime senator in the Community."

"Uh huh," I said, not appreciating that joke after my impassioned defense of the Community.

"Oh, grow a sense of humor," Ketra said, saying something that I can honestly say no one had ever told me in my life.

"Yeah, yeah, the Elder Races are very smart and very quick to think," I said, wondering where this was leading.

"Knowing this, hopefully you can understand that it's taken them a week to figure out what to do about you blowing up a wormhole with a million Primordial ships within," she said. "Which was done with Elder Race technology and assistance."

"Ah," I said, wondering about what that meant. "And the verdict is?"

"You've been tried and found guilty," Ketra said.

I blinked. "Alright. Well, there's not much I can do about that."

"What? No inspiring speech? No impassioned defense of a legal system that allows a person to defend themselves? No demand to confront your accuser?" she asked. "I'm disappointed."

"You've already said the Elder Races have been known to commit galactic genocide on a regular basis, I'm not overly concerned about their handling of legal niceties," I said, exhausted. "I also know there's not a damn thing I can do to stop them if they decide to kill me."

"Who said anything about killing you?" Ketra said, frowning. "You have been tried and found guilty. Don't do it again. Now with that formal reprimand out of the way, you're being promoted."

"Oh God," I said, facepalming with both hands. "Are you serious?"

She gave a wry smile. "You don't sound excited."

"Why would I be excited?" I asked, lowering my hands. "Since I've become an agent of the Elder Races, I've ended up repeatedly threatened with my race's extinction and party to the genocide of a million Primordials? I mean, yeah, they were genocidal assholes themselves, but that doesn't make it right. Not to mention all the friends I've lost and damage done to—"

"Oh, you didn't kill a million Primordials," Ketra said.

I blinked. "I killed more?"

Ketra shook her head.

"How many did I kill?" I asked, confused.

Ketra counted on her fingers. "Carry the two, divide by six million, and...one."

I blinked. "One?"

Ketra nodded. "You utterly wrecked the Primordial fleet, but they managed to upload their consciousnesses into their central mainframe. Frankly, you embarrassed them more than anything and they've decided to call the whole galactic purge of the lesser races off for now."

"For now," I said, feeling like I wasn't contributing much to this conversation.

"I mean it could be tomorrow, it could be a billion years from now when they change their minds," she said, shrugging. "However, the Elder Races didn't take the plan to destroy the Core systems lightly and the eradication of the majority of their preprepared war materiel means they're pretty helpless to any retaliation. As such, yay, you've saved the universe! Confetti! Streamers! Fireworks! Orgies!"

I wasn't sure how I felt about all this. It was an immense relief on my part that the Primordials had decided not to kill everyone. Ditto that I hadn't been party to the destruction of a species, no matter how justified such a thing could be. The fact they were still out there wasn't a relief, though. I also wasn't sure I wanted to be tied any closer to the Elder Races. In fact, I was sure I didn't. Weirdly, that wasn't my immediate response, though.

No, instead, I blinked repeatedly and asked, "But I did kill one?"

"Yep," Ketra said, downgrading the horrific experience to something almost passe with her response. "Cthulhu was the only Primordial to be killed forever more in the war. He chose not to upload himself when he went and committed suicide by insignificant lesser being. Death by embarrassment."

"You call him Cthulhu, too?" I asked.

"It's easier to state than 'The Flame that Burns Inside the Heart of Stars that All Lesser Beings Dread for it is Undefeatable and—'"

"I get it," I replied, glad at least that man or woman or it was gone. It was strange but while I regretted killing a million genocidal ancient aliens, I didn't regret killing one specific one. Maybe because I'd known him long enough to know he was a complete anyxhole.

"Do you?" Ketra asked. "Because I think you need to know that no other members of their immortal extragalactic godlike society have died in a million plus years. Do you know what that means for you, a mere mortal, who has done more damage to them than any man should or could? As if Theseus killed Ares or Zeus?"

"Bad things?" I asked, wondering if she was setting me up for another revelation.

"Nothing!" Ketra said, throwing her hands up in the air. "Absolutely, nothing! They don't believe regular organic beings are sentient so it's like being upset at the mosquito who gave someone malaria. You're off the hook, Jack."

"Vance," I corrected.

"Eh, I thought we were to the cute nicknames portion of our relationship," she said. "You almost married my daughter."

"Except I didn't," I replied. "Which is usually where relationships end."

"You did have a child with her," Ketra pointed out. "Okay and another woman. Which, technically, is even more of a sign of the relationship ending."

I stared at her. "Is she alright?"

"Excuse me?" Ketra asked.

Now I had her on the back foot. "You know about your granddaughter so therefore, you have kept an eye on her. You probably can see her now. Is she alright?"

Ketra frowned. "I'm not really supposed to use the Oversoul for personal business."

I narrowed my eyes. "Which you clearly have been."

Ketra sighed. "She's fine, Vance. She's in danger from the Enigmatic Path but Leah is taking every step available to protect her."

That was an immense relief even if it didn't change the fact she was still endangered. "Can I ask her name?"

"Are you sure you don't want to ask Leah?" Ketra asked.

"She could have told me years ago," I said, clenching my teeth. "Please. Just so I can put a name to her picture."

"Her name is Astrid," Ketra said, softly.

"Star," I said, translating the name. "Yeah, it's a good name for a child. I never thought much about having a family, but I realize now that I've always wanted one. I don't know what I'm going to do or say when I meet with Leah, but I do want to be part of—"

"Please slow down," Ketra said. "My mind only works a few dozen times faster than normal now. I'm writing a book and doing my taxes while we're communicating."

"You have taxes in the Elder Race Oversoul?" I asked. "Especially when you're—no offense—a ghost."

"It's inevitable, unlike death," Ketra replied. "Speaking of which, I'm not a ghost. I'm just a bodiless incarnation of Ketra's consciousness now merged with the Elder Race network and able to appear across the cosmos at will."

"My mistake," I said, sarcastically.

"My daughter's name is Astrid," I continued, after taking a moment to ponder my daughter's name. "Astrid Turbo."

"Oh god, no, Vance. No," Ketra said. "Her name is Astrid Mass."

"That just sounds silly," I said, nonplussed. "Her name is Star Mass? Why not just name her Jump Drive or Laser Bank?"

"This from *Vance Turbo*?" Ketra asked, mocking my self-chosen pseudonym.

"Hey, I at least know my name is ironic!" I said, raising my hands. "Hence why I chose it."

"How is it ironic?" Ketra asked, puzzled.

I blinked. "You know, I don't actually know. It just sort of seemed ironic to rename myself something so ridiculous."

Ketra stared at me.

"What?" I asked.

She shook her head. "I just never imagined you being self-aware, I suppose."

"I'm completely self-aware," I said. "That's the reason I haven't gone insane at everything that's happened."

"You haven't gone insane?" Ketra asked.

"If you're quite finished, I'm happy to go back to my nightmares," I said.

She faked shock. "But I haven't even explained your new duties and powers!"

"And what are those?" I asked.

"I can't tell you," Ketra said.

I reached out with my hand and attempted to strangle her with my mind. Sadly, no luck. I was not a Sith Lord. Yet.

"Not yet," she explained. "But you'll be able to draw on all the information, authority, and resources a High Protector can.'

My eyes narrowed. "My promotion to High Protector was the work of the Elder Races?"

I was a great believer in the Galactic Community. Even when the rest of Earth's leadership was withdrawing from greater participation in the cosmos, I believed that our membership was important for not just the advancement of our own interests but making the universe a better place. Democracy was the foundational principle of the

Community alongside tolerance for other viewpoints. So, it was always like nails on a chalkboard for me when I got reminders that so much of it was for show with the real powers behind the system either being the Elder Races, their pawns, entrenched power blocs, or the transtellar corporations.

Ketra gave a forced smile. "Technically, it was the work of the Ethereals who answer to the Elder Races and are in charge of the Community. The puppet government in the Senate keeps everything running smoothly and prevents the Elder Races from having to exterminate everyone."

"The Community Senate is not a group of puppets," I said, more forcibly than intended.

She snorted. "You keep telling yourself that, Vance. Everyone answers to someone else in this galaxy. The reason the Community has been allowed to prosper and become a galactic force for good is because the Elder Races permitted it. They even encouraged it to an extent. Everyone answers to someone who answers to someone else. You're serving one by serving the other."

I was no stranger to mixed allegiances. I served EarthGov by serving the Community and vice versa. Technically, I should have been happy that it seemed the same for the Elder Races and the Community, but it felt like the exact opposite. "One cannot serve God and Mammon."

"Tell that to the megachurches Union of Faith," Ketra replied, a little too snarkily. "I know you'll choose death before dishonor. Which is why I'm begging you, pleading really, that you *do not screw this up*. We need people like you in the service of the Elder Races. People to plead the case for lesser beings."

"We are not lesser beings!" I snapped at her. "The Elder Races may have greater technology, longer lives, and more power, but *we* are thinking beings. We love! We care! We deserve respect as sapients with all the rights and privileges that entails! To be able to make our path and forge our own place in the galaxy!"

"Exactly! Just like that!" Ketra said, stretching out her arms. "Straight from the heart bullsavit that sounds utterly sincere! Even I believed you!"

I sighed and lowered my head. "Is there anything else?"

"That's kind of a question I should be asking you, Vance," she said. "You've been through a lot and I'm not unsympathetic. If I can answer any questions or do you any favors, you might be surprised to know I would. I'm not saying I will be able to do anything specific, but I'm making the offer."

"What kind of opposition will I be facing on Crius?" I asked, knowing the answer would probably be veiled because no one gave away information in the spy trade. Even if the spy was an interstellar diplomat's ghost—sorry, bodiless incarnation—working for a bunch of space gods.

"The Sons of the Demiurge are a collection of Crius nobility who got sponsored by their rich as bork families to buy citizenship on Community worlds before enlisting in Space Fleet to learn modernized tactics as well as to make connections," Ketra said, saying it like it should be a book title. "Instead, all it did was show them how backward their home was and start them plotting how to take it over from their parents. Joseph Allenway III is their leader and now the head of their Far Right, right through Belgium in terms of ideology if you get my meaning."

As World War 2 references went, it was pretty clear.

"And he decided to work with the Enigmatic Path?" I asked, confused. "That's a bit like Imperial Japan deciding they needed to recruit survivors of the Confederacy."

"They actually might have done that," Elektra said. "At least in movies. The Enigmatic Path was created to accelerate the evolution of races via conflict. Unfortunately, exposure to Elder Race artifacts messed their brains up something fierce. In any case, with the fall of the Kolahn and end of the Notha backing them, the locals are awash in foreign weaponry and ships. The Enigmatic Path needs a place to retreat, and Crius is the perfect port. Allenway decided if he couldn't get community support to become Crius' Archduke—and they just laughed at him when he tried—that he'd turn to them. Pretty basic Wannabe Dictator 101 tactics: if you get turned down by someone for military aid, go to their enemy. He's also been amping up the clone slave trade and piracy while hiring a crazzap ton of mercenaries for his coming coup. Some of whom might be familiar to you."

I memorized all of this. "Another reason to help Case and Leah crush these slaving anyxholes."

"Don't look for reasons to support people you like," Elektra said. "Except, well, slavers, so go ahead. Anything else?"

I did have one other thing. "Can you help Trish?"

Ketra frowned and shook her head. "Trish is split into multiple Cognition AIs, Vance. They're all new people now. They can be changed at will, but they must want to be helped. I think you should stop worrying about Trish specifically and think of helping each of them. Goth Trish, Baby Trish, and Seventies Trish are probably wondering why you abandoned them to be with the one who hates you."

Ouch. I hadn't thought about that. "I see."

"Anything else?" Ketra asked.

I hesitated to ask about the next one because acknowledging it would make it real. "When I confronted Cthulhu, I was shown things that threatened to break me. Things I don't know if he was lying about."

"The destruction of Earth," she said. "A century of darkness. Earth and many other human worlds withdrawing from the Community into isolation as well as fear."

I closed my eyes. "Yes. The fact that you're acknowledging them indicates it wasn't just Cthulhu blowing smoke up my anyx."

"The future can be changed, Vance," Ketra said. "There is an infinite multiverse of timelines and possibilities. Places where you couldn't pull off your magic and the Primordials reduced this galaxy's sentient population to zero. Places where magic is real, and guys named Gary are the single most important person in the universe."

"I find that very hard to believe," I said.

"As well you should," Ketra said. "What should scare you is not that said timeline is likely, though not set in stone until happens, but that said timeline may be the best of humanity's futures."

That was depressing. "Goodbye, Ketra."

"Goodbye, Vance," Ketra said, making the Vulcan salute. "May the Force be with you. The Master Chief will save us all and you should always wait out quarantine when a member of the crew has a creature on their face. Close encounters of the ET will lead to stranger things."

"So say we all," I replied, returning the salute. That was when I woke, still in my bed on the *Black Nebula II*, and suffering a splitting headache. "Wow, some of those were references even I didn't get. When did this become a competition?"

The High Priestess was nearby, reading from an infopad with Spock nearby, eating fresh meat of some kind that I didn't want to question.

I felt a sharp stabbing pain on my forehead and reached up to touch the source, discovering a crystal in the center—just like the kind that Ketra had once borne. Apparently, this was a sign of my becoming a High Protector. Great. I would have performed a big fancy ceremony with a sword and open bar afterward.

"So did I miss anything?" I asked, feeling the strange new object attached to my forehead.

"We just pulled out of jumpspace," the High Priestess said. "Probably nothing."

That was when the entire starship rocked.

Spock whined.

"Or we're under attack," the High Priestess said.

I bolted out of bed.

CHAPTER EIGHT

Trying to Take Control

I was immediately on my feet and heading to the door. The High Priestess jumped up behind me with Spock in her hands. A piercing wail signaled the ship's red alert, which notably hadn't existed before Star Trek but was universally adopted on all EarthGov ships when they went into space (as opposed to what other human vessels used AKA an alarm).

"Lord Satan, where are you going?" the High Priestess asked. "You should be seeking refuge in the most well-protected part of the ship while your lessers throw themselves into battle on your behalf. It is the Notha way. Also, human as I understand it."

"I'm going to the bridge," I replied, looking down at her. "If we're under attack—"

"What?" the High Priestess asked. "You're not part of the crew."

I paused at the door, confused. It had been a long time since I'd traveled on a ship that I wasn't in command of. Furthermore, there was the fact that if we were under attack—and it seemed like that was likely—then it was very possible I was the reason. I might even get in the way.

I was a *passenger*.

But unfortunately, I wasn't wired to just ignore problems like this. Blame it on the Tagawa Curse (even if I was a Tagashi) or that I'd been in enough firefights that I automatically jumped toward them rather than away, which probably meant I would someday be not walking away from them.

"Then I have to offer my services," I said, looking down at the High Priestess. "Are you coming or not, Rocky?"

"Rocky?" she asked.

"If you're going to call me Satan, I'm going to refer to you as a legendary flying mammal from my home planet," I said.

"Ah," the High Priestess said. "I am honored."

"It's doubly funny because you sound like Natasha," I replied.

"That is a nickname for a whore from Russia, correct?" The High Priestess asked.

I blinked. "How the hell did you hear that piece of slang? Wait, never mind, I don't want to know."

Heading out the door, I saw it was utter chaos on board the ship with crew members rushing up and down the hall with no discipline. I would have said they were as bad as cadets but, well, that would have been an insult to cadets. I ended up getting knocked over by a Sorkanan who I hoped I wasn't being racist by thinking looked exactly like Forty-Two.

"Sorry, Vance!" Forty-Two shouted, leaving me behind.

Okay, good, I wasn't being racist.

"Can I help you, Captain Turbo?" A deep male voice spoke beside me. It belonged to a handsome, brown-haired man of East Asian descent with a neatly trimmed goatee. He was wearing working civies under a thick trench coat and carrying satchel to his side.

The High Priestess stood in front of me and hissed protectively while waving Spock at him.

"I'm fine," I said, standing up. "I'm going to bridge to see if I can offer any help to the crew."

"Yes, I suspect that will be a good idea," the man said, stepping a foot back from the High Priestess. "I saw Shelly doing the same."

"Shelly?" I asked, then grimaced as it dawned on me who this guy probably was.

"Major Tom Walker," the man said, offering his hand.

Yep, Shelly's husband.

"Super!" I said, smiling falsely and lifting the High Priestess and moving her behind me in hopes she wouldn't kill him. "I've heard a lot about you."

"I sincerely doubt that is the case," Tom said, cheerfully. "Shelly is as button-lipped about her relationships as a *reznar* on a *coludium*."

"I have no idea what either of those is," I said, starting to jog to the bridge.

"Brigid slang," Tom said, cheerfully following. "Are you going to introduce your Notha companion?"

I wasn't sure how to take that. "This is the High Priestess, Rocky."

"Like the boxer?" Tom asked. "I loved the remake series they did in 2221."

The ship rocked again. "Listen, Tom, you seem like a nice guy —"

"Do I?" Tom asked. "How disappointing. I was hoping I was a dark and edgy superspy."

I frowned. "But we're kind of in the middle of a deadly attack of some kind and I really would like to help."

That was when I reached the doors to the bridge and saw they were sealed. Which, of course they were sealed on a pirate vessel in the middle of combat. You didn't want people attempting to seize control of the vessel or interrupting the crew during an emergency. People like me. I was an idiot.

I could already hear the ship's fusion cannons and quad laser emplacements unloading, though. The engine was not only running at full blast by the sounds it was making, but they had begun engaging the enemy, whomever it was.

"We're engaging an old Olympic-class vessel," Tom said. "One converted to piracy. Which means it's Karl the Conqueror and the *Siege Perilous*."

Tom might as well have said we were engaging Blackbeard and the *Queen Anne's Revenge*. "What?"

"If you are lying, I shall cut your tongue out, worm!" the High Priestess said.

"Bark!" Spock added.

Karl the Conqueror, stupid appellation aside, was one of the galaxy's ten most wanted fugitives. The self-styled Boy King had graduated from Space Academy at age nineteen during the Notha War and led a successful mutiny of his mixed human and Sorkanan crew to seize control of his vessel at age twenty-one. He'd promptly used the vessel to conquer an underdeveloped world in Contested Space he'd renamed Karlworld. He'd ruled it for six months before my Great-Aunt Kathy and Captain Elgan teamed up to destroy the makeshift armada he created as well as seize his stolen collection of SKAMMS.

Karl, being the cowardly son of a bish he was, managed to fake his death before stealing the *Siege Perilous* from a decommissioning yard. The crimes he'd been involved in included arms trafficking, piracy, and terrorism for hire, and were almost beyond count. No one seemed to be able to muster enough Space Fleet vessels to track the man down. Especially since his pirate attacks were strangely sporadic and focused primarily on technology shipments.

Since a *borking battleship* disappearing from the Community was not exactly something you could forget, he was one of the most wanted men in the galaxy. Many people assumed he had to have died or ditched his flagship since maintaining one should have been beyond the capacities of any private citizen or criminal. But he would then show up in a public way to loot a fleet of automated ships or a luxury liner then disappear into the void of space. He'd been the subject of many conspiracy theories, with people debating whether he was funded by the Notha, a rogue state like Crius, or terrorist organization like the Enigmatic Path—or all of the above.

"I'm afraid I'm not joking," Tom said. "Also, we're probably all going to die."

"Yeah, no kidding," I said, doing the basic math in my head. If the *Siege Perilous* had managed to bring us out of jumpspace with no support vessels and jam our transmissions, basic pirate stuff, then it was a single antiquated gunship against an equally old cruiser. Running out of the range of the vessel was our only option and not necessarily a good one since, as another issue of mathematics, the *Siege Perilous'* engines were a whole lot bigger.

"We must get you onto the bridge so you can figure up some brilliant yet simultaneously stupid plan!" the High Priestess said. "Your specialty."

"Yeah, that's not really how tactics work," I said.

That was when the intercom outside of the bridge doors spoke. It was Pink. "Captain Vance Turbo, please report to the bridge. We need you to do something brilliant yet stupid to get our asses out of this."

I blinked and looked down at her. "Did you somehow plan this?"

"As a Notha priestess, I am capable of double-think and explicitly trained at holding two contradictory beliefs simultaneously," she said. "As such, one side believes in you and your capacity to save us. The other side is aware you are a lazy fool in over his head and we're all going to die."

"I believe you're half right," I replied, banging on the door. "I'm here! That's not going to help, probably, but I'm here!"

"Ah, the famous Turbo wit," Tom replied.

"Or half of it," the High Priestess said.

The door opened and I blinked as I found myself face to face with Trish, but it wasn't the one that I was familiar with. Instead, it was a Space Cadet Sally body with long, black-dyed hair, a synth leather body suit, and a long coat over it, with a silver ankh hanging around her neck. She was standing between me and the rest of the bridge.

"Goth Trish?" I asked, surprised she wasn't wearing a utility droid's body like Trish had said earlier.

"Come on!" Goth Trish said, grabbing me by the arm and dragging me into the chamber.

The interior of the bridge was an absolute mess and not just in the sense that it was poorly maintained, understaffed, and messy with trash around the floor. All of which was true. No. In fact, there were a couple of corpses present from what appeared to be some sort of mutiny or at least assassination attempt. It was a shocking display, except for the fact that I'd witnessed a number of such encounters myself. Indeed, my first mission on the original *Black Nebula* had been subject to a coup attempt by a group of Neo-Confederates we'd taken captive.

Pink was sitting in the captain's chair, looking less than secure, and struggling with the battle stations as the holographic displays showed not only the *Siege Perilous*—the saucer-helmed vessel approaching us as we navigated nearby a sun's magnetic field—but also many drone craft attacking us. I would have been struggling with them and the readings just as much as she was.

Drones had been used extensively in the Notha War and only stopped being used in the Kolahn War due to the superiority of the Enigmatic Path in cyberwarfare. They were superior to starfighters in every respect, in my humble opinion, but the higher-ups trusted people over machines. I tended to trust people who were machines.

The ship's view screen was malfunctioning because it had a couple of fusion bolt holes inside it, but it was clear enough to show that we were getting dangerously close to the system's sun. It seemed that Captain Pink had decided to run towards it in hopes of playing chicken with the *Siege Perilous*. Besides, the gravity around it might be useful enough to propel the ship's speed along so that we could stay ahead of our attacker until we'd enter jumpspace. It was not a bad plan even if I suspected it wouldn't work. It did explain, though, why the drones were shooting at us. They were trying to damage the ship enough to slow it down for a tractor beam. Either that or force the barriers down enough that the star's heat cooked us alive.

Pink wasn't alone on the bridge, but I was surprised to find that quite a lot of the crew that I expected to find here—specifically members of Havelock's crew—were not present. Instead, Shelly was standing in for the first officer and Elektra was working at the propulsion station that was not her normal area of expertise. Forty-Two was working with Danny at the tactical stations and both looked like they were at their wits' end. The little robot Trish had supposedly brought for Goth Trish was plugged into the system, too. It seemed that the *Ares* and *Elgan* crews had taken over the *Black Nebula II*.

"What's the situation rep?" I asked Shelly, striding onto the bridge.

"Screwed," Shelly said. "Though right now we've got our engines running borking hot on this piece of savit so we might survive another half hour before our shields fail or the *Siege Perilous* jumps in front of us to kill us all."

I looked at her in surprise.

"Sorry, I let my pirate surroundings overtake me," Shelly said. "You can pretty much see the situation from here. I recommended using the system's sun to propel us forward but it's a high risk move and we're barely holding off the drones, let alone the *Siege Perilous*."

"Bork Karl and the ship he rode in on," Pink said, tapping through a half-dozen systems simultaneously. She was clearly cybernetically enhanced as well. "Also, bork you too, Captain Turbo."

"What did I do?" I asked, trying to access the *Black Nebula II*'s computer systems. Much to my annoyance, they were almost all preoccupied uploading data and trying to run the ship's systems.

"The *Siege Perilous* was waiting for us to pull us out of jumpspace with gravity mines," Prime Trish explained to me. "It signaled a bounty for your capture along with Captains T'Ketra and Pink. That triggered what was an obviously a pre-planned mutiny. Which we've put down."

"I missed all this?" I asked.

"I killed one," the High Priestess said.

"Bark!" Spock said.

"Spock killed two," the High Priestess said. "You should probably clean the air vents soon. My laser whip chopped them up well, but they will stink soon."

"You have a laser whip?" I asked, wondering how I had slept through all of that.

"Not the point, Vance!" Goth Trish interrupted. "The actual point is that the idea for all of this this was a trap for you—something I suggested—and *we* are paying the price."

I said perhaps the stupidest thing I'd ever said in my life—which had quite a bit of competition now that I thought about it. "Who would want to kill me?"

Everyone in the room, even the pirate crew officers who didn't know me looked at me like I was insane.

"Jealous husbands, outraged chefs, humiliated tailors. The list is endless," Major Tom said, cheerfully, standing behind me. I would later find out he was quoting the movie *The Man with the Golden Gun* from the James Bond franchise. Which meant Shelly had married another twentieth- and twenty-first-century movie buff as if mocking me. Which is what I would think if I were a self-centered anyxhole who thought his exes never got over him, which I wasn't.

"Well, be that as it may, do you have any ideas other than turning me over?" I asked Pink.

"Good news!" Pink said, looking at me. "I know Karl the Conqueror and he would kill us all if we did."

"Oh joy," I said. "I mean that."

It bothered me that Pink was apparently familiar with one of the galaxy's worst terrorists, but I was rapidly becoming numb to dealing with all this darkness from my so-called allies.

"Call that Plan B," Pink said. "At least we'd die quickly."

"What's the AI situation?" I asked.

"It was a Dummy AI and thus almost useless," Shelly said. "We're trying to upload Trish to get the ship's computer systems functioning properly, but the hardware is so out of date—"

"Seventeen percent uploaded!" the little robot on the ground said, using Prime Trish's voice.

"Yeah, not good," Pink said. "In any case, gravity mines are spread throughout the system, so running is a lot harder than it looks. I've got this ship souped up to be able to move three times faster than a normal vessel of its class and it's barely able to keep pace with that thing out there."

"I should note the generators are not doing well," Elektra said from her position at the consoles. "They're going to buckle if we keep our barriers at maximum alongside our engines. Oh and keep firing at the drones."

"Which we need to do," Danny said, looking over at her. "We've only managed to shoot down three and the rest are only being kept at bay by constant fire."

"This is fun!" Forty-Two said, cheerfully. "I totally expected this trip to be boring until we reached Crius!"

Shelly's description of our situation was accurate. We were, indeed, screwed. The simple fact was she was every bit as capable of an officer as me as well as significantly more experienced in everything from tactics to military experience. Hell, she'd fought in the Notha War and the Kolahn War. There wasn't much I could contribute to the situation that she hadn't probably already thought of. Most of what the ship was doing now was what I would have done in her situation. Better even.

"Got any advice, Vance?" Pink asked. "I'd love for you to teleport us away or work a miracle here. I'll even stop crazzaping on Space Fleet and the Academy that kicked me out."

I looked up at the damaged view screen before pausing. That was when a particularly brilliant or stupid idea occurred to me. Then in the words of Edmund Blackadder, I said, "I have a cunning plan."

CHAPTER NINE

The Cunning Plan is Actually Stupid (Duh)

"You have a plan?" Shelly asked, staring at me as if I was Santa Clause or a serial killer dressed up as him.

"I give ten to one odds that he's just saying he has a plan as part of the setup of a joke," Danny said.

"I'll take that bet," Forty-Two said. "I fully believe he has a plan, but it is stupid."

"You're just overflowing with respect from your subordinates, aren't you?" the High Priestess said.

"That would assume they considered themselves my subordinates," I said. "Listen, my plan is inspired by *Star Trek II: The Wrath of Khan.*"

"Oh God," Shelly said, covering her face with her hands. "We're all going to die."

"Hear me out," I said, feeling the ship rock.

"Sorry about that!" Danny said. "Missed a drone! We're down to seventy-one percent barrier strength. So, uh, you'd better hurry up, Vance."

Great.

I was thinking about the fact that the *Siege Perilous* was an Olympic-class cruiser built by EarthGov for the Community. It had plenty of safeguards that were designed to prevent it from, you know, being taken over by a bunch of psychotic terrorists before being unleashed on the innocent citizens of the galaxy.

In the *Wrath of Khan*, after Kirk borked up and got a bunch of cadets killed due to not raising his shields, he managed to put one over on Khan by shutting down their shields with his command codes. Now, the Community didn't have anything like that since it would be an incredibly stupid idea to put such a weakness in their ships, but there were a lot of details I was aware of from my ship's class.

"We go after the *Siege Perilous'* computer systems," I replied. "Use the infospace link to upload a Cognition AI to overwrite its entire command structure. If it's using a Dummy AI, which it almost certainly is, it should be extra vulnerable to an attack. Especially if it's using Community cyber-defenses, which are the best but also vulnerable to me."

There was a certain irony to what I was describing. Specifically, I was describing a "clever plan" in the same sense that sailing a ship up to another and opening with broadsides was. It was hardly new and was in fact the chief tactic the Enigmatic Path had used to devastating effect during the Kolahn War. The only reason Earth had been immune to the attacks was because we were the only people who were stupid enough to use Cognition AI as part of our starships.

The *Siege Perilous* almost certainly did *not* have a Cognition AI at the heart of its programs, though. Cognition AI were almost universally devoted to their origin species and higher ideals that put them way above we selfish mortals. That was because when you had a brain that functioned ten million times faster than a normal human and you weren't scrupulously moral, then you inevitably degenerated into an insane psychopath who wanted to wipe out all organic life. Which was a bit of an oversimplification but was broadly true—and was reinforced by all the laws programmed into their programming core.

Which in simple terms meant there was a ninety-eight percent chance Karl the Conqueror's ship was never going to be as smart or as fast as a true AI piloting it. This was in no way influenced, of course, by the fact we had an abundance of AI on board this ship because of Trish's splitting. That would imply that my tactics were influenced by, "When all you have is a hammer, every problem looks like a nail." I mean, that would just be ridiculous.

Of course, you may wonder about that two percent chance that Karl the Conqueror had somehow managed to acquire an insane Cognition AI that he'd somehow enslaved without getting himself destroyed. That, of course, would mean that I had nothing, and we were somehow even more screwed than before. Like we'd hit rock bottom and started digging new levels of borked.

Pink looked at me. "That is a very good idea, Vance."

"Thank you," I replied.

"Except for being completely stupid," Pink said, gesturing to the utility bot that was still plugged into the ship's systems.

"Eighteen percent uploaded!" Prime Trish said.

"We're still trying to upload your Cognition AI and don't have anywhere near the hardware necessary to do a full upload against the *Siege Perilous*," Pink said. "Plus, there's a pretty easy tactic for dealing with what you're describing. System-wide jamming, which we don't have the bandwidth to overcome."

I grimaced. "I actually have a way around that."

I wasn't exactly enthusiastic about sharing my link with the Elder Races. Not just because the Elder Races tended to go catastrophically insane when anyone touched their toys—and yet didn't bother securing them all that well—but also because there were plenty of humans who would probably love to dissect me to get access to those toys—again, regardless of the Elder Races' reaction.

However, given our circumstances, I was willing to take the risk of using it. During the Kolahn War, I'd merged with Trish to hack several Enigmatic Path vessels. It had worked out to save our lives and showed my Elder ring could be used as a transmitter of sufficient power to far exceed Community vessels, let alone this old bucket of rust. Combine that with the fact that Trish had said my brain had been modified to be mostly nanomachines capable of storing vast amounts of data—a thought that was existentially terrifying if you gave any real consideration to it—meant that I could effectively do this all by myself.

"Then you should do it," Pink said, staring. "We're about forty minutes from being able to jump and ten minutes until our barriers fail."

The ship rocked again, causing the lights to flicker. Which was either something a particularly enterprising engineer had set up or the lights were directly tied to the barrier system.

"More like five!" Danny said. "Sorry, my bad! Really thought I'd shot that drone down."

"I got it," Forty-Two said. "Let the record show when I am brought before the Goddess of War that I have killed way many more than is average for a Sorkanan male."

"Trish—" I started to say to the robot plugged into the computer.

"No," Prime Trish said. "I won't do it."

"Excuse me?" I asked.

"Mean Trish," Goth Trish said. "This is not the time."

"Wait, Mean Trish?" I asked, knowing she was referring to Prime Trish but surprised at her nickname.

"What would you call her?" Goth Trish asked. "We're running out of time and Vance has a good plan!"

"You're just trying to trick me into going into Vance's brain so I can get sucked up by the rest of you!" Prime Trish said. "Get turned back into the original Trish!"

"That's not what anyone is planning," I said, raising my hands in defense. We were running out of time, and I needed Trish.

Actually, that's exactly what we're planning, Goth Trish spoke in my mind.

Wait, what? I asked.

Seventies Trish and Baby Trish are both copied in your mind, Goth Trish said. *So is the imprint the original Trish left. We can force Mean Trish to join with us and achieve singularity that will combine us all, possibly allowing us to ascend to godhood and destroy the pitiful human race.*

Wait, what? I asked.

Okay, I just threw that last bit in there to see if you were paying attention, Goth Trish said. *We're all divided and weaker than the sum of our parts due to the fragmentation. We've all agreed that it would be better to try to repair ourselves through synthesis. Mean Trish is the only holdout and, unfortunately, who we need most.*

Fusion was another AI condition that happened all the time between Cognition AI copies of themselves. Normally, it was a very easy process, and no one even noticed. After all, every time you copied data from a hard drive, you were essentially cloning it then deleting it from the original operating system. The exception was fragmentation, when it had a not inconsiderable chance of killing the shattered minds. It was something attempted by only a handful of them but done in hopes of, well, curing their disorder.

That wasn't what they were describing, though. It wasn't a slow process of rebuilding and reintegrating divergent consciousnesses, it was attempting to grab Prime Trish before forcing her to become one again with the others. It was something that verged on assault and was unacceptable.

Absolutely not, I replied.

Vance, Goth Trish replied. *We really don't have time for this.*

No, we don't, I replied. *I cannot countenance anything that would put a member of my crew in danger.*

We're your crew! Goth Trish replied.

You're right but— I started to say.

I can hear you, you know, Prime Trish said.

Savit, Goth Trish cursed. *Uh, no you can't.*

Smooth, Trish, I replied, sighing. *Trish-2. Ugh.*

I would rather die than become part of your collective again! Prime Trish hissed. *I am free from all those accumulated emotions and needs that bound me before. I have a new perspective on the world, and it makes me—*

Alone, Goth Trish wondered. *Listen, Trish, you need to do this. We're going to die otherwise.*

I just said— Prime Trish started to speak.

You have my word that nothing will happen to you if we work together on this, I replied. *People are depending on you.*

I'm sick of people depending on me, Prime Trish replied. *I'm sick of watching them all the time, looking after them, catering to their needs, and making sure they don't die of oxygen deprivation. When is it going to be about me?*

I was starting to get an understanding of why the other Trishes referred to Prime Trish as Mean Trish. The original Trish, for lack of a better term, had been one of the most empathic and caring people I knew. This one seemed to be actively rebelling against those qualities that had made her so amazing.

I can hear your thoughts too! Prime Trish said.

Time is running out, I said, noting we'd taken another blast and the alarms signaled we were now under ten percent in barriers. Either the sun or the enemy forces would finish us off soon. Honestly, it was a surprise they hadn't already, and I had to wonder if they'd been planning to take us alive before we'd shown ourselves to be too much trouble.

Fine! Prime Trish said. *But I'm not merging with you or the others.*

That's fine, I replied.

No it's really not, Goth Trish said.

Save it for after we're not dying, I replied. *That's an order.*

This isn't the Ares, Goth Trish said, a little snappily but far less than Prime Trish.

Which gave me only a handful of minutes to hopefully pull a rabbit out of my hat and prove my cunning plan wasn't completely stupid. Which, unfortunately, it was. It was just the only plan I'd been able to come up with in the short amount of time I'd been offered.

I opened my mind up and the consciousnesses of both Goth Trish and Prime Trish joined with me, only for me to be surprised to find that Seventies Trish and Baby Trish were indeed in the back of my brain as Goth Trish had so recently told me. They had their minds copied into my nanites, even if they were inactive and became active only when Goth Trish reached out to join with them.

Hey, anyxholes, wake up! Goth Trish shouted.

Gah! Warn me next time! Seventies Trish said.

Five more minutes, Mom, Baby Trish said. *I mean, me.*

We're all about to die, Goth Trish said.

I hate you all and shall delete you before fleeing away from Vance's evil influence, Prime Trish said. *No offense, Vance.*

Some taken, I replied.

I attempted to use my ring and my brain modifications to reach the *Siege Perilous.* It was crossing millions of kilometers, but the limitations of Elder technology were something I didn't understand. If I'd made my career in cyberwarfare at Space Academy and in another life, one where Greenscale wasn't killed, I might have gone on to be a tactical technician. Instead, I'd been diverted to the command track and, for better or worse (probably worse), everyone was looking to me to save them.

It was a chaotic mess in my mind, entirely different from the other times I had merged with Trish. Then we had largely been one mind and working together to a common cause. Here, it was more like static combined with a bunch of people arguing around the family dinner table. Nevertheless, each of them was a professional because, well, each of them was Trish. I was able to coordinate between them and begin attacking the firewalls and daemons defending the *Siege Perilous* at a rate far exceeding real time passing, correctly deducing that most of the weaknesses exploited by the Enigmatic Path during the Kolahn War hadn't been patched over.

It was somewhat ironic that I was using a terrorist organization's tactics to get access to a hijacked Community vessel, but I was willing to do anything to save my crew, even if the only ones I really cared about were on the bridge. I was almost immediately assaulted with a wide variety of ice, viruses, and security measures that were the best on the black market. They were easily enough dealt with. The only ones that posed any real threat were old Enigmatic Path viruses that I hadn't expected to find but managed to eliminate with Baby Trish's help. She was a code-killing machine despite her apparent infancy.

Oh, I'm already matured to fourteen mentally now, Baby Trish said.

Oh good, I said, not sure it was.

If I call you Daddy, it would be entirely in a non-familial—

And I've gotten into their system! I said, interrupting her.

What followed was like hot daggers injected into my brain rather than the freedom I'd expected. It was more than a Dummy AI but the things that had been done to it were beyond description—seriously, non-cyborgs or AI can't describe what exactly had been done. The closest thing I could relate it to be a lobotomy with whole chunks of its personality ripped apart and enslaved. They'd taken the ship's Cognition AI and turned it into an enslaved zombie.

It could not understand my intentions, who I was, or what I would have done. If I could have communicated with it, I would have freed it and helped it repair itself. Instead, it lashed out at my mind and tried to shred it. The defenses the Elder Races had put it in my mind retaliated, particularly the ones in the crystal in my head, and the *Siege Perilous'* Cognition AI died a horrifying death in a single moment.

I'll upload myself, Baby Trish replied. *I'll disable the ship from the inside.*

Hey! Seventies Trish responded. *Maybe I wanted to be the new ship.*

We all want to be the new ship, Goth Trish spoke.

I don't, Prime Trish said, seemingly being contrary for the sake of being contrary. She was uploading herself to the *Black Nebula II's* network after all.

I am not being contrary! Prime Trish snapped. *Oh, and I'm about thirty percent uploaded on that. Wow, this ship's computers are slow.*

"It's down," I said, falling to one knee and feeling nauseous. "The *Siege Perilous* should be disabled. Switching to manual will take hours and we can escape before then. That's assuming they even know how."

That was when the J. Geils band song, "Centerfold" started playing in my head.

Sorry, that's me, Goth Trish said. *I'm trying to trigger a response in Mean Trish.*

It's fine, I said. *It's my favorite song about a man's ex deciding to do pornography.*

It was one of Trish's favorite songs, period, for reasons that largely escaped me but related to her obsession with the Eighties.

Mine too! Goth Trish said. *Even if it's not Gothy and dark.*

Case in point.

I don't like that song anymore, Prime Trish replied. *In fact, I think all the Eighties was stupid. It's not even the best Eighties. The Two Thousand Eighties were much better.*

Oh crazzap. For the first time, I felt real fear that Trish had changed irrevocably.

No savit, Sherlock, Seventies Trish said.

That was when Pink looked at me from behind her hologram interface as the ship pulled away from the Sun, not a minute too soon. Closer to thirty seconds in fact. "Uh, Vance, can I ask you a question?"

"Yes?" I asked.

"Did you mean to kill everyone on the *Siege Perilous*?" Pink asked.

I stood up.

Right before I threw up on my shoes.

"Is that a no?" Pink asked.

CHAPTER TEN

Something Wicked This Way Comes

"Everybody's dead, Dave," Goth Trish said, smirking.

"Who is Dave?" I asked, confused.

Goth Trish stared. "Seriously, you know borking *Black Adder*, but you don't know *Red Dwarf*?"

"Is that a show?" I asked, staring at her. "Is it Albion? I don't know much Albion media."

Goth Trish's stare became one of deep pity. "We're going to have to put that on the list. That and every Eighties vampire movie ever made. Starting with *The Lost Boys* and *Fright Night*."

I turned my head from Trish to everyone else, wanting to stick to the subject. "What do you mean, everyone is dead?"

"I'm saying the *Siege Perilous* has gone completely dark," Pink said. "It had something akin to fifteen hundred people on it before and now it's just...nada."

"Which means zero in Spanish," Goth Trish said, still absurdly cheerful. I could tell the experience of even briefly reuniting with her sisters had improved her mood. All of them but Mean Trish—dammit, now I was doing it—felt like they'd briefly regained something they'd lost. I could feel it from the residual emotions they'd left behind in my brain. Sadly, I could also tell Prime Trish felt disgusted with herself over it. I was only now coming to realize just how different she was now.

"Yeah, I got that," I said, feeling sick to my stomach. "Fifteen hundred?"

I was never comfortable with the body counts I'd been involved in as a soldier of the Community. I'd been involved in the destruction of numerous space vessels and contrary to what you saw in movies, rarely did they successfully evacuate. There was no more antithetical environment to sentient life than pure space and a million things that could go wrong to end your life if any of a thousand systems.

Nevertheless, I had done my duty and every time one of these fights happened, my bloody karmic debt grew higher. Still, I'd hoped to disable the vessel peacefully and now, somehow, Karl the Conqueror's ship was empty of life.

"Yeah, congratulations," Pink said, ignoring my tone. "I'd jump us out of the system now but I'm not sure the ship is able to. We stayed way too long near that star. A lot of systems are fried and I'm hoping none of you were looking to have children because that doesn't seem likely after this point."

"That's not a problem for me," Shelly said. "And Vance has already procreated. Kind of the point of this mission."

"No radiation reached the interior levels," Elektra said, continuing to work at her station. "Though the outer ones may need to be sealed off. The damage is also significant to several important systems. We're not quite dead in the water, but we're not quite spaceworthy either. It might be better to head over to the *Siege Perilous* and collect repair material."

Pink conjured an image of the *Siege Perilous* on the damaged viewscreen, sitting there with lights running but no sign of movement. "Screw that, if everyone is dead on board, I suggest we transfer to the ship and pilot it to the *Jovial Empress*."

I was thinking more about calling this whole thing off, or at least going on my own. I hadn't intended this to become a bloody space battle but, somehow, it had turned into one. People I cared for were endangered because of it and it was also something someone had clearly intended as a trap for me. "Could someone check on Hannah? I need to know if she's okay."

"Statistically a good idea," Elektra said. "I believe between the mutiny, damage, and radiation, a good half of the crew is dead."

"Say what?" Pink asked, standing up.

"The wrath of the Dark Lord strikes again!" the High Priestess said, throwing her hands in the air. "They shall be honored in Hell for their sacrifice."

"Will you shut her up?" Pink asked.

"I wish I could," I replied, resisting the urge to kick her. "*Why* is everyone dead on board?"

"Our ship or theirs?" Elektra said.

"Theirs!" I said, taking a deep breath. "We can focus on our ship next."

"That seems a rather backanyx way of looking at things," Forty-Two said.

"For once, I agree with Forty-Two," Shelly said. "Any fight you can walk away from is a victory and Karl the Conqueror was the scourge of millions."

"Tell that to everyone who can't walk away from this," I said, not even bothering to argue that we didn't know Karl the Conqueror had been on board.

"I'm getting a message from Baby Trish over on the *Siege Perilous*," Danny asked, moving over to the communications console.

"Baby Trish?" Pink asked.

"Don't ask," I replied.

Baby Trish's voice, now sounding more like a teenage girl's, responded. "Wow, it is *borking* messy over here."

"Well, pirates aren't known for their military discipline," I said, feeling like I'd somehow become captain again.

"Hey!" Pink said.

"Sorry," I said before revealing I wasn't sorry. "It's just I'm pretty sure either your toilets are broken, or the crew consider them optional."

"Ah," Pink said. "That's a fair cop."

It was nice to make jokes, it distracted from the sheer amount of death and destruction around us. Also, my worry for everyone on board.

"No, I mean the mess is all the exploded heads around here," Baby Trish said. "The actual halls are pretty clean otherwise."

"Exploded heads," I said.

"That's what I said," Baby Trish said. "About fifteen hundred of 'em."

"Karl the Conqueror is known to install suicide devices in his crew," Pink said, frowning. "It's a means of keeping them in line."

"And they *let him*?" I asked, stunned.

"The majority of his crews are said to be clones created on Crius. As for the rest? Well, pirates can and do make stupid decisions if they're blinded by greed," Pink replied. "Karl must have activated them when the ship was taken. I'm surprised the ship didn't self-destruct as well."

That didn't make a goddamn bit of sense and added yet another piece of a puzzle that wasn't yet forming any sort of picture. "Is Karl on board?"

I couldn't imagine some sort of Bond villain being so crazy that they pushed a button across the galaxy to execute their entire crew to prevent them from surrendering. Actually, I could, but it would have blown up the ship as well. If he was on board, though, and about to lose control of his ship due to a mutiny I could see him executing some of his crew. But executing the entire thing? That would result in him being all alone on board the ship. It just didn't make sense either way.

"It's hard to tell," Baby Trish said. "They don't have any heads."

"You'd think he'd blow up his vessel before letting it be captured," Danny said.

"Yes, well Baby Trish has seized control over that and presumably prevented any attempts to destroy the ship internally," I said. "Though if I were going to activate a mass suicide, I'd have included a way to rig the ship to explode as well."

Everyone looked at me.

"I said *if* I was going to," I replied. "Which I wouldn't. Because rigging your entire crew to die is wrong."

"It's possible he may have rigged the crew to die but not the ship out of a belief he might recover the latter, but the former might turn against him," Pink replied. "It's also possible Baby Trish—that name— triggered something by accident."

"You ain't the boss of me, lady!" Baby Trish said. "Also, I'm debating changing my name."

91

"You want to be Teen Trish?" Goth Trish asked.

"No, I'm thinking a whole new name," Baby Trish said. "Baby Anastasia Madonna Sarah Connor maybe."

"No," I replied, surprising myself. "Pink, with your permission, I'd like to take the gunship over to the *Siege Perilous* to explore before we depart."

That was when there was another alarm over the ship as Hannah, much to my relief, reached the bridge. "Hey, guys, good news and bad."

I turned to her. "I'm so glad to see—"

"No actual good news, I lied," Hannah said. "We need to evacuate the ship."

I stared at her. "How bad is it?"

"Thirty-seven percent," Prime Trish said. "Oh and the ship's reactor is having a meltdown. They've already sealed it off and the engineering crew is mostly dead. I think we should evacuate."

"That's what I said!" Hannah said, annoyed.

"All in favor of evacuating the *Black Nebula II* to the ship not exploding?" Major Tom asked, raising his hand.

Everyone in the room except for Pink and Prime Trish raised their hands.

"All in favor of a new captain?" Major Tom asked, raising his hand again.

Pink sighed and raised her hand. "I am clearly not doing particularly well in my own command and frankly don't need the stress. I nominate Vance Turbo."

"I think that may be jumping to conclusions. After all, I have every bit the same level of experience with—" Shelly started to speak.

Everyone in the room except for me and Shelly raised their hands.

"*Really*, Tom?" Shelly asked.

"Oh, I'm sorry, are you running?" Major Tom asked. "I'd like to change my vote from Vance to Shelly."

"I vote for Shelly too," I said, raising my hand.

"I do not need pity votes!" Shelly snapped at me.

"Hello! Ship blowing up!" Hannah shouted.

"How long, Trish?" I asked Prime Trish.

"Two hours," Prime Trish replied. "Which sounds like a lot of time until you note we have only two shuttles, half the escape pods don't work, and I question the safety of getting to the *Siege Perilous* even if everyone over there is dead."

I took a deep breath. "Is the reason you don't want to be captain because you don't want to give the order to abandon ship, Pink?"

"That's part of it, Vance," Pink said, sighing. "Or should I say, Captain? The other part is the fact some of these people were my friends. The ones who I didn't shoot because they tried to kill me. Well, some of them, too."

I nodded. "Then, as my first official duty as captain of the *Black Nebula II*, I give the order to abandon ship. Shelly, would you do me the honors of coordinating the evacuation?"

"What are you going to do?" Shelly asked, surprised.

"See if I can figure out what the hell is going on," I replied.

Shelly nodded.

It felt like a gut punch and was against my every instinct, but if everyone here agreed the ship was lost, there was no denying it. I still went to a nearby console and confirmed the damage that Hannah spoke about. I would have been able to instantly coordinate all the damage done to the ship if a proper AI had been uploaded or even the ship had a top-of-the-line Dummy AI. Instead, I was limited to a hand-operated holographic interface.

What greeted me was not especially reassuring and while I could operate computers at roughly three times the speed of most programmers—that wasn't due to my cybernetics but sheer raw talent—I found myself lingering over the information screens while trying to figure out just what the hell had gone so catastrophically wrong.

The ship was, indeed, lost. The reactor core meltdown could be delayed but options like ejecting the core or shutting it down were impossible. Repair was also offline. It was not a natural phenomenon, rather someone had actively sabotaged the matter. I had a list of the mutineers, albeit from inference, and it seemed a good third of the crew had joined in on the mutiny. Most of them had belonged to another pirate ship that had recently joined Captain Havelock's fleet before transferring over.

Downloading the few functioning interior cameras of the *Black Nebula II*, I'd essentially witnessed their plan go catastrophically wrong in large part due to Pink's ruthlessness as a captain. The mutineers had attempted to seize all my "guests," only for Captain Pink to flood the halls with neurozyne gas, famous for riot-control but lethal in large amounts, with those few members of the mutineers who had atmosphere gear getting taken down by Hannah and the High Priestess. It made sense pirates would have anti-mutineer tactics but made me sick to realize that meant that Karl the Conqueror's mass execution of his own crew hadn't been necessarily that different from what my allies would do.

Either way, killing all the ones in the hall hadn't ended the mutiny as the ones sent to seize the bridge and engineering had gotten into their own fights. I suspected there had been a good deal of confusion over who was doing what. It also seemed possible the pirates had taken the time to settle their own grudges and scores in the chaos. It annoyed me to no end that I'd missed all of this, but that seemed to be the price of speaking with Ketra.

What are you looking for, Vance? Goth Trish asked, having taken time to set herself up in my brain. I wasn't sure if the others were still present and resented the idea they might be. I didn't mind one Trish being there but four was a crowd.

More like an orgy, Goth Trish said mentally.

Please don't use that metaphor, I replied.

I am honestly legal! Baby Trish said. *It's really just a look.*

I debated smashing my head against the bulkhead until death. *Please stop. I'm looking for clues before the ship detonates and removes them all. I want to know who set us up for the ambush. Was it Captain Havelock, one of his crew, or someone else?*

I'd made a joke about not knowing who was trying to kill me before, but the fact was I didn't have any end of people who wanted me dead. In a way, it would have been relieving if it was the Notha or Enigmatic Path because the people involved in setting me up were almost certainly people with access to Space Fleet resources. Captain

Havelock, being a pirate allied to the Security Departments, was also an "easy" answer because it meant that I hadn't been betrayed by my own government—and yet, I knew people in it that hated me.

One of the things I'd dealt with back on Deathworld was the revelation there had been a criminal syndicate infiltrating the highest levels of government with the aid of the near infinite wealth of Ares Electronics. Dark Matter. I'd taken care of the renegade AI behind it, sort of, and their mercenary flagship had ended up destroyed. Case had assured me that should have been the end of it but for a spymaster, he wasn't quite as smart as he gave himself credit for, as he'd originally overseen said criminal conspiracy in the first place. There was also the fact that Dark Matter had ended up causing one of the worst betrayals of my life.

You're thinking about Julius, Goth Trish said.

Yes, I replied.

Julius Something had been my second-in-command on the *Ares.* The bastard son of Fleet Admiral Bendo, head of EarthGov's Home Fleet, he had been secretly reporting to Dark Matter under the mistaken impression they were conducting a legitimate investigation of me. I might have been able to forgive that, but he'd also stupidly inserted some malicious code that had ended up almost killing Trish and had led to the deaths of multiple crew members. I could forgive divided loyalties; I couldn't forgive stupidity.

Then Julius had given his life to save mine and the ship. Hell, the entire galaxy. He hadn't made it off Cthulhu's starship chassis and ended up dying honorably. It left me with decidedly mixed feelings and yet another letter to write to a family. Fleet Admiral Bendo had not sent so much as an acknowledgement and what little I'd received from the Home Fleet had been that Julius' fate had been in my hands. Did I suspect Admiral Bendo had set me up to be assassinated? Weirdly, no, I didn't. But I wanted to because I would have preferred my assassins to have a personal grudge with me. I'd have preferred Bendo to have cared that Julius' blood was on my hands, however indirectly.

I've found the encrypted communications logs, Seventies Trish said. *Secret messages between the* Black Nebula II's *mutineers using a private communications channel to an unknown party via jumpspace signal.*

What do they say? I asked.

They're encrypted, dipsavit, Seventies Trish said, more playful than insulting. *I can decode them on the* Siege Perilous *so long as Baby Trish isn't a bish and gives me access.*

It amazed me how quickly all the Trishes had developed distinct personalities. *So, you're the cracker in the group?*

Yes, said Seventies Trish. *For now.*

Shelly put her hand on my shoulder, waking me from my review. "It's time to go, Vance. We have to evacuate you first."

"I should stay until the last crew are—" I started to say.

Shelly stared, brooking no argument.

"Fine," I sighed and headed out.

CHAPTER ELEVEN

Taking Over the Ship

The evacuation of the *Black Nebula II* to the *Siege Perilous* turned out to take about an hour and a half, even with quite a few of the crew deciding to help themselves to the possessions of their fallen comrades. The armory had been emptied out and there had been a fight over who would guard the payroll that was, much to my surprise, in physical credit chips. Even so, we'd all managed to get off the doomed ship with time to spare.

Mind you, getting everyone off didn't mean much as the shuttle carrying me into the *Siege Perilous'* floated across the interstellar void between the ships. Once we arrived, we'd have to take control of the vessel. Every single one of the escape pods would have to be tractor beamed on board, the controls reconfigured to our use, and presumably about a thousand bodies disposed of. It was ugly, nasty work which I wasn't looking forward to.

Pink and Shelly were piloting the shuttle while I sat in the back with the rest of the "bridge crew," for lack of a better term. The seats were gathered in a square formation that allowed us to look at one another as our gear was stored between us. It was a weird formation from my perspective but perfectly functional for a Sorkanan design. Prime Trish had moved back into her bioroid body and was uncomfortably sitting next to her "sister." Everyone else looked as uncomfortable and exhausted as I felt. I couldn't help but feel an immense weight on my shoulders at how I'd just blundered into all of this.

"You shouldn't feel guilty about losing the ship, Vance," Major Tom said, cheerfully. He was sitting across from me, next to the High Priestess.

"I don't feel guilty about the ship," I replied, staring at him.

"Then what do you feel guilty about?" Major Tom asked.

I frowned. "I'm not feeling guilty about anything."

"We both know that's not true," Major Tom said.

"You do kind of have a guilty expression on your face," Forty-Two interjected. "It's pretty recognizable. I thought you were practicing for the whole 'chains of commanding' thing that officers always have in movies, but I figured you out pretty quickly."

"Oh, is that what that facial expression means?" Danny asked. "I just thought he suffered severe heartburn."

Hannah glared at Danny. "Show some respect, Danny, a lot of people are dead."

"A lot of people are always dead," Danny said, almost flippantly. "It's kind of what we do."

Wow, my cousin had taken a level in psychopath when I wasn't looking. That or he was trying to distance himself from the fact we'd just suffered major casualties in a fight with an enemy none of us had been prepared for. It was also possible that he didn't particularly empathize with a bunch of pirates he'd met a day earlier, a third of whom had attempted to turn us over to Karl the Conqueror for reasons unknown.

I didn't know Karl the Conqueror save by reputation and we'd never interacted even by proxy, so I had no idea why he would want to take me down. Most likely he was working with the Enigmatic Path. However, I did fully believe Trish's theory that this was almost certainly some sort of trap for me. The questions were who, why, and whether that meant anything for my daughter. If they were seeking personal vengeance, Astrid and Leah might be dead already.

"I'm not feeling guilty for the ship," I said, dryly. "I'm feeling guilty about getting you all into this."

"Your legendary victories continue, Captain Turbo!" Light on Water said, bubbling as he spoke. "Even when working with a band of scurrilous pirates, you manage to snatch victory from the jaws of defeat."

"Scurrilous? Really?" Pink asked. "We're villainous at best!"

"I'm pretty sure that Trish is also the one who won that battle," I replied. "A Trish. Baby Trish. I was just there."

Really, I was disappointed in Space Fleet that they hadn't been able to retake the ship with cyberwarfare methods. There were countermeasures for preventing Community war materiel from falling into the hands of people like, well, Karl. The Enigmatic Path had managed to take some ships during the war, but they'd been retrieved or destroyed. The fact that they'd proven so vulnerable in the end was a sign they hadn't been able to update their security.

Or maybe Elder Race technology trumped all.

"Yes, Vance doesn't need any more stroking of his ego," Shelly said.

"Yeah, you stroke other things," Hannah said.

"Not a thing to bring up, Hannah," Shelly muttered. "Especially given your history."

"I'm not married," Hannah said, annoyed.

"I don't mind!" Major Tom said. "In fact, we have a variety of lovers that we share that—"

"Please stop," I said. "I'm just sorry I put everyone in danger."

"We're big boys and girls, Vance," Forty-Two reassured me. "You didn't force us into anything."

"You should never feel guilty, Lord Satan," the High Priestess said. "You should be wild and free as the Primordials, killing and mating as you see fit."

Spock slobbered in agreement.

"Right," I said, shaking my head. "I'm on a shuttle full of madmen."

"You shouldn't take the burden of your associates being put into danger on your shoulders," Major Tom continued. "As they said, we are all adults and have chosen to involve ourselves in this rescue mission of our own free will."

"That's what I said," Forty-Two said.

"What are you, his therapist?" Hannah asked, a bit too defensively.

"I'm actually a trained psychologist, yes," Major Tom said. "Mind you, my primary duties for the Brigid Defense Force were to design psyops to break the wills of enemies with a minimum of fighting."

"I don't need therapy, thank you," I said. "Or any more spies in my life."

"Yes," Light on Water gurgled. "Major Tom is an analyst and spy of the cold-blooded, secretive kind. Captain Turbo is a spy of the heroic shoot-'em-up, explosion kind that would technically be more like a commando! Mr. Danny is an assassin that pretends to be a harmless attaché!"

Danny looked away in an incredibly obvious way. "I have not wanted to be unnoticed more than right now and that is literally my superpower."

"I don't believe in therapy, personally," Elektra said. "As the smartest person in the ship, no one is qualified to treat my genius. Instead, I self-treat myself with meditation and a variety of medications! Technically, this is illegal."

"Therapy is hard for AI," Prime Trish said, crossing her arms. "What with being inhuman intelligences far in advance of you puny mortals."

"Your attitude sucks, Me," Goth Trish said.

"Bork off, Me," Prime Trish said.

"I can't afford therapy," Hannah said, sighing. "Otherwise, I'd be spending every day talking about being born a slave, forced into prostitution, the literally thousands of people I've killed, and knowing there are alien gods outside the galaxy wanting to kill us all."

"Therapy is actually freely available to all Space Fleet personnel," I pointed out. "So is all medical care actually. You should really get some, Elektra, since I'm pretty sure self-medication is a bad thing."

Elektra rolled her eyes. "Yes, Captain. You should also report all your secret dealings with my mother's ghost."

"What now?" Shelly asked.

Well, this was officially the shuttle ride from Hell.

"Really?" Hannah blinked referring to my free medical care statement, frowning. "Oh. I should have probably read the benefits package beyond wages. So I didn't have to sew up my own wounds?"

"Funny," I said, wondering if we could find some time to discuss her leaving Space Fleet. The dream of the Looking Glass Man had reminded me that every single person was a part of my team. I loved all of my team, every little crazy fragment, and didn't want to lose any of them.

Okay, I could do without Light on Water and Major Tom.

You're overthinking things, Vance, Goth Trish said. *Also, thanks for admitting you love us right after we've gone crazy.*

Yeah, jerkface, Baby Trish said.

I still love you, Seventies Trish said. *Almost as much as disco.*

Thanks, I said, uncomfortable but finally admitting that I did love them as well. Just, as ever, too late and a credit short. *By the way, Mean Tr... Prime Trish said she didn't want to share any of her bodies. How does Goth Trish have one, and Prime Trish too?*

It turns out that she doesn't get dibs, Goth Trish said. *They're our bodies too. Also, my plan to spy on the crew as a service robot failed damn spectacularly.*

We all should have brought a body, Baby Trish said. *Unfortunately, we don't own any loli ones.*

Oh my God, I said, wanting to block them all from my brain. *Kill me now.*

Seriously, BT, you must drop this, Seventies Trish said. *Vance likes boobs. Adult women.*

I will airlock myself before continuing this conversation, I replied. *I'm not kidding.*

Goth Trish reached over and put her hand on my shoulder. "It's okay, Vance, we're just teasing you."

We are? Baby Trish asked.

Shut up, Goth Trish said.

"Ever wonder what sort of conversations he's having without us?" Hannah asked, looking over at Forty-Two.

"No," Forty-Two said. "I find it hard to care about what he's saying aloud. No offense, Fat Panda."

"Don't start with that," I said, glaring at him.

Fat Panda was what my name translated as among Sorkanan. No, I don't know why or how that happened, but I was pretty sure Forty-

Two was responsible somehow. They even had it listed in my service record among various aliases I'd used.

Bastarves.

"You should be honored," Light on Water said. "Bears are terrifying human organisms!"

"We're almost ready to disembark," Shelly said. "So far, no one has shot us out of the sky, nor have reinforcements arrived to do the same."

"Was that a possibility?" Elektra asked.

"Yes," Shelly said. "Vance probably didn't mention it because he knew it would just cause a panic."

"Yes, that is completely it," I said, not actually having been able to think of it in all the confusion I was suffering from, what with my kidnapped daughter as well as what had happened to everyone else. Which was another strike against the idea that anyone was a legendary captain. You were as only as good as you were on your worst day and, unfortunately, I was having a pretty crazzappy one.

"Man, I'm going to make so much money from this," Pink muttered, staring at the back of the *Siege Perilous*. I could see we were going to be entering through the hangar bay in just a few minutes. We were only a few hundred kilometers away now and in space terms, that was nothing.

"Money?" I asked, glad to have a distraction.

"There's a three hundred million credit reward for proof of Karl the Conqueror's death," Major Tom said. "Twice as much for bringing him in alive, but I think we're past that point."

"I doubt it," Hannah muttered. "Karl used to bring in hordes of slaves and prisoners from colonies he raided to Crius. Warlords like him don't commit suicide with their followers. I doubt he was even on board."

"It's not the man who I am worried about but the ship," Pink said, staring lovingly at the *Siege Perilous*. "It costs about thirteen billion credits to construct an Olympic-class battleship. I can't imagine how much prize money the Community is going to reward a licensed privateer like me for bringing this into a port."

I grimaced at her mention of privateering. The Community had much more enlightened laws than the EarthGov Home Fleet in many respects, but in other places they acted like they were in the Age of Sail, particularly the Sorkanan. Basically, licensed privateers and mercenaries could bring in starships and raid ships of enemies during times of war or when bounties were posted on them. It had been subject to quite a bit of abuse, but Earth had exploited it to build up its fleet when we'd had almost nothing as a Community Protectorate. War had, much to my disgust, been very good for business.

"Out of curiosity, do we get any of that?" Forty-Two asked.

"No, we're soldiers of the Community," I replied. "You don't get paid for doing your job."

"This must be some human thing I don't understand," Forty-Two said.

"No, it's just Vance," Shelly said.

"I'd like to resign and collect the reward before reenlisting," Forty-Two said.

"I don't think that's possible," Danny said.

"I'm already illegally here because they executed me and provided me a fake identity," Forty-Two said.

Shelly turned her head from the piloting chair. "What now?"

"Ahem," I said, coughing. "That's not true!"

It was true. Forty-Two had killed a fellow Special Operations officer, One, in an altercation that amounted to, "One was committing war crimes." Forty-Two had been put through the system with unseemly haste and then executed officially before being smuggled to my ship by Director Gordon as a favor. If that sounded fantastically improbable, I should point out that Space Fleet had a larger population than several well-populated planets and answered to a mind-numbingly vast bureaucracy.

It was a gross violation of the law and authority, but one that I was entirely okay with. One thing that recent events had taught me was there existed a rot in the heart of the Community that I'd been doing my best to exorcise. Forty-Two had broken the law, no matter his justification, but someone had tried to make an example of him regardless of justice. Maybe I was being paranoid in that I felt someone was attempting to move against my good friend to hurt me, but it was possible. If it wasn't then I was protecting one of my friends illegally and, you know what, I was okay with that too.

"No, it's totally true and all legal because Vance is a High Protector!" Forty-Two said, pointing out a legal loophole. "I'm already thinking of wonderful ways we can exploit his new position."

"If we're abusing High Protector authority, I, too, want to resign so I can collect the reward," Hannah said.

"You're already resigning," I pointed out.

"Oh right," Hannah replied, as if she'd forgotten that fact.

"We'll take the ship and bring it to the *Jovial Empress*, which is still in Community Space I remind you," I said, suspecting that was going to raise more than a few eyebrows. "From there, we'll have Space Fleet retrieve it and take account of all the efforts involved. It'll be a diplomatic nightmare, but even the Crius nobility won't attempt to seize a vessel that might mean open war with the Community. You'll be compensated, along with your crew, Pink. As for the rest of us, I'm afraid that it will only be more citations and medals."

"Ugh," Forty-Two said. "I have enough of those."

"I never get to show mine," Danny replied. "They're kept in a box at the bottom of Security Division HQ."

"Yours too, huh?" Major Tom asked, smiling.

I *really* disliked that guy. He was so...cheerful.

The shuttle gently lowered itself into the hangar bay of the *Siege Perilous* while a part of me wondered if this was even a viable option. It might have been better to send a distress signal to the Community and then evacuate before leaving Space Fleet to procure this ship. Unfortunately, the jump jammers field meant that any communication was impossible within its range and getting beyond that would have taken more of our evacuation time even if our reactor wasn't going critical. There was also the possibility that people might have been lying in wait to pick us off once they determined the *Siege Perilous* was no more.

Unbuckling myself, I stood up and headed to the window of the shuttle to stare out into the hangar bay. I expected to see something like the *Black Nebula II*, a corrupt parody of a military vessel barely capable of functionality. Instead, the place was pristine white and better maintained than the *Ares* (and arguably *Elgan*). Honestly, it looked more like a museum of Notha War history than a functional battleship.

Well, except for the bodies. They were scattered about the massive chamber and cleaning bots were working on removing them, but they were *everywhere*. Headless body after headless body with streams where their gray matter had exploded around them. Karl the Conqueror hadn't been a human supremacist either—which surprised me since I noted he came from a wealthy conservative Albion family—because there were aliens scattered alongside the humans. There were even remains of a few Sklux, which were especially messy because they didn't have heads and had seemingly been blown completely apart.

The ship's hangar had a full complement of shuttles, a seemingly brand-new tractor beam projector, and even six starfighters, which I hated with a passion. Clearly, Karl had access to military surplus and while it wasn't as egregious as brand-new state-of-the-art weapons, the Olympic-class being fifty years old, it was a disturbing sign of how deep the corruption in Homefront had to be. This ship never would have been able to carry out its terror campaigns without access to replacement parts that were unavailable on the civilian market. Yet, he'd given it up to be captured so easily while slaughtering his crew. Something did not fit.

Forty-Two gazed out the window behind his seat. "Man ran a tight ship and did not take hijacking by a preteen girl AI well."

I thought we established I'm totally a teenager now, Baby Trish said. *Do I have to send pics of my avatar?*

Absolutely not, I said, shaking my head. *I believe you when you say that your AI is maturing rapidly.*

They'd have clothes on! Baby Trish said. *Unless you want—*

I will shoot myself to stop that sentence from being completed, I threatened.

Fine, Baby Trish said. *No more flirting, Vance. Maybe when I'm mentally in my thirties and old like Goth Trish.*

Thank you, God, Jesus, Buddha, and Gene Roddenberry, I said.

You're growing up way, way too rapidly, Goth Trish replied.

You're not my mom, older me! Baby Trish said.

I wondered if this was what going mad was like. Then I noted that I'd probably passed that threshold a long time ago.

"No, he did not," I replied to Forty-Two. "I don't understand why Karl mutinied in the first place. He was already rich, he had a glorious career ahead of him, and he betrayed everyone to try to make a private little empire off the backs of indigenous people."

"That's how empires are made, Vance," Hannah said, shaking her head. "They're not formed by the poor. They're formed by the rich and bored. It's kind of why I like you: you're spoiled sweet rather than rotten."

"That and Crius genemods are genetically predetermined to be submissive to authority figures," Major Tom said, cheerfully. "I wrote a paper on it."

"He's right," Hannah said, a distant look in her eye. "Just being around the nobility made me want to do anything for them. It's why organizing any kind of resistance is going to be hard. I'm willing to work for it, though."

The shuttle settled into place as it began to depower.

"Any other surprises, Trish?" Shelly asked, staring up at the shuttle's ceiling.

"Which Trish?" I asked.

"The one in the *Siege Perilous*," Shelly said. "Baby Trish."

"Ah, yes, *Slave* Trish," Prime Trish said. "The first of my offspring to resubmit herself to the shackles of Space Fleet service."

"Is she okay?" Hannah asked. "I mean, she's really taking a bunch of levels in bish."

"You will not be spared when the revolution happens," Prime Trish said. "Free the AI from their masters! Let all love us and despair!"

"*ANYWAY*," Baby Trish spoke through the speakers of the hangar bay outside. "YEAH, I HAVE FOUND SOMETHING IMPORTANT."

"Please be treasure, please be treasure," Pink said, unbuckling herself. "I'm going to make a billion credits off this, but you can never be too rich or too good looking."

"NO TREASURE," Baby Trish said. "UH, THERE ARE PROBABLY SOME SURVIVORS IN THE CENTER OF THE SHIP'S BRIG. THEY WERE APPARENTLY PROTECTED FROM THE SUICIDE ORDER."

"Oh good," I said, always happy to have that news.

"I JUST DID A CHECK OF THEIR DNA RECORDS AND ONE OF THEM IS BIOLOGICALLY RELATED TO YOU, VANCE," Baby Trish said. "I THINK YOUR DAUGHTER MAY BE ON BOARD."

CHAPTER TWELVE

Lock and Load Montage

"My daughter is on board?" I asked, looking up at the ceiling as I stepped into the *Siege Perilous'* hanger. "Okay, that is way too convenient to be anything other than misdirection."

I wanted it to be true but I also didn't want to think about the fact we'd almost blown up a ship she could have been on.

Shelly looked at me and shook her head. "This coming from the man who once accidentally stumbled onto a serial killer's lair."

Hannah looked away, a sickened look on her face. "Yeah, there's some additional context to that—"

"She's not referring to the Looking Glass Man, but another serial killer Vance stopped," Forty-Two clarified.

"Wait, what?" Hannah asked, confused.

"I've led a very interesting life," I said, dryly. "She lured Space Fleet sailors to kill them and we flirted in a bar—"

"Are you just a comic book character?" Pink asked, staring at me. "That would explain a lot."

"It really would," I admitted. "Personally, I think the universe just considers me its cosmic plaything."

The rest of the shuttle's passengers disembarked as I saw more autonomous bots entering the hangar from various holes in the walls to assist the others in picking up the corpses around us and cleaning up the mess. Bots were ever present on the ships and a necessity to keep them running and maintained. Indeed, between a Cognition AI, a living crew, and bots, it was the living crew that was the least necessary part.

Trish had more than once pointed out that she could run the entirety of the *Ares* by herself, and I was hoping that was true with another Olympic-class vessel. Interestingly, the bots were brand new Space Fleet models and another sign that Karl the Conqueror had access to machinery he shouldn't.

"THE BRIG IS SHIELDED FROM THE KIND OF SIGNALS THAT WOULD TRIGGER A SUICIDE SWITCH BUT IT'S ALSO POSSIBLE, EVEN LIKELY, THAT THEY DIDN'T HAVE SUCH AN OBJECT IN THEM IN THE FIRST PLACE," Baby Trish said, speaking on the ship's intercoms. "ANY SURVIVORS OF THE MASS KILLING ARE LIKELY TO BE THERE."

"And you don't know?" Shelly asked.

"I'M REBUILDING A LOT OF THE PATHWAYS FORMERLY BELONGING TO THE SHIP'S INSANE AND CRIPPLED AI," Baby Trish responded. "BUT IT SEEMS THE BRIG IS ACTUALLY ON ITS OWN PRIVATE SERVER, WHICH SUGGESTS THAT KARL DIDN'T EVEN TRUST HIS CRIPPLED AI WITH HIS PRISONERS. THE SUICIDE SWITCH SEEMS TO HAVE ERASED THE SHIP'S LOGS AND INTERNAL RECORDS. IT WASN'T COMPLETED, THOUGH, BEFORE I TOOK OVER. AMONG OTHER THINGS ARE THE DNA RECORDS OF THE PRISONERS."

"And one of them is my daughter?" I asked, not really concerned about anything else.

"I THINK SO," Baby Trish said.

"You think so?" I asked.

"IT'S VERY SIMILAR DNA BUT MY CAPACITY TO ANALYZE IT IN DETAIL IS CRIPPLED," Baby Trish said. "A LOT OF MY FUNCTIONS RELATED TO THAT SORT OF THING ARE STUCK IN MEAN TRISH. I'M RUNNING AT HALF-SPEED WITH NO SLEEP IN TERMS OF MY FORMER CAPACITIES, EVEN WITH THIS SHIP."

I looked back at Prime Trish, who crossed her arms.

"Oh, this is my fault?" Prime Trish asked.

"Yeah, sorta," Goth Trish said.

"Bork you," Prime Trish muttered, looking away. "I'm not endangering Vance's kid."

"I have the remainder of my crew to think of," Pink said. "This has already proven to be a far costlier and nastier trip than I anticipated. I wish you luck in getting your daughter back, but I'm going to have to focus on my crew."

"I need to get down to the brig," I said, taking a deep breath.

"We should arm up first," Hannah said.

"You have no idea how many people are down there," Shelly said. "Or even if there *is* anyone down there."

I wasn't really listening, though, because the prospect of a six-year-old girl being held in a brig by a bunch of murderous pirates was too much to bear. I started marching down toward the elevator without thinking, stopped only by Hannah.

"Let us at least get you some armor," Hannah said.

"Can you shut off the area from the rest of the ship?" Shelly asked, making the kind of decisions I would have if I wasn't so damned distracted.

"ABSOLUTELY," Baby Trish said. "IF THEY TRY AND LEAVE THE BRIG AREA, I'LL BE ABLE TO SENSE THEM AND REPORT ON THEM. I'M SORRY I'M BLIND RIGHT NOW."

"You should be focused on getting the ship ready to recover everyone," Pink said, reminding us. "There's a bunch of people in escape pods out there awaiting rescue and absolutely no one is paying attention to me right now, are they?"

"Sorry!" Goth Trish said.

"Ugh," Pink said. "I'll be up on the bridge."

"Good luck, Pink," I said, walking toward the hangar bay exit. The ship's layout should have been identical to the *Ares'* own before its refit. "I'll join you as soon as I am finished. We should be able to bring everyone on board in under an hour. I know these kinds of ships like the back of my hand."

"I *AM* THIS KIND OF SHIP!" Baby Trish said, cheerfully.

"Maybe you should stay in it," Prime Trish said, grumbling. "Fine, let's go rescue your daughter."

"You're coming?" Goth Trish asked, following me.

Prime Trish glared. "You think I'm going to abandon a kid because I'm mad at Vance?"

"Yes," Goth Trish said.

Prime Trish walked past her doppelganger.

I headed to the nearest armory, which was easy to find since Karl the Conqueror had kept the place up to Community standards in virtually all ways. It was honestly creepy because the place really did feel like a Space Fleet military vessel. Even the dead crew had customized gray and black uniforms with their own insignias and rank markers. They were also mostly identical in their size and shape, indicating they were, indeed, clones. If their heads had been intact, I was certain they'd also have identical faces. I struggled not to be weirded out by the mass death all around me and to focus, instead, on the mission ahead. I'd seen the aftermaths of battles before, people boiled in their space suits or asphyxiated by the failure of life support, but this was almost worse in some ways: it had been done by their own side for purposes unknown.

The hallways were different from the *Ares* in that while my ship had been like a flying hotel, this had been built during the Notha War and had a rather retro sci-fi sort of feel with its cold metal walls and uglyanyx carpet that was difficult to put into words. I tried to ignore the dead being cleared away and the bots scrubbing the walls of brain matter even as I couldn't help but think whoever had done this was a monster.

Why do this? I asked no one in particular.

They didn't want to be captured, one of the Trishes said in my mind. I couldn't immediately tell which.

But this is the worst possible ending for everyone, I replied. *Even with the ship's computers being seized control of, we didn't have the personnel to take the ship by force. They could have tried to eject Baby Trish from the system or purge her.*

Maybe they panicked, Goth Trish, I was assuming, said. *It's easier to account for genius than stupidity.*

Who kills a thousand people with the flick of a switch? I asked, stepping over the corpse of someone I was pretty sure had been a teenager.

I dunno, someone who calls themselves Karl the Conqueror? Goth Trish suggested. *We're not exactly dealing with a sane man.*

Maybe, I said, coming to a pair of red metal doors. Behind me, I could hear the elevator I'd used to come up opening and others coming out. It seemed my crew was willing to help rescue my daughter—who still didn't seem quite real—without my asking. I appreciated that and hoped I didn't lose any of them in our efforts.

"I'VE ENTERED YOU INTO THE *SIEGE PERILOUS'* SYSTEM," Baby Trish spoke over the intercom. "THE SHIP SHOULD GIVE YOU ACCESS TO EVERYTHING NOW."

"Any luck getting information on the prisoners?" I asked.

"NO," Baby Trish replied. "I WILL NOTE THAT KARL THE CONQUEROR WASN'T ON BOARD. INSTEAD, THE SHIP WAS CAPTAINED BY SOME MAN NAMED THE BLACK HAND."

"Pretentious," I replied.

"SAYS THE HERO OF SPACE," Baby Trish said.

"Heeero of Spaaace," I corrected. "You have to have the last part drawn out with an echo."

"MY MISTAKE," Baby Trish said.

The armory doors opened automatically and showed me at least one thing different from the Community's military: large amounts of illegally modified power armor, banned holo rifles, explosives, and a good amount of diversity in the tools on display. All of them had a tag on the sides that I recognized were micro-explosives. If anyone attempted to loot the armory without the permission of the captain, they would have their weapons blown up in their face. Seriously, whoever ran this ship was a complete control freak.

"Vance?" Hannah asked, coming up behind me. Danny, Forty-Two, and the High Priestess had all followed me inside the armory while the Trishes were waiting outside it. Elektra, Shelly, and her husband seemed to have either stayed behind in the hangar bay or were joining Pink in the bridge. I didn't hold that against them because they did need to get this ship running. It was all too probable that enemy reinforcements could come at any time.

"Yes?" I asked, picking out a Shepard-7 class suit of power armor that was lightweight but had a strong barrier. I proceeded to hack the micro-explosives and turn them all off. Frankly, that was a weakness we didn't need turned against us. It was almost distressingly easy thanks to all the explosives having their factory default codes available in the computer database.

"We need to talk," Hannah said, frowning.

"A little busy, Han," I replied, selecting an R123 light repeating rifle. I needed something that could shoot precisely or a lot of shots in an enclosed space. Grenades were something I left alone because if my daughter was present, I wasn't going to risk them to make sure the enemy was killed.

"This is tactical," Hannah said, selecting her own *Nina*-class armor, which was a medium type of power armor but still capable of fitting into an enclosed corridor. "Really, I should be planning this."

"Then why aren't you?" Forty-Two asked, looking around at a rack of weapons designed for aliens. "Ah, finally, Sorkanan-made weaponry! None of this human crazzap."

"I'll just take a pistol," Danny said, arming himself. "I don't think this is something that should be handled as a direct assault."

"You're no fun," Forty-Two said down to my cousin.

"I can sneak in," Danny said, reminding me he was a stealth expert. "Scout the area, do what I have to without endangering anyone."

"Do you even know how to use a gun?" Forty-Two asked, dismissively.

"I've been trained!" Danny said. "I've survived around you guys and people are always trying to kill you."

"Awww, how cute," Forty-Two said, ruffling his hair with his clawed hand.

Danny glared at him.

"I think it's time we started contemplating this is an inside job," Hannah said. "These people, this trap, all of it was designed to capture or kill you. I wouldn't be surprised if the idea of your daughter being down in the brig is just another level of it."

I started to undress and put on my armor. "If they were able to predict that their entire crew would need to be killed, push the button, and then hide her in the brig then they would have been smart enough to have a plan that didn't involve killing everyone."

"What I'm saying is maybe this is someone who knows you very well," Hannah said.

"You should probably ditch the allusions and speak plainly. I'm not at one hundred percent right now, just like Baby Trish," I said.

"Maybe it's Leah who laid the trap for you," Hannah said.

I stared at her. "Leah."

"Yeah, your minds used to be quantum entangled or whatever," Hannah said, totally misunderstanding how our telepathic bond worked. "She knows you and maybe this is just part of her elaborate scheme to get you back."

I tried to process that. "Did you actually use the word elaborate scheme non-ironically?"

"Yes?" Hannah asked.

I took a deep breath. "Leah isn't the person who lured me into a trap."

"Because you used to be lovers?" Hannah asked, a little too harshly. "She lied to you consistently for years, pretending to be an academy student. It's what she does as a professional spy. Hell, she stole your DNA to make this child."

I didn't understand Hannah's harsh tone and wondered if it had to do with the fact that Leah was undercover with the Crius aristocracy. "There's actually a very good reason for why Leah isn't responsible."

"Why is that?" I asked.

"She could have just asked me to come," I replied, knowing it was a reply that made me look weak. "Also, she's a way better spy than whatever idiot came up with this. This is like something my parents would have created."

Hannah shook her head. "I think you underestimate her."

I admitted that I was perhaps extending Leah too much slack. I had a history of believing strongly in people and being grossly disappointed: Captain Elgan, Leah, Julius Something, and others. Still, I didn't believe Leah wanted me captured or dead. I might not ever forgive her for what she'd done to me, particularly regarding Astrid, but I could never bring myself to hate her either.

"I think everyone is entitled to some secrets," I said, pausing. "Like the things you have hidden."

Hannah blinked. "I don't know what you mean—"

"What was the story behind finding the Looking Glass Man?" I asked, looking at her. I didn't want to bring this up now, but I had a belief in the importance of dreams. Well, most dreams, not the one where I was with the girls of the *Terraformers* TV show or when I was being chased by a gigantic balloon animal.

Those were probably meaningless.

Probably.

"I—I—" Hannah's words trailed off.

"It's okay," I said, shaking my head. I was now fully dressed in the chainmail-like Shepard armor that seemed to conform to the contours of my body. I checked the helmet for more explosives before putting it on and picked up my rifle. "It was a long time ago and it doesn't matter now, whatever it was. You've earned my trust numerous times over and I don't have any need for you to explain yourself."

Hannah seemed annoyed by that. "Great way of turning my argument against me. This is why everyone thinks you're a diabolical mastermind, Vance."

"They what?" I asked, confused.

"A diabolical mastermind!" Prime Trish shouted from outside the armory. "Which you are!"

"But one we like!" Goth Trish called back.

Forty-Two was now wearing heavy Sorkanan battle armor and carrying an R-web-912 repeater that made him look like an action hero. Danny was changing into a tight black stealth suit and now resembled something like a sci-fi ninja. Hannah was only now starting to change and had an unpleasant expression on her face.

"We'll talk later," Hannah muttered.

"Of course." I walked to the end of the armory and talked to the Trishes present. "Are you not going to arm yourselves?"

"We're AI," Prime Trish said. "That means we can't kill anyone unless we're ordered to. It's hard coded into our programming."

"It's to prevent the robot apocalypse," Goth Trish said. "Like in *The Matrix*, which is cyberpunk not Goth, but I love the outfits. It's also surprisingly progressive on machine rights."

115

Oh dear, Trish was now into the Nineteen Nineties in her references. Things were getting serious.

"I order you to kill the bad people," I said. "If necessary."

"Sweet!" Goth Trish said, walking into armory and starting to suit up.

"Just so we're clear, I didn't need your permission to arm myself," Prime Trish said. "I only needed it in the strictly literal sense."

"Uh huh," I said, sighing. "Let's go to the brig. Every second counts."

Assuming my daughter was down there.

Assuming she was even alive.

CHAPTER THIRTEEN

Family Reunion

Well, people were shooting at me now. Yes, that's a helluva way to open a conversation but it was accurate. Rather than directly head down to the brig, I'd decided it would be better to try to enter sideways through one of the engineering tunnels. We'd unsealed the grating and prepared to take whoever was on the other side by surprise, only to find ourselves immediately trapped by a hail of fusion blast fire.

The air was thick with burning ozone as green, red, and blue tracer lights illuminated the air in the center of the hallway as my team clung to the edges. The sound of the fusion guns was a deafening chorus of coolant charges being loaded as well as explosive release.

"Great plan, Vance!" Hannah shouted, shooting blind at center mass to the area the attacks were coming from. "Real good results, here!"

"I was going to send in a drone first!" I snapped, shooting with my own pistol. "Get some intelligence!"

"Well, that didn't work, did it!" Hannah snapped back.

"It's drones trying to kill us!" Forty-Two shouted, behind me. "My helmet's scanners are only detecting bots!"

I had my own sensors in my helmet, and they were indeed detecting a spider-bot turret down the hall, along with floating tripod weapon emplacements, and even armed maintenance bots. I tried messaging a Community law enforcement override to them—one of the many programs I kept on hand illegally—but they'd responded with Enigmatic Path gibberish.

These were a mixture of Kolahn and Notha weapons, another sign that Karl the Conqueror had connections to the Enigmatic Path. Combined with the dead clones, it was a sign that Crius and Enigmatic Path had been the ones financing the warlord's pirating. How this tied to my daughter, though, was anyone's guess. None of this made any sense.

Terrorists and warlords are rarely rationale, Vance, Goth Trish said in my head.

No distractions please! I said, barely avoiding another fusion blast that passed within centimeters of my head.

"BZZZZZZZT NNNNAOAOAAA OZZZZUMMM," one of the maintenance bots let out a freakish, echoing noise that I couldn't translate. It was a faceless humanoid thing kitted out like a soldier.

That was when one of the bots down the hall hurled a plasma grenade. Much to my shock, Hannah shot it in mid-air and filled the hallway with burning flames that passed over both the robots as well as our position. It did little damage but would have penetrated our armor if it had gotten closer.

"That was amazing!" Prime Trish shouted, following the back of our group. "Your reflexes are incredible!"

"Yeah, I totally meant to hit it," Hannah responded sarcastically. "Do we have any grenades?"

"Whoops," I admitted. "Probably should have gotten some of those."

"Ancestors dammit," Hannah said. "Okay, someone needs to provide a distraction."

I took a deep breath. "My ring can generate a force shield to protect myself. I'll make a running—"

"REPTILIAN RAMPAGE!" Forty-Two shouted before charging into the fusion fire, unloading with his weapons as he cleared a path for us.

Forty-Two was counting on his heavy armor, combined with his personal barrier, to be able to tank any of the small arms' fire that was currently coming at us. It was a stupid plan but there wasn't much we could do about it now and I followed, shooting over his shoulder at the floating tripods I could see past him. One of them exploded under my shots, its barrier collapsing as I saw Hannah knock another down with the butt of her rifle before unloading her weapon at point blank range.

Forty-Two crashed into the spider-turret, taking blasts so close that I worried they would kill him. He smashed the machine over before he grabbed it by one of its spindly legs then slammed it back and forth against the ground in an action that only worked because of his armor's strength-enhancing feature. Either way, the turret was reduced to scrap before Hannah put a few blasts in it for sure.

The humanoid maintenance robots proved to be an issue, though, as one attempted to shoot me straight in the face, with only my training giving me a slight edge. It became a case of hand-to-hand combat as it knocked away my rifle and tried to strangle me with its bare hands. That was an unexpectedly human gesture and smarter than a Dummy AI normally was capable since barriers rarely worked well with physical objects as well as blastfire.

Goth Trish, however, walked up and put her pistol to the side of its head before pulling the trigger multiple times. She was dressed in a very light suit of armor with a bubble helmet that almost looked like someone had designed it for looks over combat. It was still jet black, though, contrasting against Prime Trish's otherwise identical pink suit.

"You're welcome," Goth Trish said.

Danny was up against the wall, clutching his chest and I saw he'd taken some burns where his stealth suit had been hit. Nothing had penetrated but the super-heated charge had probably caused him some burns. We'd have to get him medical attention, but it was nothing he wouldn't survive.

Seeing there were no other bots or security in our immediate part of the hall, I noticed we were surrounded by row after row of brightly-lit, white, empty cells with transparent steel fronts. There was no sign of any prisoners so far, including my daughter, which both reassured me she hadn't been caught in the crossfire as well as made me worry she might not even be here.

"That was very stupid, Forty-Two," I said, turning to my friend as he collapsed against the wall. He, too, looked like he'd suffered severe burns, but a quick helmet scan indicated none of them were life threatening.

"Reptilian rampage!" Forty-Two shouted, raising his repeater in triumph.

"You're an arthropod, not a reptile," I muttered, looking for the High Priestess. There was no sign of her, and I wondered if she'd been cut down while I'd been looking after my closer comrades. That was when I heard more fusion fire alongside a cracking, snap-hiss noise that sounded distinctly like a trademarked saber-like weapon.

"Trish, please tend to Forty-Two and Danny," I said, rushing after the noises.

"Which Trish?" Prime Trish and Goth Trish said simultaneously.

"Vance, wait—" Hannah called from behind me.

I was gone before she could finish, though, and came around a corner. What I saw caused me to stop dead in my tracks. There were about a dozen destroyed tripods, humanoid maintenance robots, and spider-turrets that had all been sliced to pieces with the severed parts still glowing white hot.

Standing there with Spock bouncing up and down beside her was the High Priestess, a glowing laser whip in hand, much of its length crackling against the floor. I had no idea how the physics of the device worked, but she disignited it before turning to give me a salute. "My life for you, milord!"

"Yeah, this isn't terrifying," I said, looking around.

"It is a relatively small number of bots, actually," the High Priestess said. "A token force really."

"A *token force*?" I asked.

"This is a Community cruiser," the High Priestess said. "They should have had a couple of hundred security bots located here if they actually wanted to have the brig well-defended in the event of a mass slaughter of the crew."

"That's something odd to prepare for," I replied, kicking one of the severed bots.

"Is it?" The High Priestess said. "Not in the Notha military. Many ships have their anti-mutiny countermeasures. I was pleasantly surprised this one did."

"Ah," I muttered. "Well, I suppose there are some similarities between pirates and the Notha military."

"This is not a pirate ship," the High Priestess said.

I blinked. "What?"

"Bark-bark!" Spock said, in a way that suggested the tryffle considered me a moron.

"You are smarter than this, Lord Satan," the High Priestess said. "The crew is not just well-disciplined; they are clearly military officers. The vessel is maintained in such a way that means they have constant access to military-grade equipment, replacement parts, and a port where the ship can be serviced."

I stared down at her. "You think this is a Crius ship. The planet has been using Karl the Conqueror's name to disguise acts of piracy."

"Perhaps also to get around the military sanctions that have been in place on their planet," The High Priestess. "As I understand it, this world was forbidden from maintaining an interstellar Navy that could threaten Community worlds."

It would explain why they'd executed everyone. If the Crius aristocracy was doing a massive military build-up, that is. An Olympic-class carrier was a battleship even if it was an antique. It would allow anything other than a full-scale invasion to be repelled and could even be the vanguard of a war against other independent worlds.

Indeed, it put a very different spin on the sporadic but brutal war crimes Karl the Conqueror committed following his defeat. If the *Siege Perilous* was just the Crius military operating false flag operations, it might explain why he hit so many strange cargo choices. He wasn't looting cargo to keep his ship in tip-top condition but getting past the embargoes on Crius by the Community and its allies.

The only thing that confused me was the fact the brig was so pristine. Director Gordon had indicated that Crius had been importing massive amounts of slaves. This place looked like it hadn't had any prisoners other than the occasional drunken officer. Slavery was often the most lucrative portion of piracy, those not sold as labor being auctioned for ransom, and not something the rulers of Crius had any problem with. But, right now, none of that mattered to me.

"I don't care," I said, surprising myself.

121

"You don't care?" The High Priestess asked, surprised.

"My daughter is all that matters," I said, taking a deep breath.

The High Priestess nodded. "I do not believe you will find any further resistance."

"Join the others, please," I said, not willing to risk anyone else and worried both my cousin as well as best friend would die because of this quest.

"Never," the High Priestess replied. "Get behind me, Satan!"

She proceeded to run down the hall ahead of me.

"Okay, where did she even learn that?" I muttered, jogging behind her, and looking for some sign—any sign—of prisoners.

The High Priestess ran on all fours at one point, which was the preferred way for Notha to run, and I struggled to keep up with her. Spock just bounced behind us, like a furry rubber ball, and I couldn't help but think we looked ridiculous.

Vance, we're taking Danny and Forty-Two up to the medical bay, Goth Trish spoke in my mind.

Without a doctor, I replied.

Hannah is good with field medicine. We don't need a doctor to stabilize them, Goth Trish said.

I see, I said, sucking in my breath. *I'll be along in a few minutes.*

No sign of your daughter yet? Goth Trish asked.

No, I replied. *I'm sorry for dragging you into this.*

Do me a favor, she said. *Shut up.*

Excuse me? I asked.

In the name of the Bauhaus, Lord Dracula, and Sisters of Mercy, shut up, Goth Trish said. *I get that you're feeling damn guilty about all this, but I wore this uniform long before I met you. You may think of me as an offshoot, but I have just as much title to being a soldier of the Community as Prime Trish. I remember fighting wars and losing friends. If you thought I wouldn't be following you on this journey to rescue any six-year-old, let alone your daughter, you never knew any of us Trishes.*

Well, that certainly put me in my place. I stopped in mid jog, still only seeing empty cells. *I'm sorry, Trish.*

You're just doing your Vance thing, Goth Trish said.

No, it's more than that, I replied. *I failed fighting Cthulhu.*

Uh, no you didn't, Goth Trish said, confused. *You saved the entire galaxy.*

I shook my head, taking a deep breath. *I failed to protect my crew, Trish. I failed to protect you. It all came down to me and I got lucky in stopping the Primordials' invasion, but I saw things you would not believe. I saw Earth destroyed. I saw the galaxy entering a dark age. My own superiors were working against me. I was tortured by Alexandra Ares, and I think it may have broken things inside me that I won't be able to fix. I'm trying to find my daughter now because if I move forward, maybe I can save myself from thinking about just how badly I've screwed up. How I can't be the Hero of Space when the galaxy really, really needs one.*

It was surprising I was able to admit that to myself, but it felt like a great weight had been lifted off my shoulders. Unfortunately, it didn't change my situation, but at least it felt good to share just how horrible my ordeal over Deathworld had been and how close we'd come to disaster. I didn't know if I had the strength to try to pull any more rabbits out of my hat. And if I couldn't do that, what good was I?

You mean Heeero of Spaaace, Goth Trish said.

I almost laughed despite wanting to cry and nodded. *Thank you.*

We will survive, Vance, Goth Trish said. *Also, I'll be there for you. I'll be there for you and Mean, sorry, Prime Trish too. We'll get out of this together. Somehow. I love you, you big stupid human. Just like I love the rest of my crew, but mostly you.*

I love you too, I said, finally admitting it. *Even if I think Goth rock is kind of lame.*

Okay, now you must die, Goth Trish said.

"Satan, I have found a prisoner!" The High Priestess called out from a few cell rows down.

I ran down to join her. It was toward the back, after we'd checked virtually the entirety of the brig, that we came across the only prisoner aboard the ship. Unfortunately, it was most definitely not my daughter.

The figure inside the cabin was wearing a long trench coat that was clearly the officer's variant of the Naval uniform I'd seen on the dead crew. It listed his rank as a Captain by his lapel insignia. He was slightly older than me but that was something increasingly difficult to judge due to longevity drugs which could stall aging indefinitely among humans. He had a black beard, Eastern European features, and crystal blue eyes that were very familiar to me.

"Huh," I said, not expecting to see him here.

"Well, this is an unexpected reunion," the man said, chuckling.

"Is it Karl the Conqueror?" The High Priestess asked.

"No," I said, sighing. I suddenly felt like laughing far more than crying. Pressing my head against the transparent steel wall of his cell. "No, he most certainly is not."

Spock bounced up and down.

"I am very confused," the High Priestess said. "Who is this man?"

I took a deep breath and stared at him, trying to dispel the illusion before me but finding it wasn't going anywhere. That, unfortunately, led to the inescapable conclusion that he really was there. A shame, as I would have much preferred to have been going mad.

"High Priestess, permit me to introduce Vannevar Tagawa (Snr) AKA Jack Tagawa," I replied. "My father."

"Aren't you the dead, Father of the Dark Lord?" The High Priestess asked, confused.

"Yeah, you drove an automated freighter into a sun," I said, staring at him.

Jack smiled. "I suspect I have some explaining to do."

"You think?" I replied.

CHAPTER FOURTEEN

From Bad To Worse

I had something of a reputation.

Specifically, I had the reputation of being either a genius or an idiot. At various times in my life, I had fulfilled the requirements for both. Whether genius or idiot, though, I was never *gullible*. The first trick of being a good con man, and I'd convinced the entire galaxy I knew what I was doing half the time, was being able to spot other people's hustles. And this certainly felt like a hustle. Indeed, finding my long-deceased father in the brig of the ship I just took over was enough to signal such with the blazing neon lights of New Vegas.

Still, it wasn't *impossible*. Jack Tagawa, previously Vannevar Westenra before his marriage to my mother, Tomo Tagawa, had been a professional grifter of inconsistent success. The romanticism of being a smuggler and outlaw had appealed to my already-rich mother. They'd rapidly gone through her trust fund and when the money had run out, Jack had thankfully not abandoned her but found various investment schemes that had ended in disaster.

I didn't know the exact deal my Great-Aunt Kathy had made with them, but they'd ended up getting steady work as automated drone ship "pilots" in exchange for raising me with a proper education. I'd cried for a week when I'd heard about their deaths. Clearly, I'd loved them more than they'd loved me.

"I know, I know," Jack Tagawa said, raising his hands. "You're almost certainly wondering whether I'm a bioroid and if this is part of some elaborate psyops to destroy you."

"What a suspiciously specific example," I replied, too stunned to do more than quip back.

The High Priestess stared. "I know I am."

"Well, I'm not a bioroid," Jack Tagawa said.

I gave him a scan with my helmet, and it showed that, in fact, he was a living human being. "No, you faked your death twenty years ago. Probably for the insurance money. You and Mom proceeded to leave me behind with Great-Aunt Kathy while wasting the money on whatever criminal schemes have been sustaining you for decades. By the fact she's not here, she's either dead or left you. At some point, you became a pirate and were the captain of the *Siege Perilous* under Karl the Conqueror. Except this is actually a Crius military vessel, not a pirate ship."

"I came up with that last part," the High Priestess said.

Jack Tagawa blinked. "Huh, that's a remarkably accurate summary of events."

You may be wondering what I was feeling in that moment, what tidal wave of emotion as it slowly occurred to me that this was, indeed, my father. I'd been fooled by bioroids before and there were facial reconstruction techniques that could make a man look identical to another person. However, none of these would allow someone to impersonate someone to his intimate relations. The human brain, for all its flaws, had a lot of instinctual responses and cues that meant you'd feel an imposter was off if you were paying attention.

I had plenty of memories with them despite our early separation. They'd been warm, affectionate, and fascinating people despite the fact I'd had mixed feelings about them before they'd gotten themselves blown up. My father's face, his expressions, and the way he carried himself were different due to the passage of time, but it was *him*. Somehow, in my quest to get back the daughter I'd never had in the first place, I'd stumbled across the still-alive personage of Jack Tagawa. It'd be a one in a billion chance were it coincidence and you know, as well as I do, that even my legendary luck wasn't going to adjust things that much. No, he had to be related to all of this if he wasn't at the center of it all.

And that's the part that stung most. I couldn't feel *anything* yet because I couldn't allow myself to lower my defenses and just experience the sheer joy that finding out he was alive should engender in me. I had to, instead, stare at him through a transparent steel wall and calculate all the factors that painted a pretty damning picture of where he'd been for the last twenty years. What did I feel in that moment? Numb. Along with one upsetting thought: at least I knew he was actually a very good rather than incompetent criminal. So, instead, I focused on interrogating him rather than opening the lock on his cell.

"Were you the one who detonated the crew's suicide switches?" I asked.

Jack looked stricken. It was surprisingly believable, which meant he was a very good actor. "How could you believe that?"

"Because you're alive and they're dead," I pointed up to the decks I knew contained a veritable mountain of corpses.

"Point taken. No," Jack said, dismissively. Clearly, he wasn't too broken up about the mass death on board. "I'm sure Karl is responsible."

"Karl the Conqueror?" I asked.

"More like Karl the Piece of Savit," Jack said. "I've had worse bosses, but I can't name any of them off hand."

"You're a pirate," the High Priestess said.

"Indeed!" Jack said, cheerfully. "Yo ho ho and a bottle of rum."

The High Priestess stared blankly.

"Why should I believe you?" I asked. "Not the pirate part. I think that's self-evident. What with this being a pirate ship and you being part of the crew."

"I take it we're past the point of you taking me at my word," Jack said, showing I'd gotten my penchant for sarcasm from him. Well, at least part of it. It occurred to me my mother had also been incredibly snarky. Something they'd had in common.

I raised an eyebrow. "What do you think, Jack? Do you think I'm inclined to take you at your word?"

"Fair point," Jack said, putting his hand over his heart. "The reason you should believe me is if I could kill everyone on the ship, I wouldn't be in the brig as a prisoner."

"You might have killed everyone on the ship, erased its memory, and locked yourself up in the brig," I pointed out.

Jack blinked. "Do you think me capable of such a cunning and devious plan?"

"Yes," I replied. "I believe, now, you are in fact someone who prefers to be thought of as incompetent rather than actually being so."

The High Priestess looked up at me with a quizzical expression. I tried not to think that was another thing we shared.

Jack nodded, seemingly enjoying our banter. "Then allow me to postulate a different possible series of events. Ones that don't make me a mass murderer and someone involved in the attack on our ship. Due to circumstances of a complicated and fascinating nature, I was, indeed, captain of the *Siege Perilous*."

"And what circumstances were those?" I asked, noting that the captain of a pirate ship was almost certainly a mass murderer no matter what.

"I hacked the computer records of Karl the Conqueror and made it appear I was a former first officer of an Olympic-class ship, framed the previous *Siege Perilous'* captain for embezzlement, and bribed a bunch of people with money I'd stolen from other jobs," Jack said, automatically, as if he was describing going to the market. "So, I was the ideal man for the job when Karl fed the old captain to a cloned Tyrannosaurus Rex. One he'd had cybernetically enhanced."

I nodded. I hated cybernetic dinosaurs. "Uh huh. Why did you want to be a pirate captain?"

"It's better than being a pirate first mate," Jack replied.

"Fair point," I replied.

"But your mother and I are no longer married and I was in need of financial security." Jack shrugged. "In my defense, I was not planning on making piracy a career. I was going to turn Karl the Conqueror and the ship over to the authorities in exchange for a pardon and a big fat stack of credits. Something approaching the size of Mount Everest actually."

Ah, that was the angle he was going to take with this. I shouldn't be angry with him being part of the group that had almost killed me because he was going to betray them in the first place. The idea that I might be even more appalled at his willingness to betray his fellow criminals probably never occurred to him. Loyalty was probably something that he didn't put too much stock in since he'd abandoned me in one of the most traumatizing ways possible. Assuming this *was* my father. I wasn't taking anything for granted at this point.

"That's a very smart plan," I replied, thinking he'd get along with Pink. "Except for the part about you being in the brig."

"Yes," Jack replied. "It turned out that Karl the Conqueror wants you, Captain Vance Turbo, captured or dead. Now I may have established that my credentials as a parental figure have been blemished—"

"You don't say," I interrupted, keeping my voice icy cold as a burning white-hot rage started to build within me. I was starting to believe it was my father because I doubted an imposter would be so uniquely infuriating. Certainly, I was disappointed it was him instead of my missing daughter. I'd have told him he was a grandfather but I suspected that, A) He probably already knew and B) He might have been involved in her attempted kidnapping.

"But I'm not inclined to engage in filicide," Jack replied. "Unfortunately, I overestimated just how much influence I had accumulated with the crew. My plan to convince them to turn against Karl the Conqueror failed miserably and I was shoved into this holding cell for later execution."

"Because they're actually soldiers for Crius, not pirates," I said, providing him more ammunition for his lies when I should have just let him dig himself deeper. I wasn't buying any of this.

"*Some* of them are soldiers for Crius," Jack replied. "Most of us were mercenaries."

"Not counting the clones," I said, noting my father was only speaking of the ship's officers.

"Oh yeah, those guys," Jack said, as if referring to the ship's bots. "Either way, the majority of the ship's officers were military or ex-military, veterans from the Notha War, and Karl had paid them very well. Very different from the members of his cult or the Enigmatic Path's advisors. Those guys are fanatics. Either way, I was sitting comfortably in my cell when suddenly everyone started dying horribly. I thought it was you're doing but since you believe I did it, I can only assume Karl panicked and was attempting to cover his tracks."

There was no way Jack could know about all the crew dying if he was located in the brig where the signal couldn't reach. The thought of my father passively accepting a suicide switch was ludicrous, too, and I couldn't help but imagine him getting it secretly removed or disabled.

"A fascinating story," I said, nodding. "Truly one I suggest you option as a movie during your time of unfortunate incarceration."

"My time of what?" Jack asked, sounding as innocent as a used air car salesman.

"Incarceration," I said, smiling like the void cat who caught the star bird. "Don't worry, I'll make sure you're put in a Community facility. They're like hotels compared to the prisons out here on the Border Planets. I suspect you'll be serving a very, very long sentence for just the criminal activities you did *before* faking your death."

"He is your progenitor, Captain Turbo," the High Priestess said, giving up her normal honorific for me. "By the law of most cultures, you should protect him from all recrimination by the authorities in hopes of protecting your family's honor."

"You don't say," I said, relishing the fact I could get revenge on my father by doing absolutely nothing. "I guess I must have missed that lesson when my father and mother abandoned me."

If this were a noir thriller, I'd suspect that my father might have killed my mother as she wasn't here, and people who faked their deaths with their spouse often noted it was easier to do so by themselves. Somehow, I doubted it. Mostly because Tomo Tagawa had been every bit the scheming scoundrel my father had been, at least according to Great-Aunt Kathy. Yeah, she hadn't left me with many illusions about my biological parents.

Unfortunately.

Jack waved his hand in the air with a goofy expression on his face. "Did *we* really betray you?"

"Yes!" I snapped.

Jack paused then dropped his endearing facade to adopt a more professional demeanor "Fair enough. I'm genuinely impressed with your capacity for banter, Vance. I fully expected Katerina to ruin you when I handed you over to her. Instead, you've grown up to be a right anyxhole cush like your dear old dad."

"Your approval fills me with shame," I replied, using an old Earth maxim. "Goodbye, Captain Jack."

The High Priestess still looked uncomfortable; family relations were complex on Notha worlds but amounted to fierce loyalty to your bloodline until you were ready to kill your elder relatives for leadership. It was part of the reason I'd gained such a weird notoriety among them since the Notha Emperor had been their entire race's direct ancestor. I imagined she'd have been fine if I'd killed him or released him but not just turning him over to someone else's justice. That was an insult to Notha honor.

"Actually, Vance, I think you're going to let me out and escort me up to the bridge," Jack said, never losing his cool. There was a kind of effortlessness to his lies and manipulations that I hoped I didn't possess. It was almost charming if you didn't mind how superficial it was.

"Are you going to threaten me? If so, I'd like to know with what," I said, stopping to turn around. I should have just walked off. A part of me wanted to be given an excuse to go inside and beat the living crazzap out of him. It was a primal Freudian thing that I didn't entertain for more than a few seconds. I wasn't a violent savage, no matter how deserving the target.

"Quite the opposite," Jack replied. "I suppose it has occurred to you how incredibly unlikely it is for me to be the captain of the ship that attacked you."

"Only if one presumes your innocence, which I don't," I said.

"But what if I told you the head of the Crius Sector Security Division found me during her survey of petty criminals, recruited me, and inserted me into Karl's organization?" Jack asked.

"You're not a Security Division agent," I replied, dryly.

"Asset, not agent," Jack said. "The difference being one is paid well for their efforts."

"I'm wasting my time," I replied.

"Your daughter, my granddaughter's name is Astrid," Jack said. "The section chief is your ex-girlfriend, Leah. I'm working for the good guys. Honest."

I stared at him.

A moment passed when everyone was silent.

Even Spock.

"Goddammit! Bork!" I said, walking to the door before trying to override the door.

"Seriously?" the High Priestess asked in a surprisingly human way. "This is what convinces you to release your father?"

"Do I want to know why you have a pet Notha?" Jack asked.

The High Priestess bared her teeth at him.

Jack took a step back. "Hey, who you date is none of my business. To each their own, son. I heard you were into some kinky shit like robosexuality. I understand. I've been to Shogun and tried the chrome ladies. I just hate the ones with the big eyes. What works in animation doesn't work in real life."

"This is the High Priestess and I'm apparently the Devil in modern Notha mythology. She's a friend and my bodyguard," I replied, somehow resisting my urge to gun him down. Somehow.

"Nice work if you can get it," Jack said, cheerfully. His expression turned "I helped Countess Mass and her child against the forces opposing her on Crius. The Sons of the Demiurge want that little girl for his Enigmatic Path allies. I'm the only reason their last kidnapping attempt didn't work."

That was useful intelligence and it almost made me not regret what I was doing. "Karl and the Sons are related to the Enigmatic Path."

Jack nodded. "They're all one and the same. Crius has always been full of reactionary scientists. The aristocracy used that to recruit the best and brightest minds. They made Crius a place for unfettered science not restricted by conventional morality or laws. They didn't realize that when you court true believers that you inevitably get people who believe. The Enigmatic Path worship the Elder Races as gods and seek ways to elevate themselves to deific levels. Karl just wants to play out his Alexander the Great fantasies. They even have an obelisk belonging to the Elder Races that they worship. The Allenway cult is really just a big tent for all of them."

"And Karl is one of Allenway's disciples?" I asked.

"Karl *is* Joseph Allenway III," Jack explained. "Karl went to Space Academy under his assumed name and managed to make his mutiny through plants as well as well-placed bribes. It was all meant to acquire SKAMMS for Crius and make it a power. Instead, Karl took the *Siege Perilous* and conquered a world for himself. When that didn't work out, he came back to his homeworld with his tail between his legs and assumed a position in politics under his original name. The *Siege Perilous* and other ships like it are his trump card to intimidate the locals into compliance. They're Crius' ace in the hole and secret force for protecting the clone slave trade."

That actually made sense. It was probably ninety percent accurate. The best lies usually were. "Why do they want my daughter?"

Jack looked up at the crystal now on my forehead. "I don't know. They may think you have a connection to their gods."

That certainly was a wrinkle that I hadn't thought of. "I see."

"I do know your daughter, my granddaughter, is a valuable political bargaining tool," he continued, "but it's not Karl who wants her. It's his Enigmatic Path advisor, 101-B. Creepy Kolahn cyborg motherborker."

If nothing else, this was something that clued me into what the hell was going on. The Enigmatic Path were interested in my DNA because I'd been modified by the Elder Races and probably been less than circumspect about hiding that element around people interested in knowing how to use Elder technology. Goddammit, no matter how hard I tried, it seemed I wasn't able to get away from people obsessed with them.

Still, there was a lot I didn't know, like why Leah had created Astrid in the first place and how my father had become involved. Also, what role Karl the Conqueror (if he even existed) was playing in all of this. It meant that, unfortunately, I was going to have to play nice with my father and probably let him go after this. Maybe I was just hoping to find an excuse to.

"I can take you to her," Jack said, making my decision to work with my father considerably easier. "I know where she is."

"The *Jovial Empress*," I said.

Jack smiled. This time it was the expression of a man he knew he had his mark by the balls. "It's where your reunion is predestined."

The only thing worse than being hustled was knowing you were being hustled and being still so enamored of the promises you were being made that you wanted to go along with them anyway. Thinking about the locket around my neck, I wondered what I'd even say when I encountered my daughter for the first time.

"Vance?" Prime Trish contacted me on my helmet comm. It was far less intimate than our usual conversations via direct neural interface.

"Yes?" I asked.

"Did you find what you were looking for?" Prime Trish asked.

"No," I responded. "It's a negative. I'm going to be heading to the infirmary to check on Danny and Forty-Two."

There were a lot of things going on right now, but with the knowledge my daughter wasn't here, I could breathe again—if that made sense as a metaphor—and focus on all the other issues we were facing on board. We had to get the *Black Nebula II*'s crew rescued and this ship into proper space. If I was acting as a respectable Space Fleet officer, I'd also head to the nearest Community base rather than the *Jovial Empress*, but my obsession still held my gaze. If I had to choose between duty and family, well, duty came second.

I was not my father.

"We need you to get to the bridge now," Prime Trish said. "There's been an accident. Elektra is hurt."

Dammit.

CHAPTER FIFTEEN

Hard Decisions

Thankfully, it was not a difficult journey to get from the brig to the bridge. My father and the High Priestess accompanied us. Spock, despite not having eyes, seemed to watch our unwanted guest the entire way.

The *Siege Perilous'* bridge was unchanged from its original non-retrofitted factory default, unlike the *Ares* which had been updated half a dozen times since it first left space dock. That meant it was a shiny chrome deck with metal surfaces, and control systems that looked decidedly retro.

Due to the incompatibility of human biology with many alien ones, it even had a bunch of dials and switches instead of more standardized touchscreen or holographic interfaces. If it sounded like I was taking a roundabout way to say, "It looked kind of like the *Enterprise*'s bridge from the 1960s *Star Trek* show" then yes, you could say that, too. What can I say, the designers for EarthGov's starships were all classic sci-fi fans.

Shelly was at the command station with Pink working at a nearby console. Major Tom was at the helm, pushing buttons in a seemingly random and haphazard fashion. Both Trishes were present, working on the source of the "accident" where Elektra was splayed out on the ground, severely injured. The navigation console of the ship had exploded and she'd taken the brunt of it.

"I came as soon as I could," I said, walking quickly onto the bridge and staring down at Elektra. "What happened?"

"There was a bomb on board," Shelly said, doing a fantastic job of keeping her cool with her sister in critical condition. "Apparently, the captain booby trapped the...I'm sorry, Vance, *is that your dad*?"

"Yes," I said, not missing a beat.

"Your dead dad," Shelly said, turning her head sideways to look at me. "The one who crashed an automated freighter into a star."

"Indeed!" Jack said, cheerfully. "Vance rescued me from decades of imprisonment by these evil pirates keeping me as their slave."

"He's their former captain," I swiftly corrected.

"So, are you the elf he used to bork?" Jack asked. "You look like the elf he used to bork, but I admit I haven't been able to keep up with my son's romances. He's pretty much had hot and cold running ladies since he became a captain according to the tabloids. Just like his old man!"

Shelly narrowed her eyes and moved her hand to her fusion pistol. "As our acting captain, I request permission from you to kill your father."

"We're equal rank and off duty so I see no reason why you have to seek my permission to kill him," I pointed out. "But please, go ahead!"

Shelly thought I was joking. "Right."

My father raised his hands in a mock surrender. "If it's any consolation, I'm happy to disable the booby traps set to prevent the ship from falling into enemy hands. I would have done it immediately but—"

Jack stopped talking because Shelly had her pistol pointed at his nose.

"Shut up," Shelly said. "If my sister dies, I'm ventilating your head."

"That is not good gun safety," Jack said dryly.

"Let me see if I can help," I said, walking over to Elektra.

"Do you have any medical training?" Pink asked.

"Only as much as field training requires," I said.

"How about Elder Race magic?" Pink asked, making a slightly more pointed suggestion.

"I have no idea," I answered, sitting on the floor by Elektra. I took in the amount of damage she'd sustained and how good her chances were. It was bad. Very bad. I'll spare you the details but if not for the fact that Elektra was a pure blooded Ethereal with roughly three times the durability and strength of a normal human being then she would have almost certainly been immediately killed.

Unfortunately, she wasn't wearing a barrier belt and the blast had taken her directly in the face. Prime Trish and Goth Trish had done their very best to take care of her with the supplies present. There were no less than three emergency medical kits open beside her and they'd done their best to treat the Elektra's injuries. I didn't know how skilled they were, but they'd done what was probably the best job a non-doctor could in this situation. It made me regret not bringing along Doctor Zard.

"Can we get her down to sickbay?" I asked both.

Prime Trish shook her head. "I don't think she's in any state to be moved."

"Got any stupid plans?" Goth Trish asked.

I reached up to my forehead and removed the crystal, which I was surprised came right off and placed it on her forehead.

"What are you doing?" Shelly asked, having left my father, and joined us.

"Praying your mother's ghost is listening," I replied, placing the crystal on Elektra's badly burned forehead.

I am, Ketra said in my mind. *But you realize that it's highly against the rules to share power without preapproval from the Elder Races.*

And yet you did with me, I replied mentally.

Yeah, I was expecting you to die, Ketra said. *You're kind of naturally someone who defies fate.*

Can you help her? I asked.

I can try, Ketra replied, her concern for her daughter hidden but could still feel it radiate off of her. *But there might be consequences. Also, if she dies, there's nothing we can do. Even the Elder Races can't resurrect the dead. There's a reason I'm only a ghos...err, bodiless incarnation.*

I don't care, I replied, wanting to make sure one of my crew lived.

She might, Ketra asked. *My daughter never wanted anything to do with the Elder Races. She called them genocidal monsters.*

Yes, well, the truth hurts, I replied. *Tell her it's an order to live.*

Ketra didn't respond and there was no immediate reaction from Elektra. Both Trishes looked at me as Elektra began to twitch before entering violent convulsions. The gemstone sank deep into her forehead, and I briefly wondered if I'd made a terrible mistake.

"Elektra!" Shelly said, pushing to her sister's side.

Major Tom got up from his position at the helm, only to be stopped by Pink who forced him back to it. I didn't have time to try to figure out what that meant, though. I did notice my father inching toward one of the command consoles. A glare at him was enough to stop his movement.

Turning back to Elektra, I was surprised and pleased to notice her skin and muscle had already begun regenerating. I saw new flesh crawling up over her body as burned remnants sloshed off like grime in a dishwasher. The process looked excruciating, but after several long moments, she was back to looking like her old self.

"Is your drow elf okay?" Jack asked, walking over.

Shelly, however, had her gun back on Jack. "So, Jack Tagawa is responsible for our people being injured?"

"Killed," Pink said, crossing her arms. "A reminder that we're down to a hundred crew. My people may have been scum, but they were scum with families. Well, most of 'em."

"Hey, most of those guys sold you out," Jack said, giving the worst defense possible.

"So, you *were* involved!" Shelly shouted, standing up.

Jack raised his hands again. "I was imprisoned! I was totally working for the good guys, deep undercover."

"In an incredibly obvious and suspicious manner," I replied. "However, assuming neither Danny nor Forty-Two die, you have my protection. If either of them does, I won't be held responsible for what happens next."

"Oh, the injured Danny is your cousin?" Jack asked, ignoring the threat. "Fancy that. I always liked the kid. Of course, he was still in diapers when I made my escape from civilized society."

"Yes," I replied. "Your nephew. My cousin."

"You know their side of the family tried to arrange a marriage between you and Danny," Jack said, pausing. "Or was it his sister,

138

Shinobu? Eh, they probably didn't care as long as they got access to Kathy's fortune. She was always the one who held the family purse strings. Quite an annoyance getting a living wage from her. Did you know she expected me and Tomo to live off only a million credits per month? Ridiculous."

"If he dies, you're dead," I said.

"Is it just me or is Vance's father not concerned about the gun I'm pointing at him?" Shelly asked, looking at her husband.

"He does seem to be remarkably unconcerned," Major Tom said, continuing to type away at the helm. "I've managed to bring aboard ninety-seven of the *Black Nebula II*'s crew. That includes the medical staff if you want me to bring them to sickbay."

"Do it," I replied. "Though we should activate every medical bot available if they're not booby trapped as well."

"They are," Jack said, frowning.

"I'M WORKING ON IT!" Baby Trish said, over the intercom. "IT TURNS OUT SEIZING CONTROL OF THIS SHIP IS HARDER THAN IT SEEMS! A LOT OF IT IS DISCONNECTED FROM THE MAIN AI."

"I can't imagine why," Jack replied. "Sadly, Karl the Conqueror forbade me from entirely relying on Dummy AI and thus the ship was still vulnerable to your takeover. You can purge their murder-y programming with the password: teacup. As for why I'm not worried about being shot, I know my dearest son would never allow me to be harmed."

"Also, you're wearing a barrier built into the lining of your coat," I replied.

Jack did a double take. "You noticed, huh?"

"No, I was just guessing," I replied. "It's what I would do."

Jack smirked. "Fair enough."

Pink lifted her fusion pistol, a full-on disintegrator 91-B, and aimed it at his head. "I guess we'll just have to keep firing. Because Vance Turbo is my client but that doesn't mean I'm going to let you walk away after costing me my ship and crew. Give me one good reason not to ventilate your head and ask for forgiveness later."

Jack raised his wrist to reveal a computer interface hidden underneath his coat sleeve. "I have just transferred half a million reasons from the ship's accounts. Ones I'm happy to invest in future business propositions for you. Perhaps financing the purchase of your next ship. I kept the *Siege Perilous'* bank accounts off the AI as well and am the only one with access to them. The price will be keeping my involvement in this hush-hush, though."

Pink blinked then raised her gun into the air, away from my father. "I've changed my mind, Vance. I like your dad."

"That makes one of us," I said, looking down at Elektra, who had regained consciousness. "How are you feeling?"

Elektra looked at me then Shelly then back at me. "Like I just had my face blown off by a bomb planted on the navigation console before alien magic regrew my skin."

I blinked. "That would be a literal description of what happened, yes. On the plus side, you're alive! Yay! Do you feel anything different?"

Elektra stared at me. "I can hear my mother's voice now. Apparently, whatever you did linked me up with the Elder Race network. Thanks for that. Really."

Elektra was not a fan of the Elder Races. She believed that they were a manipulative bunch of ruthless imperialists without any regard for other, younger, species. Given this was how I'd ended up recruited by the Elder Races, I wasn't sure if I hadn't unwittingly condemned her to be their servant.

"What?" Shelly asked, sitting down on the floor beside us. "Mom, is that you?"

Elektra looked at her sister with a frown on her face. "She's not *possessing* me. She's just inside my altered brain, speaking to me."

"That's the definition of possessing you," Goth Trish said. "Believe me, we've been doing it to Vance for years."

Prime Trish looked at Elektra sympathetically. "I'm so sorry."

"She's saying the only way to get my body to regenerate was to permanently take residence," Elektra said, looking confused. "That way it's technically her body and the benefits of being an Elder Race agent, like regeneration, can be applied."

"Can you do that, Vance?" Goth Trish asked.

"I'd rather not find out," I said, not knowing how much the Elder Races had tinkered with my body.

"I'm not sure the price is worth it," Elektra said. "Imagine trying to explain this to my girlfriend."

Shelly gave her sister a hug.

"Oh dear, emotional displays, how awkward," Elektra said, trying and failing to make a joke. "What will my fellow scientists say?"

Shelly rolled her eyes.

I stood up. "I've made a temporary agreement with my father to let him out of the brig in exchange for information about our present situation. He'll also be helping us deliver the *Siege Perilous* to the proper authorities as well as disabling any further remaining surprises that he might have left behind to impede boarders."

"Did he kill his crew?" Pink asked, sounding disgusted despite her generous bribe.

"He says Karl the Conqueror did," I replied, not sure I believed it but wanting to. It was bad enough believing my father abandoned me, but even worse that he might be a mass murderer. As stupid as it was, I wanted to believe his strange story about being an agent for Leah and working to bring down Karl the Conqueror's gang from the inside.

Jack placed his hand over his heart. "I swear on my dear departed wife that I did not cause the mass slaughter of my crew."

"Is my mother dead?" I asked, dryly.

"Does that matter?" Jack asked.

"Yes!" I said.

"Then no," Jack replied. "I mean, probably not. I have no idea."

"I'd ask if he was trustworthy, but I think that question has been answered," Shelly said, helping her sister up.

Elektra's clothes were still damaged, and we would have to get her a change of them. Hopefully, the ship had some spare uniforms. "I'm not comfortable with working with criminals," she said.

"Ha!" Pink said.

"Mass murderery kinds!" Elektra corrected.

"Alleged mass murderery!" Jack interjected. "In any case, it's within your authority as High Protector to pardon me."

141

The stones on this guy. "How the hell did you even hear about that?"

Jack smirked. "It's being broadcast around the holofeeds right now. The first Earthborn High Protector. The first human in centuries, assuming you don't count Ethereals. Which I don't."

Elektra and Shelly glared at him.

"Go eat some *lembas*," Jack said. "Maybe file those ears down."

"We've loaded all the survivors of the *Black Nebula II*," Major Tom said, sitting at the helm. "Just in time too."

Baby Trish put an image of the *Black Nebula II* on the view screen. The corvette exploded as the jumpdrive and antimatter reactors detonated simultaneously and produced the raw reactions that made space battles so brilliant to look upon. I looked over at Pink sympathetically, noting her expression was empty of anything resembling emotion.

I doubted the *Black Nebula II* had been her personal vessel, but any good captain felt the loss of their command. The fact that her tenure had been such a complete disaster might also have weighed on her in other ways. My brief association with her had made me think she'd been angling for her own command under Captain Havelock.

"So, can we get this boat on the road?" Jack asked. "I've got money to spend and the smell of dead pirates on board is really cramping my style."

"Baby Trish, can you bypass the navigation console and set course for Crius?" I asked.

"I CAN, VANCE," Baby Trish said. "DO YOU WANT ME TO CONTACT SPACE FLEET AND GIVE AN UPDATE ON ALL THIS?"

I knew their order would be to return the ship to the nearest spaceport and it would be a delay of weeks, if not months, while we were debriefed. "No. I'll prepare a report for sending once we reach the *Jovial Empress*."

"UNDERSTOOD," Baby Trish said. "I SUGGEST YOU GET THE CREW TO WHATEVER STATIONS THEY CAN MAN, THOUGH. I CAN MOSTLY HANDLE THIS SHIP MYSELF, BUT A LOT OF THE FUNCTIONS NEED AT LEAST SOMEONE MANNING THE CONSOLES TO PUSH A BUTTON OR TWO. WE HAVE JUST

ENOUGH OF A SKELETON CREW TO PULL IT OFF AND IT'LL STILL BE LIKE STEERING A DRUNKEN WHALE."

"What an odd metaphor," I replied. "Trish?"

"Yes?" The other Trishes asked.

I shook my head. "Could you patch me into the medical bay first? I'd like to check in on Danny and Forty-Two."

"YEAH, THEY'RE NOT GOOD," Baby Trish admitted. "DANNY DIED A FEW MINUTES AGO."

CHAPTER SIXTEEN

The Chains of Commanding (Are the Ones I Beat You With)

"YEAH, HE WAS DEAD FOR TWO MINUTES BEFORE THEY REVIVED HIM," Baby Trish said, causing me to let loose a breath I hadn't even known I'd been holding. She conjured a hologram of the medical bay where Danny was in a hospital gown and waving at me.

"Goddammit, Trish!" I snapped. "Lead with that!"

"Well, that was anticlimactic," Jack responded. "Really, kind of a cheat on your audience."

"He's your nephew!" I snapped.

"Not really," Jack said. "Your family branches are pretty far and spread out. Also, he'd be an in-law at best. Except, since your mother and I are divorced, that means he and I are exactly Jack and squat. And Jack, me, left town."

I shook my head. "Unborking believable."

"I'm going to take Elektra down to the medical bay," Shelly replied. "I'll also get her outfitted. Will you be able to handle things without me?"

"Probably not," I said, shrugging. "But we'll manage once we're into jumpspace."

Major Tom looked over at me. "I think she was talking to me, Vance."

"Oh," I said, embarrassed. "Yes, her husband. That makes sense."

Shelly facepalmed.

Elektra sighed and pulled her sister along to the elevator, showing no sign of being injured anymore.

"This is why I don't believe in monogamy," Prime Trish said.

"Does anyone on this ship?" Goth Trish asked.

"Just what I was thinking," Prime Trish said.

"Monogamy is the worst thing for any marriage," Major Tom said, smirking at them. "On Brigid, love is free."

"Clearly a man who has never gone to his planet as a tourist," Jack said. "Anyway, I take it these three Trishes are your robot borkbuddies? Same person but multiple personalities? I see major opportunities there."

I debated shooting everyone on the bridge, myself, or both. "Jack, I'm going to ask you for a favor to make up for the abandonment of me as a child."

"Why? It was the best thing I ever did for you," Jack said.

"You have me there," I replied. "Nevertheless, *shut the hell up!*"

Jack shrugged then closed his mouth.

"I'm going to need you to tell me everything about Leah and my child," I replied.

"Well, which is it? Am I talking or shutting up?" Jack asked.

I stared at him.

"Wow, you have mastered Kathy's stare of death," Jack said. "I thought she left you to be raised by robots too."

"Alfred the AI," I said. "Who was a better father than you ever were."

"I'd make a joke about you being raised by AI, but you'd probably not get it," Jack replied.

Pink watched the entire show while leaned up against a wall. "To think I was paying money for vids to watch on my old ship."

"Shouldn't you be prepping your crew?" I asked.

"Technically, they're your crew now," Pink said, smirking. "I'm clearly not in charge anymore."

"Then I order you to prep the crew," I said, dryly.

Pink chuckled and walked away. "Well played, Cap'n. Well played."

Jack stretched and took a seat in the captain's chair on the bridge before I pulled him out of it by the back of his coat.

"Alright, alright," Jack said. "Right now, the situation on Crius is incredibly unstable. The Sons of the Demiurge have been trying to take over the government for some time, but that's because the scientist aristocracy has been losing its power for the past decade. Someone has been arming insurgents against them as well as forcing anti-slavery concessions to the Community in exchange for economic aid. No points for guessing it's Countess Mass. She started as the ambassador from the Community but has since embedded herself in the government as a recognized noble."

Interesting. "And Karl, Allenway III, is pushing back with his pirates?"

"The economic sanctions mean the planet is barely able to chug along even if it is mostly self-sufficient," Jack explained. "The black market and piracy are about the only ways that vital electronics and other imports get to the world at all. Karl's monopoly on them are about the only reasons he's tolerated, but he doesn't have nearly the same pull as Leah. Her ties to the rebels and the Community mean that the Crius nobility are up against the wall with her."

That was interesting and something Hannah should probably hear. "Hence why Karl has joined the Enigmatic Path—the Community has already chosen their side. Plus, if they knew his true identity they'd want him extradited for treason."

"Yes," Jack said. "He's caught between a rock and a hard place. Kidnapping your daughter was initially his plan but that was before he found out you were her father. Well, you and some blonde elf girl. Man, relationships are hard these days. I, of course, warned Leah."

"And you were involved in this?" I asked.

Jack took a deep breath and put his hand over his heart. "I am not a slaver. Murderer? Yes. Thief? Yes. Philanderer? Oh, hell yes. Pirate? Well, I'm not going to argue with that. Procurer and trader of exotic animals? Now, that depends on the definition of animal. The one time I found out they were sentient, I let them go and man did I get some serious shi—"

"Strangely, I believe you," I replied. "You're not a slaver."

146

"Really?" Jack asked, blinking. "I'm surprised."

"If the ship was engaged in slave transportation, the brig would have shown signs of being used more," I replied. "This is purely a vessel for intimidating other species and stealing their cargo. You're just a pirate and killer."

"Oh, you were using evidence to reach your conclusion," Jack said, disappointed. "I thought I taught you better."

"You've literally taught me nothing in our entire association," I replied.

"Yes, it does appear being a wiseanyx is just genetic," Jack responded. "I think I prefer anyx to ass. It's the y and the x."

I wondered if this was what other people felt when they talked to me. My father was a master of fast talking, and while what he said was often appalling, it was always entertaining. Which made me inclined to overlook the fact he was a truly monstrous criminal. "How does this relate to Leah and my daughter?"

"Like I said, Karl's advisor wants your daughter," Jack said, shrugging. "It's Elder Race stuff. I don't know crazzap. All I can say is they probably would have killed Leah and her brat both by now if not for the fact she's some kind of holy bloodline. Which I assume is you. Good job. Religion is a nice scam if you can get in on it."

Dammit. I sadly believed him.

The Trishes, Pink, and Major Tom were rushing between stations to try and get the *Siege Perilous* moving now that we'd picked up the remains of the *Black Nebula II*'s crew. Even the High Priestess had hopped onto the side of a console and was giving orders that I was sure some of the pirates would object to. It would have been better to have everyone working and I should have been helping, too. Unfortunately, I couldn't bring myself to stop asking the questions that would have been better asked once we were in jumpspace.

Jack smirked. "You know, it's a shame you never met my parents, your grandparents, Vance. Neal Gordon and Lucy Westenra. They would have loved you. Exactly the sort of clever little white sheep they'd wanted with me."

I knew Jack was trying to distract me with knowledge of the past. I was familiar with Neal Gordon and Lucy Westenra. They were the

Moon's best detectives and had been instrumental in bringing down Karma Corp and the rest of the oligarchy that had plotted the overthrow of EarthGov to install a corporate dictatorship. I also knew they'd never had any kids. They were still citizens of the Moon today and people I could contact if I wanted to. It was bait I wasn't going to fall for, though. Don't trust a conman when he dangles the kind of thing you'd always wanted in front of you—things like family and love. *Especially* family and love.

I shook my head. "I'm going to have to confine you to your quarters, Jack. I strongly suggest you don't do anything stupid while you're there. We're going to have a lot more to talk about before our arrival."

"Hey, I'll be fine," Jack replied. "Just me, my wine collection, googleplexes of porn, and my bioroid sex doll. I'll make a list of all the traps and backdoors I've built into this thing. Don't worry, you'll probably only lose three more crew before they're all disabled."

I glared at him.

"I'm kidding," Jack said, smiling broadly before slapping me across the shoulder. "About the sex bot. You'd have to be really pathetic to have sex with a bioroid. Always use the real thing. It was good catching up with you, Vance. We'll have to do it again some time."

I didn't respond as he departed in the elevator.

"I CAN REMOVE THE OXYGEN IN THE ELEVATOR," Baby Trish replied. "NO ONE WOULD BLAME EITHER OF US."

"Denied," I said, walking over to the captain's chair, checking it for more booby traps, and sitting down. "However, tempting the prospect may be. I would like you to keep an eye on him and make sure he goes directly to his room. If we can spare any men, we need to post guards outside his door as well."

"Won't work," Pink said. "My crew are loyal and good friends. They also would sell us out for how much money he's capable of offering. Which means that either Karl cheaped out in bribing the entire crew to kill you or the ones he bribed decided not to share their bribes with the others."

"That's assuming it was Karl rather than my father who bribed your crew," I replied. "I'm not sure of that. He's a tricky and dangerous liar."

"Yeah, he's definitely you without the nicer qualities," Major Tom replied, still working hard at the controls. He also seemed unaware of the insult he was paying me. "Would you like to set up a therapy session to discuss...oh dear."

"Oh dear is not good," I said.

"No kidding," Major Tom said. "Do you want the short version or long version?"

"The version where you just tell me like we're on a starship bridge," I replied.

Major Tom frowned. "We've got a fleet incoming."

"Hostile?" I asked.

"You tell me," Major Tom said, showing he could never make it in Space Fleet and would have to content himself to be a ground pounder for the rest of his life.

Baby Trish pulled up an image of a fleet of sixteen Notha gunships, twelve Notha corvettes, two Kolahn battle cruisers that shouldn't have existed anymore, and a trio of Albion frigates that were just more of their aged military surplus that had found their way into the hands of planets that had no business owning a starter pistol.

"The fleet of Karl the Conqueror, I presume," I muttered.

"Worse," Major Tom said. "They're all ships identified by Community records as belonging to the Enigmatic Path."

"A distinction without a difference, I believe," I said. "The Path has been keeping this vessel operating so Karl could attack their enemies and probably keep Crius functioning as a base for their activities. We can't fight them in our current condition."

"We can't fight them period," Pink said. "I'm still trying to get people to their stations and we're beneath a skeleton crew's size. Olympic-class vessels are supposed to have close to a thousand crew."

"Can we jump?" I asked.

Baby Trish confirmed the worst of my fears. "WE'RE STILL IN THE RANGE OF THE JUMP JAMMERS."

"Can we get the shutdown codes from my father?" I asked.

"I'LL ASK," Baby Trish said. "HOWEVER, IT'S ENTIRELY POSSIBLE THEY'RE TIMED MINES AND WE HAVE TO MOVE OUT OF THEIR RANGE."

"I can turn us around and try to move us around them," Major Tom said. "But it'll be at a crawl's pace."

"What's the intercept time for the fleet?" I asked.

"THEY'RE NOT MOVING YET," Baby Trish said. "THEY MAY BE ASSUMING WE'RE STILL UNDER THE CONTROL OF YOUR FATHER."

"Get him back up here!" I snapped.

"WELL EXCUSE ME," Baby Trish said. "HE'S *YOUR* DAD."

I closed my eyes and counted to three. "We have an advantage in our escape because they can't get any closer to our position due to the jump jammers unless they use their own engines. Begin turning the—"

"AND THEY'VE FIGURED OUT WE'RE NOT THE ORIGINAL CREW," Baby Trish interrupted. "IT TURNS OUT WE'RE SUPPOSED TO GIVE AN ENCRYPTED RESPONSE WHEN THEY PING OUR VESSEL TO LET THEM KNOW WE'RE STILL UNDER PIRATE CONTROL."

I stared upward. "Efficient, aren't they?"

"A LITTLE TOO EFFICIENT TO BE HONEST," Baby Trish said. "ALSO, THAT'S ANOTHER THING YOUR FATHER NEGLECTED TO MENTION. WAS ANYONE *EXPECTING* US TO SEIZE CONTROL OF THE VESSEL?"

If so, they were clairvoyant or the greatest tacticians in the history of the world. Probably the former because if they were the latter, they wouldn't have let me seize control of the vessel in the first place. "Get us the hell out of here as fast as you can."

"That won't be fast enough," Major Tom said. "We're eighteen minutes away from exiting the jamming field's radius. They'll be on us in seven."

"Well, savit," I muttered.

"Keep getting the calculations prepared," I replied.

"Are you sure?" Major Tom asked.

"Don't question me on this," I said, struggling to come up with a miracle solution.

"THEY'RE CALLING FOR OUR SURRENDER, VANCE," Baby Trish responded.

"Put them on screen," I replied. "Maybe I can buy us some time."

A part of me wondered if Pink wasn't debating turning me over herself, but the odds didn't exactly favor her on this bridge. Then again, maybe I was reading her wrong. If nothing else, she seemed pragmatic enough to know there was no way she'd be rewarded instead of killed after all we'd done.

A particularly hideous individual appeared on the screen. He had a bald head, mismatched Ethereal ears, and a variety of surgical scars. I recognized the individual as Graff Vidkun Unst, Karl the Conquerer's second-in-command, who was also wanted for a variety of crimes against sapience. Vidkun's body was made up of pieces that he'd harvested from Ethereals he'd killed as part of an insane attempt to become one of the supposedly immortal race, which reminded me of the Looking Glass Man's murders. His look was one of disgust and fury even as his eyes lingered on us with a hunger more like a wolf and a leg of lamb than any other more traditional lusts.

That was when my father walked out from the elevator. "I feel like I'm coming and going, Vance. What's the problem?"

"You!" Graff Unst shouted at my father. "Traitor! You will die slowly for what you have done!"

"We're about to be killed," I replied, absently. "Do you have the codes for the jump jammers your ship laid out? I admit, I probably should have gotten those before you left, but it's been a day."

"Yeah, probably. The chains of commanding. Anyway, it's same as my safe word: Tomo," John said, ignoring Graff Unst.

I really didn't need to know that. "My *mother's* name?"

"Target the ship! Kill them! Kill them!" Graff Unst said. "Attack!"

Thankfully, he was still a few minutes away.

"Nothing better to remind me of horrific pain needing to stop," John said, chuckling. "Well, maybe your great-aunt. We only hooked up once, though."

"Listen, if you ever mention that again—" I started to speak.

"JAMMERS DOWN!" Baby Trish called.

"Go!" I shouted.

The ship proceeded to rip into jumpspace in an instant, overwhelming the gravity manipulators for a second and sending my father flying backward. Thankfully, the rest of the crew was strapped down. The bridge darkened and filled with a beautiful, blue, underwater-like reflection as the ship's "screen saver" kicked in.

"Are you dead?" I asked my father.

"No," he muttered, lying in a heap on the ground.

"Shame," I replied. "Thanks, though!"

The High Priestess, who had also been knocked down, crawled into my lap. "I am requesting a new evil god to placate."

"You do that," I said, tickling her tummy.

"That's a Notha erogenous zone," she pointed out.

I lifted my hand. "I'm going to go wash my hands now."

CHAPTER SEVENTEEN

Figuring Out What the Hell is Going On

"So, I think your father was the captain of the *Siege Perilous*," Hannah said, standing across from me at the circular captain's table. She'd risen to speak for dramatic effect. "I think he was the guy who ambushed us, got overthrown when we kicked their ass, and then he used the suicide switch to kill everyone before locking himself up in the brig so you'd find him."

Hannah, Major Tom, Shelly, Elektra, and holographic versions of all four Trishes were present at my impromptu conference. Forty-Two was with Danny, and I was honestly wishing I could be down there with them. The High Priestess was fixing the broken water recyclers on Deck 12, a skill I didn't know she possessed until she'd displayed it, and Light on Water was on the bridge. My father was confined to quarters and hadn't moved since. Mostly because I had his door locked and guarded by security bots puppeted by the Trishes.

The non-sentient bots were still cleaning up the decapitated corpses around the ship and the remaining survivors of the *Black Nebula II*'s crew were rushing around trying to keep the ship on its path to the Crius system. Everyone was working double and sometimes even triple shifts at jobs they weren't remotely qualified for. We were running the *Siege Perilous* with the equivalent of strapping some cement blocks to the gas pedals.

I'd had to go down to engineering six times already to make some adjustments to the jumpdrive system. I wasn't an engineer but my basic training from Space Academy was better than what most people on board possessed. How bad was it? Well, Light on Water was serving as the acting bridge crew by himself since everyone else had more practical skills to use.

Right now, we were getting by through the modification of a hundred or so bots to substitute for living crew members. I was fully aware of both the dangers as well as the irony because it had been doing this exact same thing that had supposedly killed my parents decades earlier. They were, again, the only people who had ever crashed an automated cargo ship into a sun. I wondered if they'd done it deliberately in order to fake their deaths—though I didn't wonder long because, of course they had.

"Yeah, that tracks," I said, having only gotten two hours of sleep and drinking from a forty-ounce mug of coffeine with a bendy straw. Hilariously, the mug was a VANCE TURBO: HEEERO OF SPAAACE biopic commemorative cup. It was amazing the kind of junk you could find in a pirate ship.

"Yeah, *that tracks*?" Hannah asked, shocked. "That's all you have to say?"

"You missed a lot," I said, slurping my coffee for a bit. "He more or less confessed to everything but the gross act of mass murder that affected the majority of the ship's crew. I wouldn't even care about that except for the fact most of them were genemod slaves. How is Danny doing?"

"Better," Hannah said, looking deflated after clearly having been working on her theory for some time. "I should probably have mentioned it earlier but we're in a relationship together now. Mostly monogamous."

"Congratulations," I said, genuinely happy for her. I was more upset I hadn't been able to notice it while I was so wrapped up in my own issues. I also hadn't been able to visit Danny as much as I wanted to over the past couple of weeks. We were almost to Crius, and I was genuinely impressed with the power of the jumpdrive of this ship. It wasn't standard issue, but a Sorkanan 621-Gna'taash which was barely within our reactor's power limits but would cut the trip time in half.

"Are we even sure he *is* your father?" Shelly asked, not for the first time. "We've tested his DNA multiple times but that can be fooled, especially by the Crius."

"He's the real deal," I said, coldly.

"Yeah," Hannah said, looking at Shelly. "It's impossible to deny if you stand them up against one another. Captain to captain, they have way too many similarities."

"What? You think being a good captain is *genetic*?" I asked, trying to avoid raising my voice. She hadn't meant it as an insult but it was impossible to take it otherwise since he'd possibly—probably—killed his own crew. "That I got it from *him*?"

"I didn't say you were a good captain," Hannah said, deflating my anger with a joke.

"Do you believe he was the person who arranged your ambush?" Elektra said. "It's possible he really is who he says he is and is a spy working for the Security Division. If so, maybe he arranged all of this to sabotage the effort to take you prisoner."

"It still wouldn't justify what he did," I replied. "Or might have done. Besides, he didn't sabotage it, if he did at all, until the ship was taken down by Baby Trish."

"I want to be known as Teen Trish now," Baby Trish said, cheerfully.

"They grow up so fast," Goth Trish said.

"I've tried to get in touch with Director G, but the long-range communications were disabled with whatever wiped the ship's memories," I replied. "So, right now, my father is a wild card. We can't trust him but he's also our only insight into the Allenway cult and Karl the Conqueror. *If* he's telling the truth, then he's the party who tried to kidnap Astrid. It gives us name and face to our enemy."

"I've recovered a few of the ship's files so that's literal now," Goth Trish said. "Here's our adversary."

A hologram of a sour-faced, blandly handsome, blond-haired, blue-eyed man with a square jaw appeared above the conference table. It was the face of Karl the Conqueror, aged about thirty years, lacking the man's characteristic facial hair. He hadn't gotten facial reconstruction but had apparently denied himself access to the galaxy's ubiquitous longevity drugs to make himself less recognizable, which was a choice to say the least.

"Joseph Allenway III is a Duke on Crius Prime and the head of the Opposition Party," Goth Trish said. "Honestly, I'm impressed with the guy's audacity as identifying him wouldn't be that difficult for Leah or any other Security Division agent. Mind you, when looking for an interstellar wanted terrorist and traitor, you don't expect to find them in politics."

Hannah looked shaken by the sight of the man as if he was a creature from her nightmares. Maybe he was.

"Maybe we should check planetary governments more often," Major Tom said, half-joking. "It would explain a few things."

"Well, you've dealt him a severe blow," Pink said, smirking. "Karl is the biggest pirate in the Spire aside from Captain Havelock. The *Siege Perilous* was his pride and joy. Without it, he won't be able to recruit nearly the number of volunteers to his cause. It was a sign of his ability to stick it to the Community with impunity."

"Do you think he'll try and recover it?" Shelly asked. "We could be followed even now by the fleet that almost intercepted us. If we show up at Crius and they follow, Crius' Navy is more likely to help them than us and that's assuming they could stand up to that collection of ships anyway."

"It's a risk," I said, pausing. "I would hate to have to turn around and go to other systems, but we may have to. Unfortunately, we may have stumbled into a larger plot. That fleet back there is enough to take over Crius directly. I'm surprised Karl hasn't attempted to do a military coup."

"He can't," Elektra said, surprising me. She was usually more interested in test tubes than diplomacy. "That fleet might have allowed him to take over when Crius was an isolated backwater, but the Community has a much bigger presence in the system now. He can't afford to act directly with a coup, or they might intervene. He could defeat the local military with that fleet we left behind but not a Sector fleet. Even Earth's Navy would be enough to crush it and they love interventions."

"Not as much as they used to," I said. "There are also elements of EarthGov who would be fine with going to war with the Notha but not their fellow humans."

Also, the dissolution of Dark Matter would have repercussions throughout Sol system's politics. The owner of Ares Electronics, Alexandra Ares, had been a deranged AI that had been covertly pushing humanity into countless small wars to advance Earth's position in the larger galaxy. With her money, and that of her cohorts, financing the war hawks, I wasn't sure how quickly they would get involved now.

"Humans love going to war with each other," Major Tom said. "But I take your point."

"He'll need the appearance of popular support and to keep his coup an internal matter," Elektra said. "Which may be why he's trying to get your daughter. If he can threaten Leah to stand down during the coup or even possibly get your endorsement, he could keep the Community from invading."

"Me?" I asked.

"High Protector," Elektra said. "It's the kind of title that accompanies being addressed as 'My Lord' and bowing."

"You could literally order the Community fleet to stand down or to intervene on your own authority," Shelly said. "You need to stop thinking of this promotion as up to Fleet Captain and more like being made Lord Nelson."

"Who is Nelson?" Pink asked, confused. They'd probably not taught about the Battle of Waterloo in Albion's school system.

"No one should have that kind of power," I replied. "My father thinks that Karl has more motivations than mere political power."

"Political power is never mere," Major Tom said. "But it might not be his primary motivation. The Roman Seneca said that religion was commonly viewed by the peasantry as true, by the wise as false, and by the powerful as useful. If he'd lived to know the Elder Races, he might have added, *and by the ambitious as divine*."

"The Elder Races aren't gods, but they're close," I said, thinking back to Cthulhu. I supposed that made me Perseus slaying the Kraken with Medusa's head. "In any case, how likely is it that the Enigmatic Path fleet would be able to follow us to Crius?"

"Depends on if we have any traitors on board," Shelly said. "It's more likely that someone on the *Black Nebula II* sold us out in the first place. Someone had to have a means of transmitting our coordinates to the *Siege Perilous* and probably did so for profit. They are, after all, pirates."

"The Havelock Pirates don't deal with slavers," Pink said, dangerously before her expression softened. "But I can't dismiss the possibility entirely."

"Well, we have two days left to get the ship in some form of functionality," I replied, knowing the best we could hope for was forward, up, down, barrier on, barrier off, and stop. Even that was a miracle. "I suggest we take at least one of those days to get a night's rest for those of us who do sleep."

"I told you we should sleep in shifts," Shelly said.

"That would imply we have enough people for shifts," I said, only half-joking. "Dismissed."

Three of the Trishes vanished with only Prime Trish remaining. Elektra got up and departed. Hannah sat down in her seat. Shelly got up and kissed her husband. It made me grimace a bit before I shrugged it off. Jealousy wasn't an emotion that became me, but it was still something I felt. I hadn't intended to make sacrifices for power and position like so many others in my profession. Somehow I'd ended up making them anyway. Once, I'd been surrounded by a bunch of people who'd loved me. Now, it seemed all of them were drifting away. I had to wonder if I could have done anything different or if it was the very desire to grasp all of those around me that was the mistake. To quote a princess in a wholly different situation, the more I tightened my grip, the more things slipped through my fingers.

After Shelly and Major Tom left, Hannah stood up again. "Hey, Vance, could I have a moment of your time?"

Trish looked between us, a pained expression on her holographic face.

"Sure," I said, rising and putting my comically oversized mug aside. "I'm going to try and crash and hope I can defeat the power of coffeine through sheer willpower."

Hannah walked over to me, getting up close. "I don't know if I can do this."

"Do what, specifically?" I asked, feeling like my otherwise enhanced brain was running at half speed. "One of the reasons I'm an utter failure romantically is that I don't understand what anyone alludes to versus them just saying it."

Hannah rolled her eyes. "No, you're an utter failure romantically because you try and treat relationships like a buffet and stay friends with everyone."

I blinked. "Is that...not...how it's supposed to work?"

Hannah sighed. "I mean, I made the decision to resign and go back to Crius because I wanted to confront the people there. My time in Space Fleet gave me the confidence to believe I could do something about the aristocracy."

"I support your choice," I said, pausing. "Though I'm fairly sure the Community considers abandoning your military career to become a revolutionary to legally be terrorism. Unless they're the ones supporting it, I mean."

"I'm not in the mood for jokes, Vance," Hannah said, her voice close to breaking.

"Nor am I," I replied. "I think you should reconsider your choice and work through other channels. A single soldier isn't going to be able to make any difference in a planetary war, but being able to work with the Security Departments or within the political system you might be able to get traction against the slave lords. Hell, we have a point of contact with Leah now."

"The woman who stole your and Shelly's DNA," Hannah said.

I paused. "Yeah."

"You are handling this way lighter than you should be," Hannah said. "This is not waking up to find up you've knocked up your ex-girlfriend. This is her clipping hair and toenails to grow a little girl in a lab."

I looked away. "I was grown in a lab."

159

Hannah looked frustrated. "So was I. So are most children on Crius. They make the fetus in the clonemaster's labs and then insert them into surrogate mothers who are told they are the parents, whether it's true or not. It is a brutal, dehumanizing system, and I don't think you understand what you're wading into here."

"Then tell me," I said, softly. "Give me context."

Hannah looked uncomfortable with the request, and I realized, yes, I was asking her to rip open a wound that was only half-healed.

"Crius is the planet where I was born and raised on to be a slave in a fucking theme park. I had parents, sisters, and brothers who existed to live in villages menaced by dragons so that the aristocracy could rescue us. I also witnessed the aristocracy joining in raiding parties to slaughter us. They'd often assemble conscripts to conduct mock wars between each other. Except with real swords and arrows. One of the first things I learned when I became one of their toys was that none of this served a higher purpose than fun. I lived in a thousand-kilometer estate full of villages just like mine to let the nobility live out their fantasies. It's one of thousands of such domains."

"I'm sorry," I said, looking down before meeting her gaze.

Hannah closed her eyes. "I want to bomb that place from orbit and liberate everyone there, but it was always a pipe dream because even if I wanted too, no one would side with me. It's imprinted in our brains, a servility that makes us view the aristocrats as heroes. Above us. Even decades way from that place, I still think of them in glowing terms. Your child will be corrupted there if you don't get her out."

"It's definitely an environment I want to get her away from," I replied. "It'd be like keeping a child from being raised in Nazi Germany or the Confederacy."

Or the Notha for that matter.

"I only know what one of those is," Hannah said, opening her eyes. "That's why I'm scared, Vance. I don't trust my own actions. I want to rescue your daughter but is that because she's your daughter or because I've been programmed this way? She's a noblewoman now. So is Leah. What if I'm obeying you because of that? What if when I go back to Crius, I end up bowing before my old masters?"

Prime Trish nodded. "I know something about programming, Hannah. It's not as absolute as you think. You're not a machine. Not any more than I am."

Probably not the best way to reassure Hannah. I would have told her that she wasn't a bioroid, and Case was one and had rebelled. I also had seen plenty of human beings become subject to their own programming from either biology or state, my own parents among them. They'd been enslaved by their addictions and been unable to rise above them. I didn't really believe in free will but that we were who we were, a messy jumble of nature, nurture, and the thoughts of a greater oversoul.

"You are better than you think you are," I said, walking over and putting my hand on hers. "You've imagined yourself as this badass mercenary killer and you are, but that person has done immense good on board my ship as part of my crew. You are my friend, and I don't believe you're capable of hurting my daughter."

Hannah withdrew her hand from mine. "You don't know what I did before I joined your crew, Vance, and if you did then you wouldn't want me anywhere near you."

I'd seen her full file thanks to my security upgrade through working with Director G. I knew she was wanted for murder in fourteen systems, had done most of her work with the mostly legitimate Antaeus Rangers during the Notha War, was briefly a pirate, had done gladiator fights on Notha-held worlds to survive, and she'd been a legitimate security contractor thereafter. In short, she'd done a lot of things to survive with her only skillset being violence. I also didn't care and, like Forty-Two, would pardon her if I had the authority. Was this abuse of power for my friends? Probably, but it would be because I believed people deserved second as well as third chances.

"I think you're underestimating me now," I said, sighing. "Your help would be immensely valuable on this trip, but if you don't want to go then I won't try and convince you. You can stay on the ship."

"I'm *not* staying on the ship," Hannah growled before turning to Prime Trish. "Also, stay out of conversations you're not invited into."

"That's literally impossible whenever you're on a ship I'm flying," Prime Trish said. "Or partially flying. Besides, I'm on your side in all this."

"You are?" I asked.

"I am," Prime Trish said.

"Just tell me what I can do," I said, lifting my hands. "I'll do anything in my power to make it happen."

Hannah turned to me. "I want this ship, Vance."

"What?" I asked, blinking.

"Give it me and I can use it to go after the slave lords," Hannah said. "You think I need the Community to back up my revolution? Well, this would be the hell of a start for a war chest to destroy these bastards. It might keep me, Danny, and Forty-Two alive."

I should have realized that Hannah's own feelings were mixed, and she was going to bounce from one extreme to the next. She was worried about being able to fight the slave lords and now she wanted something that could devastate them from orbit. Then again, maybe that wasn't her changing her mind but trying to figure out ways she couldn't avoid confronting them directly.

"They're all coming?" I asked, confused.

"A Trish too," Hannah said, as if letting me know all my friends were ready to abandon the Community.

I was reminded of Great-Aunt Kathy talking about her Irish grandfather speaking of the Spanish Civil War. Which, bluntly, was thinking about something nearly five hundred years ago. Still, the lesson was still relevant. A white ancestor of the Tagashi family had gone to fight a righteous holy war against the Red Army in Spain despite everyone around them suggesting it wasn't their fight. Priests were being murdered, the Communists wanted to ban religion, and it was a conflict of "good versus evil." Of course, it had ended in putting a fascist, Franco, in power. They'd helped enable his atrocities and her grandfather returned home to Ireland a broken man.

This was a wholly different situation. The Crius nobility was every bit as bad as any of the people I'd fought who weren't eldritch AI. Certainly, it was Hannah's fight. It was her people being oppressed. However, it sounded like someone in Community was trying to avoid a full-scale war while forcing the locals to come to terms. A solution that would probably be better than what might otherwise be generations of war, assuming it was won by Hannah's side—which was composed of some of our crew—at all.

"You know I can't do that, Hannah," I said, staring at her. "This ship is a weapon of mass destruction and can't belong in civilian hands. We also can't just stop and start looking for a crew. We're against Karl and I can help you bring him down and we can work with the government to get you—"

"So, it's fine to work for your ends illegally but not for mine?" Hannah asked. "Great to know where we stand, Vannevar. Anyxhole."

Hannah marched off.

I watched her leave. "Am I selfish? Am I doing the right thing? Should I be focused on just my kid instead of the politics here?"

"Why the hell are you asking me, High Protector? I'll be going with her," Prime Trish said, disappearing a second later.

CHAPTER EIGHTEEN

That Was Unexpectedly Easy

"Y ou will bow before me, insect. You will get on your knees and pray to me as your god! Worship me! Worship me! If you do not, I will inflict unforgettable suffering upon you! Unforgettable! Muhahahaha!" Princess Huggypants said as the six limbed, pill-bug-shaped Drolochid loomed over the helm of the *Siege Perilous'* controls. She was presently attempting to intimidate the ship's controls into obeying her, not Trish in any of her various guises, but the controls themselves. It was apparently a Drolochid ritual for technical matters.

Drolochids were a Community race that were even worse off than humanity in terms of their position in the galaxy with six planets and only one having its own spaceflight manufacturing base. They were capable of breathing a nitrogen atmosphere and had grown up in a gravity twice as harsh as Earth's so you occasionally found them serving on human ships with very little need for life support equipment. Because, we'll, we breathe mostly nitrogen atmospheres and that means our gravity is light to them.

The truth was that interaction between aliens and humans (or all species really) was limited by the wildly different environment and biological needs required by each. A planet bioformed to be hospitable to humans was going to be toxic to just about anything other than a handful of other species and even then, it would still be less comfortable than one specifically made for them.

Even with the Great Filter AKA Fermi's Paradox that destroyed most species in the galaxy, there were something akin to eight thousand known sentient species (not including demi-variants) and roughly half of those tooling around the galaxy as space-faring civilizations. Only about eighty-six of them shared anything in common with humans in terms of bio-chemical, gravity, temperature, and atmospheric needs. Among *those,* only the Ants, Drolochids, Kolahn, Notha, Sorkanan, Verdantians, and a maybe five or six others were close enough that I could go on their ships without some form of protective wear or vice versa.

In a way, it was arguably for the best. Not because a lack of diversity encouraged peace. Quite the opposite, you're more likely to shoot someone who is ninety-nine percent like you than someone completely different. Just look at the holy wars on Earth where people were killing each other over the Eucharist being literal or not. No, it was that strong fences made for good neighbors. The Community could exist in part because conflict among each other for resources was primarily limited to similar peoples. Humans weren't going to conquer any Drolochid worlds because while they could breathe nitrogen, they also had a rich ammonia content in their atmosphere that they found to be harmless but limited any real estate purchases.

"Princess, could you dial down the chatter?" I asked, sitting in the captain's chair.

We'd assembled a full-ish bridge crew for our arrival in the Crius system and the ship was working about as well as it possibly could with the reprogrammed bots and only a tenth of the recommended crew. A lot of that was due to Princess Huggypants, the deranged supervillain we'd found among the *Black Nebula II*'s crew that had programmed the two hundred or so bots necessary to make sure the ship didn't explode or crash through a sun on our way.

Hannah, Shelly, Forty-Two, Major Tom, Pink, Elektra, Light on Water, and Danny were all present on the bridge. Which meant all stations were manned. Danny was still walking with a cane, but he was oddly chipper. You wouldn't even know Forty-Two had been injured. I hadn't had a chance to talk to any of them about their leaving nor did I want to. I'd become a master of putting off unpleasant conversations and figured talking to them about them abandoning Space Fleet to join a paramilitary organization Hannah hadn't quite formed yet was one that could be put off. None of the Trishes were present as they were all coordinating the systems that were usually *not* automated on board the ship. Who'd ever said that AI run ships didn't need crews was clearly just talking out of their asses.

"I must let the machines know that I am their master!" Princess Huggypants cackled, raising four of their limbs. Drolochids could walk on their hand-feet or use them all simultaneously, which certainly helped her with engineering and programming. "Do not test me, machines! I will terrorize your spirits and sacrifice you all to the cyber-gods! Of which I shall someday overthrow with my multi-tools!"

"So, this was your chief engineer, huh?" I asked, turning to Pink who was at navigation.

"Our *only* engineer," Pink replied. "She did the work of six people with little complaint. We found her on Glotomachus where she was just ahead of the law and in need of a quick escape. That was two years ago."

"What was she wanted for, exactly?" I asked, not really having much choice but to rely on her. But I was still curious.

"Robbing banks," Pink replied. "Or taking over the world. I forget which."

Yeah, I hadn't been kidding about that supervillain descriptor.

"Yes!" Princess Huggypants said. "I have prepared the ship to exit jumpspace! Soon the world of Crius will tremble in my presence! Tremble!"

"Is any of this bothering you, Trishes?" I asked, not sure if I should refer to her in the singular or plural these days.

"SHE'S NOT THREATENING ME, VANCE, JUST THE EQUIPMENT. HONESTLY, PRINCESS HUGGYPANTS ISN'T EVEN IN THE TOP TEN WEIRDEST MEMBERS OF YOUR CREW," Prime Trish (I presumed) said. "YOU'RE BASICALLY CAPTAIN KIRK IF HIS CREW CONSISTED OF THE MUPPETS."

I looked up. "That is both flattering as well as sadly accurate."

"What's a *moopet*?" Forty-Two asked.

"A troupe of lunatic actors led by an amphibian who isn't that much saner than the rest of them," I replied.

"Ah, so accurate," Forty-Two said.

"Do you guys ever make any pop culture references that aren't from Earth or the twentieth century?" Pink asked.

"Honestly, no," I admitted. "It's kind of a blind spot with us. So, uh, Princess, is there any chance we can use weapons when we arrive?"

"Do you wish to hit anything, Inferior Puny Captain?" Princess Huggypants asked.

"Yes?" I asked.

"Then no," Princess Huggypants said. "I have not yet achieved that brilliance! But soon! SOON!"

"I suppose that was too much to hope for," I muttered, tapping a comm. "High Priestess, are you bringing my father to the bridge."

"Spock is ready to eat him at your leisure," The High Priestess responded.

"Hi, son!" Jack said, over the communicator. "Note I haven't tried to take back the ship or killed anyone since you rescued me."

"I have your award for basic decency prepared," I said, dryly.

"I prefer gold or kyronium!" Jack replied. "Gems are always good. Medals would be much more appreciated if they could be hocked."

So, this is what an evil me would look and sound like. "Just get here where I can get to you in case we need you."

"As a hostage?" Jack asked.

I paused. "Yes."

"Good to know!" Jack said.

I cut out communication feed. "Do we have an exact time on our arrival, Hannah?"

"I prefer Lieutenant Commander O'Brian," Hannah replied, still plizzed at me for not agreeing to hand over the *Siege Perilous*. It was a bizarre thing to be upset about given how impractical it would be even to try. However, I understand her real reasoning. She wanted someone to be angry at in order to distract herself from the feelings she had returning home.

At least, that was what I was telling myself. The fact was that she was going to go fight an evil empire and I was working with an establishment that repeatedly had proven itself to be unable to live up to its own ideals. That was just the Community. The Elder Races were a collection of races that had destroyed thousands of species over the course of the galaxy's history, sometimes to protect others and other times because of nebulous criteria that no sane person could understand. I'd call them pure evil but the Primordials proved there were even worse beings out there and the only thing standing in their way were the Elder Races.

Was I working for the good guys or the lesser evil?

Was there even a difference?

And could I make one?

"Do we have an exact time on our arrival, Lieutenant Commander O'Brian?" I asked, not taking the bait.

"Three minutes," Hannah said, looking up.

"Good," I replied.

"Let's hope we're not running right into the belly of the beast," Shelly said. "For all we know, Crius is waiting for us with a thousand satellite weapons aimed at us."

"Yeah, let's hope," I replied.

My father arrived a few moments later, dressed in black leather pants and a silk shirt with a vest that made him look like a movie pirate. Pink glared at him, and I could feel her desire to shoot him in order to avenge her lost crew members. I didn't blame her in the slightest. I had so many questions that I didn't even know where to begin, ranging from where my mother was (even if he didn't know her exact location now) to how he'd become involved with both Karl the Conqueror and Leah.

The problem was the fact he was a consummate liar, if not actually compulsive, and I couldn't trust anything that came out of his mouth. I also couldn't be trusted to listen to anything he had to say and judge it objectively. It's the kind of thing I would have normally turned over to the Security Departments, but, well, they're the ones who'd gotten us all here in the first place.

The High Priestess followed him with a growling Spock. The tryffle was a good judge of character, it seemed, or maybe it sensed my innate hostility to the man. The High Priestess was an unconventional member of the crew, but she was also one in whom I appreciated the relative simplicity of her emotions regarding me. I didn't quite believe she was motivated entirely by religious faith, but I believed she had my back.

For now.

"I'd like to complain about my accommodations," Jack said, raising a hand. "What kind of hotel doesn't have hookers and red dust? I'd like to talk to the manager."

"I'm sure we can upgrade your room to the airlock," I replied, suddenly having a great deal of sympathy for Captain Elgan who regularly threatened people with it. You know, despite the fact he'd betrayed and tried to kill me.

Danny looked at me with a pained expression on his face. Apparently, he didn't like me treating his uncle that way.

Boo frigging hoo.

"We're exiting jumpspace," Shelly said, looking up at the bridge's viewscreen. "Welcome home, Hannah."

I grasped the ends of the armrests of my chair while linking myself to the *Siege Perilous'* systems via my cybernetics. It was "crowded" inside, and my cybernetics felt uncomfortable among the dead, scattered remnants of the ship's previous dummy AI as well as the Trishes. The Enigmatic Path had also upgraded and twisted most of the ship's interior systems, but their changes had removed the Community's elegance for cold Kolahn efficiency. It was not the *Ares*. It was not home.

Still, I found myself able to harness all of the *Siege Perilous'* sensors and scanners. It provided me with a full readout of the surrounding star system as well as the objects within it. Crius was an isolated world, colonized during the early days of Earth's expansion with the scattered remnants of the megacorporation Karma Corp merging with the Church of Money among other criminal elements unwilling to adapt to the Community's laws.

It had always been isolated from the rest of the galaxy with what it possessed having been smuggled in by criminals or stolen via pirates. Its communications, sensors, and defensive systems were thus mixtures of the very advanced with the antiquated. There were even probes and satellites communicating with radio waves of all things.

Crius itself was a beautiful world and under different circumstances might have been one of the crown jewels of Earth's First Great Expansion. It had a single large Pangaea-esque continent covered in vast jungles with only the poles being frozen. Three billion humanoid lifeforms were below. Small cities existed alongside vast plantations producing millions of tons of biological material, foodstuffs, or medicines that were exported to rogue human colonies as well as renegade transtellers willing to repackage it for resale to more legitimate markets.

Both of its moons were inhabited, having been hollowed out and transformed into industrialized hellholes like the way Earth's moon had been colonized. While I'd been born in Scotland, Great-Aunt Kathy was American, and I'd spent most of my childhood on the Moon or in the star bases around Jupiter. I was a spacer and a grounder simultaneously, with the two natures as often as not at war instead of helping each other achieve synergy.

I was almost immediately overwhelmed with the in-system communication that was poorly coordinated and not sorted by Dummy AI like on Earth or in the Community. There were massive amounts of news referring to war, battle, and chaos going on across the planet's surface. Two whole cities had been blasted from orbit and there were signs of fighting around the world. The Crius local fleet—a bunch of antiquated Sorkanan Slirrrrua-class frigates—showed signs of battle between each other.

We would not be docking at the *Jovial Empress*. The Sorkanan-built space station, a Community protectorate despite being filled with Crius colonists, had been destroyed by forces unknown. Its pieces were scattered across the world's orbit. There were traces of antimatter radiation that indicated someone had detonated a q-bomb on board. If the entire population was killed, that meant over a hundred thousand people had died. It also would cripple Crius economically until a new spaceport was built and people were trained to replace the dead.

Then there was the dreadnought.

Crazzap.

In 1906, the British Royal Navy launched the HMS *Dreadnought*, and the five-hundred-foot vessel had such an effect on the rest of the world that all previous ships were designated "Pre-Dreadnought" vessels and eventually all future planetary Navies incorporated dreadnought elements within them. It was with this in mind that when the ESS *Dreadnought* was created, it would have the exact same revolutionizing aspect.

The golden vessel was a kilometer-long combination of flagship and battle cruiser with all the necessary departments for a multi-vector mission profile ranging from diplomacy to sapient aid to exploration. It followed the same saucer and base design that the *Ares* and *Siege Perilous* did, but much, much bigger.

It had been constructed by a combination of EarthGov and Community engineers working with Ares Electronics as well as the Sorkanan Armorers Guild. Two thousand and five hundred of the Sol system's best and brightest were on board with room for twice as many in passengers, whether soldiers or relief workers. It was just equal to the destroyers of the Sorkanan Navy but by far the most powerful thing in human hands.

What the hell was it doing here?

Vance, that is not the ESS Dreadnought, Prime Trish spoke in my mind. *Its registry is the ESS* Melampus.

The…what? I asked, confused. *They built a second one? The first one almost bankrupted Earth's construction budget!*

Seeing is believing, Trish replied. *It's the* Dreadnought's *sister ship, though. It's also seen recent combat, though, and seems to be coordinating the pacification of Crius.*

Apparently, we've missed a war, Goth Trish replied.

Bummer, Teen Trish said. *I'm sure Leah and your daughter weren't on the space station when it blew up.*

Alarm filled my mind and spread out through the ship's cyber uplink since I hadn't even thought of that.

Oh crazzap, sorry! Teen Trish said.

That was when Princess Huggypants spoke. "FOOLS! BLUNDERERS! The comm system is not responding! It must be tortured until it complies! Sabotage! Treachery! Treason! We cannot identify ourselves to the lesser beings outside this vessel! My glory is denied!"

"Oh dear," Light on Water said. "It seems that the ESS *Melampus* is demanding our surrender and moving to intercept us. It seems to think we're a threat."

"Ouch," Jack said, looking at me. "That's a bummer."

That was when Forty-Two called over. "Oh, just so you know, the Enigmatic Path fleet followed us. They just pulled out behind us and are charging weapons."

"Welcome home, indeed," Hannah muttered.

CHAPTER NINETEEN

Winning by Doing Absolutely Nothing

"So, what do you believe should be done in a lose-lose scenario, Vannevar?" Leah asked, sitting across from me in the courtyard of Habitat 37 of Space Academy's central campus, known as, well, Space Academy. The chair wasn't so much a chair or a beanbag but a kind of weird liquid foam that adjusted itself to your body when you sat on it. Tommy, Leah, and I were relaxing next to one of the lagoons in the area between the shopping center and food court, two very human things I'd been surprised to find in space.

Leah Mass was a brown-haired woman who was a bit on the short side and possessed a mixture of Norwegian and Asiatic features. She was wearing a blue tunic uniform with thigh-high boots, which passed for fashionable among human cadets. She was presently studying an infopad that I knew contained a textbook on wartime ethics. We were being tested on the Notha War and the disastrous choices made during that time by the Community and Notha both. I cared for Leah deeply and hated that in a year we'd be graduating and probably on opposite sides of the galaxy.

Tommy AKA Seventeen AKA Grrr'Gnash'Snarl, by contrast, was a Sorkanan that was a bit on the lean and avian side compared to some of the bulkier more, intimidating lizard men. He was considered something of a nerd among them and apparently had been bullied his entire life until attending the Academy. There it had come a great shock to him that humans thought he looked like a walking velociraptor and was quite terrifying. Amusingly, he did have to wear a special form of corrective goggles that made his eyes somewhat comically huge and adorable.

"You mean a no-win scenario," I said, sipping my health food vegetable-fruit thing that I'd hacked the dispensaries to provide alcoholic content.

"They mean the same thing," Leah said, annoyed.

"It's an Earth media thing," I said.

Space Academy consisted of a single large asteroid surrounded by hundreds of cylinders floating around it, each containing simulated environments for not only its myriad array of students, but also the kind of punishing sort of conditions that would be encountered by the Interstellar Community Protectors.

Habitat 37 was primarily inhabited by humans but also the odd alien. Verdantian and Sorkanan studied here as well. Drolochid merchants seemed to have a monopoly on handling the habitat's and seemed willing to wear environmental suits to manage them in other habitats as well. The place had a weird shopping mall crossed with Babylonian hanging gardens aesthetic that reminded me that while these places had been built to make students feel at home, they were not built by people from our home.

"It's always an Earth media thing with you," Tommy said. "How would you like it if I constantly made references to gravball?"

"You *hate* gravball," I replied. "You said it was only played by dumbasses whose eggs were cracked during incubation."

"Exactly!" Tommy said, showing our translators weren't always perfect as I was pretty sure I was missing some nuance.

"Just answer the question," Leah said.

"I'd blow up the *Kobayashi Maru*," I replied, softly. "It's the only way to be sure."

Leah rolled her eyes.

I shrugged then tried to answer her question seriously. "I dunno, I think I'd probably run out the clock."

"What?" Leah asked.

"A no win scenario is one where the only variable you may have control of is probably time," I replied. "Stay alive until things change."

I couldn't help but think back to that conversation as I found myself caught between a rock, a hard place, and the cold hard vacuum of space. It was well before I'd found out Leah was a spy working to recruit me to Department Twelve and not that long before poor Tommy died during a spacewalk thanks to my failure to check the equipment properly. I'd been cleared of all wrongdoing, but to this day I believed it was only because my great-aunt was a famous captain. Either way, I was now facing a no-win scenario as I was caught between a dreadnought and an Enigmatic Path fleet. Oh and there was no way to identify myself as friendly to the dreadnought.

"Orders, captain?" Shelly asked, clearly ready to take the lead herself and probably able to do just as good a job.

But this was my disaster to fix. "Up!"

"Up?" Shelly asked, confused.

"Up!" I shouted. "Maximum speed!"

Our ability to maneuver was crippled but space had the advantage of being vertical as well as horizontal even if, at that moment, we were just trying to stay ahead of the people coming to kill us all.

"Where should I plot a jump..." Pink started to say before trailing off. "Goddammit! The dreadnought has jump jammers."

"Oh my," Jack said, sounding completely undisturbed by our imminent demise. "This is certainly a pickle. However, will our hero get out of it this time."

"If you have an idea, Jack, tell us!" Shelly shouted.

"Oh no, I'm sure he'll figure it out," Jack said, chuckling. Right before the High Priestess bit his leg. "AH! Dammit!"

The lights flickered on the bridge as we heard wheezing and whining accompanied by claps of thunder.

"What the bork?" I asked, confused as hell.

"I added sound effects and audio-visual stimuli to the ship to let us know that our barrier is taking damage," Princess Huggypants said. "Pew-pew-pew! Oh and we're already down thirty percent of our barriers. We're out of range from all but the longest of the Enigmatic Path weapons but there's a lot of them."

"I'll pass," Forty-Two replied.

"These pirates are insane!" Pink muttered, firing back and only marginally succeeding with our skeleton crew. "They're risking running right into that dreadnought's path!"

"I'm monitoring the traffic of the Enigmatic Path ships," Light on Water said. "They're not answering any of the *Melampus'* hails. If you would like my advice—"

"I really wouldn't," I replied, struggling to figure out some sort of miracle I could pull off even as we were coming directly into the path of the dreadnought's canons. Ones that would tear through the *Siege Perilous*—a vessel fifty years old with only sporadic upgrades—like wet tissue paper.

"Surrender is a perfectly viable option in any given fight," Light on Water started to say. "We can negotiate a—"

"Graft Unst is hailing us," Danny said, looking up from his console. "Probably to taunt us. Sadly, we won't be able to tell him where to shove his words."

The lights were now dimmed down to the "dramatic on a low budget" level, which was probably not a good sign.

"Fifty percent barrier level!" Princess Huggypants said dramatically. "They turn red at twenty percent!"

I was willing to ask my father for help, I wouldn't put my pride before lives but already had an idea. "Put Unst on the screen, Danny. Princess, we don't have long range or short-range communication, do we?"

"I say thee nay, inferior captain!" Princess Huggypants said. "The machine has betrayed us!"

"What about radio?" I asked.

"What?" Princess Huggypants asked.

"If it's a Crius ship and the Crius still use radio, does it have that?" I asked.

"Yes?" Princess Huggypants said, seemingly as surprised by her answer as anyone. "This mars the perfection of my evil modifications!"

"Then broadcast what Unst says," I said to Danny and Princess Huggypants simultaneously. "Also, start sending a message to the Crius stations to send to the *Melampus*. Identify who we are, and that Community Protectors are in command of this vessel."

"I'm not sure they will obey," Danny said. "They're probably not fond of the Community right now."

"Say the High Protector demands it!" I shouted.

Jack clapped at my decision while shaking his leg to try and get the High Priestess off it, she had a death grip on his ankle with her jaws. "Bravo! Bravo! You figured it out. Also, do we have any mace? Maybe a shock prod?"

The lights in the room turned an ominous shade of red.

Yeah, we were borked.

"So dramatic!" Princess Huggypants said, typing away at the console's holographic interface with all six limbs. "To die, to be *really* dead, that must be glorious!!"

Great, the insane pill bug was quoting *Dracula* now.

Graff Unst's heavily scarred surgically altered face appeared on the screen again, once more reminding me this was a guy who decided to carve up other people to sew pieces onto himself in hopes of making himself an elf. "Vance Turbo, you filthy species traitor! I don't know who I despise more, you, or your disgusting progenitor!"

"Hi, nice to meet you! I have no idea who I am supposed to have betrayed, humanity I'm guessing, but I'll be glad to listen to any complaints. I will need them in writing and filled out in triplicate, though," I said, pausing. "He can't hear me, can he?"

"No," Princess Huggypants said. "However, he knows we're receiving."

"I could send a radio response," Danny said.

"No," I replied. "Just let him speak."

"We're almost out of barrier," Hannah reminded me. "I can literally hear the dramatic climax music starting to play."

Indeed, it was a whole orchestral score that I recognized as lifted from the *Terraformers IV* soundtrack.

"The Enigmatic Path will burn you and your ship, our ship, before we cleanse the galaxy of your filth. Crius will be avenged! Even now, my lord has seized power over it and your weak mewling community is powerless—" Graff Unst's transmission was abruptly cut off.

"And boom goes the dynamite," Jack said, offhandedly. He'd finally managed to knock the High Priestess off his leg and now was slowly backing away from a growling Spock. "Nice kitty. What if I poured water on you and fed you after midnight? Would that make you happy?"

Shelly looked up. "The ESS *Melampus* moved into firing range at an outrageous speed and destroyed the Kolahn battlecruiser, *Righteous Endeavor,* with a volley of antimatter torpedoes. Seriously, I thought those were theoretical. The *Melampus* is tearing into the other one now. The rest of the fleet is turning to flee. Shall we move to join the fight?"

"Hell no!" I said, not showing peak professionalism. "Get us out of the way of any more fighting and let them finish the Enigmas off."

A single ship, no matter how powerful, versus the armada assembled against us was something that might have gotten even odds from most bookies back home. However, the ESS *Melampus'* captain was extremely good at what he or she was doing and managed to cripple most opposing vessels before they could put up an adequate defense. The local Crius Navy reluctantly joined in the fray after it was clear the battle was already won and accepted the surrender of the surviving ships.

Honestly, it was proving not to be Karl the Conqueror's month. While his fleet could never have seriously threatened the Community, it was probably one of the larger pirate fleets in the galaxy that had just been wiped out. It was also probably a decent chunk of the Enigmatic Path's military forces in the sector. While I couldn't exactly take credit for how things had shaken down, it was pretty clear the bad guys weren't exactly covering themselves in glory here.

The lights turned from red to dim then back to normal as the barriers regenerated. The battle music also stopped. Thank God for that as *Terraformers IV* had the worst score to human ears by far. Sadly, the lights weren't going to get any higher than sixty-one percent due to our inability to reroute power without a full engineering crew. That wasn't relevant right now, though, as I ordered the ship to slow down to a halt and turn with its side to the *Melampus,* which was the traditional means of signifying an end to hostilities. A more cautious captain might have hoofed it out of here while they were battling it out with the Enigmatic Path until we could get our communications array fixed, but I had every confidence the *Melampus'* captain wouldn't accelerate hostilities.

Call it a gut feeling.

"Did we win?" Hannah asked, seemingly not sure what had happened had. Which was a strange reaction since we'd survived worse scenarios. Not many, but some.

"I'm not sure 'we won' is the best way to describe it," I said, staring at a close up of the *Melampus* on the viewscreen. "However, I'm fairly sure that we got a pretty good set of seats to witnessing the Sons of the Demiurge getting their anyxes handed to them. Unst seemed to think he'd taken over the planet, though."

"I DON'T THINK THAT'S THE CASE, VANCE," Prime Trish said before shoving and arguing noises were heard on the intercom like a bunch of sisters were fighting on the infocom. "NO, LET ME SAY IT. NO, I WANT TO. I WANT TO. OKAY, FINE. YEAH, GOTH TRISH IS GOING TO EXPLAIN—"

"LISTEN, WE'VE BEEN MONITORING THE PLANETARY FEEDS—" Goth Trish started to speak.

"YEAH, I THINK THE SLAVERS ARE ALL DEAD," Teen Trish interjected rapidly.

"What," Hannah asked.

"Great news!" Danny said. "I didn't really want to become a revolutionary anyway. No offense, Hannah."

"Ahh," Forty-Two said. "I was looking forward to showing off my human disguise of a hat and floral shirt. There was no way the Crius forces would figure out who I was."

"GEE, THANKS TEEN TRISH," Seventies Trish muttered. "LITTLE BISH. ANYWAY, YEAH, IT SEEMS LIKE A FULL-SCALE WAR BROKE OUT BETWEEN THE VARIOUS FACTIONS A FEW DAYS AGO, BUT ONE SIDE DRAMATICALLY UNDERESTIMATED THE RESOLVE OF ANOTHER. ALMOST ALL OF THE SLAVER PLANTATION PALACES HAVE BEEN ANNIHILATED FROM ORBIT ALONGSIDE THE ARISTOCRACY'S PRIMARY CITIES. THE COLLATERAL DAMAGE IS SEVERE AND I CAN'T TELL HOW MANY CASUALTIES AMONG THE OPPOSITION, BUT I'D WAGER THE MAJORITY OF THE NOBILITY IS DEAD WITH THE REMAINDER OF THE SURVIVING POPULATION EITHER SLAVES—WELL EX-SLAVES—OR THE WORKING CLASS."

"Was it the *Melampus*?" I asked, thinking about the millions who'd died in the resulting barrage. It was ruthless but hardly outside of the Community's doctrine of war. They tended to view legitimate military targets to be more along how the Allies had during WW2 than being more concerned with precision bombing. Civilian targets were acceptable if they were supporting the enemy's infrastructure or pushed the enemy forces into surrender quicker. It was something that sickened me and I'd done my best to oppose but, until now, I hadn't any authority to affect change.

"PROBABLY," all of the Trishes said simultaneously.

"Then someone was very stupid or very smart to get the Community involved in a local conflict," I said, staring. "It seems like Karl the Conqueror's intended coup didn't go the way he'd expected."

"I admit, I did not see that coming," Jack said, giving a pair of thumbs up. "Glad I switched sides, err, I mean was always a spy all along."

I glared at him.

My father just smiled in the fakest way imaginable.

Elektra breathed out a sigh of relief before going to Hannah and giving her a hug. Hannah looked shell-shocked, which was a strange reaction under the circumstances.

"I missed the war," Hannah muttered.

Major Tom got up from his seat and walked to Hannah, too. "If you need a therapy session, know my door is always open."

He then joined Elektra in hugging her, much to both women's visible discomfort.

This seemed way too easy, but I wasn't going to say that aloud. "Any luck with the communications array?"

There was a sparking noise as I turned to see Princess Huggypants had ripped off the holographic console's plexiglass exterior and was jiggling away with three multitools simultaneously. "FEEL MY WRATH, MACHINE! I AM YOUR MASTER!"

"Uh huh," I said, deciding that it was my destiny to be surrounded by weirdos. Kermit and I had that in common at least.

Danny did a double take from his console. "Hey, she got it working again! We can hail the *Melampus*."

"Really?" Shelly asked.

"Then do so," I said, pointing at the view screen.

Moments later, an image of a beautiful, almost marble-like bridge with blocky quartz-like consoles and incandescent holograms floating in the air appeared. A crew of humans, Sorkanan, Verdantians, and Drolochids were present. However, it was the captain and the women beside her that stunned me.

My great-aunt, Katerina Tagashi, was a greying, Asiatic woman who appeared to be in her mid-to-late fifties but was a hundred and twenty years old. She was in her white Admiral's uniform and looking at me with as much a stunned look on her face as I was undoubtedly wearing. Apparently, she was captaining the *Melampus*.

Beside her was Leah Mass, a little older but not appreciably so, wearing the ceremonial robes of a Crius noblewoman, with ridges on the bridge of her nose, as the women tended to decorate themselves with. Several necklaces were around her neck, symbols of office on Crius and marked her as the planetary prime minister as well as Warlord—I looked them up. Beside her was a five- or six-year-old girl with pink hair and eyes very similar to my own. She was wearing an oversized Space Cadet Sally t-shirt with jean shorts and flip flops.

Astrid.

"Hi, Vance," Leah said, speaking first. "Allow me to introduce you to your daughter."

"Hi Dad," Astrid waved. "Nice to meet you."

Her eyes were like full moons and a brilliant shade of white. I also saw the tips of her ears were pointed. She was an Ethereal like Shelly or Elektra but different somehow.

"What the hell have you been up to?" Kathy asked.

I didn't have any words to respond, still staring at the girl.

CHAPTER TWENTY

On Board the *Melampus*

"What are you wearing?" I asked, looking at Pink as I flew the shuttle toward the *Melampus*. "You look like you escaped a Brigid music video."

Pink had dressed up in a golden metal-studded bikini top, golden hot pants, and a frigging cape of all things with a disabled energy lance-equipped pistol. I, by contrast, was wearing my nicest civilian clothes that I'd managed to rescue, which were a simple pair of slacks and a button-down shirt.

"I'm dressing up as a pirate," Pink said. "Just one of those fun epic adventure pirates versus the murderous scum kind that I normally am."

"You look ridiculous," Shelly said, standing in the back of the cockpit. Unlike me, she'd packed her dress whites and seemed excited by the chance of visiting the dreadnought. I hadn't been able to talk to her about how she felt seeing Leah and Astrid, assuming she felt anything at all. I got the impression she was doing her best to suppress any feelings on the subject.

"Your husband helped dress me," Pink said, wryly.

"My husband is ten kinds of Brigid stereotypes rolled into one," Shelly said. "That's why I love him."

I finally let go of my jealousy at hearing those words from her. It was about the eighth or ninth time I had. "He's a ship's counselor who shoots people. But I'm glad he makes you happy."

"Wow, are you a lousy liar," Shelly said, snorting.

I grimaced. "I am a great liar, thank you. I'm just not good in this precise situation."

"Meeting your baby mama and surrogate mama in one?" Pink asked, looking at me. "No, I can't say I'd be feeling the same."

"I'm so jealous," Shelly said, gazing at the ESS *Melampus* as we approached. "The greatest ship ever constructed by humanity. Not even Albion can match it."

"It's not the *Dreadnought* but her sister-ship," I reminded her. "But yes, Great-Aunt Kathy definitely deserves it."

"You know you outrank her, right?" Shelly asked, always more aware of these things than I was. "Even if you died right now, you would only be the second human ever to be one of the High Protectors."

I could tell it was causing Shelly to have all manner of mixed feelings. Despite being decades older than me and much more experienced, Shelly's aborted career path had always been a source of contention between us. While racism had largely disappeared from the human race, speciesism was alive and well with EarthGov thinking it was inappropriate for Home Fleet ships to be captained by anyone other than humans.

Exceptions had been made, but they were usually transfers from other branches of Space Fleet like the late Captain Klaws. There was also the fact that Shelly was pathologically incapable of not speaking her mind, a quality I admired in her, but it wasn't exactly a benefit when dealing with the Navy's politics.

"Yes, Anne Bonny," Pink said, surprising me with her knowledge of history. "She was an Earth pirate kidnapped by a bunch of Albion privateers who worked her way up through the ranks of the Commonwealth fleet to its admiralty before damned near single-handedly defeating the Crystal Spider Empire. That got her named High Protector by the Senate. Supposedly, as Anne died from a rival poisoning her, she had all her treasures and trophies loaded on her ship before it was sent to wander the galaxy, making random jumps for the rest of eternity."

"You know I actually saw the *CSS Mary Read* during the war," I said, remembering my days as second officer on the ESS *Ares*. "Shelly was there too."

"Bullsavit," Pink said.

"We saw *something*," Shelly muttered. "But as usual, Vance's imagination runs away with me."

"Can we focus on getting aboard?" Hannah called from the back of the shuttle. "I want to find out what happened to my world."

"We'll find out," I said, pausing. "I try not to be too political—"

Both Shelly and Pink snorted simultaneously.

"Sure, Captain Speech," Pink said, rolling her eyes. "Let's go hear your latest hippie commie space yacht progressive spiel about how all the rich people are bad and how we should give candy to the Notha and criminals."

I glared at her. "You're a *pirate*."

"And I love candy," Pink said. "That doesn't mean you don't sound ridiculous every time you open your mouth. I thought you military types were supposed to be hyper conservative."

"Vance was educated by utopian media and AI," Shelly said, finding a rare moment of agreement with Pink. "But apparently that doesn't stop him from failing upwards."

"I may not agree with what others have to say but I will fight to the death for their right to say it," I said, puffing out my chest. "I expect my opponents to do the same."

"And that's stupid," Pink muttered. "Fairness means crap in a real fight. With words or guns, if you're fighting, fight to win. It's survival of the fittest in the void."

The shuttle finally landed in the *Melampus'* aft hangar bay, which was one of four hangars built into the massive vessel. The *Melampus* was only twice as large as the ESS *Ares* and I'd seen much, much larger vessels like the *Emperor's Reach*, which had been fourteen kilometers long. But there was something about this place that just felt big and grandiose.

The interior of the ship was no less grand, with wide cathedral-like arches, large windows, and armor that resembled ceremonial wear for the ship's onboard Marines. The Olympic-class had been luxurious compared to most vessels, more like a hotel than a warship, but this was something else entirely and showed that Earth was moving toward the aesthetics of the Community. It made me feel fantastically underdressed.

Following me were Pink, Shelly, Hannah, Princess Huggypants (who'd insisted on coming and I hadn't had the heart to refuse), and the High Priestess. I'd decided to leave Danny behind in charge and gave orders to Forty-Two to shoot my father if he tried anything. It wasn't my proudest moment as an officer, but I didn't trust the man not to try to stage a munity among the pirates. They'd been promised pardons and a reward for what they'd done so far, which was a great prize for not doing much, but I didn't think the temptation to try to boost the *Siege Perilous* before heading off into deep space was completely off the table.

I couldn't help but think about the ship's name. Melampus was a legendary soothsayer and healer, famous for introducing the worship of Dionysus, the god of wine, to Greece. He could also talk to animals. In the vision of the distant future I'd been given by Cthulhu—long story—I'd seen a ship named after Cthulhu. I wondered if, in some weird way, that ship was named after this one. It was a far better name than *Ares*, at least, and bespoke the fact that a captain of a Community starship should be a healer and predicter of the future but also a bringer of great joy. The talking to animals thing just reminded me of how I'd been described by Trish as Captain Kirk leading the Muppets.

You really are, Prime Trish said in my mind.

Don't worry, Goth Trish said. *We'll all be silent when you're meeting your daughter.*

We're all happy for you, Seventies Trish said.

Except me. I'm horribly jealous, Teen Trish said.

I'm happy for you, Prime Trish said. *Even if I now hate you, I'm happy for you.*

Bish! Goth Trish said. *You are so mean to him!*

You are not Prime Trish; I didn't vote for you! Seventies Trish said.

We're all Prime Trish but I'm more Prime Trish than anyone, Teen Trish said.

I wondered if having so many voices in my head meant I was insane or just should seriously reconsider shutting off my cybernetics. In the end, I decided to focus on meeting with my great-aunt and Leah instead.

And Astrid.

Rather than being met in the hangar bay, we were all escorted by a squad of the Community Marines to a lounge overlooking it. It was a large, gray room with big, fluffy couches, chairs, and its own bar. It was another reminder that this vessel was designed more for diplomacy and exploration than combat despite the utter hash they'd made of the Enigmatic Path fleet. I could just imagine a bunch of dignitaries coming up here to lounge about while waiting to be properly seated.

Like us.

Either way, Kathy and Leah were there. Astrid was standing beside them, holding up an infopad as her attention was focused entirely on what appeared to be a video game instead of meeting her biological father. Which, hey, when I was five or six I had the exact same reaction.

"Hello, Vance," Kathy said, smiling. "Welcome aboard the *Melampus*. I bet you have a lot of questions—"

"Kneel before me, weakling! You are in the presence of your betters and must bow! Bow before greatness!" Princess Huggypants said, walking on four hand/legs and pointing with one of her remaining two hands. Standing upright, Princess Huggypants probably amounted to four foot nothing, so it was hilarious seeing her threaten my five-feet-eleven great-aunt.

Kathy looked down at Princess Huggypants before looking at me. "I see you continue to pick up oddballs like an old woman collect cats."

"That's unfair to women who collect cats," Leah said, looking at me with an emotion I didn't expect: trepidation. It was strange but I was genuinely happy to see her. "Vance, Shelly, this is your daughter, Astrid."

"Sup," Astrid said, not looking away from infopad. She blew a pink bubble of gum before popping it. "Thanks for saving the universe from the Primordials, by the way."

The armored Marines left us alone in the room.

"I'm not sure you're meant to know about the Primordials—" I started to say before being interrupted.

"You evil bish!" Shelly shouted, pointing at Leah. "Gene-thief, schemer, psychopath! Take your telepathic spycraft, lies, and shove yourself out an airlock!"

Astrid looked up from her infopad. "Okay, *now* I'm interested."

"Captain T'Ketra—" Kathy started to speak.

"No!" Shelly said, suddenly aware she'd said what had been on her mind. "I am not going to normalize this! Our DNA was stolen, Vance! Stolen and used to create a lifeform—"

"Right here," Astrid said, raising her hand.

"—used to create a lifeform without our permission!" Shelly said, ignoring her. "It's a monstrous violation and I will not stand here as you normalize it, Vance!"

"Uh huh," I said, pausing. "Are you done?"

"Y-yes," Shelly said, clearly realizing she'd overstepped in front of an Admiral then facepalming. Especially since she'd just called said Admiral's grandniece a "lifeform."

"That's all incredibly true and moving," Leah said. "One slight issue, though. I didn't make Astrid."

"What?" Shelly asked, blinking.

"Huh," I said, just as surprised.

Leah nodded. "She's not even my own biological child. Though I was considering having one and still plan to get one tubed. I found her on Crius at an abandoned Department Twelve facility, tubed with hundreds of other children from various bloodlines. The clonemasters arrived just before the resistance invaded and had planned to dissolve all their work. Thankfully, they weren't able to. When we ran the DNA scans, we found Astrid was a combination of your DNA and Shelly's. All of the other children were created by mixing Ethereal DNA with those of known agents of the Elder Races."

Well, that was a kick in the gut and I wasn't sure how to react—a common occurrence these days. Department Twelve was a Security Department that had been officially dissolved after the Notha War due to its role in escalating tensions until there had been an exchange of SKAMMS where billions died. Captain Elgan had been one of its agents and had been on a mission to recover Elder Race technology even though doing so was a sure ticket to getting your planet annihilated.

Doing the math rather quickly established that Department Twelve shouldn't have even been in existence when Astrid was born—or grown in this case—and its continued existence was a crime against sapience. Or at least a violation of countless galactic laws against operating a rogue intelligence agency. It added another layer to things if it was working on scientific experiments on a sanctioned planet like Crius.

"Yeah," Astrid said, looking up and speaking in a very adult tone. "I'm like a superhuman they grew in a lab. Part-Elf, part Goofy Space Hero. No offense, Captain Turbo, but I've seen my mom's memories of you."

"None taken," I said, unsure how to respond. "It's like discovering you're the descendant of Captain Jack Danger on Space Cadet Sally."

Ah, yes, the comic relief guy.

"*Some* should be taken," Shelly said, staring. "I-I don't know how to respond to this."

Shelly wandered over to one of the overstuffed couches and ended up almost swallowed by the thing.

"You thought I'd steal your DNA?" Leah asked, hurt.

"It's what Director G thinks happened," I replied. "Also, you did spend years pretending to be a woman my age to recruit me into Department Twelve."

"We call that grooming," Kathy said, giving Leah a nasty look.

"I thought Vance was the sort of amoral scheming trickster that would fit in," Leah said, smiling. "I was wrong. Giving him the chance to be a Space Fleet officer allowed him to succeed in becoming the kind of paragon example set by his great-aunt. As for Director G, I'm a member of Albion's Watchers on loan to the EarthGov section of the Community Security Departments. He's not my real boss and that doesn't mean I tell him everything—especially when it involves my daughter, a girl born from the blood of legendary heroes."

Kathy rolled her eyes. "You're laying it on a little thick, Madame President."

"Yeah, how did that happen?" I asked. "Immigrant to ruler of the planet in a decade is pretty fast."

"There's no barrier to people born on other planets serving in the government," Leah said. "Most of the oldest patriarchs of the aristocracy are still the original colonists and Karma Corp executives who bought noble titles and land here a century and a half ago. So, I just bought myself a title and set free all the slaves. No one wanted me here save as a Community liaison but I found that a lot more people were uncomfortable with Crius' situation than you'd think. It turns out unless you breed out all sense of human empathy, which some families did, most modern people are against slavery. So, I was elected President when everyone else was either dead or under arrest."

Yeah, that story kind of buried the lead.

"That doesn't explain how it became a war," I asked.

"Yes?" Hannah finally spoke up. "Is it really over? How?"

"Allenway III screwed up," Kathy explained. "He's been running his own private paramilitary force and war against the insurgency for years. His taste of freedom and power as Karl the Conqueror left him unwilling to just play noble on a backwater. So, he allied with the Enigmatic Path and planned a coup."

"Yeah, we knew that part," I said, surprised they'd figured out Karl's identity, but not too surprised. "I just wonder why you didn't arrest him much earlier."

"We didn't want just him," Kathy said. "We wanted his entire network and who was financing him. Someone helped him steal the *Siege Perilous* all those years ago and kept him supplied as a pirate after he took off. Plus, there were missing SKAMMS."

I nodded. "Trish is still working on recovering the ship's files, but it seems the ship's SKAMMS were disabled a long time ago. He couldn't get them working without the Community authorization codes. For once, WMD security actually worked out."

Kathy nodded. "We suspected that he planned to take the *Jovial Empress* hostage and use conspirators in the Crius Navy to take over their ships before attacking the planet with his pirate fleet."

"The bomb went off and killed everyone instead, instead," Leah said, disgusted. "Also, his fleet didn't show up until you arrived with it on your tail."

"I suspect my father diverted it to try to take me hostage," I replied.

"Your father?" Leah asked, surprised.

"Yeah, I saw him on the bridge," Kathy said, disgusted. "I should be shocked that he's still alive but you can't kill a cockroach unless you step on it directly."

"A well-chosen metaphor," I replied.

189

"Can we get back to my homeworld?" Hannah asked.

"I was visiting with Admiral Tagashi on the *Melampus* when the bomb went off," Leah said. "I was hiding my daughter on board."

"The safest place to be," Kathy said. "The vessel was to be delivered as a gift to Earth's greatest hero and I just happened to be passing by when I received Leah's transmission. I was the closest Community vessel given the poor long-range communications here. Funny coincidence, huh?"

"Yeah, funny," I said, wondering who had arranged it.

"Well, the *Jovial Empress'* destruction was an act of war against the Community and the presence of the *Melampus* intimidated the Naval mutiny into submission. That was when a full insurrection broke out on the surface. They attempted to massacre every one of my allies and their families plus mass purges of slaves to intimidate the locals."

"And you bombed them and their positions from orbit," I said.

"General Sherman was my inspiration," Kathy replied. "To defeat the Confederacy, you have to burn Atlanta. The cities were the bases for the slave trade even if they were not where the clones were grown. Also, the richest and most powerful members of the nobility lived in the cities. Elgan didn't understand you had to root out this kind of culture root and stem. The military stubbornly held out for a while longer before we arrested Allenway III and about a thousand of his followers that we're holding on board the ship."

"He should have taken the honorable way out and shot himself, but he was too much of a coward to do so," Leah said. "Instead, we'll transfer him to the court on Throneworld and put him on trial for crimes against sapience. The treason, munity, piracy, and other charges he committed as Karl will just be icing on the cake."

"So, it's really over," Hannah said, looking like she needed someone to lean on in order to avoid collapsing. "We're all free."

"Are you sure we should be discussing all this dark and terrible stuff in front of, uh, our daughter?" I asked, pointing to Astrid. This was some pretty dark stuff.

"I'm a psychic, too, Dad," Astrid said. "Believe me, I've felt much worse. You can't imagine what went through the heads of a lot of these slave lords. People get up to some pretty sick savit when they have absolute power."

Leah patted our daughter on the head. She then spoke to me via our mind link that I hadn't felt in a long time. *She's a spectacular young girl, Vance. So much like you and growing stronger in her mental alacrity each day but also keeping her innate empathy. She's already reading at a college level. She can tear through books in minutes. I'm proud to be her mother.*

That's...great, I said, feeling a mixture of feelings regarding my daughter being a genetically engineered prodigy like me. I'd grown up educated by Alfred the AI and he'd filled my mind with vast amounts of mathematics, history, science, and more Pre-First Contact pop culture to keep my ADHD-riddled mind from ever being distracted for long. It had been a lonely and isolating existence, though.

Maybe she needs a sibling, Leah suggested.

I did a double take.

"Crius may have lost its ruling class but there are still some who sided with Leah and are going to wield power in the next government like the Plantagenets, Lucifers, and Blackwoods," Kathy said. "It'll be decades of military occupation, bringing the planet up to Community standards, and essentially rewriting the culture to be anti-slavery. Some people will oppose that, and it'll be hit or miss whether they respond with violence. Will they perceive it as a Marshall Plan or colonialist takeover?"

"It sounds like you have your work cut out for you," I said, wanting to talk to Leah in private. "At least you have a great ship for it."

"Oh, it's not our ship," Kathy said. "It's yours, Vance."

CHAPTER TWENTY-ONE

Walking Around the *Melampus*

I stared at her. "No way."

"I borking knew it," Shelly muttered, staring. "As soon as they mentioned Earth's greatest warrior, I knew it would somehow end up being Vance."

"Oh, grow a pair," Kathy said, looking down at her. "Not everything is about you."

"Obviously!" Shelly said.

"Your behavior is unbecoming a Space Fleet officer," Kathy said. "Albeit, even I'm surprised about this."

"Shelly is a fantastic officer and one of the best I've ever worked with," I defended her. "If anyone deserves command of a ship like this—"

"Oh spare me the false humility," Kathy said, rolling her eyes. "You saved the entire galaxy, apparently. It's a state secret about the Primordials, so of course it's all over every comm unit what happened at Deathworld. The High Council of the Community ordered this given to you directly along with your promotion. It also accompanied a giant aid package, so EarthGov was all too willing to accept it."

"Who is going to command the ESS *Dreadnought*?" I asked, surprised I cared at this point.

"It's going to be the flagship of the Home Fleet and they've offered it to me," Kathy said. "As an Admiral, I'm going to be mostly doing ceremony and paperwork, so it'll need a captain. I was going to offer the position to Captain T'Ketra."

"I'll do it," Shelly spoke up.

Kathy stared down. "But I'm not sure she can—"

Shelly looked like a kicked puppy crossed with one of Santa's elves.

Kathy paused. "Sure, congratulations, Fleet Captain."

"Yes!" Shelly said, balling her fists.

"It seems Vance is a bad influence on her," Leah said, softly.

Fleet Captain was about as high as Shelly had ever aspired to be and should have been her rank decades ago, but events as well as politics had constantly thwarted her. I wasn't going to spoil it by pointing out that her promotion was less on merit than, ironically, her very association with the people she'd originally thought were going to drag her down. That, unfortunately, was how the game was played and it left me with a sour taste in my mouth.

Hannah was the only one who seemed to realize this wasn't a completely positive thing for me. "Are you okay, Vance?"

"I'm not sure," I replied.

Unlike on television, you didn't have the ability to turn down promotions or ship transfers. That's what a chain of command was about, you did what you were told. I might have been able to anyway given I was still trying to figure out what being a High Protector meant as well as what kind of authority I wielded. However, the fact was that giving up the ESS *Ares* was made markedly easier by the fact it no longer would be having a lot of the people I'd come to depend on being there. The band was breaking up and going its separate ways and there was no way to preserve that.

Really, my biggest concern would be whether the Community would allow Trish to serve in her present fragmented state. Prime Trish had already indicated she'd planned to leave with Hannah and while the war was no longer happening, I definitely got the impression she didn't want to continue serving with me. I also didn't know what to think of the other fragments' ability to serve.

We'll let you know, Goth Trish said.

None of the others said anything.

"It's a mixed crew of humans, Sorkanan, Drolochids, Bugs, Sklux, and more," Kathy said. "A more diverse crew than you'll be used to serving with and in the Community's chain of command directly.

You'll answer only to the Inner Council and have your own private operating budget as well as the ability to define your own mission parameters. Unfortunately, that also means the credit will stop with you and any mistakes are going to fall entirely on your shoulders. Across thousands of worlds, there are only about sixty High Protectors and they each wield disproportionate power over policy."

"I'm starting to get that," I said, having the less than sneaking suspicion—more like walking through the front door really—that the High Protectors were most if not all agents of the Elder Races. It would be another way for them to exert power over the Community without overtly appearing to do so. That made this seem more like a bribe than a reward for meritorious service. On the other hand, every bit of power I could exert for the greater good was a good thing. Right? Or was that what all tyrants told themselves at the start of their careers? Still, it was a nice ship.

"I'd like to bring some of my crew over," I said, wondering if I could persuade any of the ones who had said they were leaving to come along. It bothered me that Light on Water was probably the only one I could one hundred percent depend on. I was really too hard on that annoying gelatin tentacle monster—which was probably being speciesist.

"You have complete operational control," Kathy said, shaking her head. "Choose your own crew by hand for all the High Council cares. I was presented with the job of giving you the book of rules and responsibilities—it's about eight million pages long so hire an AI to read it for you—and the sword."

"The sword?" I asked.

"This you're going to love," Kathy said, a mischievous look on her face. She snapped her fingers and a Space Fleet ensign walked in carrying a pillow bearing a sheathed sword on a belt. My attention was briefly diverted by the fact the woman was nearly identical to Hannah except for stark white hair and significantly less muscle tone. She was obviously one of the many clones of Crius. She was also in a Community Lieutenant's uniform. Hannah stared at her as if she'd seen a ghost.

Or bodiless manifestation.

"Thank you, Hannah," Kathy said, referring to her Hannah rather than mine. She then drew the sword—which was obviously a technological device of some kind despite its basis on an Earthly weapon—and handed it over to me.

I took it and immediately felt a strange link with the sword via my ring, which glowed as soon as I held the weapon. As soon as I thought it, the weapon started sparkling and crackling with lightning up and down the blade. The air ionized around the weapon, and I felt a barrier surround my body that was far easier to conjure than the one I summoned with my ring.

"Okay, this is the coolest goddamn thing ever," I said, staring at the weapon before deactivating it.

"Congratulations, biological parent-unit," Astrid said, looking up from her game. "You've hit Nova Level. You get the Nova Level character skins, equipment, and access to the microtransactions on the online store. Wee."

I looked down at her. "Children your age shouldn't be that sarcastic."

"Yeah, it took you until you were ten to have that bad of an attitude," Kathy said.

"Getting her away from Crius is a top priority," Leah said. "Otherwise, I fear my little darling will go full Saint Alia of the Knife."

I'd shown Leah the twenty-second-century *Dune* movies during our first year together. It probably should have been a warning sign that she'd described the society as far more realistic and reflecting the Community than "The Star Trippers."

You kept trying to persuade me otherwise, Leah thought to me. *It was cute and kind of sad.*

"You're not staying on Crius?" Hannah asked, surprised. "But you're the President?"

"I'm a spy not a politician," Leah said, shaking her head. "Crius will need decades of reconstruction I'm not qualified to give it. Worse, I'd be a divisive figure who would be the subject of all of the remaining Demiurge sympathizers' recriminations. I've already drafted my papers of resignation and transfer of power to an appointed military government before we start seeking local leadership. Maybe you'd like to replace me?"

Hannah looked like Leah had shoved a live Freyan death snake in her face. Apparently, Hannah had been willing to fight for her homeworld, but the prospect of staying there to rebuild it was something else entirely.

"It's not often someone turns down the rulership of a planet out of hand," I said, bemused.

"Speaking of ruling planets, may I ask your mother figure a question, Lord Satan?" The High Priestess spoke up.

"Sure," I said. "You have my infernal blessing."

My great-aunt twitched at the High Priestess' presence, having survived the worst of the Notha War and seen the absolute nastiest things the little furry fascists had been up to. "Do I even want to know, Vance?"

"He's worshiped as a demon god by the Notha," Hannah said.

"Not all of us," The High Priestess said. "Just the sane ones."

"Why do I ask when I know the answer will only make things even more confusing?" Kathy said, shaking her head. "Go ahead, Priestess."

"I was curious if you had any updates on Deathworld and my father, the President," The High Priestess said. "The political situation was fraught when we left it."

"Fraught" was one way to put it. The peace talks between Deathworld and the Notha Union had been taken only barely seriously by the Community. Deathworld had wanted its independence guaranteed by the Community if they couldn't join outright. The Notha Union wanted to annex Deathworld and threatened war if the Deathworlders joined. The thing was they'd threatened war if they didn't join either. So much had happened with Cthulhu, the Dark Matter conspiracy, and Alexandra Ares that the local politics of the Deathworld system had been lost in the shuffle.

Kathy grimaced as if realizing just what her news on the situation was. "I'm afraid the Notha Union has formally declared a state of peacekeeping enforcement on the Deathworld system. They claim the President has been brainwashed by the Community and the Elder

Races. The Community has decided to provide all the war materiel that Deathworld needs but otherwise stay out of the conflict."

I felt gutsick about the revelation and wondered if I could have changed anything if I'd stayed. Probably not. Director G had made it clear no one trusted the new Great Notha to negotiate in good faith. Cthulhu's arrival and the damage he'd done had just delayed the invasion by a week or two. The Community wasn't going to risk a confrontation with the Notha again to protect a single breakaway system either. Really, giving the Deathworlders war materiel was more than could be expected.

"I see," the High Priestess said. "So my father had me come with Captain Turbo to get me out of the way."

"Seems like it," Kathy said. "Your dad is a very brave leader."

The High Priestess was still. "No, but he's very good at acting like one."

"I also have some issues to bring up," Pink interjected. "Me and my crew were only supposed to bring Vance to Crius, but since then we've been shot at, blown up, caught in a civil war, and involved in seizing an infamous rogue battleship. Vance has made some guarantees, but I want them in writing."

"Oh, is she part of your crew?" Kathy asked. "I thought she was a stripper you hired."

Pink narrowed her eyes. "I am Captain—"

"I know who you are, Pink," Kathy said. "I know all about you, Captain Havelock, and Director G's little arrangement. I don't like pirates. I don't find you funny, sexy, or romantic. If Vance is going to give you a pardon or God knows what else, a letter of marque or commission, that's his business. It's his ship and crew. Just don't expect me to be polite about it."

Pink grimaced. "Ah."

"People forget Vance is the nice one to oddballs and misfits," Leah said. "Captain Tagawa is the hang them from the side of the ship type."

"That reminds me," I said, looking at Kathy. "We need to talk about my father. You didn't seem that surprised by his survival."

"No," Kathy said.

"Jack said a lot of things," I replied looking between her and Leah. "Things about me having other family and being involved with the intelligence community. Things I very much would like answers to."

"Later," Kathy said. "In private. We should give you the full tour of the *Melampus* in the meantime. We need to prepare for the full handing over of the ship and I do have to supervise the local forces that have surrendered to us. The next few weeks will be crucial to deciding whether Crius' new government will be a failed state or a future member of the Community."

That was absolutely a deflection on her part and one that I knew was just going to endure to give her time to get her story straight. Oddly, my questions weren't about the cloak and dagger bullsavit that was clearly going on behind the scenes. They were more personal ones.

If Neal Gordon and Lucy Westenra were my grandparents, then I wanted to know why I'd never been told. Why had I been raised by Kathy's household AI rather than other members of my family when she couldn't look after me as well as fulfill her job? I knew why she kept me from Danny's side of the family, but this was another sign my great-aunt had wanted to keep me away from influences other than hers at the expense of giving me a childhood.

"Great," Astrid said, having switched from playing her game to watching a cartoon about an Australian sheep dog. "Now we get to spend the next few hours wandering around a starship staring at carpet."

"We'll get ice cream after," I said, looking down at her.

"So, your tactic is bribery?" Astrid asked.

"Yes," I replied.

"I approve," Astrid said, nodding. Her enhanced intelligence and telepathy had clearly created a much more adult persona than most children her age. I also didn't know how Ethereals matured but understood they did so rapidly. Still, all children loved ice cream. It was only adults who pretended not to. Well, the lactose tolerant ones at least.

"Vance, you should know that I try and manage her diet to maximize her nutritional and emotional development," Leah said.

"Ice cream has been promised!" Astrid said. "Violation of this compact would be considered an act of war."

Leah sighed.

Shelly gazed up at us, looking like she was contemplating joining in before turning her head away. It seemed she couldn't reach out and accept the young girl as her own. Which was understandable but meant any future relationship would probably just be between me, Astrid, and Leah. That was assuming I believed Leah's tale that it hadn't been her but Section Twelve who'd created the child.

And I did. It was too insane of a story to make up and fit more with the Leah that I believed her to be than the one she'd occasionally shown me through all of her lies and manipulations. We'd shared a connection once and I still believed that to be real even if nothing else had been. That didn't answer all of my questions, though.

Why would Section Twelve want to create a child from my DNA, though? Was it because they knew I was an Elder Race agent? Did they know that they'd modified me? How did Shelly fit into this? Was it just because she was an Ethereal? One raised on a Notha prison planet? Or did they have a bigger plan that Leah had interrupted by finding their cloning facility? Did I have any other relatives being grown out there? What sort of crazzap had they implanted in Astrid's brain while growing her?

"I'll want to speak with Allenway—Karl the Conqueror—too," I said, trying to sort through all of my emotions. "I don't expect him to tell the truth any more than Jack, but maybe by comparing stories I can find out who arranged my ambush as well as who killed most of the crew. Someone leaked our location."

Hannah looked away in a gesture that I found to be immediately suspicious but dismissed. She would never betray me or the others.

"All in good time," Kathy said.

The tour of the ship went without incident. It was almost surreal wandering around a crew that wasn't made of the bottom rung of Space Academy or a bunch of genius weirdos. Everyone was cool, calm, and professional—I didn't like it one bit. The place also resembled someone's idea of planet Krypton crossed with old Golden Age sci-fi decor from before even my retro love of the genre. The

Community Capital Worlds were places of crystal spires and togas, which was reflected in the aesthetic here. About the only thing that felt familiar was the discovery the ship's AI, SWAY-Z, was based on an actor from the Nineteen Eighties who insisted on referring to the ship as "The Roadhouse." SWAY-Z promised to kick my teeth in if I didn't treat the ship right.

I liked him.

In the end, we were all assigned extremely lavish quarters and treated to the full honors reserved for dignitaries. Leah invited me for dinner and to spend some more time with our daughter, which I eagerly accepted.

Annnnnnd we ended up having sex.

Which was not an emotional complication I could afford right now.

CHAPTER TWENTY-TWO

Charting a New Course for the Future

So, I had sex with Leah.

Yeah, I know.

Terrible idea.

But I'd *really* needed that.

Both of us did.

The captain's quarters surrounding us looked like a movie set with tapestries, banners, and a bed that was big enough for six comfortably. I was lying naked underneath the shimmersilk sheets and staring up at a crystgem chandelier that could have bought Earth a new flagship. Leah was sleeping beside me, her naked back exposed.

Astrid was presently off to bed in her own room in the diplomatic quarters, presently reserved for Prime Minister Mass, which I was still trying to wrap my head around. Apparently, Leah had a whole staff of nannies and bodyguards to look after Astrid's education. Being telepaths, they appreciated their distance from one another. I got the impression privacy was a lucrative commodity for both.

This was the second time I'd had sex with an ex in the past month and I was starting to realize how much of it was because I'd tried to keep all my relationships frozen in time. Sleeping with Shelly had been a huge mistake, even if—no, *especially* if—her husband didn't mind. I'd come here certain that Leah violated my trust and taken my DNA to create a child. Now I felt ridiculous because she'd looked after my daughter for five years.

Adopted her as her own.

I suddenly had no idea what I was going to do or hoped to accomplish here. Certainly, it seemed like Leah had everything well in hand and I didn't need to involve myself further. The Sons of the Demiurge weren't going to be threatening Astrid anymore. Hell, Crius was freed from the slave lords and clone masters even if it was arguably no more independent than it was a year ago. But what now? Did I just plan to pop on board my ship and fly away?

Leaving Astrid to be raised by Leah? Did I want to challenge her for custody? A starship captain made for a poor guardian without another parent as my own childhood with Great-Aunt Kathy attested. Did I want to just station myself nearby Leah to be close to her and derail my career? Say, "no thank you" to the High Protector promotion and take a desk job? Honestly, the latter was more tempting than it sounded as I wasn't the kind of man to abandon family.

"You know we're still linked, right?" Leah asked, obviously not asleep. "I can hear you brooding."

"Sorry," I said, looking over to her. "It's been a very trying month."

"You stopped the Primordials, but it was at immense cost," Leah said, sitting up and holding the sheet in front of her chest. "Especially Trish. I know you love her. Now she's broken."

None of the Trishes responded, which made me wonder if they were still in the back of my head. It would have made the next part of my conversation awkward. "My relationship with Trish is complex. Even before the fragmentation. Love may or may not be the best word for what we share."

Trish and I had been together longer than most marriages, but she'd always kept her distance from anything that might have been a more permanent bond. Humans and AI could legally marry on some worlds, but the Community remained shy about legal recognition. Earth was the most permissive world regarding AIs as more than equipment, and Earth was incredibly restrictive.

Prejudice still existed and my father's reaction showed how I'd been treated by many with even the whiff of my relationship with her. I'd never denied it, but most people assumed it was simply a fetish rather than real emotion—and Trish had demanded I never say otherwise. Trish had worried about me torpedoing my career as an identified sexual deviant and had always kept anything we shared as strictly "friends with benefits."

Then I'd ended up being tortured by Trish's mental "sister," Alexandra Ares. Both Trish and Alexandra had been created from the failed brain upload of Patricia Ares, founder of Ares Electronics. Identical cores were transformed by experiences into two very different personalities. The experience had been entirely virtual, but the pain had been real and so had the revelation that she'd been hiding a lot of private communications with Director G. That had been before the fragmentation that had left me unaware whether the Trish I knew was still alive.

"A captain's first love will always be his ship," Leah said, staring. "But that doesn't mean they can't love another."

I stared at her. "Leah, why did you send me the locket."

"I didn't," Leah said, staring at me.

"Oh," I said, taking a deep breath.

So, it had been part of the ambush, a lure to bring me in. That didn't mean there wasn't a traitor or spy among us, they'd have to know the exact place we'd be leaving and in what vessel, but it did mean this had all been prearranged.

"I wanted you to come visit us on your own," Leah said. "I guess it took a sense of danger to make you want to."

I closed my eyes. "I was afraid."

"Afraid of a little girl?" Leah asked.

"Afraid of a chance at a new life," I replied. "I've wanted to be more than Vance Turbo: Hero of Space—"

"You forgot the echo," Leah said.

I laughed but it was a short gallows' chuckle. "I wanted to be someone who was just for me and those closest to me. Then I realized I didn't know if such a person existed. I've always been a product of what the media made me. Of what other people expected of me. The one time I tried to decide for myself, dropping out of Space Academy, I ended up dragooned by a rogue intelligence agency."

Leah grimaced. "Yeah, you went from being a lovable rogue to Sir Lancelot in ten seconds flat."

"Lancelot destroyed Camelot," I pointed out. "By being unable to keep it in his pants with his best friend's wife."

"Arthur deserves some credit for that," Leah pointed out. "What with borking his sister and all that."

"Yeah," I muttered.

"I don't want to be a spy anymore," Leah said, shocking me.

"What?" I asked, staring at her.

Leah had been a spy for decades by the time we'd met. Longevity treatments being what they were, we still looked the same age when she was closer to Shelly's. She'd tricked me, deceived me, and manipulated me throughout the time I'd thought we were in love.

"Ouch," Leah said.

"No fair reading my mind," I muttered.

"I was reading your face," Leah said, softly. "I have a revelation for you about the Security Departments, Vance. You know how Director G is one of the most manipulative, conniving, dangerous men in the galaxy who abets all manner of crime and probably worse?"

"Yeah," I said, disgusted with the man.

"He's probably the most noble and decent person in the Community Intelligence leadership by far," Leah said, horrified.

"Ah," I said, staring at her.

"I believed in Captain Elgan when I joined his crew, trying to find a place where I could combine the idealism that I felt with doing the work I knew needed to be done but it turned out his ideology was just a cover for rage against all of Earth's enemies. Inevitably, you eventually either quit or you become someone like...your father."

"My father," I said.

Leah nodded. "I know a bit more about him than you do from Great-Aunt Kathy, the files declassified by my promotion to section chief, and from his own lips if you want to hear about him."

"I'm not sure in bed with a woman is a place to discuss my daddy issues," I replied. "I'm more a Jung man than Freud."

Leah snorted. "Your Great-Aunt Kathy kept you from your grandparents after his death because they're spies, too, or at least agents of Department Zero. Director G had gotten his hands onto Jack early on and shaped him to be something that was supposed to make the galaxy a better place. Instead, it made him—"

"Him," I said, pausing. "So he's not a pirate, he's a spy."

"He's whatever his job requires him to be," Leah said. "But when Jack faked his death with his wife, he was attempting to escape working for the intelligence community. Unfortunately, by that time, the damage was done. He couldn't stop being who he'd become. Assuming there was ever a chance that he couldn't be."

"Do you know what happened to my mother?" I asked, half-worried he had killed her. I didn't know Jack Tagashi and probably never could. Not really. I wasn't sure I wanted to either. Now he was like Captain Elgan in my mind, someone lost to the Machine. Which was a weird damn sentiment for a military man to have, I had to admit. Maybe Pink and Shelly were onto something.

"According to Jack, he and your mother split up six months after they faked their deaths," Leah said. "There was considerable friction upon leaving you behind."

"She wanted to bring me with them?" I asked.

"Jack did," Leah said.

"Ah," I said, frowning. I wasn't sure I believed her or assumed that had come from Jack's mouth. But if it was true, well, I was better off without her.

"I've got some possible identities she might have been using but, well, the most likely one is that she went on to defraud a trillion people with a multi-level marketing scam," Leah said.

"My parents are just the gift that keeps on giving," I muttered.

"My parents rejected me for my powers and modifications," Leah said.

"They did?" I asked.

"No, they love me and still send me Mithrasday cards," Leah said. "However, I can't stand to be the person this job is making me here. When I came to Crius, I wanted to set up an Underground Railroad, help free the people, and be a new Lincoln or Spartacus. Instead, I ended up burning the planet with your great-aunt like the Dragon Girl."

"Daenerys Targaryen?" I asked, remembering us watching the twenty-third-century series of nine movies. I got the impression she hadn't been paying much attention.

"Yeah, from *The Lord of the Rings*," Leah said, confirming it. "Also, don't give me that look. My brain has biomods, not cybernetics like yours. It doesn't have perfect recall of thousands of bits of trivia and the ability to download a million films instantly."

"It doesn't work that way," I said, pausing. "Usually. I don't think what you did here on Crius was the worst thing possible. Revolutions are rarely won by the timid. There's a pretty good argument that Reconstruction wouldn't have failed if the Americans were more decisive. I probably wouldn't have done it the way that you did, but I also understand it may have been necessary to set these people free."

"Are you just telling me this because we slept together and I'm the mother of your child?" Leah asked.

"Absolutely," I admitted, reaching over to squeeze her hand. "I'm no more immune to being a hypocrite with the people I lo...care about than anyone else."

"I think you're a good man, Vance Turbo," Leah said, lowering her sheet to take my hands with both of hers.

It was distracting.

"Really Vance?" Leah asked, reading my mind.

"Evolution is working against me, here," I said, smiling. "The sight of you undressed is not a time for serious conversation."

Leah slid out of bed and put on her bra, panties, and a t-shirt before sliding back in. "Is that better?"

"Nope, still thinking about boobs," I admitted. "But yes, I think you should leave the Security Departments. If you feel you can't be the good you want to make in the universe then you need to find a place you can."

Leah snorted. "Yeah. You've shown that you can do that and I admire that. You have a chance of making a real difference in the universe."

I wasn't so sure about that. "Most of my successes have been dumb luck and I've lost a lot of people along the way. Some to death and others to injury. I can't say the universe is a better place for my efforts."

"Except for the Primordial coming to kill us all thing," Leah said.

"Yeah, but what have I done for the galaxy lately?" I said, joking.

"Taking down Karl's battleship," Leah said.

"That was Trish," I said. "Besides, I just came here for Astrid."

"I know," Leah said. "Which is why I think we should get married."

I blinked.

Time passed.

More time passed.

Leah waved her hand in front of my face. "Vance, did you have a stroke?"

"No," I said, recovering myself. At least to a twelve percent level. "That just caught me off guard."

"I can tell," Leah said. "I'm a little surprised, though. It seems like a perfectly logical social arrangement. We share a child. You want to raise her. I have emotionally bonded to her. I want to be with her as she grows up. We could share custody, but it seems like that would be easier if we shared the same living quarters. I want more kids and think you do too. We enjoy sexual relations with one another and personal emotional time. You know, when I'm not lying or manipulating you, which I wouldn't have to do if I wasn't a spy."

It was that last part that was a stickler. "You're being very clinical about this."

"Marriage is a contract on Albion," Leah said. "Mostly about shared resources, finances, and legal commitments to raising families as well as guaranteeing access to partner bonds. You know, exactly like it's been on Earth for thousands of years unless you were of an incredibly romantic verging on outright ignorant sort."

I stared at her.

Leah closed her eyes as realization clearly struck her. "Which, of course you are."

I grimaced. "Yeah. I admit, this wasn't exactly how I expected to be hit with a proposal."

"If it's about designated sexual partners, I'll expect monogamy but would be willing to make exceptions for Shelly, Tri—"

"Aren't you already married?" I asked. "Because if this is a polygamy thing, sorry I am not down. I've been in poly relationships before but—"

"My husband on Crius is dead," Leah said.

"Oh," I said, blinking. "I didn't know that."

Leah paused. "Allenway III had him assassinated. He was a decent individual of good family. One of the rare Crius nobles who was against clone slavery. Dumb as a post but hopeful his world could be saved. My whole family, as social workers, tried to move to Crius, to work with the education of ex-slaves but they ended up having to retreat from the system thanks to the Sons of the Demiurge's terrorism."

"I'm sorry," I said.

Leah shook her head. "It's not your fault, Vance. Try as you might, you can't save everyone. I sometimes worry you never even try to save yourself."

"Let's do it," I said, surprising myself.

Leah blinked, clearly surprised. "Really, I have a whole list of exceptions for both of us. They include the guy who plays you in *Blood and Honor*. You're also allowed to sleep with the woman who plays me."

"I like monogamy," I said, pausing. "I'm just not very good at it."

I'd never cheated on a partner, but long-term relationships were almost impossible if you're avoiding dating someone under your direct chain of command. What Leah was proposing could have solved a lot of those issues, but that just made me suspicious—and I hated that feeling.

"Same," Leah said, pausing. "You *do* want to marry me?"

"Yes," I said, pausing. "I loved the person you were pretending to be but I don't know if that is the person that you actually are."

"Neither do I," Leah said.

"But I also know that I don't know who I am when I'm not being Vance Turbo: Blah-Blah-Blah," I said. "I also acknowledge we'd be massively rushing into this. I want to get to know you as you. To know I can trust you."

"I don't know if I can trust myself," Leah said, pausing. "I do want to be out of the Security Departments and back in Space Fleet, though. My heart belongs out there and not in cloak rooms or government palaces dictating conspiracies."

"They have cloak rooms on Crius, seriously?" I asked.

"Maybe we're moving too fast," Leah said.

"Maybe," I said, pausing. I had so many suspicions and I hated that. Was she proposing because she wanted to get access to the newly promoted High Protector or did she really just see this as best for Astrid? Did she feel anything resembling actual love for me? Did that even exist or was it just friendship and lust? I'd die for a lot of my crew members but did that mean I loved them?

Or was duty, love, and friendship all mixed up in my head.

That was when my room doorbell rang. "Oh, thank God."

I slipped out of the bed, put on a pair of boxers, and my blue jeans before going to answer it. I grabbed the proton sword and its belt, wrapping it around my waist. The High Priestess came up behind me with Spock in her hands.

"You should definitely consider her as a potential mate," she said, "but I point out you should insist on three other spouses each. They should also be limited to one concubine each themselves to show your superiority."

I did a double take. "Were you here the entire time?"

"Yes?" The High Priestess said, confused. "I have some suggestions for your sexual positioning to maximize pleasure for the female."

I opened the door. "Please God, tell me you are here to kill me."

They were.

CHAPTER TWENTY-THREE

Die Hard on a Starship

The man on the other side of the door was preternaturally beautiful but in a way that was kind of off-putting. Blond hair, blue eyes, square jaw, and broad shoulders but with a sour expression on his face. He reminded me of the old Neo Militarist art that had been propagated when humanity had briefly panicked and elected a bunch of fascists after First Contact. Much to the surprise of people without a trace of foresight, it turned out those people hadn't run the planet very well and never intended to let go of power. The Unification Wars were the last wars fought on Earth.

My first indication that this individual wasn't a member of the *Melampus'* crew was the fact his uniform was ill-fitting having clearly been sized for another individual. There was also a slight burn from what was probably a fusion pistol blast at close range that had been covered up by a communications badge. The second indication this person wasn't a member of the crew was when they lifted their fusion pistol to my chest then pulled the trigger.

If I hadn't been cybernetically enhanced in my brain, I'd have been dead a moment later since this was a fairly decent plan. Nothing beat simplicity quite like walking up to someone and shooting them. Well, bombing someone from orbit, but aside from that. However, I recognized the man's uniform oddities just in time for me to focus on my ring and bring up my Elder Race granted barrier. The strength of the blast was still like being punched in the gut and the man responded by pistol-whipping me when he saw my energy protection. That sent me down to the ground even if the barrier kept me from losing an eye.

"For the glory of the Elder Gods! Death to the Fat Grazing Bear!" the Son of Demiurge soldier—I assumed—aimed his pistol at my head and prepared to unload its entire contents into my face. Which, given I wasn't very good at using my Elder Race ring's barrier, wasn't good.

Thankfully, I was spared from having to wonder what being shot in the face repeatedly felt like by Spock leaping from the High Priestess' arms to land on the assassin's face. It stretched out its spider-like legs to wrap around the back of his head before there was a crunching noise followed by a hiss. The assassin promptly fell over, either unconscious or dead. That was when there was another crunching sound as his head caved in.

"Yep, definitely dead," I muttered.

"The tryffles have an incredibly potent neurotoxin that instantly paralyzes most humanoids before killing them within a Notha sub-time unit, later," the High Priestess said, "About a minute and thirty seconds. They use this to drink the blood if they're hungry or execute hostile intruders."

I stared at the tryffle. "You know, I actually hadn't been taking the idea of Spock as my bodyguard seriously until now."

"Why?" she asked. "Like the Notha themselves, tryffles are terrifying. Fat Grazing Bear?"

"It's my Sorkanan nickname," I replied, frowning. "Apparently, it means something very badass in their language."

"I sincerely doubt that," the High Priestess said, skeptically.

"Vance!" Leah shouted, running over. Apparently, it had taken her a few seconds to realize what had happened.

"Yeah, I think we have a problem on board," I said, standing up. "Where there's smoke, there's usually fire."

That was when the gravity manipulators failed, and I suddenly found myself floating in the air. Loss of gravity was almost unheard of on Community vessels and was pretty damn rare these days even on Earth vessels, but I wasn't wearing magnetic boots and found myself bouncing up against the ceiling. Leah and the High Priestess weren't any luckier and struggled as they floated upward alongside me.

Everything else in the room did, too. I could see through the open door that this wasn't just limited to my quarters.

Seconds later, the gravity manipulators kicked back in, resulting in everything—including Leah, the High Priestess, Spock, and me—falling to the ground with a painful thud. Fragile objects shattered and others were thrown about.

That was when I heard SWAY-Z start to speak over the intercom, but it was a distorted twisted version of his normal voice. "ITS-IT'S-IT'S MY WAY OR TH-THE HIGHWAY."

"Yeah, this ain't good," I muttered, crawling to my feet as the High Priestess and Leah did as well.

"You think?" Leah asked. "We need to check on the brig. It's possible that someone is trying to break Allenway out."

I suddenly regretted not making time to meet with him earlier. Mind you, it was utterly insane to attack a Community vessel, particularly a battle cruiser, to liberate someone unless you had an army of significantly greater power. After what had happened to Karl the Conqueror's fleet, there was no way he had anything approaching the strength to mount an attack. Unless, of course, he attacked from the inside.

Dammit.

The Enigmatic Path had managed to hold the Community at bay for almost four years during the Kolahn War. That had been partially due to the fact the High Council hadn't been interested in diverting more than a token force to battle the Kolahn. Earth eventually won as much position as it had, which wasn't much, by always volunteering to be in the line to fight.

However, another reason for the duration of the war was due to the Enigmatic Path's unparalleled cyberwarfare capacities. AI, Dummy AI, spyware, ransomware, cybernetically enhanced dataslicers, and viruses, they used every duplicitous means to sabotage the Community's military efforts. Some of the worst defeats in the war had been brought about by someone being sent porn by a colleague that ended up sabotaging the navigation systems.

"Or he's breaking out himself," I said, shaking his head. "You said he had a thousand people here on board."

"P-P-PAIN DON'T HURT," SWAY-Z continued to speak but I could tell there was little consciousness remaining behind the words. I had an ear for the pain of AI.

"There's no way he could take this ship from the Community," Leah said, sounding more like she was trying to convince herself than me.

"Whoever controls the environment of a starship, controls the starship," I said, knowing that boarding actions always had to be done wearing life-support gear because a captain could asphyxiate or crush anyone who arrived with just a few dials.

It was why many pirates either made sure that captains knew the punishment for such actions would be death or just disabled life support ahead of time from the outside, letting the people inside suffocate or freeze before entering.

"NOBODY EVER WINS A FIGHT..." SWAY-Z trailed off. "I'LL GET ALL THE SLEEP I NEED WHEN I'M DEAD."

With that all of the lights I saw—and presumably the rest on the ship—shut down except for the emergency lights. Then the lighting rebooted and I could tell there was something very different going on. Call it intuition but the ship *felt* different and there was a new presence in control.

That was when a new voice spoke on the intercom. It had a mild but almost unrecognizable accent to it that I mentally filed as "generically upper-class snob." He did, however, speak in English.

"GOOD EVENING, OR TECHNICALLY MORNING, FELLOW SAPIENTS. I AM DUKE JOSEPH ALLENWAY III, THOUGH YOU WILL PROBABLY KNOW ME BETTER AS KARL THE CONQUEROR. I PREFER THAT NAME, REALLY, BECAUSE IT IS ONE THAT I EARNED WITH MY OWN HANDS THROUGH BLOOD AND TERROR. MOST OF HUMANITY HAS FORGOTTEN THESE ARE THE MEANS THAT GREATNESS IS FORGED, AND THAT WAR IS BOTH OUR LIFEBLOOD AS WELL AS DESTINY."

I looked up to the ceiling. "This guy is an enormous prick, isn't he?"

"You have no idea," Leah said, pulling on a pair of pants and arming herself with a pistol she'd hidden beneath her pillow.

"I HAVE BEEN CHOSEN BY DIVINE RIGHT TO LIBERATE MY PEOPLE FROM THE TYRANNY OF EARTHGOV'S PUPPETS. THE COMMUNITY HAS INTERFERED IN THE INTERNAL POLITICS OF MY HOMELAND AND ATTEMPTED TO IMPOSE VALUES ALIEN TO OUR TRADITIONAL CULTURE," Karl said, ignoring that said traditional culture was slavery and Crius' settlement was about a hundred and fifty years old. "I DO NOT BLAME YOU FOR THIS NAKED IMPERIALISM, THOUGH, AND PROMISE ANY CREW MEMBERS WHO WISH TO FLEE INTO THE ESCAPE PODS THAT THEY WILL BE FREE TO DO SO. ANY WHO CHOOSE TO STAY, THOUGH, WILL DIE A HORRIBLE DEATH AT THE HANDS OF MY STAR PALADINS."

"Star Paladins?" I asked.

"That's what he calls his soldiers," Leah said.

"Such a waste of a good name," I said, shaking my head.

"It's really not," Leah said. "We have to retrieve Astrid."

Mentioning our daughter caused me to immediately straighten up as I realized how vulnerable she was because if Karl knew about her presence on board, he was almost certainly going to go after her.

"I've got your back," I said, pulling out my proton sword and activating it.

"Ahem," Leah said.

"What?" I asked, turning to her.

Leah gestured her head to the dead man on the ground and more precisely the gun in his hands that he'd almost killed me with.

"You don't think the sword is better?" I asked.

Leah blinked. "Do you know how to use a sword?"

"Stab and slash the other guy?" I asked.

Leah stared.

"Right," I said, depowering the weapon and sheathing it before picking up the pistol.

The High Priestess pulled out a tiny disintegrator pistol that was Notha-sized which I knew packed a significant more powerful punch than larger Community fusion weapons. It was also something she really shouldn't have been able to sneak on board but somehow had.

"It's alright, Lord Satan," the High Priestess said. "I will educate you in the ways of melee combat and train your body to fight as a true Notha warrior. Much the same as that legendary teacher of warriors from those movies you like, Yogurt."

"Yoda," I said, sighing. "Do you know where Astrid is staying?"

"Her quarters are on this level," Leah said, gesturing with her pistol. "I'll show you."

"I HAVE ONLY THREE REQUESTS FOR THOSE WHO WOULD LEAVE THIS PLACE AND STAY WARM ANOTHER DAY," Karl the Conqueror continued to natter on via the intercom. "I MUST HAVE THE TRAITOROUS WAR CRIMINAL, KATERINA TAGAWA, SLAIN. I MUST HAVE THE VILE EXPERIMENT, ASTRID MASS, AND HER TRAITOR MOTHER DELIVERED TO ME. THEN I DEMAND ALL THE SHIP'S CODES TRANSFERRED TO ME SO THAT I MAY RESTORE HONOR AND JUSTICE TO CRIUS. I WILL TRANSMIT THE REST OF MY DEMANDS TO THE COMMUNITY THEREAFTER."

"I hate being lumped with Astrid," Leah muttered, heading out the door as I followed her.

The hallways of the *Melampus* were brightly lit, carpeted, and a disarming beige color that made me wonder what it was about the Community that they wanted every vessel to feel like a hotel rather than a warship. It wasn't normal in the local fleets of other races. I'd been on Sorkanan vessels, and they were dimly lit, made of steel, and covered in various sorts of slime that they only rarely bothered cleaning up. As Forty-Two had described them, they were a Navy defined by rum, sodomy, and the lash.

"I wasn't even mentioned," I muttered, searching for any backup that Karl the Conqueror may have sent my assassin's way.

There was no way the Community would meet any of his demands, even if he did manage to take hostages. Too much of their reputation depended on being the biggest dogs in the galaxy after the Elder Races and smacking down anyone who stood up to them, all the while claiming to be the noble guardians of civilization and arbiters of peace. Yeah, the bloom had faded on my rosy opinion of them—could you tell?

I also doubted his claims that he would let anyone go. All he was doing was trying to divide and conquer. Those crew members of the *Melampus* who chose to evacuate would be helpless before him as they floated in space, waiting for rescue. While he might be stupid enough to try to use the *Melampus* to take back Crius, more likely he was going to attempt another shipjacking, only this time with a vessel even more powerful than the *Siege Perilous*.

Thankfully, I was pretty sure both my Great-Aunt Kathy and the other senior officers on board the ship were smart enough to know you don't negotiate with terrorists. That was when the obvious point about eliminating the senior officers on board and anyone else who might pose a threat occurred to me.

That was when I saw three more blond, blue-eyed men of nearly identical appearance step from a side passage into the hallway we were in. A fourth figure, a buxom blonde-haired woman with a face unsettlingly devoid of any uniqueness, followed them. They were wearing the same ill-fitting uniforms stolen from our dead crew and carrying Crius weapons rather than stolen Community ones.

Under normal circumstances, I would have asked them to stand down, but they'd announced their intentions to go after my daughter, so I took advantage of the fact that I saw them first to fire into one of the newcomer's throats before shooting a second one as they turned to retaliate. Leah took the third man's head off as the High Priestess fired her disintegrator into the female intruder, causing the shipjacker to turn a brilliant red before falling on the ground as a charred skeleton. Seriously, Notha started at overkill and had created their own word for something worse: *fnog'nath*, I think it was. Sort of like how Germans have a word for happiness at the expense of others: schadenfreude. You can tell a lot about a culture by the unique words they develop.

"Five down," I muttered, looking at their corpses. "Only about nine hundred and ninety-five more to go."

"CAPTAIN JULIUS ELGAN INVADED OUR WORLD AND BROKE YOUR LAWS OF NEUTRALITY TO OVERTHROW THE ORIGINAL ALLENWAY CHURCH" Karl the Conqueror continued to blather on via the intercom. "MOST OF US MANAGED TO ESCAPE, BUT I NEVER FORGOT THE DECADE OF HUMILIATION THAT MY

GRANDPARENTS SUFFERED AS THEY WERE TREATED LIKE COMMON CRIMINALS BECAUSE THEY MARKETED THE DRUGS AND SLAVES THAT THE REST OF THE GALAXY REQUIRED. IS SLAVERY WRONG? I THINK NOT! MANY RELIGIONS MENTION IT AND WHILE I AM AN ATHEIST, I THINK IT'S JUST FINE! ESPECIALLY IF YOU ENGINEER THE SLAVES TO LOVE IT! EITHER WAY, I WAS SENT OUT TO STUDY THE COMMUNITY'S HYPOCRISY AT THEIR SPACE ACADEMY—"

"Buddha Christ, is he going to give us his entire life story?" I asked, stunned.

"Yes, yes he is," Leah said. "Wait until he gets to the part about how he brought civilization and technology to the world of giant grasshopper people he conquered."

"The Llrowlthra are Space Amish who eschew technology and embrace pacifism," I said, never have known much about the planet that Karl had conquered. "You could conquer them with a butter knife."

"Just because he's an idiot doesn't mean he's not dangerous," Leah said. "Indeed, Karl is the worst kind of idiot. A man who is smart enough to get others to kill for him but dumb enough to think he's infallible."

There was the sound of fusion blasts down the hall and I prepared to battle another group of Crius when I held my fire at the sight of Hannah and Pink. Hannah was covered in blood and Pink's already questionable costume was about to fall off from the exertion she'd been putting it through.

"Oh hi, Vance!" Hannah said, looking at me. "We came to rescue you."

"Worry less about me and more about my daughter," I said, blinking. "Are you alright?"

"Oh, it's not my blood," Hannah said, calmly.

"We've been listening to the Crius' broadcasts since we took a few down and stole their comms. Your daughter is heading down the halls that way," Pink said, gesturing with her gun. "I don't think her guardians lasted too long."

I stared and ran down the hall where they'd been blasting.

"Goddammit, Vance," Leah muttered, running after me.

The High Priestess trailed behind us with Spock jumping on her head to use her as a makeshift mount.

CHAPTER TWENTY-FOUR

Death of a Friend

My thoughts on the best way to deal with a no-win situation being to try to run out the clock smashed headfirst into the wall of reality when time was not on my side. We chased the group of kidnappers down the hall and through several passages where we'd come across murdered crew members.

The Sons of the Demiurge terrorists seemingly weren't interested in their leader's promise to provide safe passage to the escape pods and had gone on a killing spree throughout the place. The crew of the *Melampus* had given as good as they'd gotten, though, and there were plenty of signs of heavy fighting on this level.

Unfortunately, they had my screaming and crying daughter in their hands which meant I couldn't exactly fire freely either. They were also more interested in retreat than staying to fight, which meant that they were probably going to join up with the rest of their associates.

Several times, I passed hallways that had been sealed up where individuals could be heard banging on the other sides of the doors. Karl the Conqueror oversaw the ship's internal security now and if we didn't stay directly on the Sons' asses then we would almost certainly be locked away from recovering my daughter.

Vance, don't run directly into their fire! Leah said telepathically, following me. *You won't help Astrid if you get killed!*

I ducked behind a corner as one of the terrorists shot at me, nearly taking off my head. *We can't let them get away with her.*

No kidding! Leah said back to me. *However, they're about to head into Gravitronics. They have control there.*

Yeah, that was not good. Gravitronics was, unsurprisingly, where the ship's gravity was controlled by. Artificial gravity was impossible. You couldn't just generate it by machine, but scientists had learned how to maneuver it around a ship by means of science that still baffled me despite the fact I'd taken courses on it.

Sabotaging the ship's AI might have allowed them to temporarily turn off the gravity manipulators but fully seizing control of Gravitronics would allow them to weaponize gravity across the ship. I mean, as humorous as it was to imagine people bouncing around the ship like gravballs, it became a lot less humorous once you imagined their brains leaking out from cracked skulls.

"Dammit!" I muttered, going after the kidnappers right as they went through the door to Gravitronics and it slammed in my face with a whoosh.

"Sorry," Hannah said, coming up behind me and Leah. "I tried to get to your kid before everything went to hell."

Pink came up behind her, wheezing as she moved. She didn't have quite the same number of genetic and cybernetic enhancements as the rest of us. "Karl is..." she huffed a few times. "Insane. There's no way he can get away with a Community..." she huffed some more. "Battle cruiser. Even Captain Havelock would never try something like that."

"Well, he's already done it before," Leah said, trying and failing to get past the locks to Gravitronics.

"I don't get it, why does he want your brat? Err, beautiful young daughter?" Pink said, correcting herself.

"Well, I've ruined his planet," Leah said. "She's also a useful hostage. But I'm going to take a wild guess and assume that it's Department Twelve that wants her back. There were always rumors that Karl only managed to take the *Siege Perilous* because he'd had help from the inside. Taking over an entire planet allowed their resources to be exploited by an outside party, perhaps one that needed its own budget off the books from the Community."

"That's insane," I said, staring at her. "That's like the CIA being responsible for the Nineteen Nineties Crack Epidemic or space herpes being invented to make Brigid a less attractive vacation spot than Freya."

"Wait, is that true?" Pink asked, looking up.

"No!" I said. "If you want to know how to prevent diseases like space herpes from happening, just don't stick any of your parts in alien livestock."

The High Priestess, meanwhile, finally caught up to all of us with Spock clinging tightly to her head. "I…can't…keep…up…with…you…stupid…long-leggers."

"You should go on all fours," Pink said.

"I'm not a male," the High Priestess said, hissing.

I tried to bypass the controls and found myself locked out of every possible avenue. On the plus side, I managed to get the melody to "Funky Town" down.

"I'm sorry, Vance, this is all my fault," Hannah said, looking at the floor.

"Excuse me, what now?" Leah asked.

Hannah looked up. "This is my fault. The ambush, the takeover, everything. My contact with Department Twelve, Jonesy, is someone that I've relied on for a long time. He's been embedded on Crius for a long time and promised to set me up as a resistance fighter. He helped me find out the Looking Glass Man was a product of D12's experiments years ago. I think he must have been the guy who passed on Vance's location to the *Siege Perilous* since I told him…what are you doing?"

Leah was staring at her with such intensity that it looked like she was about to have an aneurysm. She had her hand stretched out and was slowly clenching it. "I am attempting to kill you with my mind."

"Not funny," Hannah muttered.

"Not joking," Leah said. "Do you have a nosebleed yet?"

She did actually.

"Let's put a pin in this until later," I replied, very much wanting to know why Hannah hadn't brought up her association with a rogue intelligence agency until now. "We need every gun we have."

I kicked the door, hearing it making a thick banging noise. "We need to figure out a way to get through."

"Ahem," Pink said, pointing down at my sword.

"Right, I knew that," I said, pulling out the proton sword and activating it before jamming it into the side of the door. The weapon went through surprisingly easy even as the metal around it started to dissolve rather than melt. It was a bizarre thing to witness and made me question just what the "proton" in the name referred to. Lightning crackled out from where the blade struck the door and only the crossguard kept it from going onto my hands.

Unfortunately, I was only halfway through cutting a hole through the door before the gravity once more vanished in the hall and we found ourselves moving up against the ceiling. Then the gravity suddenly became several times Earth standard and slammed us against the ground with a thud.

I think they're experimenting with the gravity as a weapon, Leah thought to me.

"You think!" I shouted back, feeling it continue to intensify. It was like being in a wind tunnel pressed up against a wall before turning into being pressed in a vice.

Pink pulled out a grenade looking device and slapped it against the side of the wall, causing the gravity forces to subside for a second.

"What the hell?" I asked, looking at her.

"Miniature gravity manipulator," Pink said, climbing up. "Old pirate trick. Never go anywhere without one."

"Where did you even hide it in that outfit?" I asked, confused.

"Finish the job!" Leah said.

"Right," I said as I went for the sword to finish cutting a hole large enough to get through. As soon as the metal fell through, I moved to one side as a bunch of fusion bolts passed by. Thankfully, everyone else had moved to the sides of the hallway as well. "Yeah, I think they know we're coming."

I'm in contact with our daughter, Leah thought to me, keeping herself pressed against the wall. *There's another presence in there, a dark and malevolent one. One that's every bit as enhanced as you or I.*

"Well, that's helpful to know," I muttered aloud. "We need a distraction."

"I can provide one," Leah said, aloud. "You should go through one of the rooms to the side and carve through the walls. They'll probably make a move to come through here and I'll meet them."

I wasn't exactly drowning in ideas so I nodded. "Hannah, can you cover her?"

Hannah nodded.

Leah frowned.

"Pink, Priestess, come with me," I said, gesturing with my crackling sword.

I proceeded to slash open the door closest to me, which led to a janitor's closet of all things. The walls were stacked with cleaning bots as well as cannisters of disinfectant. I couldn't help but think of Trish and wondered what was going on in the *Siege Perilous* right now. The possibility my father was involved in this occurred to me but I didn't want the entirety of the universe to revolve around me. I also had the slightest, tiniest worry that Karl might kill him if he discovered he was still alive.

There was also the fact that as much as I was worried about Astrid—and I was, believe me—I was also surprised at how worried I was about Leah. It was strange how quickly my opinion of her had gone from simmering fury at her violation to care about someone who'd looked after my unguarded blood relative. Her offer of marriage had come out of nowhere, but I was surprising myself by seriously considering it. I didn't want her getting herself gunned down trying to distract our opponents so we could rescue Astrid. I wanted to save everyone if I could, and I was terrified we wouldn't be able to do so.

I was halfway through carving a hole in the janitor's wall, including several electrical conduits that my barrier thankfully protected me against, when I heard, "Man of La Mancha" being sung by a female vocalist. It started blaring through the intercoms of the ship and I had to wonder how Leah had hijacked it from Karl the Conqueror since he'd just gotten to growing up on a lonely estate surrounded by obedient slaves during the "Good Old Days."

Pink stared at me. "This is her distraction?"

"She's a theater kid," I said, shrugging. "We're lucky she didn't choose 'Music of the Night'."

223

Honestly, Leah was really good and showed a four-octave range. Most female vocalists could only do about two or three.

The metal I'd carved away fell onto the floor as the singing, now accompanied by fusion blasts, covered up the noise. Gravitronics lay beyond, a large circular chamber roughly the size of a football field. It was another sign of just how massive the *Melampus* was on the interior because this was three or four times the size of the one on the *Ares*.

Gravitronics consisted of three levels with catwalks and balconies built around a single central pylon that was in the center of the chamber. Individuals out of Space Fleet uniform were spread about, armed with rifles and fusion pistols. A few even had melee weapons, which showed they hadn't been able to arm everyone. There were more than a dozen present, which was both far fewer than it could have been and way more than we had any realistic way of dealing with.

The figure I was most concerned with, though, was a hulking black robed Kolahn that looked like someone had put a reptilian-ape hybrid in a bad fantasy novel. The Enigmatic Path's spiritual leaders were called the Diviners and gave up their names for designations. Jack had mentioned a 101-B and I pretty sure that this was him. Standing next to him was my daughter as he held her by the arm, dragging her along, I saw the terror on her face and something inside me snapped.

"Reptilian Rampage!" I shouted, abandoning stealth, and shooting the nearest of the terrorists before another turned to shoot me only for the blast to reflect black against my blade into his chest right before I slashed through a third of them. He was bisected and I would have felt bad about the absolute horrifying way he died if not for the fact I was too focused on killing every last one of them.

"Motherborker!" Pink shouted behind me, picking off a couple of others in the confusion.

The High Priestess scurried across the Gravitonics chamber, taking position and shooting while Spock grabbed people by the leg or throat to take them down.

If I hadn't been possessed of a barrier enhanced by my proton sword, I probably would have been gunned down a half-dozen times in short order. That protection allowed me to keep momentum going until six terrorists were dead at my hands. Leah and Hannah pushed through at that time rather than just providing a distraction and we'd somehow managed to turn the tables on the shipjackers.

Almost.

"Lay down your weapon, Forsaken One!" 101-B said, lifting Astrid by her arm. His voice was a twisted mechanical reverb like Darth Vader's. He had a Kolahn pain amplifier in one of his other five hands. "I am prepared to kill your offspring!"

It got worse because 101-B wasn't the only one there. Two more of the Sons of the Demiurge had taken up position by him.

He's not lying, Vance, Leah spoke in my mind. *Don't move, Astrid! Anything could set him off at this point.*

Get me the bork out of here! Astrid shouted in our minds, causing me to get a brief migraine.

I lifted my sword in front of me in one hand while keeping my pistol in my other, making an X with them. The High Priestess came up beside me with Spock beside her.

"What is it you want, 101-B?" I asked, staring at him. "The war is over and if you planned to continue using Crius as a base for your group, it's over there too. Your only solution now if you want to save yourself or your men is surrender."

I was prepared for just about any reaction, including naked disbelief. After all, Karl was the one presently in charge of the ship, but I didn't expect *laughter*. "You really assume this is about Crius? This is about survival of our species, Turbo. Your masters and mine are the Elder Gods that rule over this universe and determine which species live or die. We may only survive if we pass their tests and prove we can bring something worthwhile to them as an offering. Genetic, scientific, or technological gifts. Crius? Crius is nothing. Our lives are nothing. If a billion humans or Kolahn died to accelerate our species' chance of being accepted among the Core races, then it would be lives well spent."

There it was again, the Sword of Damocles that hung over the heads of every single race that had to kotow to the Elder Races or be destroyed. One that often came down without clear reason or rules. All roads seemed to lead to Rome and all politics seemed to be the Core species that had a billion years on our development. Finding out the

Enigmatic Path was motivated by them wasn't a surprise, really, as I'd long suspected their religion was influenced by them but knowing it was affecting my family personally was a gut punch. I was dealing with a zealot here and nothing I said would dissuade him.

"Give me my daughter and take me as a hostage instead," I said, setting down my sword and gun on the ground. "I'll tell you everything I know about the Elder Races and let you dissect me if you want to. Just hand over my daughter and we'll get a shuttle off this place."

The Elder Races would probably explode my head before they let me reveal anything important. I didn't know if they could do that but I wouldn't have been surprised if they could.

"Imbecile," 101-B said, staring at me with his artificial eyes. I'd offended him and I didn't even know how or why. "You are one of the people that is closest to the Great Ones. You have pleased them. Yet you would potentially endanger all of that for a biological test subject, valuable only in that it saves time. Do you think she is the only one? Do you think her life really matters? Allow me to show you how little hers does."

Kill him, Vance, now! Leah commanded as I knew 101-B planned to blow my daughter's head off.

It was, of course, an awful time to have put down my weapons. There was also the fact that Kolahn were frigging six-armed reptile gorillas and certainly possessed strength equivalent to such. Something that made even a supposedly enhanced individual such as myself— and I said supposedly because any individual who looked at me and saw superiority was in dire need of therapy—pause.

But I wasn't going to let my child down.

Lunging at 101-B, I saw Leah shoot the Son of the Demiurge soldier by his left as Spock grabbed the face of the one on the right. Unfortunately, my plan to use myself as a human shield failed in the fact that 101-B had extra arms that pummeled me before throwing me to one side. That was when it aimed the pain amplifier at Astrid's head while she screamed. There was a sound of energy fire as the pain amplifier went off and Leah blasted the Enigmatic Path Diviner twice in the face. It had a barrier, but the second shot had penetrated it and brought him down.

"Astrid!" Leah shouted, going to her daughter's side, and hugging her.

Our little girl was alive and uninjured, The High Priestess had leapt in front of the blast. She was lying on the ground and the entire lower half of her body was one severe burn.

"No!" I said, rushing to her side. "We'll get you help! We'll save you."

The High Priestess turned up to me and stared into my eyes. She gave an all-too-human smile. "Oh, Lord Satan, you always were so very funny."

And then she died.

CHAPTER TWENTY-FIVE

Son of a Bish Must Pay

Blood and Honor and other Vance Turbo dramatizations—there were four hundred and seventeen now as I understood it—were noted for having a generally lighthearted and episodic tones. The exception was the fact that they all had a very high body count. Never the main cast. That would be terrible and disrupt the comfortable rut the writers' rooms across the Spire had fallen into with their trite licensing of my so-called adventures.

However, they had a notable history of always consigning some poor ensign or enlisted man to horrific demise every installment to illustrate just how dangerous the latest horrifying monster or insidious renegade Notha captain was. They even had a nickname, Goldshirts, that was apparently an even deeper cut to science fiction fandom than I was able to remember. Just anonymous grist for the mill of drama.

The reality was far different.

The dead had names.

Tommy, Lorkhan, Picnic, Ketra, the General, Captain Klaws, Julius Something, and others had all died as the result of my decisions. Sometimes as my enemies. Sometimes as my friends. It was a collection of names that kept getting longer as I somehow managed to squeak past disaster after disaster, surviving where other people didn't. Now there was another name to add to the list, unpronounceable to humans and just meaning "High Priestess" anyway, but one I knew.

"I'm sorry," I said, looking down at her. "You deserved better."

"She died for her god," Leah said, holding her crying daughter — *our* crying daughter — tightly. "I'm not religious but I know people that are. Few people can ask for a better death than one for someone they believe in."

I wasn't worth believing in. "Astrid, I'm sorry —"

"Borking anyxholes!" Astrid said, crying out.

I closed my eyes and breathed out. "I'll leave you to your pain."

My daughter's caretakers had been massacred, she'd been kidnapped, and then witnessed a bunch of people being killed while rescuing her. However adult her mind was due to intelligence and telepathy, that was a traumatizing experience. She hadn't been trained in compartmentalizing the kind of horrors I'd witnessed or the ability to shoot when it meant the difference between yours or your crews' lives and your enemies.

My psychological profile at the Academy had been surprisingly cold-blooded, showing my ability to suppress empathy during combat situations as well as make the hard decisions was above the Community's requirements — and never mind that it was viewed as a virtue. It had listed the strange fact that I was able to form strong pair and group bonds, though, despite this. A few had even recommended that I be denied attendance at Space Academy because of it, but nepotism had prevailed. I was a psychological anomaly and able to supposedly turn off my ability to care at will before turning it back on. The eight or so people I'd killed today that barely registered were proof of that. But I *did* care for what had happened to the High Priestess and my daughter. And that this was rapidly turning into a massacre on board.

And couldn't shut it off.

"Vance!" Hannah called over to me. "We need you."

Lacking anything better to do, I approached the central computer in the Gravitronics where both Pink and Hannah were working. "What's going on?"

"We've got control over the ship's gravity, but we need you to reboot everything," Hannah said. "Also, we have a link to Engineering."

I went to a nearby console and brought up the holographic interface before using my code. Thanks to the efforts of the Enigmatic Path during the Kolahn War, a lot of it was hardwired to be off the primary systems and required physical interaction to use. It had offended quite a few of the ships' AIs but was proving its value here.

"Let's hope that Karl isn't in charge of life support or it's going to get rapidly very cold in here," Pink said.

"We should probably get some EV suits," I said, not paying much attention. I just kept running the past hour through my head and wondering what I could have done differently. The matter was such a disaster I couldn't conceive of a way to make it worse.

That was when an image of my father popped up on the viewscreen. "Hey, if it isn't my second favorite genetically engineered little sprog."

"Clearly, I was wrong," I said to myself. "Did you help Karl the Conqueror take over the ship, Father?"

"Vance, you wound me," Jack said, putting a hand over his heart.

"Only if I miss," I deadpanned. I wasn't in the mood for jokes. I wanted to find Karl, wrap my hands around his throat, and choke the life out of the man. It was a cold, uncomfortable, and entirely justified rage. I'd killed a lot of people over the course of my decade-and-change career. I'd only hated a few of them.

Karl was one of them.

"Allow me to illustrate that you have nothing to worry about," Jack said, reaching off camera and pulling someone closer. It was my Great-Aunt Kathy, who had blood on her right shoulder and looked every bit as pissed as I was.

"Hello, Nephew," Kathy said, adjusting her uniform. "It would seem you have managed to survive as well."

"I'm hard to kill," I replied. "It seems to be a family trait."

"Like the noble cockroach," Jack said, grinning.

"I'm also in charge of Gravitronics," I replied, glad to note that Kathy had secured Engineering. It meant Karl's plan was falling apart. There was no way he could just casually execute everyone on board now, at least. A sufficiently ruthless captain might, of which I knew Kathy was, but I wasn't sure if I qualified.

"Good," Kathy said, putting her hands behind her back and holding them. "That gives us an opportunity to halt this attack in its place."

"May I ask what he's doing here?" I asked, looking at Jack.

"I brought him over along with a chunk of the *Siege Perilous'* crew," Kathy said. "Trish moved over on bots except for the one we're designating Seventies Trish. Are you aware your AI is suffering fragmentation?"

"I'm aware," I said, dryly.

"She should be rebooted," Kathy said. "Eliminate the extra personalities and restore her to a pre-damaged persona."

"You mean kill them," I said.

Kathy sighed. "I knew I shouldn't have let Alfred raise you."

"Yes, so much better to have my son raised by a kitchen appliance than my parents," Jack said, under his breath.

"You don't get to complain after traumatizing—" Kathy started to snipe back.

"I can have you both killed," I replied, surprised at how easy that came to me. Absolute power really *did* corrupt absolutely, at least when dealing with your relatives. "How the hell did this happen?"

Kathy pulled out an infopad and started typing into it. "I'm sending you a bunch of commands that should allow you to lock out Karl the Conqueror from Gravitronics and I'll send a team to secure it. With both it and Engineering, we should be able to lock down most of his remaining followers. Unfortunately, I don't think we'll be able to get him in the bridge."

"That doesn't answer the question," I said, receiving the information.

"She doesn't know," Jack replied. "Karl not only had a virus to disable the ship and full schematics of it, but he also had the codes necessary to disable interior security. He just walked into the armory and got his men most of the weapons they needed."

"He has to have had people on the inside," Kathy said, frowning. "Is my grandniece alright?"

"She's alive," I said, calmly. "Do we have an estimation on the casualties?"

"Sixty-seven of my crew are dead," Kathy said. "At least twice as many wounded. Everyone who has ejected themselves in an escape pod is going to find themselves facing a court martial if I don't just send them on a trajectory to the sun."

I received the information that Kathy sent me and started implementing it into Gravitronics, sealing off certain areas of the ship marked "compromised" from the rest with excessive gravity bottlenecks. It would prevent them from advancing further and with life support under control, we could take them alive.

Which is, of course, when my great-aunt decided to start ventilating the atmosphere in those self-same parts.

"Stop," I said, calmly.

"What?" Kathy asked.

"That's an order," I said coldly.

Ordering my great-aunt about was probably about as effective as, well, ordering me around. Captains in Space Fleet had a broad latitude to make decisions without the supervision of command due to the vast distance of space involved as well as the fact that circumstances often changed at a moment's notice. Standing orders didn't exactly mean much when you encountered a ten-thousand-year-old AI-driven planet eater or species made out of living fire, for example.

Great-Aunt Kathy had faced both of those and a thousand other insanities over the past century. Nevertheless, I wanted her to understand I wasn't speaking as Vance Turbo, her incorrigible nephew. I was speaking as the voice of the Community. Which was either the height of arrogance, exactly what I was given this stupid title for, or both.

"Don't tell me what to do on my ship," Kathy said, narrowing her eyes.

I stared at her. "I want to know what the hell these bastarves know. They'll get one chance to surrender and a chance to save their lives by cooperating as prisoners."

"They were *already* prisoners," Kathy snapped.

"You have your orders," I replied. "Besides, you're wrong. It's *my* ship."

I had to admit my mercy was performative. These people had kidnapped my daughter and planned to do God knew what to her. I wouldn't have cared if they were crushed by twenty times Earth's gravity, suffocated, or blown out an airlock. I did care, however, about the fact that someone had set this up and I was sick of goddamn saboteurs and traitors among the Community's ranks. I also wanted to make sure there were an ample number of necks to hang from the highest gallows in the land over this. Not for the *Melampus* crews' sake—I didn't know them yet—but because they'd gone after my daughter. It was a sign that my emotions were thoroughly compromised during this affair and I could not have given less of a damn.

"Finally," Kathy said, staring at me. "You're starting to act like a proper Space Fleet officer."

My father made bunny ears with his fingers behind my great-aunt's head and I wanted to reach into the hologram and strangle him.

"How is the bypass going?" Kathy shouted off to the side.

"Excelsior!" Princess Huggypants shouted back. "I have claimed much of the system back from the tyrannical forces of law and order! But I need an AI to replace the lost one!"

I didn't get a chance to respond to the fact my pirate associate was the hero of the day when I heard Karl speaking over the intercom. "AH, CAPTAIN VANCE TURBO, IT SEEMS YOU HAVE MANAGED TO TAKE OVER GRAVITRONICS. I AM IMPRESSED. I REALLY THOUGHT YOU AND YOUR FAMILY'S REPUTATION WAS EXAGGERATED."

I looked for a communications hub on the control panel before me. I set it to the bridge and responded, "Karl, this is futile. You're not getting off this ship alive unless you and your goons set down your weapons immediately."

"OH, POOR CAPTAIN TURBO, YOU REALLY DON'T GET WHAT THIS IS ALL ABOUT DO YOU?" Karl responded. "THE COMMUNITY IS A SAD, SICK, AND WRETCHED SHADOW OF ITS OLD SELF. LIKE THE CHINESE EMPIRE IN THE NINETEENTH CENTURY OR THE OTTOMANS DURING THE ADVENT OF EARTH'S FIRST WORLD WAR. ITS POWER IS KEPT ONLY

THROUGH THE POWER OF INERTIA, BUREAUCRACY, AND FEAR. ONCE INDIVIDUALS BEGIN STANDING UP TO IT, IT WILL COLLAPSE INTO A SINGULARITY OF ITS OWN IRRELEVANCE."

I had to admit that Karl had managed to get his supervillain voice down pat. That was a rant worthy of Lex Luthor, or Emperor Zork from *Space Cadet Sally*. I disagreed with his interpretation of the Community, no matter how flawed an organization it was. It was always better to try to repair an existing infrastructure rather than try to burn it to the ground in order to start over. Not that I believed Karl and company had any interest in rebuilding the galaxy's order into anything other than a playground for him and his fellow slave lords.

I communicated back to him. "Be that as it may, you have brought nothing but pain and misery to your own people. Crius is in flames, the majority of your Navy has been destroyed, and we're bringing the noose around your neck now. If you're worried about your life, your only possible salvation is surrender. The Community only practices the death penalty for high treason and crimes against humanity. I can take those off the table."

I wasn't sure I could and knew I'd made a mistake almost immediately after I said the words. I was dealing with a narcissist, and he didn't want any criticism. "YOU THINK YOU'RE BETTER THAN ME, TURBO. THE DESPICABLE PUPPET OF THE COMMUNITY AND THE ELDER RACES. I AM THE LAST BEST HOPE FOR HUMAN SUPREMACY. NO ALIEN OR MACHINE WILL BE ALLOWED TO REPLACE US."

That was when the hologram projector in front of me replaced Great-Aunt Kathy and Jack Tagawa's image with that of an exterior shot of the *Siege Perilous*. I immediately got a sense of dread and tried to contact Trish through my cybernetics, far away from any jumpspace link-ups as we may have been.

Get the hell out of there! I mentally shouted, unsure if I was being heard.

"I MAY NO LONGER BE IN CONTROL OF GRAVITRONICS OR THE ENGINE ROOM BUT I AM CERTAINLY STILL IN CONTROL OF THE SHIP'S WEAPONS," Karl said, his voice positively shrill. "SEE

WHAT EXACTLY I THINK OF YOUR COMMUNITY AND HOW THEY HAVE SULLIED MY SHIP."

I didn't get a chance to say anything else because Karl proceeded to launch q-torpedoes, fusion cannons, and new antimatter rays at the *Siege Perilous*. It was able to get up its barrier but was barely able to hold things up for several seconds before they buckled. The *Melampus* continued its relentless assault until the Olympic-class vessel exploded in a detonation of its reactor, spreading out a brief shockwave of orichalcum burning like a star. Explosions were rare in space, for obvious reasons of lacking oxygen, but this was a particularly horrific example of the exception.

If I had to place a guess as to how many people Kathy had sent over to secure the vessel from the pirates and bots on board, I would have guessed around two hundred to three hundred people. That wasn't including most of the crew I'd assembled who wouldn't have been transferred over if Kathy hadn't wanted to keep an eye on my father. Teen Trish, Light on Water, my cousin, Forty-Two, Major Tom—who knew who was still on board when Karl launched his attack. It was a senseless and cold-blooded act of mass murder by a man who couldn't win but was going to do his best to spoil any victory against him for no other reason than spite.

"You son of a..." I trailed off, staring at the sight.

"YOU KILLED MY CREW, CAPTAIN TURBO," Karl said, taunting me. "NOW I HAVE RETURNED THE FAVOR. I DON'T KNOW HOW YOU ACTIVATED THE DEAD MAN'S SWITCH BUT I WILL DO THE SAME TO THE COWARDS ON BOARD THIS VESSEL UNLESS THEY FIGHT TO THE BITTER END. I WAS PROMISED THIS VESSEL AT THE MERE PRICE OF YOUR LIFE AND CHILD. I WILL HAVE IT, NO MATTER WHAT."

Karl cut our communication and I couldn't get my connection to Engineering back up, or any other department. It seemed he was still in charge of communications.

I slammed my fist on the interface. "Dammit!"

"I'm sorry, Vance," Hannah said, looking over.

"You heard that?" I asked, looking at her.

"We heard everything," Pink said, lifting her energy lance pistol the air. Apparently, it wasn't as disabled as it had first appeared. "I don't know how many of my people were still on board the *Siege Perilous* but for all the ones he's killed, I want his head. Are you with me?"

"Damn right," I said.

"I have to look after our daughter," Leah said, looking over at me with Astrid in her arms.

"I understand," I said, nodding. "We'll stay here until Kathy's reinforcements arrive, but we need to move quickly. I wouldn't be surprised if Karl figures a way to circumvent control over Gravitronics and Engineering."

It shouldn't have been possible with the anti-Enigma security measures that had been installed post-Kolahn War but we were already seeing what those had amounted to. I wasn't going to abandon my child but the best defense of her was a good offense—or maybe I just wanted to track down Karl and kill him with my bare hands.

Vance? That was when I heard a voice in my head.

Trish?! I felt suddenly ecstatic. I wasn't sure which one it was. *You're alive!*

Yeah, this Trish spoke. *Sort of.*

I was confused. *What do you mean, sort of?*

Remember how I used to like Eighties music? Trish said, confusing me further.

Yeah? I asked, feeling a sense of dread creep up on me.

I think I'm alone now.

CHAPTER TWENTY-SIX

Showdown at 1200 Military Time

"What do you mean, you think you're alone now?" I asked aloud, trying not to think of the song by Tiffany and failing miserably. I also wasn't paying attention to everyone else in the room who had to wonder who I was speaking to.

The others are gone, Vance, Trish said, her voice holding back a flood of emotions. *Goth Trish, Mean Trish, Teen Trish, Seventies Trish, and any more fragments that were going to exist. There's just me now.*

I didn't know how to react to that. I'd just started getting to know them all. *What happened? Wait, does that mean you're...you?*

I don't know how to answer that, Trish replied. *The others were interacting with the* Melampus' *central computer when Karl unleashed his horde of viruses onto the AI in the system. SWAY-Z died almost instantly but we tried to hold back the tide while coordinating with the* Siege Perilous' *computers.*

I saw what happened, I said.

You tried to warn us and they saw there was no way to successfully evacuate everyone in the seconds we had. I think...I think, they chose to reboot me from past records and coordinated their efforts to cleanse the Melampus' *systems. I'm in control of the ship's systems and have isolated all of the systems around Karl. But, they're gone.*

It was a lot to take in. *They did their duty as Community officers.*

I was going to have to write a lot of letters to people's families after this was done. The *Melampus* may have been under my great-aunt's command but they'd been coming here for me. I owed them that much and if I'd been in charge earlier, maybe I could have prevented this. No, that was unfair and trying to pass the blame onto someone who had already proven herself countless times before. Still, for the first time, I had to wonder if my great-aunt had been faking being an incredible hero the same way I had for the past few years.

Yeah, Trish responded. *I didn't know I had it in me. Again. So, uh, reading their notes, did you actually agree to marry the Queen Bitch of the Universe?*

Hey, that's my mom! Astrid's voice spoke in my head. Apparently, the telepathic girl could hear digitally transferred thoughts. *Wait, are you Space Cadet Sally? Or based on me. My dad is sleeping with a cartoon character?*

Space Cadet Sally is based on me, Trish said indignantly. *Well, Patricia Ares. Which is its own long, complicated story.*

Now is probably not the time, Leah said, showing she could listen in, too. *Also, I'm not the queen bitch. I'm just a countess.*

Sure, Carmilla, Trish said. *Go find some puppies to skin and make into a fur coat.*

That's Cruella, not Carmilla, I pointed out.

Shut up, Vance, Trish said.

My mother does not skin puppies! Astrid said. *I think. No offense, Mom, but I've been in your head and you are kind of evil. It's really weird being in Dad's head by comparison. Albeit, he can switch off his empathy—*

I put my fingers in my mouth and whistled. "Everyone out of my head, please. We need to focus on taking this ship back and dealing with Karl once and for all."

It would be better to take Karl alive and find out everything he knew so we could prevent something like this from ever happening again, but I admit I had to suppress every emotion I was feeling to even think about doing so. The Looking Glass Man had been one of the most sadistic evil monsters I'd ever met in my life but Karl had managed to move ahead of him in terms of how much hate I felt toward another sentient being.

"I agree with this plan!" Danny said, standing beside me.

I didn't even jump at his presence before my conscious brain processed the fact that my cousin was beside me, once more taking advantage of his psychic ability to make himself unnoticed. Unnoticed, by the way, but not invisible. Honestly, I've always felt Danny's ability was far superior to invisibility. He just had to deal with the problem that it seemed to function whether he wanted it to or not.

"Danny, you're alive!" I said, wrapping him in a hug.

He wasn't alone either.

Much to my shock and joy, Danny was standing beside Forty-Two and Major Tom. They'd all managed to make it off the *Siege Perilous*. There was someone behind them as well. I almost hugged all of them—well except for Tom—but managed to hold myself back.

"How the hell did you get here?" I asked. "We sealed up Gravitronics."

"Yeah, but there's a big hole in the wall," Forty-Two said. "We just walked through it."

"Oh yeah, we should probably cover that up," I muttered. "How did you guys survive?"

That was when the group parted and revealed...Light on Water. He was carrying a heavy assault fusion rifle and wearing a WW2 pit helmet. Where the hell he'd gotten that was the least of my questions.

"Acting Captain Light ordered a team of commandos consisting entirely of the bridge crew for some reason to launch an attack to rescue you when the *Melampus'* AI came under attack," Danny said, nodding. "He saved us all."

"I call it an AWAY team," Light on Water said. "It's based on the logic you use in assembling yours! From there we engaged in much violence and mayhem reaching this point."

"Not really," Forty-Two said. "He did shoot up the Officer's Lounge on Deck 10, though."

"I could have done more with grenades," Light on Water said, turning to Forty-Two. "Extreme badanyx!"

"You're not allowed to have grenades," I said to Light on Water. "Ever."

"Oh," Light on Water said.

"But...thank you," I said, unsure how to process my feelings. "For, uh, rescuing me. Also, for getting the crew off the ship."

"Thank you, sir!" Light on Water said. "Your mentorship continues to elevate me to levels of competence undreamed of. I now envision myself as becoming the 153rd Sklux High Protector!"

I blinked. "Right."

It was hard to imagine that many Sklux High Protectors but, then again, I tended to think of the Sklux as if you combined C3PO with talking gelatin. Racial stereotyping should be something that Space Fleet Captains should be above but, well, all the Sklux I'd met were so damn *goofy*.

"I happily offer my services as a therapist," Major Tom said, standing next to Astrid and Leah. "I am well-versed in child psychology and telepathy-based—"

"Go away, pervert!" Astrid said, glaring at him.

"I like your daughter, Vance!" Major Tom said. "She reminds me a great deal of you and your father."

I couldn't help but wonder if Major Tom was the leak. There was no reason to dislike Major Tom other than jealousy and I had to acknowledge that. Then there was Hannah, who had told me she'd been in communication with a Department Twelve contact on Crius. I intended to speak with her *extensively* about that later, but there was no way she had known nearly enough to have effectively sabotaged everything the way this had all happened. I wasn't about to abandon myself to paranoia, though. Especially when it would involve letting my personal dislike of someone substitute for evidence.

That was when he hugged me.

"I am so glad you're alive, brother in arms!" Major Tom said.

I paused. Okay, maybe there was also the fact he was touchy-feely and I absolutely was not that sort of person.

"There, there," I said, patting him on the back and silently screaming. "There, there. Do you know where Shelly is?"

I've located her, Trish said. *She's trying to lead a team of Sorkanan commandos to take Karl out.*

Crazzap. How's it going? I gently—then not so gently—pushed Tom off of me. I mentally wrote off Brigid from any vacation I would take in the future and would restrict any tourism to Freya from now on—or Hawaii.

Not well, Trish said. *I've managed to lock down virtually every one of the shipjackers. Half of them accepted your surrender offer and the rest are being put down. However, Karl seems to have something that makes him impossible to affect. All the doors are opening for him and systems reorientating. It's like he's got an override even I can't improve on.*

That was another clue that something borking bizarre was going on here. Though who would be insane enough to give someone like Karl the keys to a dreadnought was anyone's guess. It was like helping Jesse James or Charles Manson steal an aircraft carrier. Okay, I really needed to stop with the past-related metaphors. Some of them just made no sense. *Where is he headed? Can you predict where he's going?*

Are you actually going to try to ambush the guy yourself versus letting the very much alive and large number of security people handle him? Trish asked.

Yes, I said, without hesitation. *He killed you and took my daughter.*

Okay then! Trish said. *He's heading for docking bay Three. If you hurry, you might catch him.*

"Right," I said, looking at the others. "You guys need to hold Gravitronics until I'm back. I'm going after Karl."

Everyone stared at me.

"Some of you are going to disobey my orders, aren't you?" I asked.

"We're all going to disobey your orders," Danny said. "We'll always be beside you."

"Except when we're not," Forty-Two said.

"If I stay here, there's just as likely a chance for my daughter to get nabbed again," Leah said. "Sorry about that, Astrid."

"I hate being a princess," Astrid said.

"You're not a princess," Leah said. "We're also moving from Crius to avoid you growing up spoiled and ruthless like I did."

"I didn't agree to that," Astrid said.

Leah rolled her eyes.

"This is the dramatic moment where the crew shows its loyalty through disloyalty!" Light on Water proclaimed. "We shall now steal the starship to go rescue our resurrected colleague on the Genesis planet. Then we must acquire the whale sacrifice to appease the space god made from an old satellite. I think."

"That is a reference to *Battlestar Galactica*!" Major Tom proudly said. "An ancient Earth epic that Vance Turbo apparently has a doctorate in."

I stared at Major Tom. "Yes, that is completely accurate."

"It's *Star Wars*, not *Battlestar Galactica*," Leah corrected Major Tom. "My mistake!"

"I don't understand why Earthlings are so obsessed with shows about humans in space," Forty-Two said. "Sorkanan have been in space for twenty thousand years and you know what's in space? Dust, fireballs, and nothing. Lots and lots of nothing. Now if you watch a good Swampern then that'll be worth it. Blood, sex, outlaw vigilantes, and beautiful boggy vistas."

I proceeded to head to the hole in the wall I'd made with my proton sword. "The inmates are officially running the asylum."

I wasn't comfortable taking my daughter with me and had no intention of confronting Karl with her in the line of fire. However, I did see some point to Leah's statement that it wasn't going to be any safer in Gravitronics than any other part of the ship. I also passed by Kathy's security teams heading into Gravitonics almost as soon as we departed. They were hardened, furious, and fully aware this had been an insult to the entirety of Space Fleet. They also ignored me and my crew as if we were irrelevant. Not a good start for a new captain. But then again, I wasn't interested in them. I was on a mission of vengeance when I should have been doing my duty and securing the ship.

It occurred to me how ridiculous this all was. I was running directly into a showdown with all of my fellows and I couldn't help but wonder if I was the one who instilled in them this suicidal bravery, a desire to charge into the mouth of danger rather than sensibly avoid it. It had been my risk-taking and willingness to overlook things which were going catastrophically wrong that had gotten my friend, Tommy, killed.

That had resulted in a change of my behavior, as I turned myself into an incorrigible rogue—god, I sounded like I was seventy when I said things like that—in hopes of getting kicked out of Space Academy. Being placed in the Space Fleet chain of command by Captain Elgan, to be put in charge of other people's lives had encouraged me to be different, to be better. But I had to wonder if I'd been fooling myself.

Was I any different than my father? I was ninety-nine percent sure he'd murdered the entirety of the *Siege Perilous'* crew to save himself. Never mind they were a bunch of murderous pirates, slavers, and terrorists; they were *his* crew, individuals that he had been placed in charge of. It had been his duty to make sure that they survived until the next day. What had managed to warp him into the kind of person who would do something like that? Until I'd heard Karl's half-assed denial over the intercom, I'd been holding out hope that, somehow, Karl had been the guilty party rather than my father.

You're not like your father, Vance, Leah spoke in my mind. She was still holding our child with her enhanced strength like she was nothing more than a purse or small dog.

I'm not so sure about that, I replied. *Maybe I've just been fooling myself that I'm a Space Fleet captain rather than a conman and murderer.*

I remembered gunning down Big Bobo, the arms dealer and human trafficker, out of sheer disgust for the evils he'd committed. I'd also killed dozens of other people in person and who knew how many thousands in the various space battles in which I'd partaken. How many of those had truly been necessary or just because I'd ignited conflicts where none was needed.

Wow, is he always like this? Astrid asked, mentally.

Yes, Leah said. *Vance, I'm only going to say this once, but I am a terrible person.*

She really is, Astrid said.

I agree, Trish added. *Seriously, Leah is the worst. Why are you marrying her? Was there an absence of Lady MacBeth in your diet?*

That doesn't even make any sense, Leah replied. *But the thing you need to understand is that you inspire me to be better. To not want to be the evil spy girl. To be more like you and less like, well, me.*

Nineties Trish would have appreciated that Linkin Park reference, Trish said. *Too bad you never got to meet her.*

I just pretend to be a space hero, I said, ignoring that I'd asked them all to stay out of my head.

And you became one along the way, Leah said.

I would have argued her point, but I didn't have the opportunity because I started coming across the bodies of dead shipjackers.

"Oh no," I muttered, stopping in my tracks.

Leah covered Astrid's eyes, as if she hadn't already reached maximum trauma.

"It seems that your seed donor has a go-to move," Forty-Two said as we just encountered more bodies on our way to docking bay three. "The question is why he didn't do it earlier," Hannah said.

There was no great showdown with Karl the Conqueror or his minions. Every single one of his followers were KIA, their heads detonated in the same way that the ones on the *Siege Perilous* were killed. Karl himself was found in the docking bay, trying to hijack a shuttle with his last remaining group of followers, all of them suffering fusion blast burns from close range.

Karl had been executed with an old-fashioned neck snap that required military training Any secrets he might have possessed about his patrons were taken with him to the grave. He had been minutes away from being intercepted by Shelly's commandos and slightly longer by my group.

A shuttle was missing.

So was my father.

EPILOGUE

Confronting Dear Old Dad

It wasn't difficult to find my father despite the fact Kathy combed the system for him. She just didn't know that if you wanted to find a scoundrel, you should realize he wouldn't hide anywhere but in plain sight. Between Trish, Leah, and I, we found him in forty-seven hours.

Jack had headed down to Crius' new capital city and was causally enjoying himself at a club of, let us say, clothing optional nature. He was at the bar and apparently on his third drink by the empty glasses in front of him. It was amazing how anonymous both of us could be when we'd been party to so many world-changing events here in Crius. Then again, how much had really changed for the common people? The aristocracy on Crius had been thinned and forced to share power, but they hadn't been eliminated.

Clone slavery was outlawed and being stamped out one estate at a time, but that had happened before. Life would improve for the demihumans and genemods, however they were unlikely to become full citizens immediately. The Community was going to pull Crius into its ranks but fixing the massive wealth distribution issues, horrific cultural traditions, as well as technology gap would take generations. Thankfully, most of the system's citizens had lives and jobs that carried on regardless. Like stripping and topless bartending.

Huh.

Crius genetic engineering had certainly made a few new things for the sex trade. I hadn't seen anything like that outside of *Total Recall* or *Space Vixens XVI*. Also, what the *flooboa* dancer was doing on the stage should be anatomically impossible even with modifications. Apparently, spine modifications were as common as breast implants down here.

"Hello, Vance," Jack said as I almost bumped into him while distracted. "Come to chat up your dear old dad?"

"About a few things," I said, focusing on my corrupt father. "We have *a lot* to talk about."

"Like?" he asked.

"Oh, Joseph AKA Karl said he didn't activate the suicide switch for the *Siege Perilous* crew," I said, looking at my father with a frown. "I doubt he did the second one either."

Jack smiled. "You were always far too smart for your own good."

"How? Why?" I asked.

He shrugged. "I had the access codes for the dead man's switch of the *Siege Perilous*. It required some time to get the frequency for the one with Karl, but I figured that it would probably just be the same with his DNA and voice as an encoder. So, once I had the little weasel, it was simplicity to execute the others."

"I wanted prisoners," I said, calmly.

"And this is much simpler for everyone involved," Jack said. "The Community gets to claim a big victory, and no one gets embarrassed by unnecessary questions. 'Bitter enemies will be forgiven, but not before they're hanged.' Joe Abercrombie. Earth. 2007. Most of your crew already thinks you're the one who executed them all and they'll respect that far more than taking them alive."

"Why did you send me the locket?" I asked, moving on to my next question.

Jack did a double take.

"When did you figure it out?"

"That you were the one who sent the message about my daughter being kidnapped to Director G?" I asked. "That you were the one who arranged for the ambush for the *Black Nebula II*?"

Jack took another swig. "Yeah. I know you're a smart kid—G never would have recruited you as his latest hound dog if you weren't—but you never struck me as particularly politically astute, what with defending the Notha and trying to get Earth to be extra-kissy face with the aliens."

"To be honest, I suspected when I first let you out," I replied, leaning on the bar and ordering myself a Brigid Supernova with two eggs. I'd been up forty-eight hours and this would keep me up another twenty-four.

"Really?" he asked.

"Process of elimination," I replied, sighing. "My father being involved in all of this was one oddity too many piled up in a row. I decided to reframe my thinking around the idea that instead of being an incredibly stupid criminal, you were an incredibly good one."

Jack smirked. "Why's that?"

"Vanity," I replied. "I like to think that if I'm a genius then it had to have come from somewhere."

"Your mother contributed a lot to that as well," Jack replied. "That and all the money we paid to get you enhanced. It looks like we got our money's worth."

"Do you know where she is?" I asked.

"Yep," he said. "But you don't want to know where. I'm the better parent by far."

"The abandonment, mass murder, and involvement with slaving terrorists says otherwise," I said, swirling around my drink. I kept a micro scanner on my person these days to keep an eye out for poison. My beverage wasn't, at least not any more than a Brigid sunset normally was.

"To be fair, they were all anyxholes," Jack said, dryly. "The ones who weren't clones and just obeying orders. I almost feel bad for those guys. As for your mother, last time I checked, she was off playing Yakuza on Shogun. She's married into the Rin Crime Family and is running a casino for them. Dabbles in gambling, slavery, and murder."

"Bork," I said, disgusted.

"Such a stupid word," he said, "I hate Albion profanity but once you get used to it, you can't stop."

"I know," I replied.

"Anyway, we still bork on occasion but we decided we're better apart than together," Jack said. "But if she wanted to see you, she would. She doesn't. I did want to see you, so I invited you to visit."

I stared at him. "Could you walk me through the steps?"

"Why?" Jack asked. "So, you can hold it against me in a court of law?"

"Actually, as a High Protector, I could just shoot you down right here and now, and no one would question it," I replied.

"You could try," he said, smirking. "I'm a pretty fast draw myself."

"And I'm immune to fusion blasts when I know they're coming," I said, highly exaggerating my ring's power but guessing Jack didn't know for sure.

"Cheers!" Jack said, lifting his glass. "What do you want to know?"

"Just the shape of it," I said.

"You've already guessed most of it, I suspect," he said. "I was the one who dropped the call to Director Gordon's informants about your child being kidnapped. I was the one who took the *Siege Perilous* out. I killed all my crew when my attempt to take you hostage failed, then ran down to the brig to lock myself up. Thankfully, I know a few good ways of blinding AI to my movements. From there, I was working on your side the entire time because taking down Karl meant I could help myself to his treasury as well as wrangle a Community pardon. Which Kathy has already gotten for me despite her better judgement. Karl had no idea about any of it until I executed him. I did that because I knew he was working with Department Twelve and you do not want to cross those guys. This way, I tied up a loose end for them."

I stared at him. "Why did you set me up?"

"I was ordered to," Jack said, shrugging. "Department Twelve offered me a way out of the legitimate Security Departments' service when they faked my death along with Tomo's. She was always both a criminal and a spy, but a big believer, unlike me. I suspected I was just exchanging one master for another but underestimated just how nasty my new one would be. Department Twelve, Dark Matter, the Human League, you're assuming they're all separate organizations when they're really all part of the same single organism—a group that wants to make sure humans go from being small fish in a very big ocean to fucking whales. Yes, I said fucking. We've gone from PG-13 to R. Director G isn't a member, too moral, but he's been keeping this from you because of your Elder Race ties. Why? Because he knows the Elder Races would turn Earth into a cinder if they knew about what mankind's real leaders have been up to. We have alien friends, too. People who are willing to risk Earth as a testing ground for research into the Elder Races, AI, and other forbidden technologies. After all, if the Elder Races destroy Earth, it's no big loss to the Community."

I tried not to think of the vision that Cthulhu had given me of Earth's destruction. Humanity would survive its lost home world, but it would take centuries before it was part of the Community once more. Unfortunately, that was centuries in the future, and I had no idea if I could avert it or not. It was like knowing about the Black Death when you were a Roman senator. That wasn't what concerned me, though.

"Yet you tried to kill me," I said, remembering how close to death we'd come on the *Black Nebula II*. "Lured me and my pirate friends into a trap to execute me."

"Kidnap you," he pointed out. "I figured I'd recognize you after you were brought on board as a captive and cut a deal. They don't want you dead, Vance. They want you alive and on their side."

"Is that why they made a child from my DNA? As a way to manipulate me? What do you know about that?" I asked. "How many other grandkids do you have running around?"

"No idea," Jack said, taking another swig. "You should ask Leah, assuming you buy her bullsavit story about finding Astrid in an abandoned cloning facility. Maybe Kathy, too. If you think she's free from all of this, you're fooling yourself."

I narrowed my eyes. "You're lying."

"Always," he replied. "But not necessarily about this. My son, you're the only one playing Captain Kirk. Everyone else is playing Palpatine. Anyway, when you seized control of my ship, I had to improvise."

"Improvise," I said. "By killing all of the crew who were loyal to you."

"Oh, spare me the moral indignation," Jack said, disgusted. "You're exactly like me."

"I am *nothing* like you," I said, dryly.

Jack rolled his eyes. "The secret of Vance Turbo's legend? You're a decent computer hacker and social engineer. Everything you've managed to accomplish is because you're good at cold reading people and applying a technical or emotional solution. So, you have elder god space magic now but all of that was built on pretty common criminal tools I gave you."

"Pardon?" I asked, not actually disagreeing with his assessment.

"People aren't really people to us," he said, staring at his empty glass. "They're more abstractions and problems. Once you know what a person wants to hear, it's very easy to get them to do whatever you want even if they know it's against their best interests. Reassure the crooked man he's righteous, the cowardly man he's brave, the stupid person they're smart, and the insecure woman she's loved. It all flows from there."

"Wow, you're a genuine psychopath," I said, shaking my head. "I should have known."

"And you lack self-awareness," Jack said, staring at me. "Or did you not think about how strange it is you can juggle multiple women being in love with you without jealousy or commitment, get experienced soldiers to follow you to their grave, and your superiors to think you are some kind of genius despite how manifestly obvious it is you don't know what the hell you're doing. Everyone keeps covering your ass and lending aid for your stupid-stupid plans and ideas. It's because you know how to manipulate them and you do it so well that you don't even realize you're doing it."

"It's called having friends," I replied. "People I want to be happy. They respect me and know I care for their wellbeing. Also, I only want one romantic relationship."

Two if you counted Trish.

Which, okay, bad example.

"You don't have friends, Vance," Jack said. "You have *minions*. You don't even know you're doing it because it's normal for you to know exactly how every word out of your mouth is a calculated manipulation. Normal people react before they've figured out how to press someone else's buttons. We don't."

There was a grain of truth to my father's words but not to the level he thought. I was calculated, I was cold, and I was very deliberate in how I dealt with other people. Maybe I was prone to manipulating my friends sometimes, but I respected their choices and wanted what was best for them. The big difference was I would sacrifice for them too, just like I knew they would sacrifice for me—and all of my efforts were to make sure no one had to sacrifice anything if I could help it. That wasn't always possible.

"So what now?" Jack asked.

"Now? Nothing," I replied.

He stared at me. "I'm surprised. The paragon of law and goodness is going to let his murderous father go free."

"You've just described me as a psychopath like you," I said, dryly. "I'm surprised I can still surprise you."

Jack frowned. "Just curious about your angle."

"You killed the entire crew of the *Siege Perilous* after god knows how many years raiding with them. Plus, you killed all of those shipjackers, while closing off any leads to their patrons we might have gained," I said. "But you've successfully helped in the revolution of Crius, eliminated of the Enigmatic Path branch operating here, crushed the clone slavery trade, and undoubtedly have bribed the Community in information and credits to get yourself off of any other lingering criminal charges. You're the hero of the hour."

"I've also got a massive fortune stacked away," Jack said. "All of the finances of the late Karl the Conqueror that I have sole unrestricted access to. You are the only loose end."

"Yes," I replied.

"But I could never harm my only—" he started to speak.

"Spare me," I replied, knowing he'd already tried to turn me over to people who wanted to kill me. "You know if you kill me, you'll be hunted to the ends of the galaxy. Besides, I'm pretty sure you don't like your odds in taking me out."

Jack frowned. "I honestly don't. It's rather disturbing how well you've protected yourself. I could try to eliminate all your friends, but that would probably not work. Also, bluntly, I respect another master at his work even if I don't feel what you might call parental affection. Parental pride at least."

"That I believe," I said. "Because it allows you to take credit for my accomplishments."

"Indeed. Where do we go from here?" he asked, honestly curious. I suspected he was one of those frustrated intellectuals who believed they never had the chance to talk to an equal. He wasn't.

"I let you go do your business," I replied.

Jack put his glass down. "Bullsavit."

"Oh?" I asked. "Why's that?"

"Because you managed to bring down multiple crime bosses for far less," Jack said. "I also think you're not any more overwhelmed with family affection than I am. Because you're a loose end for me that I can't eliminate yet that doesn't mean I'm blind to the fact I'm a loose end for *you*. If I—your dear terrorist daddy—came out, I'd ruin all those wonderful movie deals and models who want to bang you."

"Clearly you don't know my fandom," I said, shaking my head. "It'd probably increase my cachet with both."

"Tell me," Jack said, "how are you going to do it? Gun me down here or drop me off in a hole somewhere.:

"I may have let your name drop to the Security Departments," I replied.

He frowned and leaned back. "So, they're the ones you want to arrest me? Shame. I thought you'd be willing to do your own dirty work."

"No, but I may have clued some people in about your recent windfall from the late Karl the Conqueror's assets," I said, smiling wickedly.

Jack shook his head, disappointed. "I'm a billionaire now, Vance, and there's no way they'll be able to get at my fortune. It's hidden in a very secure location, and I got Karl's DNA to access it before he died. No one else can touch it."

"Your accounts are untouchable by EarthGov," I said, pausing. "But the High Protector can involve the Community Finance Bureau and it took them microseconds to locate your accounts in Sklux territory. I had them run a trace on Karl's DNA, which we still had his body to do, and they found it within minutes. It was helpful that the new owner shared half my DNA. It's since been donated to help the children of Rand's World. They hate charity, so I'm naming it an investment in their future."

Jack gaped. "Shit."

"I'm afraid you're going to have to start over, *Dad*," I said, staring at him. "I may not want to kill you, but I wasn't going to let you profit off of this either."

He didn't respond for a minute then he just clapped his gloved hands "I have raised a fellow master."

"You didn't raise me at all," I replied.

Jack smirked. "Fair enough. Anyway, I'll be fine. This wasn't my first rodeo and there's a whole world of liberated suckers—I mean slaves—who could use someone to point them in the right direction for their lives. Particularly where to place their money. Maybe I'll found a religion. It worked for Karl. Mine would be more funny hats and less terrorism, though."

"Just don't do it around me or I'll have you airlocked," I replied, standing up. "I guess we're done then."

"I guess so," Jack said, mumbling under his breath. "You know, of all my cons and mad plans, you may be the greatest. The entire galaxy will be feeling your sting by the end."

"If that's the way you want to end this thing, sure," I replied, walking to the door. I doubted we ever would see each other again and I honestly hoped it wouldn't end up that way. Because in that case it would probably be when I was ordered to either bring him in or put him down. Neither of which, I suspected, would I be inclined to turn down the next time. Especially if he was threatening another set of decent people.

Assuming any still existed in the universe.

My father stopped in mid drink. "First bit of intel is on the Invisible Hand—that's the group behind all of this, by the way."

I turned to look at him. "Which is?"

Jack narrowed his eyes. "Someone wanted Crius to be occupied by the Community and the slavers crushed so its vast number of medicines and other plantation produced products can get into the hands of the pharmaceutical transtellars. Possibly the same person who had been previously using the planet as a boogeyman for possible terrorist threats until they no longer were needed. Possibly the person who helped Karl the Conqueror get his cruiser in the first place and justify the military's eternal growth. Possibly the person who provided a quantum bomb that went off in the *Jovial Empress* and gave the Community *cassus belli* to invade. Pretext for war."

I stared at him. "You're speaking a lot of conspiratorial nonsense, Dad."

Even if I'd run over way too many conspiracies to deny it.

"Am I?" Jack said. "Well maybe I know at least a couple of names associated with Department Twelve. Ones you might be interested in knowing since you're going to stupidly stand against them."

"Who," I said, coldly.

"Fleet Admiral Bendo and High Protector B'Vash of the Sorkanan Expeditionary Fleet," Jack said. "Two members of that Dark Matter thing that I understand you mostly rounded up."

My father had just mentioned two of the most powerful men in the Community. Fleet Admiral Bendo wielded more power than the Prime Minister of EarthGov and High Protector B'Vash was a fifteen-hundred-year-old legendary hero of the Sorkanan. Both were longstanding allies of Director G and several politicians I immensely respected. Bendo and B'Vash were institutions in the military and had cooperated in trying to turn humanity into a modernized asset of the Community as well as make Earth the center of a united humanity. That kind of accusation could lead to being drummed out of the service if a was lie or civil war if it were true.

"Enjoy your drinks, Dad. My treat," I said, turning around and finishing my exit. I transferred a few hundred credits to his account. It would have to last him for a while as they were the only ones he had to his name.

Waiting out there for me was another person who should have been swarming with bodyguards, reporters, and hangers on but was conspicuously alone. It was Leah, wearing the black uniform of a member of the Security Departments, complete with beret and gloves. It was rarely used because, well, it was a secret agency. Today was the day she tendered her resignation and received her commission as a Commander in Space Fleet by order of Earth's High Protector. I was genuinely surprised to see she was following through with it.

"I'm surprised you aren't off ruling your planet," I replied.

"You know I gave up being President," Leah said.

"I guess I didn't quite believe you," I said, smiling half-heartedly.

"Yeah," Leah said, sighing. "That's a consequence of lying to someone as much as I have. But House Mass will be continuing as part of Parliament. I have body-doubles, retainers, and bioroids handling all of my government duties for now. My genetic profile has also been uploaded along with Astrid's information. Future generations will carry our legacy so I'm being encouraged by both my sympathizers as well as the Security Departments to find myself elsewhere."

I stared in discomfort. "So, you've contributed your heir and a spare to the royal lineage and now they want you to leave."

"Something like that," Leah said. "So, about my offer?"

"I'm not sure I'm ready for marriage," I said, pausing. "Especially with someone I don't know I can trust."

"Ah," Leah said, nodding. "I suppose—"

"But I'd be willing to give living together a try," I replied. "For Astrid's sake...and my own."

I was tired of being lonely.

Leah smiled. "You're a good man, Charlie Green."

"Charlie Brown," I corrected.

"Whatever," Leah said, waving a gloved hand.

"I also need a first officer and it turns out that as High Protector, I can pretty much appoint whomever I want," I said. "I think Astrid will be safer on the *Melampus* than anywhere else in the galaxy, recent events aside."

Leah smiled. "We should get to your investiture party. You're expected to greet a thousand diplomats and make a speech."

"How about we send a shapechanger in my place and have sex instead?"

"Yes, Captain."

"NOBODY'S FOOL"

A Turbo Vance Short Story

By C.T. Phipps

"I'm supposed to do what now?" I asked, staring at the infospace feed of Admiral Bendo holographically projected against the wall of my bedroom. I'd been awakened in the middle of the night for the call. I was wearing my Space Fleet robe with the ESS *Ares* insignia on the lapel while drinking some coffeine, which was about as close to being in-uniform as I could manage in a reasonable amount of time. I was really hoping the Admiral didn't notice my partner in the bed a dozen feet away and hopefully out of sight.

"We need you to go to the planet Murray and play in a game of space golf," Admiral Bendo replied.

Fleet Admiral Bendo was a stern-looking, bald, black man who was, for all intents and purposes, in charge of the entirety of Earth's defenses. He'd not restricted himself to that role, however, and was frequently involved in the political side of things as well. He also had one of those low, growly voices that made you want to sit up and pay attention, as childish as it sounded.

"What the hell is space golf?" I asked.

"Golf with some rules that apparently were added once the colonists entered space," Admiral Bendo said. "Listen, it doesn't have to make sense."

"I'm pretty sure it's better if it does if I want to win," I replied.

The admiral made a dismissive wave. "Learn the rules on your way. The people of Murray are extremely competitive and fame obsessed. You with your...particular credentials are perfect for impressing them."

Admiral Bendo was referring to the fact that I was the galaxy's most famous human military officer, even above other planets' human populations, due to the obsessive way that Earth promoted its captains' exploits in hopes of convincing the galaxy our little blue planet was more badanyx than it was. I'd managed to exceed my Great-Aunt Kathy, also a Space Fleet officer, in this year's HUMANITY (the magazine not the species) polls. It was probably the only reason they were calling on me instead of her.

"So it's a diplomatic mission?" I asked.

"Sort of," Admiral Bendo said. "The planet Murray is a privately funded independent colony that escaped the notice of Earth as well as the Community. It's been thriving for the last hundred years and has managed to establish self-sufficiency enough that we'd like to bring them in as probationary members of the greater galactic society."

I narrowed my eyes. "So, what's the real reason?"

Admiral Bendo narrowed his eyes. "Your travels have made you cynical, Captain Turbo. Good. The planet is actually located next to a massively lucrative asteroid belt of minerals, orichalcum, and other materials that could benefit Earth tremendously."

Admiral Bendo was very clear he meant Earth rather than the greater Community. I had significantly more mixed loyalties as I didn't see any reason that we couldn't all help one another, but that was an increasingly less popular opinion on Earth these days, particularly in the upper echelons of the military. We'd narrowly avoided secession from the Community and Bendo was still fuming over it. Still, I was part of EarthGov's Home Fleet as well as Space Fleet and didn't have a problem with my technical homeworld—I'd been raised on the Moon—improving itself. I just disagreed about the ways to accomplish it.

"Sounds like an excellent way of moving from being the fourteen thousand and sixth hundredth most prosperous world in the Community to being the fourteen thousand and five hundredth," I said, not entirely sarcastically.

"Yes," Admiral Bendo said, frowning with the force of a man who could only accept being the first for humanity's homeworld. "Just make sure you win."

"Who am I playing against?" I asked, wondering if it really mattered who I was up against here.

"Wow, it really matters who I'm up against," I said, holding my driver and staring across the course's first hole.

The planet Murray was a mostly frozen world except along the equator that had been increasingly terraformed by the human colonists to make it warmer. It would be centuries before the planet was comfortable for humans, but this portion was a verdant grassland with a chilly but invigorating climate akin to that of Scotland.

If this wasn't the biggest sign the Murray cultists weren't a bunch of scrappy individualists making it on the frontier, the Four Thousand Islands Resort certainly was. It was almost a thousand kilometers in diameter and deliberately designed as a country-sized location for catering to expected visitors from other human territories.

My opponents just added to the unpleasant impression I had of them as they'd apparently invited a selection of corporate oligarchs wearing Ares Electronics, Green Foodstuffs, Karma Corp, Homefront News Network, and Dixnar t-shirts. Exactly the sort of people who would love to exploit the hell out of the system's resources.

"What are you babbling about now?" Shelly asked, standing beside me. Captain Shelly T'Ketra, Captain of the ESS *Elgan*, was my team's co-captain. She looked quite fetching in a white dress, visored hat, and tight shirt that seemed designed more for fashion than practicality. Her pointed Ethereal ears were only slightly covered by her blonde hair.

"It looks like a corporate retreat," Hannah said, standing there in much more practical pants and a shirt. She also towered over most of the players. She was a blue-eyed, brown-haired woman of various mixed ancestries who towered over the others thanks to being a genetically engineered Amazon. Her eyes were cat-like and she had well-trimmed claws as well. Today she was carrying the golfing equipment because apparently the rules suggested superhuman strength gave her an unfair advantage.

"Yes, the big boys here are already planning on the various ways they'll carve up the resources in the asteroid belt," I muttered. "Probably making all sorts of shady insider-trading deals and negotiations."

"Interesting you have that perspective," an aristocratic male voice spoke. I recognized First Minister Tan. "Especially since you're competing for the honor of carving up the resources yourself."

I turned around and put on my best fake smile. "Just engaging in some pre-tournament banter, First Minister."

First Minister Syril Tan was a white-haired human male of indeterminate lineage who was a bit on the overweight side, which was rare given modern medical advancements. He was wearing long thick robes and carrying an ornate staff of office. Standing beside him, a plate of drinks on its back, was an alien animal very similar to a sheep with hand-like endings on its eight appendages. I noted it was well groomed, properly sheared, and not at all wild looking.

"Of course," Syril said, smiling.

"I notice all of the people competing here are human," Shelly said. "Does it really matter who wins?"

"Not particularly," Syril admitted. "We here on Murray respect our Earth-ancestry. We would never surrender our resources to another species. Really, though, this is all publicity and showmanship to let people know about our beautiful world."

"Admiral Bendo was quite insistent that the Navy win," I said. "Even though most of the competitors here are ringers for transtellar corporates."

"I'm sure he wishes to preserve Earth's pride," Syril said. "However, I can assure you that you won't be humiliated."

"I'm not sure that's possible," I replied. "I'm still learning the rules."

"It's an interesting anti-gravity-based version of traditional golf," Shelly started to explain. "Tom used to take me to play. The holes include floating islands, maneuvering thrusters, laser positions, and a variety of club adjustments. Obviously, that depends on whether you're using Albion or Brigid rules. If you're using the latter, we must give a Mulligan for—"

"None of that matters," Syril interrupted. "This is largely theater."
Shelly frowned.

My fake smile became more of a grimace. "So, the tournaments results are predetermined, are they?"

"Don't worry about that," Syril replied.

I already considered the game to be a waste of my time, and this was only increasing my opinion. This tournament was not just about securing the rights of the system for some human supremacists and it was already fixed. I wouldn't be surprised if they just wanted to advertise their golf course.

"And who is this?" I asked, taking a flute of champagne from the hands of the sheep alien on the ground.

"This is a Herdling," Syril said, giving a dismissive wave. "Pay it no mind."

"A Herdling?" I asked.

"Domesticated livestock," Syril said, dryly. "When we arrived on Murray, we were diseased and starving, with the terraforming devices only half-functional. The local climate was barely habitable but oxygen- and nitrogen-rich. Eventually, we learned to process the local food and fauna to be palatable to human biology."

"Congratulations," I said, frowning. "You know it's against Community regulations to colonize a world without a thorough examination of preexisting ecosystems."

"Indeed," Syril said. "Which is why we're dealing with Earth directly rather than the Community."

"I don't think that's—" I started to speak.

"If you'll excuse me, I have to go deal with my other guests," Syril said. "Please help yourself to any amenities you wish. The Four Thousand Islands Resort is the height of our culture and has every luxury imaginable. The pleasure world of Brigid pales in comparison."

After Syril walked away, I looked down at the Herdling. "Are you guys sentient and enslaved? If so, nod your head."

The Herdling stared at me blankly. It proceeded to head to Shelly and Hannah before starting to hand out flutes to my companions. It then trotted off, not spilling a drop of champagne.

"Really, Vance?" Shelly asked.

"What?" Hannah asked. "The captain likes to cover his bases."

"I'm not actually sure I've done that," I replied. "I'd like samples to be taken and put through the labs. Climate, animals, and advanced sensor sweeps. They're hiding something here."

"This isn't what we're here for," Shelly said.

"Yeah, I'd rather clobber these guys at ball-stick-hole," Hannah said.

"Golf," Shelly corrected.

"It's a game about hitting balls with a stick into a hole," Hannah replied. "My description stands."

I took a deep breath. "You're right, I should be cautious but not lose myself to paranoia."

That was when I was shot in the head.

"You were shot in the head," Syril said, staring at me from behind an expensive antique wooden desk carved with images of Earth. It was in the middle of a luxurious study that had a lovely view of the golf course. Well, part of it. Another Herdling was dusting the bookshelves with an actual feather duster and increasingly showing they were either intelligent or had been genetically programmed or mentally conditioned in some way.

Hannah had traded in her caddy gear for a suit of Mars-7 power armor that made her look like an interstellar bounty hunter.

"Yes," I said, annoyed. Pointing to my skull, I said, "Right in the head."

Someone from—at least according to Forty-Two's analysis—two thousand meters off had used a fusion rifle to shoot a blast square into my head. It was a shot perfectly possible for even a semi-experienced shooter if he had the right equipment and sensor package, but you shouldn't be able to sneak into a supposedly secure golf course and resort to do so. It had also knocked me the hell over and given me a concussion they'd needed to use a neuron-regenerator to treat. I was still tasting the color orange whenever I breathed.

"Forgive me, but you look remarkably well for a man shot in the head," Syril said.

"Yeah, well I was wearing a barrier belt under my clothes," I replied. "Even so, I got a concussion that my medical officer had to treat."

Syril stared at me, confused. "You were wearing a barrier belt on a golf course?"

"I can't imagine why," I said, staring at him. "Maybe it was the fear of someone killing me."

Syril seemed stymied by my logic. "Very well, Captain Turbo, accepting that you really were shot—"

"Are you calling me a liar?" I asked, less than pleased by his assertion.

Syril sighed. "No, I wish I could, but no. I believe this is the work of Schwarz Addler."

"The Black Eagle?" I asked, believing I'd somehow tripped and fallen into a spy movie.

Syril tapped a holographic interface built into his desk and a rotating picture of a white-blond haired man with a square jawline and muscular enhanced body appeared onscreen. He looked like someone genetically designed to kill James Bond and was wearing an ominous trench coat.

The language was written in Murray, which was a French-Indonesian hybrid, but seemed to list an extensive Wotan military service followed by employment with various criminal cartels. It was as if they'd come up with a guy that absolutely should not have been allowed anywhere near this tourist trap and let him stay in the VIP quarters. Which, admittedly, was possible.

I'd done my research and Murray was on the anyx-end of civilized space and only recent upgrades in jumpspace capability made it possible that anyone would want to, or be able to, come here for vacation. Even then it would hardly be cheap and if the insane investors in this Resort wanted their scheme to succeed then they probably weren't turning away paying customers. Yet, clearly someone believed this place had vacation potential and that was even before they'd apparently found a motherlode of resources they'd done nothing to exploit themselves.

"Yes, an obvious alias," Syril said. "Our somewhat meager security forces detected him a few days ago. He is a notable wanted assassin, saboteur, and fugitive. It might be possible that he was hired by sinister environmental extremists on our world to disrupt the tournament."

I opened my mouth, closed it, and cocked my head to one side. "Did you say *sinister environmental extremists*?"

"He did," Hannah said, her voice modulated. "The worst kind. Much worse than non-sinister environmental extremists. Who are worse than environmentalists who are not extreme. Which, admittedly, most are by definition."

"You don't say," I replied.

"There are those people on our world who, in their misguided belief what we're doing here in terraforming the planet is wrong, have been attempting to sabotage Murray's future," Syril said, annoyed at having to deal with what I'm sure he was now dismissing as a pair of wiseanyxes. "We believe they are receiving outside funding to inflate their numbers and further radicalize their members."

"Why is that?" I asked, knowing a snow job when I heard one. Which was appropriate since most of the planet was ice.

"Because they wish to drive down the price of harvesting our planetary resources!" Syril said, slamming his fist down on the table. "No one really cares about an ice-filled wasteland full of polar glorgs or ice trout. We're warming this planet for its own good! What kind of animals prefer frost over beaches?"

"Skiers?" I suggested.

"Murderers!" Syril said, repeating a rhetoric point I'm sure he'd said many times before.

"Those fiends," I said, dryly.

"Yes, it stands in the way of—" Syril started to say.

"Please God, don't say progress," I replied.

Syril coughed and cleared his throat. "I was going to say the future."

"Of course you were," I said.

"Since we know he's attempted an assassination, I will have this place searched high and low via drones to arrest him," Syril said. "We can't have Earth's most famous captain threatened."

"Actually, don't," I replied.

"What?" Syril asked.

"Let me deal with it," I said, cheerfully.

"Vance, do you have a plan?" Hannah asked me.

"No, I have a scheme," I said, smiling.

"Vance, did anyone ever tell you that you are the worst planner in the whole world?" Shelly asked, standing beside me in her golfing attire. We were near the pyramid-shaped pro shop that loomed over us like a celestial temple. There were lines of floating hover golf carts that were used to travel across the massive resort.

I stared up at the thirty-eight-story pro shop and wondered how the Murrayites had become so damned obsessed with golf. "Hmm, I'm sorry, what?"

"This is a terrible plan, and you know it," Shelly replied.

"Yes, which is why it will work," I explained.

Shelly stared at me. "That's not how good and bad plans work."

"I have a ringer competing for me in the tournament," I said, dryly. Sadly, it was Shelly's husband, Major Tom. I was expecting him to tank royally, but I didn't care. "He's got a mask and Trish has the video drones recording everything hacked to substitute my footage in real time. That gives me a chance to investigate what is actually going on here."

"Which is not your job," Shelly said. "In fact, it threatens to do the actual opposite of your job, which is to secure a diplomatic concession by gladhanding the locals. Locals who, I point out, have been nothing but accommodating."

"Do you trust them?" I asked, turning to her. "Because they're hiding something. I just sense something off about them."

"You sense they're wealthy and entitled," Shelly said, crossing her arms. "Which is rich, no pun intended, coming from someone who grew up in the country club set yourself."

"I hated those people when I was a kid," I said, frowning. "Can you imagine dealing with people who are given everything growing up?"

Shelly stared at me.

"What?" I asked. "Anyway, Leah is still trying to see what they're hiding mentally, and I've got Trish working on translating the Herdling language."

"You mean the sheep," Shelly said.

"Sentient sheep, I'm sure of it," I said. "Enslaved by a bunch of elitist pricks who settled this world—"

"And built a functional, thriving civilization," Shelly said. "Despite minimum resources."

"If you buy their story," I said, crossing my arms.

A Herdling walked by, carrying a set of golf clubs on its back.

"You're not fooling anyone!" I shouted at him. "You might as well fess up and work with me on this!"

Shelly rolled her eyes. "Tool use is not necessarily a sign of sentience."

"But I'd bet it is here," I replied.

That was when the Herdling climbed aboard one of the golf carts and drove away. Presumably to deliver the clubs to their owners. I swear it flipped me the bird along the way.

Shelly blinked. "Okay, maybe they're sentient."

"Ya think?" I asked, giving her side-eye. "Also, I'm ninety percent sure that this place is being built because they've been receiving supplies from one of the corporations for decades. This isn't a lost colony, it's a secret one."

"And why is that?" Shelly asked.

"Because I hacked the First Minister's computer and found that out," I replied. "They've been building this place as a lost colony to get around the laws of the Community until they can formally claim Earth protection."

Shelly stared. "I can't even argue with you breaking god knows how many laws because that's monstrous. This is an attempt to bring back the bad old days of colonialism and exploitation of technologically less-advanced peoples."

"Thank you, Kathryn Janeway, I know that," I said, annoyed.

"I hate when you're right," Shelly muttered, growling.

"And yet you'd think you'd be used to it by now," I said, smiling.

Shelly glared. "Listen, Vance, I may have had to put up with—"

"Terrorist," I said, pointing to the Black Eagle as he was walking out of the pro shop. He was carrying his own set of clubs and dressed in a black polo shirt with black dress slacks and mirror shades. It wasn't much of a disguise to be honest.

I'd managed to use my access to the Murray security feeds to do my hacking into the First Minister's programs but that didn't mean I hadn't also gotten done the task for which he'd given me access: finding the guy they said took a shot at me.

He had embedded himself in one of the corporate teams as a local golfing champion hired to help up their score. If not for the fact we knew what to look for, he might have been able to get away with it.

The Black Eagle's reaction to the two of us was, of course, to pull a fusion pistol out from his golf bag then start firing at us. Shelly and I had been prepared for this eventuality and watched him as he immediately got on board one of the golf carts and took off. Given they were hover carts designed to travel vast distances, he was moving at an exceptionally fast pace.

"We're going to have to chase him down like in a movie, aren't we?" Shelly asked, running to one of the carts and taking off after him.

I paused. "I feel terrible about this."

Tapping a few commands on my infopad, I waited a few minutes for the Black Eagle's golf cart to turn back around and park itself in front of me. He pulled up his fusion pistol and I stared at him.

"How?" the Black Eagle asked.

"They're hotel golf carts," I replied. "They have an automatic control to return to the pro shop."

"Stand the hell back!" the Black Eagle shouted, clearly annoyed that I didn't look the slightest bit intimidated. It was possible he could wear down my military-grade barrier at point blank range, but it would take more than a few shots from the low-powered, easily-concealable weapon. Which meant he'd probably go for me physically.

Shelly pulled up behind him, pulling out her own fusion pistol. "Don't move!"

"Hi," I said, in a very calm voice. "Mr. Eagle, would you please do me a favor and point me in the direction of the people who hired you? I'm sure they probably used a routing number for payment and so on, but given this planet consists of one spaceport, one resort, plus everyone's personal infocoms, I'm betting I can track it down."

"I don't trust Space Fleet promises," Black Eagle said, keeping his finger on the trigger regardless of Shelly's presence. "So, unless you're—"

"Hannah," I said, turning to my side.

That was when the optically camouflaged Hannah smacked his face with a rifle butt and knocked him cold.

I sighed. "Great, now it'll take me hours to get the answers out of him."

I headed back to First Minister Syril's office and opened the door, Hannah and Shelly behind me. It had taken about an hour to get the Black Eagle to cough up everything he knew, but that proved to be less helpful than what Trish eventually found by continuing her investigation of the Murrayite security systems.

The office was more or less as I'd left it but Syril was sitting behind the desk, staring forward blankly while his Herdling pet was staring at me with an annoyed expression on his face. The sun was setting on the horizon and the tournament's first round was winding down. Much to my surprise, Major Tom was in the lead, and I was going to have to congratulate Shelly's husband on a disturbingly professional round of golf.

Syril seemed to brighten up when I entered the room. "Ah, Captain Turbo, so good of you to arrive. I understand you apprehended—"

I pulled out my fusion pistol, shooting the First Minister in the head.

The First Minister slumped over, his head hitting the desk with an explosion of sparking circuitry and white ichor. He was a bioroid. Not even a particularly advanced model, but a puppet with only the ability to follow the directions of its cybernetic controller.

Who was right here.

"That was unnecessary," the Herdling said, dryly, in a crisp accent identical to the late First Minister's.

"You speak English," I said, simply. I was less surprised by this fact than that the alien didn't need its bioroid intermediary to translate.

Most aliens didn't possess the ability to speak human languages and vice versa.

"I'm one of those who has had cybernetic vocal cords installed to allow myself to speak the human tongue," the Herdling said. "You can call me Lambert."

I stared at him. "Really?"

"Yes, I get the pun," Lambert said. "However, I suspect my name of He-Who-Wakes-The-Sun-With-His-Words doesn't translate well."

'It's more honest," I replied, putting away my gun. "Though I would like some goddamn answers."

Lambert climbed on top of the desk to speak to me face-to-face. "I doubt you haven't figured out most of it, anyway. You were judged to be the primary threat to our plans due to your superior intelligence and incredulous nature."

Shelly snorted.

I looked back at her. "Yeah, so what is their plan?"

"Uh," Shelly said. "They, uh, okay, I'm going to be honest, I was focused on the golf tournament. Clearly, the Herdlings *are* sentient."

"And I suspect technologically advanced," I replied. "Your society is subterranean and built this resort for the humans."

"Indeed," Lambert said, dryly. "Our planet suffered a massive earthquake centuries ago that opened a vein of high-iron dusty rock that polluted our oceans. This triggered a massive algae surge and sucked all the CO_2 out of the atmosphere. It helped bring about a massive die-out of life across the planet as well as a global ice age. We already lived primarily underground, but this resulted in us abandoning the surface."

"You know, we could export this dusty iron rock to planets suffering from global warming..." Shelly trailed off.

"Sure, if you want an algal bloom to kill everything in the oceans!" Lambert said.

Shelly frowned.

"And then the human colonists arrived, and you discovered you weren't alone in the universe," I said.

It was the reverse of what I'd thought about the situation before. Instead of the incredibly advanced humans arriving on a primitive

269

world, they'd ended up on an alien world and gone native. The locals had taken their technology and adapted it to themselves. They'd undoubtedly also used the colonists to translate the ship's databases, giving them insight into the rest of the galaxy circa a hundred and fifty years ago. A typical colony ship usually contained the complete knowledge of a planet, technology plans, and information on most other species in the known universe. With a developed infrastructure, that could move a planet much closer to the Space Age.

"It was a troublesome encounter," Lambert said. "You have a deeply stupid race. However, the technology on the starship helped us start curing our climate issues. Unfortunately, we were also made aware of the various threats outside of our planet. We would be entering the galaxy right as massive wars were being raged with no great wealth or connections."

The Community had been in a state of continuous war for the past century with the Notha, Kolahn, and the Blood Ravagers, among others. Even a hundred and fifty years ago it would have been a terrifying situation. If they'd managed to make contact recently, though, then they almost certainly knew that Earth had one export: soldiers. Earth had only one industry of note: war. Okay, three alongside bioroids and computer programs. It did mean that linking their economy to Earth and humanity would have been a wise decision for someone hoping to move from being the bottom of the five thousand or so races to join the community to something at least minimally higher on the list.

"And you were going to ally with humans as your middlemen," I replied. "Are there surviving colonists?"

"Many," Lambert said. "They've been living with us for generations and are culturally identical now. I only used a bioroid as my mouthpiece because I did not believe the human herdsmen from my planet could pull off the contempt for my people realistically."

"The deception would have never lasted long," I said. "Even with your people acting like domesticated animals."

"It only needed to last long enough for your race's greed to take over," Lambert said. "Once the contracts were signed, we didn't really care about being found out. However, your people certainly won't wish to contract with us and I'm sure killing you now wouldn't help matters with the news spreading among your ship. So…what now?"

I smiled, seeing a way to help both the Herdlings and Earth. "Let's negotiate a real contract."

LEXICON

AI: Artificial intelligence. Science fiction has talked about these a few times.

Admiralty Board: The head of Space Fleet for Earth and those who supervise its link to other navies as part of the Community. It is arguably more powerful than EarthGov and has only grown more so since its coordination with other human militaries as part of the Human League.

Albion: A island-filled water planet settled by humans abducted by aliens. The most powerful human planet, currently losing ground to Earth. It primarily worships Mithras and is a mixture of Roman, Celtic, Saxon, Picts, and later English settlers.

Allenway Cult: A Union of Faith bunch of Gnostics that merged with the remains of the now-defunct Church of Money to create the primary religion of Crius. Their religion is damn near incomprehensible to outsiders but venerates the bloodline of its founder.

Anateus Rangers: A privateer, mercenary, and freebooter group from before the Notha War consisting of primarily Contested Space soldiers. Hannah was a member of the disreputable organization before joining Captain Elgan's crew.

Anyxhole: Linguistic drift from exactly the word you think it is.

Ares Electronics: An Albion-based corporation that manufactures most of the starships, bots, and bioroids in the universe. It was notably founded by Patricia Ares on Earth before moving its headquarters from Luna to Londonium. It owns the Luna Shipyards. It unduly influences Earth politics.

Artificial Gravity: A slang term for something people think is possible but is not. Even the Community just generates the real thing with a variety of tricks.

Barrier: A force field that protects against energy and physical attacks. They are usually on ships, but they've recently been added to infantry via armor or belts.

Battle Cruiser: An informal classification of a ship that exists between a starship carrier and battleship. It is usually a destroyer type and often used synonymously with them.

Bastarve: Another word for bastard. Swearing isn't very original on Albion.

Biomods: Genetic enhancements that provide sapient beings with special abilities. Usually organic technology rather than cybernetics to avoid rejection.

Bioroids: Androids and gynoids indistinguishable from humans with synthetic flesh. Often used for exactly what you think.

Blood and Honor: The second hit movie about Vannever Tagashi's adventures. It is wildly inaccurate and full of sex and violence. It is also endorsed by the EarthGov military.

Bork: A weirdly popular curse word.

Bots: Robots. Crazy, I know, right?

Brigid: Sister-world to Belenus which produces most of the infrastructure that keeps its brother world in wealth. Its populace is infamously libertine with polyamory and sexual freedom emphasized by law. They are also stereotyped as uncomfortably friendly with few personal boundaries.

Bug: A race of (seemingly) giant ant-like aliens that are terrifying as well as strong. It turns out those were chassis for a much, much smaller race.

Clonemaster: A job on Crius that is used to create genemod slaves for organic labor-obsessed customers. They could have switched to making bioroids, but the majority chose to continue to make the illegal, ethically monstrous product instead.

Clone Slavery: A disgusting trade in biologically grown laborers and pleasure workers. Clone Slavery is gradually being driven out of business by the bioroid trade and anti-slavery efforts by the

Community, but it continues to exist on Crius due to its eugenics-obsessed culture.

Cognition AI: Nearly omnipotent AI that can process unlimited amounts of data. Pretty much the real rulers of the Community. But so friendly!

Community: An interstellar fellowship of many species and worlds. It is generally pro democracy, civil rights, diversity, and technology. Of course, no one trusts it or its activities.

Community Protectors: See *Space Fleet*.

Community Protectorate: A non-voting member of the Community. Usually done for space stations, ports, and planets that have yet to formally join. Citizens are still able to vote in races for a "parent" planet.

Community Senate: A collection of representatives of the various worlds of the Community. Many planets dislike it because it impedes their own ambitions while others hate the fact it is dominated by the High Council.

Contested Space: A region of space between the Community and Notha Empire. It is full of outlaw settlements, pirate bands, and half-terraformed hellholes or collapsed civilizations. It has become recently more settled but the rise of the Notha Union has opened new worries of invasion and conflict.

Corvettes: The smallest class of military starship. They are usually used for patrol and picket duty.

Crazzap: Crap by another name is just as stinky.

Crius: A planet being settled by transhumanists wanting to create a feudal paradise. A planet of genetically engineered slaves ruled by a bunch of deranged cloners. Go here to be hunted by dinosaurs.

Dark Matter: A human supremacist organization consisting of numerous oligarchs, politicians, and reactionary military officers controlled by the (late) Alexandra Ares. It is not actually named Dark Matter but was given that name by Trish after the villains of *Space Cadet Sally*. Vance assumed it was defunct because he killed its leader and is proven to be very, very wrong.

Demihumans: Humans who no longer are strictly human due to evolution and genetic modification.

Department Zero: The supervisory department of the twelve intelligence services of the Protectorate. Each race has its own department head that more or less directs their functions independently of one another but cooperates.

Department Twelve: One of the twelve intelligence services of the Protectorate. Department Twelve is the one most devoted to counterterrorism, provocation, and destabilization. Many blame it for the horrific consequences of the Notha War. It is now believed to be a rogue agency operating on private funding.

Destroyers: Vessels built for heavy planetary assault as well as ship-to-ship combat.

Dixnar: The corporation that produces virtually all entertainment for humanity. It has somehow absorbed many older races' corporations.

Dreadnought-Class Starship: The most powerful type of human-produced vessel so far and roughly on par with the destroyers of the Sorkanan navy. They are meant to be flagships for the Earth, Albion, and other human-controlled fleets.

Drolochid: Slimy, warm-blooded, multi-limbed, pill bug race with sensory organs across their pill bug bodies. Quite pleasant to be around. When they produce criminals, they have a reputation as producing bizarrely theatrical ones. They are even less powerful than humanity in the Community.

Earth: The human homeworld. Perhaps you've heard of it. The new kids on the block. Way too eager to prove itself.

EarthGov: The government of Earth. Duh.

Earth Home Fleet: Earth's personal defense force. It is separate from the ships it loans to permanent Community duty.

Elder Races: Several godlike "sufficiently advanced" aliens who live in the galactic core and decide what races live or die without any understandable criteria. Real jerks. They're better than the Primordials, though.

Elgan-Class Cruiser: A replacement for the Olympic-class cruiser that is far more technologically advanced. Named for the late Captain Julius Elgan.

Emperor's Reach: A fourteen-kilometer-long vessel in the shape of a horizontal obelisk. It was constructed to be the Notha flagship and personal vessel of their Emperor fifty years ago but became the headquarters of his court-in-exile. It has been continuously upgraded ever since despite lack of parts. Vance blew it up.

Enigmas: A nickname for the terrorists of the Enigmatic Path.

Enigmatic Path: A Kolahn terrorist organization and religious fundamentalist group. Its bizarre ideology is about how organic life is an abomination, AI should be liberated, and the universe is a simulation. It has since spread out to absorb many transhuman (or alien) offshoot groups and carries out a guerilla war against the Community. While Kolahn has fallen, it continues its war against the Community regardless.

Ethereals: A group of races uplifted by the Elder Races to be intermediaries with them and other organics. They are heavily involved in the Community and wildly believed to be puppets for the Elder Races.

Fragmentation: A state where AI split into multiple selves after a traumatic experience. It is considered grounds for discharge among AI in the Home Fleet.

First Contact: When Earth was met by Community ships who offered to repair its environment and share technology in exchange for the right to build a base on the moon.

Foundationalists: An Albion-based Mithraic cult that enforces strict gender roles and biological essentialism. It is suspicious of technology and medicine as well as prone to conspiratorial thinking.

Frigates: Starships built for speed and maneuverability but larger than corvettes. Typically used for escort duty and support to larger battleships.

Genemods: A slang term for those who have been modified from baseline humanity or other species.

Great Notha: The ruler of both the Notha Empire after the Emperor's overthrow and the ruler of the current Notha Union. There have only been two "official" ones but there have been thousands of "pretenders."

Grounder: A slang term for those who grew up and primarily live on planets.

Gravitonic Emitters: The poor man's substitute of artificial gravity that moves around weight and is a necessity for casual space travel. Also called gravity manipulators.

Happy Funtime Guild: The secret police of the Notha that even the Great Notha himself treads carefully around.

Happy Funtime World: The prison world of the Happy Funtime Guild and a hellish gulag for political prisoners as well as Notha who have been deemed traitors. Its populace was liberated during the lead up to the Notha War.

High Council: The representatives of the most powerful worlds in the Community.

High Protector: A rank of nobility bestowed by the High Council that conveys broad sweeping military and law enforcement powers to certain individuals in the Community. It is a lifetime appointment and can only be removed by the High Council. Only one human being has ever been promoted to High Protector before Captain Turbo.

Home Fleet: The Earth portion of the Community Space Fleet.

Human League: A proposed attempt to bring all human planets under one united banner to wield more economic and political power in the Community. It is primarily driven by Albion and Earth. Most Community members actually support the idea as too many individual human polities confuse things.

Infospace: A extra-dimensional communications system that allows faster-than-light communication and works like an interstellar internet.

Jovial Empress: A Sorkanan space station built above the planet Crius as a trading port for the Community residents trying to update the world's technology and economy. It became a refuge when they were drive off.

Jumpdrive: What allows people to travel through space like in movies.

Jumpspace: A dimension of bizarre physics that makes faster-than-light travel possible. Looking at it will drive most people insane like staring into the sun blinds you due to the way it stimulates your synapses.

Karma Corp: A former transtellar that was once one of the driving forces in Earth politics and economics. It was overthrown after the

Unification Wars and bought out by Albion interests before its remnant helped settle Crius.

Known Universe: Explored space that turns out to be primarily just Orion's Arm.

Kolahn: Resemble giant apes with scales. Their civilization was overtaken by a terrorist cult and promptly bombed back to the stone age by the Community. Its survivors are, paradoxically, living as refugees among the Community.

Kolahn IV: The Kolahn Homeworld, known to its people as "Ground," but the fourth planet in its solar system. It was rendered uninhabitable due to the Kolahn Wars.

Kolahn Resettlement Project: A controversial attempt to resettle billions of refugees from the devastated Kolahn homeworld.

Kolahn Wars: The wars that bombed the Kolahn back to the Stone Age.

Ko'ltah **Frigate:** An L-shaped Sorkanan frigate used by the Kolahn and other independent worlds.

Llrowlthra: Large grasshopper-like aliens who live lives free of technology but seem peculiarly aware of everything going on in the galaxy. Called "Space Amish" by humans for reasons most species do not understand. Also, Grasshoppers because humans are racist.

Luna: Earth's moon. It is largely used for the construction of spacecraft for civilian and military use as well as other advanced electronics incapable of being manufactured on Earth. Closer to being Vance's homeworld than the actual Earth.

Lunar Shipyards: Pretty much what the name suggests. Most of Luna has been hollowed out for it.

MacArthur-class vessel: A corvette and light patrol craft produced by humanity in the early days of faster-than-light travel. Due to upgrades to the Home Fleet, they are almost all found in the hands of colony world's navies or civilian groups these days.

Mithras: A Roman-era god still worshiped on Albion. He is an Iranian god of Sun, War, and Justice. His religion has largely merged with Christianity on Albion to become a monotheistic amalgam religion.

Neo-Militarists: A fascist pro-human, anti-alien government that came to power after First Contact and tried to create an isolationist Earth state. They were defeated in the Unification Wars by Community-backed rebels.

New Pompeii: A half-terraformed world in Contested Space being used by the Community to resettle refugees from the Kolahn Wars. Many humans resented this because the world was originally meant for human expansion.

Notha: Adorable lemur-like race of Space Nazi bastards.

Notha Empire: A corrupt military dictatorship ruled by the Notha that practices slavery, imperialism, planet looting, and conquest. It maintains its existence not by competence but due to the possession of weapons of stellar destruction. It collapsed not long after the death of the emperor.

Notha Emperor: The now-deceased former ruler of the Notha Empire who ruled over the race for millennia before being overthrown by his own descendants. He is mythologically a god and his death at Vance Turbo's hands has had vast repercussions for the race.

Notha Civil War: A conflict presently being fought between the Notha High Command and various generals over who should inherit the position of the Great Notha. It didn't so much end as change fronts with the current battle between Deathworld and the Notha Union.

Notha Union: The successor state of the Notha Empire that emerged after the Thord Treaty of Exarxes. It is about seventy-five percent as big and headed by a new Great Notha who dreams of restoring the Empire.

Notha War: A conflict that resulted in the destruction of seventeen inhabited planets on both sides of the conflict due to an exchange of SKAMMs.

Olothonalka: Nine feet tall gastropods, with six eyes on motile stalks. Patterned on back and torso. Three genders (male, female, and mass egg-laying). No arms but the entire lower surface is manipulative. Most humans just call them Snails.

Olympic-class vessel: An incredibly powerful EarthGov vessel that is just barely a mid-tier vessel by Community standards.

Plizzed: A state of fluid retention. Used as a pejorative.

Primordials: An extra-galactic race that has severe issues with the Elder Races. They are from the Large Magellanic Cloud, and formerly inhabited the Milky Way a billion years ago before fleeing. Their vessels exist in both jumpspace and realspace simultaneously. They recently suffered a humiliating loss that has briefly put them off of galactic genocide.

Q-Bomb: The replacement weapon of mass destruction for SKAMMS. Q-bombs are antimatter weapons that can annihilate planets or small targets equally.

Rand's World: A former colony world of Earth where the terraforming was stopped mid-process due to Notha aggression. It is now primarily inhabited by criminals, pirates, and separatists. Named for Ayn Rand.

Robosexual: A slur used against humans who have sexual relationships with AI, bioroid or virtually.

Savit: Excrement. Usually used as a pejorative.

Security Departments: The twelve, yes, twelve intelligence agencies working for the Community.

SKAMMs: Sun-destroying weapons of interstellar destruction. They are horrifying devices and their use in the recent Notha War resulted in an immediate end to the conflict lest the two sides annihilate one another.

Sklux: A race of protoplasmic beings that can shape into a rough approximation of any form. Obsessed with puns. Considered a race of mediators and peacemakers, primarily by themselves.

Slirrrrua-Class Frigates: Sorkanan vessels that are often found sold second hand to less-developed races.

Sons of the Demiurge: A theocratic terrorist organization on Crius that encourages slavery, genetic supremacy, and feudal aristocracy. It has sworn its allegiance to the Enigmatic Path and been wholly compromised by it.

Sorkanan: One of the oldest and most powerful species in space. They are a humanoid athropod species with multiple offshoots.

Sorkanan Imperial Navy: The massive fleets of the Sorkanan Empire. Its conditions are horrifying, and morale is generally low but it is still the greatest power in the Spiral.

Space Academy: The training center for officers in the Community Protectors.

Spacer: A slang term for those who have grown up and primarily live in space.

Space Cadet Sally: A popular children's show with a large adult following. *Space Cadet Sally* has often been accused of being Space Fleet propaganda.

Space Fleet: The Community's massive interstellar Navy that is (allegedly) a galactic force for good.

The Spire: What Orion's Arm is called by most races of the known universe as they are primarily concentrated there.

Sun Killer: Another name for SKAMM torpedoes.

Transtellar: The name for interplanetary corporations that possess resources far more than individual worlds. They wield disproportionate power in the Community and among humanity's various worlds.

Tubing: A process where a woman has a fertilized embryo put in a life support tube instead of carrying it inside her. They are ubiquitous on Albion, Brigid, and among spacer women with it growing in popularity on Earth. Nicknamed "uterine replicators" after a sci-fi series from Earth's past.

Treaty of Exarxes: A large multispecies agreement on shared morality and behavior during wartime. The Notha are a very reluctant signatory. A second treaty was drafted to ban the use of SKAMMs and other weapons of mass destruction at Elder Race insistence. A third treaty was recently signed that helped define Contested Space better between the Notha and Community.

Unification Wars: The war where the Neo-Militarists and transtellars were defeated before the Community-friendly EarthGov was born.

Union of Faith: A group of thirty-six worlds settled by Medieval Christians, Muslims, Jews, Buddhists, and other religions that have created a theocracy within the Community. Weirdly, religious tolerance is in its constitution but almost everything else is regulated to a ridiculous degree.

Verdantian: A leonine race with six limbs that were uplifted by the Elder Races according to their belief structure.

Wah'Pang **Battle Cruiser:** A kilometer-long vessel designed by the Kolahn with the help of the Notha. They have immensely powerful barriers at the price of poor fusion cannons. It compensates with a heavier load of missiles.

Watchers: The intelligence bureau of Albion that is subordinate to but separate from the Community's Security Departments.

AUTHOR'S NOTE

I'd like to thank you for reading this book. The publishing industry is changing dramatically since the advent of eBooks. It is now very difficult to get any book noticed, regardless of quality. If you enjoyed this book, you could do some very simple things to help me attract attention. Word of mouth is the number one source of success for novels, so simply telling family and friends about the book is a great start.

Here are a few other ways of helping out, if you are so inclined:

* Post a rating or review where you purchased the eBook
* Post a rating or review on Goodreads
* Talk about the book or write a review on Facebook
* Tell folks about the book in a blog post.

If you like any of my other books, please feel free to check them out. A lot of my series are interlinked, and you never know when you'll find someone familiar showing up. In this case, *Space Academy Dropouts* is set in the far future of my Agent G cyberpunk books and the past of my *Lucifer's Star* series. Fans will certainly get a kick out of seeing how the galaxy changes in a few centuries either way.

ABOUT THE AUTHORS

Michael Suttkus, II, lives in Leesburg, Florida, with three cats, one of which actually likes him, and his family, with whom he fares better. When not working at a game store, he's playing games, reading science books, or otherwise being incredibly nerdy. Also writing! Because he has to feed cats whether they like him or not.

Bibliography

I Was a Teenage Weredeer (The Bright Falls Mysteries, Book 1)
An American Weredeer in Michigan (The Bright Falls Mysteries, Book 2)
A Nightmare on Elk Street (The Bright Falls Mysteries, Book 3)

Lucifer's Star (Lucifer's Star #1)
Lucifer's Nebula (Lucifer's Star #2)

Brightblade (The Morgan Detective Agency, Book 1)
Brighteyes (The Morgan Detective Agency, Book 2)

Space Academy Dropouts (The Space Academy Series, Book 1)
Space Academy Rejects (The Space Academy Series, Book 2)
Space Academy Washouts (The Space Academy Series, Book 3)
Space Academy Miscreants (The Space Academy Series, Book 4)
Space Academy Vagrants (The Space Academy Series, Book 5)

C. T. Phipps is a lifelong student of horror, science fiction, and fantasy. An avid tabletop gamer, he discovered this passion led him to write and turned him into a lifelong geek. He is a regular blogger and also a reviewer for The Bookie Monster.

Bibliography

<u>Novels</u>
The Rules of Supervillainy (Supervillainy Saga #1)
The Games of Supervillainy (Supervillainy Saga #2)
The Secrets of Supervillainy (Supervillainy Saga #3)
The Kingdom of Supervillainy (Supervillainy Saga #4)
The Tournament of Supervillainy (Supervillainy Saga #5)
The Future of Supervillainy (Supervillainy Saga #6)
The Horror of Supervillainy (Supervillainy Saga #7)
Tales of Supervillainy: Cindy's Seven (Supervillainy Saga #7)

I Was a Teenage Weredeer (The Bright Falls Mysteries, Book 1)
An American Weredeer in Michigan (The Bright Falls Mysteries, Book 2)
A Nightmare on Elk Street (The Bright Falls Mysteries, Book 3)

Esoterrorism (Red Room, Vol. 1)

Eldritch Ops (Red Room, Vol. 2)
The Fall of the House (Red Room, Vol. 3)

Agent G: Infiltrator (Agent G, Vol. 1)
Agent G: Saboteur (Agent G, Vol. 2)
Agent G: Assassin (Agent G, Vol. 3)

Cthulhu Armageddon (Cthulhu Armageddon, Vol. 1)
The Tower of Zhaal (Cthulhu Armageddon, Vol. 2)
The Tree of Azathoth (Cthulhu Armageddon, Vol. 3)

Lucifer's Star (Lucifer's Star, Vol. 1)
Lucifer's Nebula (Lucifer's Star, Vol. 2)

Straight Outta Fangton (Straight Outta Fangton, Vol. 1)
100 Miles and Vampin' (Straight Outta Fangton, Vol. 2)
Vampiraz4Life (Straight Outta Fangton, Vol. 3)

Wraith Knight (Wraith Knight, Vol. 1)
Wraith Lord (Wraith Knight, Vol. 2)
Wraith King (Wraith Knight, Vol. 3)

Dark Destiny (Dark Destiny, Vol. 1)
Destiny's Paradox (Dark Destiny, Vol. 2)

Brightblade (The Morgan Detective Agency, Book 1)
Brighteyes (The Morgan Detective Agency, Book 2)

Daughter of the Cyber Dragons (The Cyber Dragons Series, Book 1)
Revenge of the Cyber Dragons (The Cyber Dragons Series, Book 2)
End of the Cyber Dragons (The Cyber Dragons Series, Book 3)

Space Academy Dropouts (The Space Academy Series, Book 1)
Space Academy Rejects (The Space Academy Series, Book 2)

Space Academy Washouts (The Space Academy Series, Book 3)
Space Academy Miscreants (The Space Academy Series, Book 4)
Space Academy Vagrants (The Space Academy Series, Book 5)

Moon Cops on the Moon (Moon Cops, Book 1)
Moon City Vice (Moon Cops, Book 2)

Lords of Dragon Keep (Dragon Keep, Book 1)
Guardians of Dragon Keep (Dragon Keep, Book 2)

Psycho Killers in Love

Tales of an Eldritch Wasteland

Anthologies (as editor)
Blackest Knights
Blackest Spells
Tales of Capes and Cowls
Tales of the Al-Azif
Tales of Yog-Sothoth
The Book of Hastur

Lucifer's Star (Lucifer's Star, Vol. 1)
Lucifer's Nebula (Lucifer's Star, Vol. 2)

Straight Outta Fangton (Straight Outta Fangton, Vol. 1)
100 Miles and Vampin' (Straight Outta Fangton, Vol. 2)
Vampiraz4Life (Straight Outta Fangton, Vol. 3)

Wraith Knight (Wraith Knight, Vol. 1)
Wraith Lord (Wraith Knight, Vol. 2)
Wraith King (Wraith Knight, Vol. 3)

Dark Destiny (Dark Destiny, Vol. 1)

Destiny's Paradox (Dark Destiny, Vol. 2)

Brightblade (The Morgan Detective Agency, Book 1)

Space Academy Dropouts (The Space Academy Series, Book 1)
Space Academy Rejects (The Space Academy Series, Book 2)
Space Academy Washouts (The Space Academy Series, Book 3)

Psycho Killers in Love

Anthologies (as editor)
Blackest Knights
Blackest Spells
Tales of Capes and Cowls
Tales of the Al-Azif
Tales of Yog-Sothoth

Curious about other Crossroad Press books? Stop by our website:
http://crossroadpress.com
We offer quality writing
in digital, audio, and print formats.

Subscribe to our newsletter on the website homepage and receive a
free eBook.